The Fire Court

Andrew Taylor is the author of a number of crime novels, including the ground-breaking Roth Trilogy, which was adapted into the acclaimed TV drama *Fallen Angel*, and the historical crime novels *The Ashes of London*, *The Silent Boy*, *The Scent of Death* and *The American Boy*, a No.1 *Sunday Times* bestseller and a 2005 Richard & Judy Book Club Choice.

He has won many awards, including the CWA John Creasey New Blood Dagger, an Edgar Scroll from the Mystery Writers of America, the CWA Ellis Peters Historical Award (the only author to win it three times) and the CWA's prestigious Diamond Dagger, awarded for sustained excellence in crime writing. He also writes for the *Spectator* and *The Times*.

He lives with his wife Caroline in the Forest of Dean.

 @AndrewJRTaylor
www.andrew-taylor.co.uk

By the same author

Fireside Gothic
The Ashes of London
The Silent Boy
The Scent of Death
The Anatomy of Ghosts
Bleeding Heart Square
The American Boy

A Stain on the Silence
The Barred Window
The Raven on the Water

THE ROTH TRILOGY: FALLEN ANGEL
The Four Last Things
The Judgement of Strangers
The Office of the Dead

THE LYDMOUTH SERIES

THE BLAINES NOVELS

THE DOUGAL SERIES

ANDREW TAYLOR

The Fire Court

HarperCollins*Publishers*

HarperCollins*Publishers* Ltd
1 London Bridge Street,
London SE1 9GF

www.harpercollins.co.uk

First published by HarperCollins*Publishers* 2018
18 19 20 LSCC 10 9 8 7 6 5 4 3 2

A catalogue record for this book is available from the British Library

ISBN: 978-0-00-811913-3 (HB)
ISBN: 978-0-00-811911-9 (TPB)

Typeset in Fournier MT by Palimpsest Book Production Ltd, Falkirk, Stirlingshire

Printed and bound in the United States of America by LSC Communications

For more information visit: www.harpercollins.co.uk/green

For Caroline

THE PEOPLE

Infirmary Close, The Savoy
James Marwood, clerk to Joseph Williamson, and to the
　　Board of Red Cloth
Nathaniel Marwood, his father, widowed husband of
　　Rachel; formerly a printer
Margaret and Sam Witherdine, their servants

The Drawing Office, Henrietta Street
Simon Hakesby, surveyor and architect
'Jane Hakesby', his maid, formerly known as Catherine
　　Lovett
Brennan, his draughtsman

Clifford's Inn and the Fire Court
Lucius Gromwell, antiquary
Theophilus Chelling, clerk to the Fire Court
Sir Thomas Twisden, a judge at the Fire Court
Miriam, a servant at Clifford's Inn

I

Pall Mall
Sir Philip Limbury
Jemima, Lady Limbury, daughter of Sir George Syre
Mary, her maid
Richard, Sir Philip's manservant; also known as Sourface
Hester, a maid

Whitehall
Joseph Williamson, Under-Secretary of State to Lord
  Arlington
William Chiffinch, Keeper of the King's Private Closet

Others
Roger Poulton, retired cloth merchant; late of Dragon Yard
Elizabeth Lee, his housekeeper
Celia Hampney, his widowed niece
Tabitha, Mistress Hampney's maid
Mistress Grove, of Lincoln's Inn Fields; who lets lodgings
  to Mistress Hampney
Barty, a crossing-sweeper in Fleet Street, by Temple Bar

CHAPTER ONE

RACHEL. THERE YOU are.

    She hesitated in the doorway that led from the Savoy Stairs and the river. She wore a long blue cloak over a grey dress he did not recognize. In her hand was a covered basket. She walked across the garden to the archway in the opposite corner. Her pattens clacked on the flagged path.

That's my Rachel, he thought. Always busy. But why did she not greet him?

You are like the river, my love, he had told her once, always moving and always the same.

They had been sitting by the Thames in Barnes Wood. She had let down her hair, which was brown but shot through with golden threads that glowed in the sunlight.

She had looked like a whore, with her loose, glorious hair.

He felt a pang of repulsion. Then he rallied. A woman's hair encouraged lustful thoughts, he argued with himself, but it could not be sinful when the woman was your wife, joined to you in the sight of God, flesh of your flesh, bone of your bone.

Now the garden was empty. There was no reason why he should not go after her. Indeed, it was his duty. Was not woman the weaker vessel?

He used his stick as a prop to help him rise. He was still hale and hearty, thank God, but his limbs grew stiff if he did not move them for a while.

He walked towards the archway. The path beyond made a turn to the right, rounding the corner of one of the old hospital buildings of the Savoy. He glimpsed Rachel ahead, passing through the gate that led up to the Strand. She paused to look at something – a piece of paper? – in her hand. Then she was gone.

She must be going shopping. A harmless pleasure, but only as long as it did not encourage vanity, a woman's besetting sin. Women were weak, women were sinful, which was why God had placed men to watch over them and to correct them when they erred.

The porter in his lodge took no notice of him. A cobbled path led up to the south side of the Strand. The traffic roared and clattered along the roadway.

He looked towards Charing Cross, thinking that the shops of the New Exchange would have drawn her like a moth to a blaze of candles. No sign of her. Could he have lost her already? He looked the other way, and there she was, walking towards the ruins of the City.

He waved his stick. 'Rachel,' he cried. 'Come here.'

The racket and clatter of the Strand drowned his words.

He followed her, the stiffness dropping from his limbs, his legs gathering strength and momentum with the exercise. On and on she walked, past Somerset House and Arundel House, past St Clement's and under Temple Bar into Fleet Street and the Liberties of the City.

He kept his eyes fixed on the cloak, and the rhythm of his walking lulled his mind until he almost forgot why he was here. By the Temple, Rachel hesitated, turning towards the roadway with its sluggish currents of vehicles and animals. She looked down at the paper in her hand. A painted coach lumbered to a halt on the opposite side of the road. At that moment, a brewer's dray, coming from the other direction and laden with barrels, drew up beside it. Between them, they blocked the street.

Rachel slipped among the traffic and threaded her way across the street.

The brewer's men were unloading the dray outside the Devil Tavern. A barrel broke free and crashed into the roadway. The impact shattered the staves on one side. Beer spurted into the street. Two beggars ran whooping towards the growing puddle. They crouched and lapped like dogs. The traffic came to a complete halt, jammed solid by its own weight pressing from either side.

A sign, he thought, a sign from God. He has parted this river of traffic for me just as it had pleased Him to part the Red Sea before Moses and the Chosen People.

He walked across the street, his eyes fixed on Rachel's cloak. She turned to the left in the shadow of the square tower of St Dunstan-in-the-West.

Why was she leading him such a merry dance? Suspicion writhed within him. Had the serpent tempted her? Had she succumbed to the devil's wiles?

An alley ran past the west side of the church to a line of iron railings with a gateway in the middle. Beside it, a porter's lodge guarded the entrance to a cramped court. Men were milling around the doorway of a stone-faced building with high, pointed windows.

Rachel was there too, looking once again at the paper in her hand. She passed through the doorway. He followed, but the crowd held him back.

'By your leave, sirs, by your leave,' he cried. 'Pray, sirs, by your leave.'

'Hush, moderate your voice,' hissed a plump clerk dressed in black. 'Stand back, the judges are coming through.'

He stared stupidly at the clerk. 'The judges?'

'The Fire Court, of course. The judges are sitting this afternoon.'

Three gentlemen came in procession, attended by their clerks and servants. They were conducted through the archway.

He pressed after them. The doorway led to a passage. At the other end of it a second doorway gave on to a larger courtyard, irregular in shape. Beyond it was a garden, a green square among the soot-stained buildings.

Was that Rachel over there by the garden?

He called her name. His voice was thin and reedy, as it was in dreams. She did not hear him, though two men in black gowns stared curiously at him.

How dared she ignore him? What was this place full of men? Why had she not told him she was coming here? Surely, please God, she did not intend to betray him?

On the first floor of the building to the right of the garden, a tall man stood at one of the nearer windows, looking down on the court below. The panes of glass reduced him to little more than a shadow. Rachel turned into a doorway at the nearer end of a building to the right of the garden, next to a fire-damaged ruin.

His breath heaved in his chest. He had the strangest feeling that the man had seen Rachel, and perhaps himself as well.

The man had gone. This was Rachel's lover. He had been watching for her, and now she was come.

His own duty was plain. He crossed the court to the doorway. The door was ajar. On the wall to one side, sheltered by the overhang of the porch, was a painted board. White letters marched, or rather staggered, across a black background:

XIV
6 Mr Harrison
5 Mr Moran
4 Mr Gorvin
3 Mr Gromwell
2 Mr Drury
1 Mr Bews

Distracted, he frowned. Taken as a whole, the board was an offence to a man's finer feelings and displeasing to God. The letters varied in size, and their spacing was irregular. In particular, the lettering of Mr Gromwell's name had been quite barbarously executed. It was clearly a later addition, obliterating the original name that had been there. A trickle of paint trailed from the final 'l' of Gromwell. The sign-painter had tried ineffectually to brush it away, probably with his finger, and had succeeded only in leaving the corpse of a small insect attached to it.

Perhaps, he thought, fumbling in his pocket, temporarily diverted from Rachel, a man might scrape away the worst of the drip with the blade of a pocket knife. If only—

He heard sounds within. And a man's voice. Then a second voice – a woman's.

7

Oh, Rachel, how could you?

He pushed the door wide and crossed the threshold. Two doors faced each other across a small lobby. At the back, a staircase rose into the shadows.

He listened, but heard only silence. He caught sight of something gleaming on the second step of the stairs. He stepped closer and peered at it.

A speck of damp mud. The moisture caught the light from the open door behind him.

'Rachel?' he called.

There was no reply. His mind conjured up a vision of her in a man's chamber, her skirts thrown up, making the two-backed beast with him. He shook his head violently, trying to shake the foul images out of it.

He climbed the stairs. On the next landing, two more doors faced each other, number three on the right and number four on the left. Another, smaller door had been squeezed into the space between the staircase and the back of the landing.

Number three. Three was a number of great importance. There were three doors and three Christian virtues, Faith, Hope and Charity. Man has three enemies, the world, the flesh and the devil. Mr Gromwell's number was three, whoever Gromwell was.

In God's creation, everything had meaning, nothing was by chance, all was pre-ordained, even the insect trapped in the paint, placed there to show him the way.

He raised the latch. The door swung slowly backwards, revealing a square sitting room. Late afternoon sunshine filled the chamber, and for a moment he was transfixed by the loveliness of the light.

A window to God . . .

He blinked, and loveliness became mere sunshine. The light caught on a picture in a carved gilt frame, which hung over the mantelpiece. He stared at it, at the women it portrayed, who were engaged in a scene of such wickedness that it took his breath away. He forced himself to look away and the rest of the room came slowly to his attention: a press of blackened oak; chair and stools; a richly coloured carpet; a table on which were papers, wine, sweetmeats and two glasses; and a couch strewn with velvet cushions the colour of leaves in spring.

And on the couch—

Inside his belly, the serpent twisted and sunk its teeth.

Something did not fit, something was wrong—

The woman lay sleeping on the couch, her head turned away from him. Her hair was loose – dark ringlets draped over white skin. Her silk gown was designed to reveal her breasts rather than conceal them. The gown was yellow, and also red in places.

She had kicked off her shoes before falling asleep, and they lay beside the couch. They were silly, feminine things with high heels and silver buckles. The hem of the gown had risen almost to the knees, revealing a froth of lace beneath. One hand lay carelessly on her bosom. She wore a ring with a sapphire.

But she wasn't Rachel. She didn't resemble Rachel in the slightest. She was older, for a start, thinner, smaller, and less well-favoured.

His mind whirred, useless as a child's spinning top. He had a sudden, shameful urge to touch the woman's breast.

'Mistress,' he said. 'Mistress? Are you unwell?'

She did not reply.

'Mistress,' he said sharply, angry with himself as well as with her for leading him into temptation. 'Are you drunk? Wake up.'

He drew closer, and stooped over her. Such a wanton, sinful display of flesh. The devil's work to lead mankind astray. He stared at the breasts, unable to look away. They were quite still. The woman might have been a painted statue in a Popish church.

She had a foolish face, of course. Her mouth was open, which showed her teeth; some were missing, and the rest were stained. Dull, sad eyes stared at him.

Oh God, he thought, and for a moment the fog in his mind cleared and he saw the wretch for what she truly was.

Merciful father, here are the wages of sin, for me as well as for her. God had punished his lust, and this poor woman's. God be blessed in his infinite wisdom.

And yet – what if there were still life in this fallen woman? Would not God wish him to urge her to repent?

Her complexion was unnaturally white. There was a velvet beauty patch at the corner of her left eye in the shape of a coach and horses, and another on her cheek in the form of a heart. The poor vain woman, tricking herself out with her powders and patches, and for what? To entice men into her sinful embrace.

He knelt beside her and rested his ear against the left side of her breast, hoping to hear or feel through the thickness of the gown and the shift beneath the beating of a heart. Nothing. He shifted his fingers to one side. He could not find a heartbeat.

His fingertips touched something damp, a stickiness. He

smelled iron. He was reminded of the butcher's shop beside his old premises in Pater Noster Row.

Was that another sound? On the landing? On the stairs.

He withdrew his hand. The fingers were red with blood. Like the butcher's fingers when he had killed a pig on the step, and the blood drained down to the gutter, a feast for flies. Why was there so much blood? It was blood on the yellow gown: that was why some of it was red.

Thank God it was not Rachel. He sighed and drew down the lids over the sightless eyes. He knew what was due to death. When Rachel had drawn her last labouring breath—

The cuff of his shirt had trailed across the blood. He blinked, his train of thought broken. There was blood on his sleeve. They would be angry with him for fouling his linen.

He took a paper from the table and wiped his hand and the cuff as best he could. He stuffed the paper in his pocket to tidy it away and rose slowly to his feet.

Rachel – how in God's name could he have forgotten her? Perhaps she had gone outside while he was distracted.

In his haste, he collided with a chair and knocked it over. On the landing, he closed the door behind him. He went downstairs. As he came out into the sunshine, something shifted in his memory and suddenly he knew this place for what it was: one of those nests of lawyers that had grown up outside the old city walls, as nests of rooks cluster in garden trees about a house.

Lawyers. The devil's spawn. They argued white into black with their lies and their Latin, and they sent innocent, God-fearing men to prison, as he knew to his cost.

Birds sang in the garden. The courtyard was full of people, mainly men, mainly dressed in lawyers' black which reminded him again of rooks, talking among themselves. Caw, caw, he murmured to himself, caw, caw.

He walked stiffly towards the hall with its high, pointed windows. At the door, he paused, and looked back. His eyes travelled up the building he had just left. The shadowy man was back at the first-floor window. He raised his arm at the shadow, partly in accusation and partly in triumph: there, see the rewards of sin. Fall on your knees and repent.

Suddenly, there was Rachel herself. She was coming out of the doorway of the blackened ruin next to Staircase XIV. She had pulled her cloak over her face to cover her shame. She was trying to hide from him. She was trying to hide from God.

Caw, caw, said the rooks.

'Rachel,' he said, or perhaps he only thought it. 'Rachel.'

A lawyer passed her, jostling her shoulder, and for a moment the cloak slipped. To his astonishment, he saw that the woman was not Rachel, after all. This woman wore the mark of Cain on her face. Cain was jealous of his brother Abel, so he slew him.

Not Rachel. His wife was dead, rotting in her grave, waiting among the worms for the Second Coming of the Lord and the everlasting reign of King Jesus. Nor had Rachel borne the mark of Cain.

'Sinner!' he cried, shaking his fist. 'Sinner!'

The bite of the serpent endured beyond death. Perhaps he had been wrong about Rachel. Had she been a whore too, like Eve a temptress of men, destined to writhe for all eternity in the flames of hell?

Caw, caw, said the rooks. Caw, caw.

CHAPTER TWO

I T IS MARVELLOUS what money in your pocket and a toehold in the world will do for a man's self-esteem.

There I was, James Marwood. Sleeker of face and more prosperous of purse than I had been six months earlier. Clerk to Mr Williamson, the Under-Secretary of State to my Lord Arlington himself. Clerk to the Board of Red Cloth, which was attached to the Groom of the Stool's department. James Marwood – altogether a rising man, if only in my own estimation.

That evening, Thursday, 2 May, I set out by water from the Tower, where I had been a witness on Mr Williamson's behalf at the interrogation of certain prisoners. The tide was with us, though only recently on the turn. The ruins of the city lay on my right – the roofless churches, the tottering chimney stacks, the gutted warehouses, the heaps of ash – but distance and sunlight lent them a strange beauty, touching with the colours of paradise. On my left, on the Surrey side, Southwark lay undamaged, and before me the lofty buildings on London Bridge towered across the river with the traffic passing to and fro between them.

The waterman judged it safe for us to pass beneath the bridge. A few hours later, when the tide would be running faster, the currents would be too turbulent for safety. Even so, he took us through Chapel Lock, one of the wider arches. It was a relief to reach open water at the cost of only a little spray on my cloak.

London opened up before me again, still dominated by the blackened hulk of St Paul's on its hill. It was eight months since the Great Fire. Though the streets had been cleared and the ruins surveyed, the reconstruction had barely begun.

My mind was full of the evening that lay ahead – the agreeable prospect of a supper with two fellow clerks in a Westminster tavern where there would be music, and where there was a pretty barmaid who would be obliging if you promised her a scrap of lace or some other trifle. Before that, however, I needed to return to my house to change my clothes and make my notes for Mr Williamson.

I had the waterman set me down at the Savoy Stairs. My new lodgings were nearby in the old palace. I had moved there less than three weeks ago from the house of Mr Newcomb, the King's Printer. Since my good fortune, I deserved better and I could afford to pay for it.

In the later wars, the Savoy had been used to house the wounded. Now its rambling premises near the river were used mainly for ageing soldiers and sailors, and also for private lodgings. The latter were much sought after since the Fire – accommodation of all sorts was still in short supply. It was crown property and Mr Williamson had dropped a word on my behalf into the right ear.

Infirmary Close, my new house, was one of four that had been created by subdividing a much larger building. I had the smallest and cheapest of them. At the back it overlooked the graveyard attached to the Savoy chapel. It was an inconvenience which was likely to grow worse as the weather became warmer, but it was also the reason why the rent was low.

My cheerfulness dropped away from me in a moment when Margaret opened the door to me. I knew something was amiss as soon as I saw her face.

I passed her my damp cloak. 'What is it?'

'I'm sorry, master – your father went wandering today. I was only gone for a while – the night-soil man came to the door, and he does talk, sir, a perfect downpour of words, you cannot—'

'Is he safe?'

'Safe? Yes, sir.' She draped the cloak over the chest, her hands smoothing its folds automatically. 'He's by the parlour fire. I'd left him in the courtyard on his usual bench. The sun was out, and he was asleep. And I thought, if I was only gone a moment, he—'

'When was this?' I snapped.

She bit her lip. 'I don't know. Upward of an hour? We couldn't find him. Then suddenly he was back – the kitchen yard. Barty brought him.'

'Who?'

'Barty, sir. The crossing-sweeper by Temple Bar. He knows your father wanders sometimes.'

I didn't know Barty from Adam, but I made a mental note to give him something for his pains.

'Sir,' Margaret said in a lower voice. 'He was weeping. Like a child.'

'Why?' I said. 'Had someone hurt him?'

'No.'

'Has he said anything?'

Margaret rubbed her eyes with the back of her hand. 'Rachel.'

I felt as if someone had kicked me. 'What?'

'Rachel, sir. That's what he said when he came in. Over and over again. Just the name. Rachel.' She stared up at me, twisting a fold of her dress in her hands. 'Who's Rachel, sir? Do you know?'

I didn't answer her. Of course I knew who Rachel was. She was my mother, dead these six long years, but not always dead to my father.

I went into the parlour. The old man was sitting by the fire and spooning the contents of a bowl of posset into his mouth. Margaret or someone had laid a large napkin across his lap. But it had not been large enough to catch all the drops of posset that had missed his mouth. He did not look up as I entered the room.

Anger ran through me, fuelled by love and relief, those most combustible ingredients, and heating my blood like wine. Where was my father in this wreck of a human being? Where was Nathaniel Marwood, the man who had ruled his family and his business with the authority of God's Viceroy, and who had earned the universal respect of his friends? He had been a printer once, as good as any in Pater Noster Row, a man of substance. Politics and religion had led him down dangerous paths to his ruin, but no one had ever doubted his honesty or his skill. Now, after his years in prison, only fragments of him were left.

The spoon scraped around the side of the empty bowl. I took the bowl from him, meeting only the slightest resistance, and then the spoon. I placed them both on the table and considered whether to remove the soiled napkin. On reflection, it seemed wiser to leave it to Margaret.

Eating and the afternoon's unaccustomed exercise had tired him. His eyes closed. His hands were in his lap. The right hand was grimy. The cuff of his shirt protruded from the sleeve of his coat. The underside of the cuff was stained reddish-brown like ageing meat.

My anger evaporated. I leaned forward and pushed up the cuff. There was no sign of a cut or graze on his wrist or his hand.

I shook him gently. 'Sir? Margaret tells me you went abroad this afternoon. Why?'

The only answer was a gentle snore.

Four hours later, by suppertime, the posset was merely a memory and my father was hungry again. Hunger made him briefly lucid, or as near to that state as he was ever likely to come.

'Why did you go out, sir?' I asked him, keeping my voice gentle because it upset him if I spoke roughly to him. 'You know it worries Margaret when she cannot find you.'

'Rachel.' He was looking into the fire, and God alone knew what he saw there. 'I cannot allow my wife to walk the town without knowing where she is. It is not fitting, so I followed her to remonstrate with her. Did she not promise to obey me in all things? She was wearing her best cloak, too, her Sunday cloak. It is most becoming.' He frowned. 'Perhaps it is too becoming. The devil lays his traps so cunningly. I must speak to her, indeed I must. Why did she bear the mark of Cain? I shall find out the truth of the matter.'

'Rachel . . . ? My mother?'

He glanced at me. 'Who else?' Even as he spoke, he looked bewildered. 'But you were not born. You were in her belly.'

'And now I am here before you, sir,' I said, as if this double time my father inhabited, this shifting confluence of now and then, were the most natural thing in the world. 'Where did my mother go?'

'Where the lawyers are. Those sucklings of the devil.'

'Where, exactly?' The lawyers congregated in many places.

He smiled. 'You should have seen her, James,' he said. 'Always neat in her movements. She loves to dance, though of course I do not allow it. It is not seemly for a married woman. But . . . but how graceful she is, James, even in her kitchen. Why, she is as graceful as a deer.'

'Which lawyers were these, sir?'

'Have you ever remarked how lawyers are like rooks? They cling together and go caw-caw-caw. They all look the same. And they go to hell when they die. Did you know that? Moreover—'

'Rachel, sir. Where did she go?'

'Why, into the heart of a rookery. There was a courtyard where there was a parliament of these evil birds. And I followed her by a garden to a doorway in a building of brick . . . and the letters of one name were most ill-painted, James, and ill-formed as well. There was a great drip attached to it, and a poor creature had drowned therein, and I could have scraped it away but there was not time.'

'A creature . . . ?'

'Even ants are God's creatures, are they not? He brought two of them into the ark, so he must have decided they should be saved from the Flood. Ah—'

18

My father broke off as Margaret came into the room bearing bread. She laid the table for supper. His eyes followed her movements.

'And then, sir?' I said. 'Where did she go?'

'I thought to find her in the chamber with the ant. Up the stairs.' He spoke absently, his attention still on Margaret. 'But she wasn't there. No one was, only the woman on the couch. The poor, abandoned wretch. Her sins found her out, and she suffered the punishment for them.'

The fingers of his left hand played with the soiled shirt cuff. He rubbed the stiff linen where the blood had dried.

Margaret left the room.

'Who was this woman?' I said.

'Not Rachel, thanks be to God. No, no.' He frowned. 'Such a sinfully luxurious chamber. It had a carpet on the floor that was so bright it hurt the eyes. And there was a painting over the fireplace . . . its lewdness was an offence in the eyes of God and man.'

'But the woman, sir?' I knew he must have wandered into one of his waking dreams, but it was wise to make sure he was calm now, that he would not wake screaming in the night and wake the whole household, as he sometimes did. 'This woman on the couch, I mean. What was she doing there?'

'She was a sinner, poor fool. Displaying herself like a wanton for all the world to see. Tricked out in her finery, yellow as the sun, red as fire. With a coach and horses too. Oh, vanity, vanity. And all for nothing. I closed her eyes, I owed her that at least.'

Margaret's footsteps were approaching.

My father's face changed, scrubbed clean of every expression but greed. He turned his head to the door. Margaret stood there with a platter in her hand. 'Come, James, to table,' he said. 'Supper is served. Can't you see?'

I learned nothing more from my father that day. Experience had taught me that there was little purpose in talking to him after supper, not if you expected replies that made much sense. Nor was I convinced that there was anything more to learn.

Besides, why bother? My father's memory was unpredictable in its workings and, by and large, he was now more likely to recall events from the remote past than more recent ones. If he remembered anything at all. For much of the time he lived among his dreams.

'Come to me later in my chamber,' he mumbled, when he had finished eating. 'We must pray together, my son.'

'Perhaps, sir.' I did not like to look at him. There was a trickle of dribble at the corner of his mouth and his coat was speckled with crumbs. He was my father. I loved and honoured him. But sometimes the sight of him disgusted me. 'I have business to attend to.'

My mind was busy elsewhere. Something might be salvaged from my plans for the evening. I calculated that if I took a boat from the Savoy Stairs, my friends should still be at the tavern. And, if fortune smiled on me, so would the pretty barmaid.

Accordingly, after supper, I left Margaret to deal with my father. I had grown prosperous enough to keep two servants – Margaret Witherdine and her husband Samuel, a discharged sailor who had suffered the misfortune of losing part of a leg in his country's wars against the Dutch. Samuel had fallen into poverty and then into debt, partly because of his country's inability to pay him what he was owed. Nevertheless he had done me a great service, and I had discharged his debt. In return, I believed, Sam and Margaret served my father and me from loyalty as well as for their board and lodging and a little money.

All this was agreeable to me. God help me, it gave me a good opinion of myself. I was as smug as the cat who has found the larder door open and eaten and drunk his fill. And like the cat, sitting afterwards and cleaning his whiskers in the sunshine, I assumed this happy state of affairs would last for ever.

So I did not see my father after supper that day. Sometimes I went into his chamber when he was ready for bed, even if I had been out late. But not that night. I did not admit it to myself but I was irritated with him. Because of his folly, I had been obliged to forgo my evening on the river. To make matters worse, when I had reached the tavern, my friends were not there and the pretty barmaid had left to be married.

So Margaret must have settled him in his bed, listened to the mumbled nonsense that he believed to be his prayers and blown out his candle. She must have sat with him in the dark, holding his hand, until he fell asleep. I knew that would have happened because that was what she always did. I also knew that my father would have preferred his son beside him when he said his prayers, and that he would have liked his own flesh and blood to hold his hand, rather than a servant.

The following morning, I had arranged to go into the office at an earlier hour than usual. Mr Williamson wanted my notes from the Tower interrogations as soon as possible. Besides, I was behind in my task of copying his correspondence into his letter book, and there was also my regular work for the *Gazette*. The press of business was very great — the *London Gazette*, the twice-weekly government newspaper which Mr Newcomb printed here in the Savoy, was another of Williamson's responsibilities, and he delegated much of its day-to-day administration to me.

My father was already awake. He was in his chamber, where Margaret was helping him dress. As I left the parlour, I heard his voice, deep and resonant, booming in the distance; like his body, his voice belonged to a healthier, stronger man, a man who still had his wits about him. I persuaded myself that I could not spare the time to wish him good morning before I left.

I did not give my father another thought until after dinner, when my servant Samuel Witherdine came to Whitehall and knocked on the door of Mr Williamson's office. Sam was a wiry man with a weathered face and very bright blue eyes, which at present were surrounded by puffy eyelids. He wore a wooden leg below his right knee and supported himself with a crutch.

Something was amiss. It was unheard of for him to come to the office of his own accord. I thought the puffy eyes meant he was hungover. I was wrong.

CHAPTER THREE

THE DOOR OPENED.
    'Mistress?'

On Friday morning, a woman lay on her bed in a new house on the north side of Pall Mall. She clung to the shreds of sleep that swirled like seaweed around her. Drown me in sleep, she thought, six fathoms deep, and let the fish nibble me into a million pieces.

The door closed, and was softly latched. Footsteps crossed the floor. Light and quick and familiar.

'Are you awake?'

No, Jemima thought, I am not. She fought the creeping tide of consciousness every inch of the way. To be conscious was to remember.

She had been dreaming of Syre Place, where she had grown up. It was strange that she knew it to be Syre Place because it had seemed not to resemble the real house. The real Syre Place was built of brick, of a russet colour like a certain apple that her father was fond of. As a child, she had assumed that the house had somehow been built to match the apples, which was all part of the rightness of things, of the patterns that ran through everything.

But the Syre Place in her dreams was all wrong. It was faced with stone, for a start, and designed after the modern fashion that Philip liked. (Philip? Philip? Her mind shied away from the thought of Philip.) It was a house in the modern fashion, a neat box, with everything tidy and clean both within and without, and a roof whose overhanging eaves made it look as if the building were wearing a hat.

'My lady? My lady?'

In Syre Place, the real one, there was a park where her father used to hunt before he lost his good humour and the use of his legs. Down the lane was the farm, whose smells and sounds were part of life, running through every hour of every day. In this Syre Place, however, the park was gone, and so was the farm. Instead there was a garden with gravel paths and parterres and shrubs, arranged symmetrically like the house. But – now she looked more closely at it – there was nothing neat about the garden in the dream because weeds had sprung up everywhere, and brambles criss-crossed the paths and arched overhead.

Nettles stood in great clumps, their leaves twitching, desperate to sting her. Her brother had thrown her into a bed of nettles when she was scarcely out of leading strings, and she still remembered the agonizing, unfair pain of it. How strange and unnatural it was, she thought, that a plant should be so nasty, so hostile. God had made the plants and the animals to serve man, not to attack him.

Nature was unnatural. It was full of monstrous tricks. Perhaps it was the work of the devil, not God.

'Come now, madam. It's past eleven o'clock.'

Time? What time of year could it be? In the garden at Syre Place, the gravel paths were carpeted with spoiled fruit. Brown apples and pears, and yellow raspberries, and red strawberries and green plums, as if all fruitful seasons existed at once. They lay so thickly on the ground that she could no longer see the gravel. The smell of decay was everywhere. Jemima raised her skirts – good God, what was she wearing? just her shift? But she was outside and in broad daylight, where anyone might see her – but the pulpy fruit splashed stickily against the linen and spattered the skin of her bare legs.

There were wasps, too, she saw, fat-bellied things cruising a few inches above the ground and feeding on the rottenness. What if one of them flew up inside her shift and stung her in her most private and intimate place?

In her fear, she cried out.

'Hush now,' Mary murmured, the voice floating above her. 'It's all right. Time to wake up.'

No, no, no, Jemima thought. Despite the wasps, despite everything, it was better to stay asleep, her eyes screwed shut against the daylight. She wanted to stay for ever in Syre Place where once, she thought, she had been happy.

What was happiness? Rocking in Nurse's lap as she sang. Sitting beside her brother Henry when, greatly condescending, he guided her as she stumbled through her hornbook. Or, better still, when he perched her up before him on the new brown mare, with the ground so far beneath that she had to close her eyes so she wouldn't see it.

'I'll drop you, Jemima,' her brother had said, his arms tightening around her. 'Your skull will crack like an eggshell.'

Oh, the sweet, delicious terror of it.

Someone she could not see called her name.

No. No. Go to sleep, she ordered herself: down, down, down into the deep, dark depths where no one can see me. To the time before that fatal letter, before the Fire Court, before she had even known where Clifford's Inn was.

Something was buzzing. It must be a wasp. She moaned with fear.

There was a sudden rattle of curtain rings, brutally unexpected, and she was bathed in brilliance. The bed curtains had been thrown open. It was as if someone had thrown a bucket of light over her. She squeezed her eyelids together but the light glowed pinkly outside them. A current of cool air swept over her, bringing the scents of the garden.

'Close the curtains, you fool,' she wanted to say, 'shut out the light.' But she couldn't, wouldn't speak.

She was lying on her back, she knew, on her own bed in her own bedchamber. If she opened her eyes she would see the canopy above her, blue and silver, silk embroidery; the bed was in its summer clothing; the winter curtains and canopy were made of much heavier material, and their embroidery was predominantly red and gold, the colours of fire. The curtains were hers, part of her dowry. Almost everything was hers. Everything except Dragon Yard.

She didn't want to know all this. She wanted to be asleep in the dark, in a place too deep for dreaming, too deep for knowledge.

'Master's coming,' said the voice. A woman's. Her woman's. Mary's.

A wasp. Buzz, buzz, buzz. Why can't it go away?

'Any moment he'll be here. I can't put him off.'

Her brother Henry had had a waistcoat like a wasp: all

yellow and black. Jemima wondered what had happened to it. Perhaps it had been lost in the fire. Or perhaps it was down, down in the deep, dark depths, where Henry was presumably lying himself. Anything the fishes had left. Philip had served with Henry in the Navy in the Dutch wars. That was how she had met her husband, as her brother's friend.

The latch rattled again, shockingly loud. The buzzing stopped.

'Isn't she awake yet?'

Philip's voice, achingly familiar, and horribly strange.

'No, master.'

'She should be awake by now. Surely?'

'The draught lasts longer for some people than for others.'

Heavy footsteps drew closer to the bed, closer to her. She could smell Philip now. Sweat, a trace of the perfume he sometimes wore, the hint of last night's wine.

'Madam,' he said. Then, more loudly: 'Madam?'

The voice made something inside her answer to it. Her body's response was involuntary, beyond control or desire. She knew she must continue to breathe, and that she must give no sign that she was not deeply asleep. Yet she wanted to cry out, to scream at him, to howl in agony and rage.

'Hush, sir. It's better to let her be.'

'Hold your tongue, woman,' he shouted. 'She's pale as a ghost. I'll send for the doctor.'

The buzzing returned. To and fro, it went, nearer and further. She focused her attention on it. A distraction. She hoped it was not a wasp.

'She's always pale, sir,' Mary said, almost in a whisper. 'You know that.'

'But she's slept for hours.'

'Sleep's the best cure. There's no physic can mend her faster. It's always been the way with her. I went out this morning and fetched another draught from the apothecary in case she needs it tonight.'

'You left her alone? Like this?'

'No, no, master. Hester was watching over her. I wasn't gone long, in any case.'

'Devil take that fly,' Philip muttered, his attention fastening on another irritation.

The buzzing stopped abruptly. There was the sound of a slap, followed by a muffled oath.

'Hush, sir,' Mary said. 'You'll wake her.'

'Hold your tongue. Or I'll put you out on the street with nothing but a shift to cover your nakedness. Has she said anything yet?'

'No, sir. Not a word.'

'Stand over there. By the door.'

The heavy footsteps drew nearer. She kept her eyelids tightly closed. She heard the sound of his breathing and knew he must be stooping above the bed, bringing his face close to hers.

'Jemima.' His voice was a whisper, and his breath touched her cheek. 'Can you hear me?' When she said nothing in reply, he went on, 'Where were you yesterday afternoon? Where did you go?'

Philip paused. She heard his breathing, and a creaking floorboard, the one near the door, where Mary must be standing.

'What made you so distressed?' he said. 'What did you see?'

After a few seconds, he let out his breath in a sigh of exasperation. He walked away from the bed. 'Mary? Are you sure you know nothing?'

'No, sir. I told you – she left me in the hackney.'

'I'll whip the truth out of you.'

'That is the truth.'

The door latch rattled. 'Send for me as soon as your mistress wakes. Do you understand?'

'Yes, master.'

'Don't let anyone else talk to her until I have. Not Hester, not anyone. And not you, either. Is that clear?'

'Yes, sir.'

The door closed. The footsteps clattered down the stairs.

She listened to Mary moving around the room and the buzzing of the fly. After a moment she opened her eyes. Daylight dazzled her. 'I thought he would never go,' she said.

Jemima spent Saturday and Sunday in bed. Mary tended to her needs. Mary was her maid. She had come with her from Syre Place. Her father was a tenant farmer on the estate, a man with too many daughters. Sir George had charged Mary to take special care of her mistress when she married Philip, and to obey her in all things, not Philip.

Mary sometimes slept with her when Philip did not come to her bed, especially in winter.

When Mary wasn't in the room, she sent Hester in her place. Hester was a stupid little girl, fresh from the country. When she was obliged to speak to her mistress, she blushed a cruel and unforgiving red that spread over her face like a stain. She blushed when her master was in the room too, but he never spoke to her.

'My lady?' Mary said on Monday afternoon. 'We need to change the sheets.'

She opened her eyes and saw Mary standing over her with

an armful of bedlinen. She allowed herself to be helped out of bed and placed in an armchair by the window. It was a fresh, clear afternoon. Her bedchamber was at the back of the house. The trees at the bottom of the garden shielded the brick wall behind them and the fields stretching up to Piccadilly.

The window was open, and she heard hooves, hammering and sometimes distant voices. The trees blocked out most of the view, but occasionally she glimpsed a flash of colour through the leaves or wisps of smoke, rising higher into the empty sky until they dissipated themselves in the empty blue of heaven.

If one went to heaven after death, Jemima thought, how eternally tedious it would be if it were nothing but blue and infinitely empty. Better to be nothing at all oneself. Which was blasphemy.

Philip came up to see her while she was sitting there.

'Madam,' he said, bowing. 'I'm rejoiced to see you out of your bed at last.'

He glanced at the maids, who had continued at their work but were making themselves as unobtrusive as possible, as servants should. 'Mary says you remember nothing of your – your illness.'

'No, sir.' She and Mary had agreed it was wiser this way, wiser to bide one's time. 'I had pains in my head when I woke up.'

'The doctor called it a sudden inflammation of the brain. Thanks to his treatment, it came and went like an April shower. Can you remember how it happened?'

'No. It is all a perfect blank to me until I woke up in my bed.'

'You and Mary went out for a drive in a hackney coach,' he said slowly, as if teaching a child a lesson. 'After you'd dined – on Thursday. Remember?'

'No.'

'The fever came on suddenly. You were insensible, or very near to it, when Mary brought you home.'

'I remember nothing,' she said, though she remembered everything that mattered. She remembered every inch of the way to Clifford's Inn, every step up the stairs of Staircase XIV. For now, however, it was better to pretend to forget.

Philip's hand touched her arm. 'The doctor said that sometimes sufferers are much troubled by dreams when the fever is at its height, and believe all sorts of strange fancies. But thank God all that is passed now.'

'I am much better, sir,' she said. 'I feel quite refreshed.'

'Good. In that case, will you join me at supper?'

'I think not. I will take something here instead.'

Jemima watched him as she spoke, but his expression told her nothing. Her husband was tall, lean and dark-complexioned – like the King himself. He was not a handsome man but usually she found his face good to look at, because it was his. But now his face had become a mere arrangement of features, an array of hollows, projections, planes, textures, colours. He was a stranger to her.

A familiar stranger. A treacherous stranger, and that was the very worst sort of stranger.

'Tomorrow, then,' he said, smiling. 'For dinner. We shall have guests, by the way – a brace of lawyers. One of them's Sir Thomas Twisden, the judge.'

It seemed to her that he spoke more deliberately than usual, enunciating the words with precision as if they were especially significant. He paused – only for a second, but she knew that the pause meant something, too. He knew that she didn't like people to come to the house.

The maids had finished making the bed. Hester left the room, her arms full of dirty linen. Mary remained, tidying the pots and bottles on the dressing table.

'And I've asked Lucius Gromwell to join us,' Philip said.

Jemima caught her breath, and hoped he hadn't noticed. Gromwell, of all people. The sly, twice-damned, whoreson devil. How dared they? She stared at her lap. She sensed he was looking at her, gauging her reaction to Gromwell's name. She was aware as well that, on the very edge of her range of vision, Mary's hands were no longer moving among the litter on the dressing table.

'It will be good to have you at the table,' he went on. 'You must make sure they send up something worth eating. We must do our best to keep Sir Thomas amused. We want him to look kindly on us, after all, don't we?'

His voice sharpened towards the end, and she looked up. He wants me to twitch like a hound bitch, she thought, to the sound of her master's voice.

'Yes, sir,' she said.

'He's a Fire Court judge,' Philip reminded her. 'He's down for the Dragon Yard case.'

He smiled at her and made his way towards the door. He paused, his hand on the latch.

'Lucius is writing a book, by the way. He is mad for it. It's called *The Natural Curiosities of Gloucestershire*, and it will have many plates and maps, so it will cost a great deal to produce. I promised him I would pay for the publication, and he assures me it will make me a handsome profit when the edition sells out, as well as enshrine my name for posterity.'

Gromwell, she thought. I hate him.

'You remember him, don't you? My old friend from school and Oxford.'

She nodded. Gromwell will look at me tomorrow and know my shame, she thought, and I shall look at him and know that he knows it. He arranged it all. None of this would have happened without him. Gromwell, who dared to stand in my way at Clifford's Inn.

'Poor Lucius, eh?' Her husband lifted the latch and laughed with what seemed like genuine amusement. 'I doubt he'll ever finish the book. He is a man of many parts but he finishes nothing he begins. He was like that at school, and he's never changed.'

CHAPTER FOUR

MY FATHER HAD been run over in Fleet Street by a wagon bearing rubble removed from the ruins of St Paul's Cathedral. The weight had broken his spine, killing him instantly. It was a miracle that the pressure had not cut him in half.

Infirmary Close was full of wailing women. Margaret persuaded herself that his death had been her fault, for she had left him in the parlour while she was making dinner, believing he was no longer capable of managing the locks and bolts of the door into the lane. The neighbours' maids wept in sympathy. The laundry woman came to the house to collect the washing; she wept too, because tears are catching and death is frightening.

After he brought me home in the hackney coach, Sam went into the kitchen yard and chopped wood as if he were chopping down his enemies: one by one, with deliberation and satisfaction.

As for me, I went into my father's bedchamber and sat beside him, as I should have done last night. He lay with his eyes closed and his hands folded over his chest. Someone had covered the great wound with a sheet and bound up his jaw. His face appeared unmarked. Sometimes the dead look peaceful. He did not.

I could not pray. I did not weep. The weight of his disapproval bore down on me, for I had strayed from the godly path he had ordained for me, and now it could never be put right. Worse still was the shame I felt about how I had behaved to him and how I had felt about him during the last few months, when he had become as vulnerable as a child.

Something shifted inside me, as an earthquake ripples and rumbles through solid earth and rock, bringing floods and ruin in its wake. Nothing would be the same again.

That was when the memory of Catherine Lovett came into my mind. She was a young woman with a strange and independent cast of mind. I had done her a service at the time of the Fire, though I had not seen her since; she was living in retirement and under an assumed name. As it happened, I had been with her when her father died, and I had seen what she had done. She had taken his hand and raised it to her lips.

I looked at my father's hand. Flesh, skin and bone. The fingers twisted like roots. The nails discoloured and in need of trimming. Death had robbed his hand of its familiarity and made it strange.

I lifted the hand and kissed it. The weight of it took me by surprise. The dead are heavier than the living.

'I am truly sorry for your loss,' Mr Williamson said the following morning.

I thanked him and requested leave of absence to bury my father and settle his affairs.

'Of course.' Williamson turned away and busied himself with the papers on his desk. 'Where will you lay him to rest?'

'Bunhill Fields, sir.'

Williamson grunted. 'Not an Anglican burial ground?'

'I think not. He would not have wished it.'

Bunhill Fields was where the Dissenters lay, and where my father belonged. Williamson returned to reading letters, occasionally annotating them. The two of us were alone in the Scotland Yard office, which lay just to the north of the Whitehall Palace itself. Williamson had two offices, one close to my Lord Arlington's, and this one, which he used for the *Gazette* and for other concerns that required more privacy.

A few minutes later, he spoke again, and his voice sounded harder than before, closer to his northern roots, which was often a sign of irritation in him. 'You must look to the living, Marwood, as well as the dead.'

'Yes, sir.'

'You would not wish anything to reflect ill on this office. Nor would I.'

I bowed my head. I knew what Williamson intended me to understand. Before his mind lost its bearings, my father, Nathaniel Marwood, had been a Fifth Monarchist. As a result of his allegiance to that dangerous sect, he had been imprisoned for treason. He had considered the Church of England as the next best thing to the Church of Rome with its Papist ways and its foul plots against honest men. He had hated all kings except King Jesus, whose coming he had devoutly waited for.

'After all,' Williamson said, staring grimly at me, 'you

would not want to lie in Bunhill Fields yourself when your time comes. At least, I hope you would not.'

'Of course not, sir.'

Nowadays I served the King; and it was politic for me to have a care for what I did and said, and to choose wisely whom I associated with. I made sure the world knew that I went to church regularly and that I took communion when it was fitting to do so, according to the rites of the Established Church and the instruction of its bishops. But there was always the danger that, through my father, I might be considered guilty by association, by blood.

'So you will change your mind, Marwood? No doubt your father would have wished you to think of your best interests in these changed times.'

'Yes, sir. But I must also think of his.'

Williamson gave a laugh – short, sharp and mirthless, like the bark of a dog. 'You're obstinate in your folly.' He lowered his head over his papers. 'Like father, like son, I suppose.'

For some reason, that last remark comforted me as nothing else did.

Two days later, on Monday, we laid Nathaniel Marwood in his grave. There was no reason for delay – the death had been an accident; it was easy enough for an old man to stagger on the crowded pavement and fall under the wagon. He had been notably infirm in mind, if not in body, and quite possibly did not even know where he was. Such deaths happen every day.

We took the body to Bunhill Fields. Apart from the minister, the bearers and the diggers, the only mourners were Sam and myself. Margaret was debarred by her sex from coming, which was unkind, for her grief was in its way deeper and truer than my own. She still wept for my father at the slightest provocation, despite the fact that in life he had been a burden to her.

After the interment, Sam and I took a hackney coach around the walls of the ruined city, a wasteland of blackened chimney stacks, roofless churches and sodden ashes. I told the driver to set us down in Fleet Street. We went to the Devil, the big tavern between Temple Bar and Middle Temple Gate, where Sam stuffed himself with as much as he could eat and I made myself swiftly and relentlessly drunk.

Memory is a strange thing, fickle and misleading, as treacherous as water. My memories of the rest of the day are like broken glass – jumbled, largely meaningless and with sharp edges liable to wound. But I remember perfectly one snatch of conversation between us, partly because it happened early on, and partly because of what was said.

'Do you know the crossing-sweeper here, master?'

I was too busy drinking to reply.

'He knows you,' Sam went on.

'Do I?' Of course I gave the sweeper a penny occasionally. If you used a crossing regularly, you would be a fool not to. But I could not for the life of me remember what the man looked like.

'His name's Bartholomew,' Sam said. 'Like the prophet. Barty.'

I was not attending to what he was saying. I was trying to attract the attention of the waiter and order more wine.

'He's the one who brought your father home. The day before he died.'

I forgot the waiter and looked at Sam. 'Yes – I remember.

Margaret told me. I should give him something for his trouble.'

Sam touched the side of his head with his forefinger. 'Barty said he didn't know the old man's wits were wandering. Not at first. I mean, seeing him from the outside, who would? He didn't look as if he had an addled brain.'

It was a fair point. Nathaniel Marwood had looked what he was – an old man in his sixties, but hale enough. It was only if you tried to talk to him, and you heard the nonsense that poured out of his mouth, making little more sense than the babble of an infant, that you realized his infirmity.

'There's an archway up beyond the church, sir. Barty said that was the way your father came.'

'An archway?' I thought he meant the great gateway that divided the City from Westminster, and Fleet Street from the Strand. 'You mean he came through Temple Bar?'

'No, no. This archway's off the street. To the north, by St Dunstan-in-the-West.' Sam leaned forward. 'It's the way into one of these lawyers' colleges. Clifford's Inn.'

Suddenly my father's words were in my mind. The last words, nearly, that I had heard from him, and possibly the last words that contained some fragmentary elements of lucidity. 'Where the lawyers are. Those creatures of the devil.' He had hated and feared lawyers since they helped to put him in prison and take away his property.

'Isn't that where the Fire Court is sitting? Why would he go there?'

Sam shrugged.

Have you ever remarked how lawyers are like rooks? They cling together and go caw-caw-caw . . . And they go to hell when they die.

So there had been, after all, a single fragment of fact among my father's ramblings, buried in all the nonsense about my mother. He had been to Clifford's Inn, among the lawyers.

'Did Barty say more?'

'He was weeping,' Sam said. 'Barty told me that. So he walked him home, but he couldn't make head nor sense of what your father was saying.'

I hammered my fist on the table. 'Then I shall go to Clifford's Inn and find out.'

The waiter mistook the gesture and was at my elbow in a trice. 'Beg pardon, master, didn't mean to keep you waiting. Another quart of sack, is it? You will have it directly.'

'Yes,' I said, frowning at him. 'Very well, a drink before we go, to godspeed us and drink to my father's memory.' I glared at Sam. 'He should not have been weeping. He should not have been unhappy.'

Sam stared at the table. 'No, sir.'

'And why in God's name did he go to Clifford's Inn? Did someone drag him there?' All my guilt, all my sorrow, had at last found an outlet. 'I shall have the truth of it, do you hear, and I shall have it now. Find me this Barty and I shall question him.'

'Yes, sir,' Sam said.

There was the waiter again, back already. Before I was an hour older, I was too drunk to have the truth of anything.

CHAPTER FIVE

THE DAY AFTER the funeral I woke with a headache that cut my skull in two.

My mouth tasted as it had in the first few weeks after the Great Fire when everything had turned to ashes, from the air we breathed to the water we drank. Every breath and every mouthful was a reminder of what had happened. Every footstep raised a grey cloud that powdered our clothes and our hair. The destruction of a city and the death of an old man tasted the same: ashes to ashes.

It was early. I wrapped myself in my gown and went down to the kitchen, tottering like an old man myself: in fact just as my father used to do when his limbs were stiff after sleep. Death, I think, must have a sense of humour.

The kitchen was at the back of the house, a gloomy room partly lit by a leaded casement which looked over the graveyard. Margaret was already there. She had lit the fire and was busying herself with the preparations for dinner. She took one look at me, pointed at the bench by the table and went into the pantry.

The kitchen smelled of smoke and old meat. Now I was

here, I wanted to leave, but I lacked the strength. In a moment Margaret returned with a jug of small beer and a pot to put it in. Without speaking, she poured a morning draught and handed it to me.

The first mouthful made me retch. I fought back the rising nausea and took a second mouthful. I kept that down and ventured cautiously on a third.

'I put juice of the cabbage in there too,' Margaret said. 'A sovereign remedy.'

I retched again. She went back to stirring the pot over the fire, the source of another smell. I watched a rat skim along the bottom of the wall from the larder and slip through the crack below the back door. I lacked the energy to throw something at it.

Taking my time, I drank the rest of the pot and let it settle. I felt no worse for it. At least my mouth was less dry.

Margaret refilled the pot without my asking. Sam had a tendency to take too much drink, and she knew how to deal with it.

I closed my eyes. When I next opened them, Margaret was standing over me. She was a short, sturdy woman with black hair, dark eyes and a high colour. When hot or angry, she looked as if she might explode. She looked like that now but I wasn't sure why. My memory of the later part of yesterday was blurred. Clearly, I had been very drunk. That probably meant that Sam had been very drunk too.

'Master,' she said. 'Can I speak to you?'

'Later,' I said.

She ignored that. 'Your father's clothes, sir. I—'

'Give them to the poor,' I croaked. 'Sell them. I don't care a fig what you do with them.'

'It's not that, sir. I tried to clean his coat yesterday. The one he was wearing.'

I winced and looked away, reaching for the pot.

'It's a good coat,' she said. 'There's a deal of use left in it.'

'Then get rid of it somehow. Don't bother me with it, woman.'

'I emptied the pockets.'

Something in her voice made me look up. 'What is it?'

For answer, she went to the shelves on the wall opposite the fireplace and took down a small box without a lid. She set it on the table.

Inside was my father's frayed purse and a piece of rag. The purse contained two pennies — we had never given him more because his money tended to be stolen or lost, if he had not given it away first — and four pieces of type, the only surviving relics of his press in Pater Noster Row. His folding knife was there too, with its handle of wood, worn and stained with constant use. At the bottom was a crumpled sheet of paper, smeared with rust.

Not rust, of course. Dried blood. Just as there had been dried blood on the cuff of his shirt.

Yesterday's conversation with Sam flooded into my mind. The crossing-sweeper. Clifford's Inn. *Where the lawyers are. Those creatures of the devil.* And, before that, my father talking deluded nonsense about my mother, and the woman on the couch, and closing her eyes.

I picked up the paper and smoothed it out. It was a strip torn from a larger sheet. Written on it were the words 'Twisden, Wyndham, Rainsford, DY'.

Margaret refilled my pot. 'It wasn't there last week, master.'

'Are you sure?'

She ignored the question, treating it with the contempt it deserved.

My brain was still fighting yesterday's fumes. I screwed up my eyes and tried to focus on the words. First, the three names. Then two initials. DY — a name so well known that initials sufficed for it?

'Bring me a roll and some butter.'

She went away. I sat there, staring into nothing. Clifford's Inn. A scrap of paper stained with blood. A few names. It unsettled me that my father's ramblings had contained a grain of sense. He really had strayed into a place of lawyers. But he could have picked the paper up anywhere.

The door from the yard opened and closed. There were footsteps in the scullery passage, and the tap of a crutch on the flagged floor.

Sam appeared in the kitchen doorway. He jerked his head towards the scullery passage and the back door. 'Barty's in the yard.'

I stared at him.

'He won't get any scraps out of me at this hour,' Margaret said tartly. 'Tell him to come back after dinner.'

'Hold your tongue, woman.' Sam looked at me. 'Barty, master. The crossing-sweeper who saw your father. You told me to find him for you. Do you remember? In the Devil?'

Suddenly I was sober, or I felt I was. I stood up, knocking over the bench. 'Bring him in.'

'Best that you go out to him, master.' Margaret wrinkled her nose. 'If you'd be so kind. He stinks.'

'You'll give him something to eat,' I said. 'Take it out to him.'

'Something you should know, sir,' Sam said. 'Barty says he saw your father again.'

44

'What the devil are you talking about?'

Sam's voice was gentle. 'On Friday morning. As well as on Thursday.'

There was a moment of silence. My mouth was open. Margaret stood with a pan in her hand, leaning forward to put it on the fire, as still as a statue.

I swallowed. I said slowly, 'Last Friday, you mean? The day my father died?'

Sam nodded.

'Did he see what happened?'

'He'll only speak to you. I'm no use to him. You're the one with the purse.'

Margaret whimpered softly. She set the pan on the fire.

'Why didn't he tell us sooner?'

'He was taken up for debt that very afternoon. It's only yesterday evening his mother raised the money to get him out of prison.'

Sam hopped down the passage and into the yard. I followed. Over his shoulder, I saw the crossing-sweeper sitting on the side of the trough that caught the rainwater. He was huddled in a filthy cloak with his hat drawn low over his ears. He was a crooked man with a sallow countenance.

When he saw us, he sprang up and executed a clumsy bow. Then he shrank back into his cloak as if he wanted to make himself as small as possible.

'Sam says you saw my father on the day he died,' I said. 'As well as the day before, when you brought him back here.'

Barty nodded so violently that his hat fell off, exposing a bald patch covered in scabs, below which a fringe of greasy hair straggled towards his shoulders. He licked his lips. 'You won't make me go before a justice, master? Please, sir.'

'Not if you tell me the truth.'

'I done nothing wrong.' He looked from me to Sam with the eyes of a dog that fears a beating.

'Tell me,' I said. 'You won't be the poorer for it.'

'It was like Thursday, master. He came out of Clifford's Inn again, down to Fleet Street. He was in a terrible hurry, and he knocked against a bookstall there, and the bookseller swore at him . . . '

Sam nudged him with his elbow. 'Tell his honour the rest.'

Barty screwed up his face. 'He was looking back over his shoulder. As if someone was chasing him.'

'What?' I snapped. 'Who?'

'Couldn't see, sir. There was a wagon coming down from St Paul's, and a coach coming the other way, under the Bar. But I thought I'd go over and give the old fellow a helping hand, like I done the other day.'

'Hoping it would be worth your while,' Sam said. 'You don't have to tell us all that. Go on.'

'Well . . . ' Barty looked at me, and then away. 'That's when it happened. The old man tripped – fell into the road – in front of the wagon. But I heard . . . '

I seized his collar and dragged him towards me. Part of me wanted to shake the life out of him. 'What did you hear?'

'His screams, master. His screams.'

I let the wretch go. He fell back against the trough. I was trembling.

'And next?' I said.

'All the traffic stopped. I went over the road to see if . . . '

'If there were pickings to be had?'

He tried to give me an ingratiating smile. 'He was alive still, sir. Just. There was a crowd around him. But he looked up and he saw me there among them. I swear he saw me, master, I swear he did. He knew me. I know he did. He said . . . *Rook. Where's the rook?*'

'Rook,' I said. 'Rook? What rook?'

Barty stared up at me. 'I don't know what he meant, master. But I know he was scared of something.'

'What else?' I demanded.

'That's all he said, master. Then he was gone.'

Later that morning there was a knocking at the door. Sam announced that the tailor had come to wait on me.

I had quite forgotten the appointment, perhaps because I did not want to remember it. Death is a dreary business, time-consuming and expensive, and so is its aftermath. But it would not be right in the eyes of the world if I went abroad without visible signs of my bereavement.

Some of these signs were cheap enough to arrange – before the funeral, I had ordered Margaret to dull the metal of my buckles, attach black silk weepers to my hatband, and blacken my best brown shoes – including the soles, on Margaret's advice, for they would be visible when I knelt to pray.

I had borrowed a suit of mourning for the funeral but I needed to have my own. On Saturday, I had visited the tailor's shop to be measured, and to choose the material and discuss the pattern. Now the man had come to fit the suit and to try to persuade me to buy a black silk sash to set off the new clothes.

By the time all this was done, my head was clearer, and my stomach had returned to something approaching normality, though the very thought of sack made me feel queasy.

Death has this consequence: it jerks a man from the rut of

routine: it throws him back on his own company at a time when he wants it least. All this time, as the tailor prattled away and my mind became my own again, I could not concentrate on anything but the one word: 'rook'. There was nothing to distract me from it.

But what could I do? Find the nearest justice and lay the information before him? What was there to say? That a foolish old man had strayed into Clifford's Inn, and afterwards he had fallen under the wheels of a wagon in Fleet Street. A crossing-sweeper had told me that his last words had been to ask where the rook was.

What crime had been committed? Whom could I lay information against? But I had to do something, for my father's sake.

No. That was a lie. I had to do something for my own sake as much as his. In the hope of easing the grief, the guilt.

When the tailor was gone, I took the tray of my father's possessions upstairs to his chamber. The bed had already been stripped to its mattress and the curtains removed. The floor had been scrubbed and the room aired; Margaret was a vigorous housekeeper.

My father's clothes, such as they were, lay folded in the press. His smell clung to them, faint and unsettling. An old man's smell, musty and familiar. He had left little else behind him apart from his Bible and the contents of his pockets.

He had had the Bible as long as I could remember. It was a Geneva Bible, the old translation favoured by those of a Puritan persuasion. When he had been taken up for treason, he had had the book in prison with him and he read it over and over. When I was a child, he had ordered me never to touch it in case I sullied the sacred volume with the sinful touch of my grubby fingers. Until now, I had obeyed him.

Now the Bible was mine. I took it down to the parlour and laid it on the table, where the light fell on it from the window. I turned the pages, which were brittle and torn. Without my father there, the book had lost its significance. It was still a Bible, of course – the Holy Book, more precious than all the world. The Word of God. I did not dispute that. The volume was dense with wisdom, crammed with essence of holiness. But at the same time it was just a book, a small, shabby copy of something available in its tens of thousands across the country. It needed my father to lend it weight and value.

Fixed with a rusty pin to the back cover was a fold of paper. Inside, I found a lock of light brown hair, the strands twisted together and held in place with a knotted red thread.

Memory ambushed me, swift and vicious as a footpad. 'Rachel . . . how graceful she is, James, even in her kitchen. Why, she is as graceful as a deer.'

I touched the curl of hair, the fragment of my mother, a relic of someone who had been alive, whom my father had once loved and desired. I could not imagine him courting her. I could not imagine my parents being young together, younger than I was. But it seemed that her youthful self had remained so vividly alive in his memory that the image of her had lured him into Clifford's Inn, had lured him among the lawyers.

My father hated them. Lawyers were agents of Satan, servants of the Antichrist. They had helped to put him in prison. Yet desire for his dead wife had cast out all fear of them.

CHAPTER SIX

S T DUNSTAN-IN-THE-WEST WAS partly clothed in scaffolding. The church projected into the street, forcing the roadway into a bottleneck before it passed under the Bar into the Strand. Shops and booths huddled as if for protection against the south aisle wall, blocking more of the pavement and constricting the foot traffic. Though the Fire had not destroyed the church, it had come close enough to cause minor damage and blacken the stonework, particularly at the east end.

The entrance to Clifford's Inn lay at the west end of the nave, squeezed between the square tower of the church and the wall of the neighbouring building. I walked along a flagged passage that took me past the churchyard to a gate. A small, dingy courtyard lay beyond, much wider than it was deep, surrounded by a series of buildings of different sizes and ages.

The hall was directly opposite, filling the right-hand half of the northern range. I followed the path to the doorway at its left-hand end, where people were standing and talking in low voices. Some were lawyers and their clerks. Others were ordinary citizens, both men and women.

They ignored me as I passed like a ghost among them, through the doorway and into the passage that ran through the range to another doorway. The passage was crowded too, though the people were much quieter than those in the courtyard. The door to the hall itself was on the right. It was closed. A porter with his staff stood in front of it.

'Hush, sir,' he said in a savage whisper. 'The court's in session.'

I went out by the further door. I found myself in a much larger courtyard, which had a garden beyond. Over to the left, through another gateway, was Serjeant's Inn, with Chancery Lane beyond, running north from the Strand. To the right was an irregular range of buildings, leading to a further court and then another gate, which gave on to an alley off Fetter Lane. The lane had marked the western boundary of the Fire last September, but the flames had left their mark on both sides of the road. One of the Inn's buildings had been gutted – a block just inside the gate on the north side of the court. The roof was gone and the upper storeys had been partly destroyed.

Clifford's Inn as a whole had an air of dilapidation like an elderly relation in reduced circumstances left unattended in the chimney corner. There was one exception to the general neglect: a brick range facing the garden, on the far side of the blackened ruin.

What had my father said?

'I followed her by a garden to a doorway in a building of brick.'

It was strange indeed. Here was another grain of truth

among my father's ramblings on his last evening. First a place full of lawyers, and now a building of brick beside a garden.

The building had four doors at regular intervals along its length, with a pair of windows on either side overlooking the garden. I sauntered across the courtyard towards it in an elaborately casual manner. Each doorway led to a staircase, on either side of which were sets of chambers. The names of the occupants had been painted on a board beside each doorway.

I paused to examine the nearest one. There was something amiss with the lettering. I had spent my early life in the printing house, and I noticed such things. My father had made sure of that.

XIV
6 Mr Harrison
5 Mr Moran
4 Mr Gorvin
3 Mr Gromwell
2 Mr Drury
1 Mr Bews

'The letters of a name were most ill-painted, James, and ill-formed as well.'

My skin prickled at the back of my neck. It was extraordinary. The board was just as he had described it. One name had obviously been added more recently than the others, and by a painter with little skill, and with no inclination to make the best of what skill he had. Gromwell.

'There was a great drip attached to it, and a poor creature had drowned therein.'

It was as if my father's ghost were beside me, murmuring

the words into my ear. Yes, there was the ant, trapped below the last 'l' of 'Gromwell', decaying within its rigid shroud of white paint.

Horror gripped me. If my father had been right about all this, then what about the woman he had seen displaying herself like a wanton in a chamber above? The woman with her coach and horses. The woman whose eyes he had closed in the chamber with the ant.

Gromwell's chamber?

I opened the door and climbed the stairs. I did not hurry, partly because I was scared of what I would find. On the first landing, two doors faced each other, numbers 3 and 4. I waited a moment, listening.

'I thought to find her in the chamber with the ant . . . up the stairs . . . '

I knocked on number 3. I heard movement in the room beyond. A tall, florid-faced man opened the door. He wore a morning gown of dark blue plush and a velvet cap. There was a book in his hand, with a finger marking his place. He frowned at me, raised his eyebrows and waited.

'Mr Gromwell?' I said.

It must have sounded like 'Cromwell' to the man's ears. Or perhaps he was merely oversensitive, which was understandable as Oliver Cromwell's head was displayed as a dreadful warning to traitors on a twenty-foot-high spike over Westminster Hall.

'It's Gromwell,' he said, drawing out the syllables. 'G-r-r-romwell with a G. I have no connection with a certain Huntingdonshire family named Cromwell. The G-r-r-romwells have been long established in Gloucestershire. G-r-r-romwell, sir, as in the plant.'

'Whose seeds are used to treat the stone, sir?' I said, remembering a herbal my father had printed.

The eyebrows rose again. 'Indeed. A thing of beauty, too. As Pliny says, it is as if the jeweller's art has arranged the gromwell's gleaming white pearls so symmetrically among the leaves. Sir Thomas Browne calls it *lithospermon* in his *Pseudodoxia Epidemica*.'

I bowed in the face of so much learning. Behind Mr Gromwell was a table piled high with books.

'Forgive me for disturbing your studies.' I shifted my stance, so I could see further to the left. I couldn't see a carpet. All I could make out was an expanse of bare boards and a grubby rush mat. 'My name is Marwood. I wonder if my late father called on you last week.'

Gromwell frowned, and I guessed he was taking account of my mourning clothes for the first time. 'Your late father?'

Over the fireplace was a dusty mirror in a gilt frame that had seen better times, but no trace of a painting, lewd or otherwise.

'He died the day after he came here.'

'I am sorry to hear it.' Mr Gromwell did not look prosperous but he had a gentleman's manners. 'But I have been away. My rooms were locked up.'

He took a step back. His arm nudged the door, which swung further open, revealing most of the room. There wasn't a couch of any description, let alone one with a body on it. None of the furnishings could be called luxurious. I felt both relieved and disappointed. It was remarkable that my father had recalled so much. Once he had entered the building, his imagination must have taken over. But I persevered.

'I am much occupied with business at present,' Gromwell said in a stately fashion. 'I bid you good day, sir.

'Does the name Twisden mean anything to you, sir?' I asked. 'Or Wyndham? Or Rainsford?'

He shook his head. 'Forgive me, sir, my studies—'

'Or the initials DY?'

Gromwell's face changed. For an instant, he looked surprised, jolted out of his stateliness. His features sharpened, which made them look briefly younger. 'No,' he said, more firmly than he had said anything yet. 'Good day to you.'

He closed the door in my face. I knocked on it. The only answer was the sound of a bolt being driven home.

CHAPTER SEVEN

THE YOUNG WOMAN sat in the gallery taking short-hand. Her real name was Catherine Lovett, but most of the time she tried very hard to forget that inconvenient fact. Now she was Jane Hakesby, a maidservant attending the Fire Court at Clifford's Inn to serve her master, Simon Hakesby, who was also a second cousin of her father's. She was a maidservant with accomplishments, equipped with some of the advantages of gentle breeding, though few of them were much use to her at present. In her new life, only Mr Hakesby knew her true identity.

She did not intend to be a maidservant for ever. On her knee was a notebook held flat with the palm of her left hand. A steadily lengthening procession of pencilled marks marched across the open page, meaningless except to the initiated.

In the hall below, the court was in session, dealing with the last of the day's cases. There were three judges at the round table on the low dais at the east end. The clerks and ushers clustered to one side, making notes of the proceedings and scuttling forward when a judge beckoned, bringing a book or a letter or a fresh pen. The petitioner and the defendants, together with their representatives, stood in the space immediately in front of the dais.

There was a lull in the proceedings – perhaps five seconds – during which no one spoke, and the court seemed to pause to draw breath. Her mind wandered. Her pencil followed. *His wig's crooked*, she wrote. *Judge on left.* Then a lawyer cleared his throat and the talking and arguing began again.

The hall was cramped and shabby. Clifford's Inn was not a grand establishment on the scale of the Temple, its stately colleague on the other side of the Fleet Street. Even in May, the air was chilly and damp. In the middle of the floor, a brazier of coal smouldered in the square hearth. The heat rose with the smoke to the blackened roof timbers and drifted uselessly through the louvred chimney into the ungrateful sky.

Jane Hakesby was sitting in the gallery at the west end, though a little apart from the other women. Her notebook rested on a copy of Shelton's *Tachygraphy*. She was in the process of teaching herself shorthand, and the Fire Court provided her with useful practice. Most of the women were in a whispering huddle at the back, where the judges could not see them. Sometimes they glanced at her, their faces blank, their eyes hard. She knew why. She did not belong among them so they disliked her automatically.

'All rise,' cried the clerk. 'All rise.'

The court rose to its feet as the judges retired to their parlour to confer on their verdict. Jane Hakesby looked down at the floor of the hall. Below her was a bobbing pool of men's hats. Benches had been fixed along the side walls, and it was here that the elderly and the infirm sat. From her vantage point at the front of the gallery, she saw the brim of Mr Hakesby's best hat and the folds of the dark wool cloak he usually reserved for church and high days and holidays. Even his best cloak was shabby.

Hakesby did not have a direct interest in the case under consideration. He was here on behalf of the freeholder to keep watch over his interests. The dispute itself was an involved and bad-tempered affair between the leaseholder and three of his subtenants about which of them would be responsible for rebuilding their houses after the Fire, and how the cost of doing so would affect the terms of their leases and sub-leases. The Government had set up the court solely for the purpose of settling such disputes, with the aim of encouraging the rebuilding of the city as soon as possible.

Mr Hakesby's white hand rested on his leg. Even at this distance, she made out that the fingers were trembling. A familiar sense of dread crept through her, and settled in her stomach. She had hoped that as the weather improved, his health would improve with it. But if anything his ague grew worse.

And if it grew so bad he could not work, what would become of her?

In a while the judges returned with their verdict, which found in favour of the subtenants but varied the terms of their leases in the leaseholder's favour. The judges departed and the hall began to empty.

Jane Hakesby allowed the other women to leave before her. She kept her head down as they filed past her to the stairs, pretending to study a page of *Tachygraphy*. It was improbable that any of them would recognize her, or rather recognize her as who she had been, but old habits died hard. In a moment she followed them down to the passage at the end of the hall.

There were doors at either end of the passage, one to the small court bounded by the Fleet Street gate, the other to the garden court that contained most of the other buildings of Clifford's Inn. Mr Hakesby emerged from the hall and touched her arm. She took his folder of papers and offered him her arm. He pretended not to see it. Leaning on his stick, he made his way slowly towards the north doorway, leaving her to trail behind him.

He was a proud man. It was one thing to show weakness to his maidservant, but quite another to show it to the world, especially to that part of the world that knew him. But she was learning how to manage him.

'The sun is out, sir,' she said. 'I found it so cold in the hall. Would you permit me to sit in the garden for a moment?'

But he wasn't attending to her. He stopped suddenly. 'Good God,' she heard him say.

She looked past him. Her eyes widened. Without thinking, she took a step backwards, ready for flight. Here was someone who belonged to her old life.

'Mr Marwood,' Hakesby said, his voice trembling. 'Your servant, sir.'

She recognized him at once, which was strange. James Marwood looked different from before – he seemed taller, and he was dressed in mourning. He was also out of place at Clifford's Inn. He belonged among the clerks of Whitehall, not here among the lawyers. Most of all, though, her instant recognition was strange because she had seen him properly only once, and then by the light of candles and lanterns, and at a time when she had other things on her mind. She wondered who was dead.

Mr Hakesby glanced over his shoulder at her. He turned back.

'Good day to you, sir,' Marwood said, his voice cautious as though he was uncertain of his welcome. His eyes slid towards her but he did not greet her.

'And to you . . . ' Hakesby hesitated and then went on in haste, as if to have the information off his chest as soon as possible. 'And here is my cousin Jane. Jane,' he repeated with emphasis, as if teaching a lesson, 'Jane Hakesby. She's come up to London to be my servant at the drawing office.'

She dropped a token curtsy. Four months earlier, Marwood had saved her life in the ruins of St Paul's. Apart from Hakesby himself, only Marwood knew that Jane Hakesby was really Catherine Lovett, the daughter of a Regicide who had died last year while plotting against the King.

'And what brings you here, sir?' Hakesby asked.

'An enquiry, sir. And you?'

Hakesby nodded towards the hall. 'The Fire Court has been in session.'

'Do you often attend?'

'As occasion requires. When I have clients whose interests are concerned.'

Marwood drew closer. 'I wonder – indulge me a moment, pray – do the names Twisden, Wyndham or Rainsford mean anything to you?'

'There's Sir Wadham Wyndham – he's a justice of the King's Bench, and he sits sometimes at the Fire Court. In fact, he was one of the judges sitting there today. Could it be him?'

'Perhaps. And the others?'

'I don't know the names. Could they be connected with the Fire Court as well? You should ask Theophilus Chelling. He's the Fire Court's assistant clerk. He will know if anyone does.'

'I'm not acquainted with him.'

'I'll introduce you now, if you wish.' Hakesby's eyes moved to his maid and then back to Marwood. 'I believe there can't be any harm in it.'

Marwood murmured his thanks, and Hakesby led the way to a doorway in the building that joined the hall range at a right angle. Marwood walked by his side. Jane Hakesby trailed after them, as a servant should.

They climbed stairs of dark wood rising into the gloom of the upper floors. Hakesby's trembling increased as they climbed, and he was obliged to take Marwood's arm. The two doors leading to the first-floor apartments were tall and handsome modern additions. On the second floor, the ceilings were lower, the doorways narrower, and the doors themselves were blackened oak as old as the stone that framed them.

Hakesby knocked on the door to the right, and a booming voice commanded them to enter. Mr Chelling rose as they entered. His body and head belonged to a tall man, but nature had seen fit to equip him with very short arms and legs. Grey hair framed a face that was itself on a larger scale than the features that adorned it. The top of his head was on a level with Jane Hakesby's shoulders.

'Mr Hakesby – how do you do, sir?'

Hakesby said he was very well, which was palpably untrue, and asked how Chelling did.

Chelling threw up his arms. 'I wish I could say the same.'

'Allow me to introduce Mr Marwood.'

'Your servant, sir.' Chelling sketched a bow.

'I am sorry to hear that you're not well, sir,' Marwood said.

'I am well enough in my body.' Chelling puffed out his chest. 'It's the fools I deal with every day that make me unwell. Not the judges, sir, oh no – they are perfect lambs. It's the authorities at Clifford's Inn that hamper my work. And then there's the Court of Aldermen – they will not provide us with the funds we need for the day-to-day administration of the Fire Court, which makes matters so much worse.'

Uninvited, Hakesby sank on to a stool. His maid and Marwood remained standing.

Chelling wagged a plump finger at them. 'You will be surprised to hear that we have already used ten skins of parchment, sir, for the fair copies of the judgements, together with a ream of finest Amsterdam paper. Scores of quills, too – and sand, naturally, for blotting, and a quart or so of ink. I say nothing of the carpenter's bill and the tallow-chandler's, and the cost of charcoal – I assure you, sir, the expense is considerable.'

Hakesby nodded. 'Indeed, it is quite beyond belief, sir.'

'It's not as if we waste money here. All of us recognize the need to be prudent. The judges give their time without charge, for the good of the country. But we must have ready money, sir – you would grant me that, I think? With the best will in the world, the court cannot run itself on air.'

Chelling paused to draw breath. Before he could speak, Hakesby plunged in.

'Mr Marwood and I had dealings with each other over St Paul's just after the Fire. I was working with Dr Wren, assessing the damage to the fabric, while my Lord Arlington sent Marwood there to gather information from us.' When he had a mind to it, Hakesby was almost as unstoppable as Mr Chelling himself. 'I met him as I was coming out of court just now. He has a question about the judges, and I said I know just the man to ask. So here we are, sir, here we are.'

'Whitehall, eh?' Chelling said, turning back to Marwood. 'Under my Lord Arlington?'

Marwood bowed. 'Yes, sir. I'm clerk to his under-secretary, Mr Williamson. I'm also the clerk of the Board of Red Cloth, when it meets.'

'Red Cloth? I don't think I know it.'

'It's in the Groom of the Stool's department, sir. The King's Bedchamber.'

Mr Chelling cocked his head, and his manner became markedly more deferential. 'How interesting, sir. The King's Bedchamber? A word in the right ear would work wonders for us here. It's not just money, you see. I meet obstructions at every turn from the governors of this Inn. That's even worse.'

Marwood bowed again, implying his willingness to help without actually committing himself. There was a hint of the courtier about him now, Jane Hakesby thought, or at least of a man privy to Government secrets. She did not much care for it. He moved his head slightly and the light fell on his face. He no longer looked like a courtier. He looked ill.

She wondered who was dead. Had there been a mother? A father? She could not remember — she had probably never known. For a man who had changed her life, she knew remarkably little about James Marwood. Only that without him she might well be dead or in prison.

'Mr Marwood has a question for you, sir,' Hakesby said.

Marwood nodded. 'It's a trifling matter. I came across three names – Twisden, Wyndham and Rainsford. I understand there is a Sir Wadham Wyndham, who is one of the Fire Court judges, and—'

'Ah, sir, the judges.' Chelling rapped the table beside him for emphasis. 'Mr Hakesby has brought you to the right man. I know Sir Wadham well. Indeed, I'm acquainted with all the judges. We have a score or so of them. They use the set of chambers below these, the ones on the first floor, which are larger than ours. We have given them a remarkably airy sitting room, though I say it myself who had it prepared for them, and also a retiring room and a closet. Only the other day, the Lord Chief Justice was kind enough to say to me how commodious the chambers were, and how convenient for the Fire Court.'

'And do the judges include—'

'Oh yes – Sir Wadham is one, as I said, and so is Sir Thomas Twisden. Sir Thomas has been most assiduous in his attendance. A most distinguished man. I remember—'

'And Rainsford?' Marwood put in.

'Why yes, Sir Richard, but—'

'Forgive me, sir, one last question. Do any of the other judges have the initials DY?'

Chelling frowned, and considered. 'I cannot recall. Wait, I have a list here.' He shuffled the documents on his table and produced a paper which he studied for a moment. 'No – no one.' He looked up, and his small, bloodshot eyes stared directly at Marwood. 'Why do you ask?'

'I regret, sir, I am not at liberty to say.'

Chelling winked. 'Say no more, sir. Whitehall business, perhaps, but I ask no questions. Discretion is our watchword.'

Marwood bowed. 'Thank you for your help, sir. I mustn't keep you any longer.'

'You must let me know if there is any other way I can oblige you.' Chelling tried to smile but his face refused to cooperate fully. 'And if the opportunity arises, I hope you will not forget us.'

'You may be sure of it, sir.'

'If the King but knew of our difficulties, especially with our governors who—'

'Mr Gromwell, is it?' Hakesby interrupted, beginning to rise to his feet. 'Is he still putting obstacles in your way?'

'Gromwell, sir?' Marwood said. 'The name is familiar.'

'Then I pity you, sir.' Chelling waved his hand, as if consigning Gromwell to a place of outer darkness. 'It would be better for the world if he were entirely unknown.'

'Why? What has he done?'

'He is one of our Rules – that is to say, the members who are elected to govern the affairs of Clifford's Inn. He is particularly charged with overseeing the fabric of the place, and its maintenance. I regret to say that he's no friend to the Fire Court.'

'But you are paying something for the use of the hall, I suppose?'

'Of course we are – and for these chambers – but he thinks we do not pay enough for the privilege. He ignores entirely the *pro bono* aspect of the matter.' Chelling pointed out of the window. 'The other day I asked if we could use the fire-damaged staircase over there for storage. It would ease our lives considerably, and cost him absolutely nothing. It's no use to anyone else at present. But he refused point-blank.'

Marwood bowed again. 'I'm sorry to hear it, sir.'

Chelling returned the bow, and almost toppled over. 'If only the King were aware . . . '

By this time, Hakesby had managed to stand up. She came forward to offer her arm – he was often unsteady when he had been sitting down – but Marwood was before her. The three of them said goodbye to Mr Chelling and went slowly downstairs.

'Poor man,' Hakesby murmured. 'Clinging to his duties at the Fire Court as a drowning man clings to a straw. Chelling has many excellent qualities, but he's been unfortunate all his life, partly because of his stature.'

They emerged into the sunlight. Marwood looked at Jane Hakesby and, she knew, saw Catherine Lovett.

She stared back at him, hoping he would leave them.

Hakesby turned towards them. 'Will you dine with us, sir?'

CHAPTER EIGHT

THE LAMB WAS in Wych Street, just to the north of the Strand and set back in a court. It was an aged building with blurred, blackened carvings along the bressumers supporting the upper storeys. It lay conveniently between Mr Hakesby's drawing office at the sign of the Rose in Henrietta Street and the house where he lodged in Three Cocks Yard. Shops lined the ground floor, and the tavern was above.

The landlord conducted them to a small chamber, poorly lit by a mullioned window overlooking a yard. Hakesby ordered their dinner, with wine and biscuits to be brought while they waited. Jane Hakesby worried about the cost.

Marwood slipped on to a bench that faced away from the light. She set down her basket and sat opposite, beside Mr Hakesby who took the only chair. She examined him covertly. His face was pale, the skin stretched tight over the high cheekbones and smudged with tiredness beneath the eyes.

He had agreed to come with them, but without much enthusiasm. It was as if it didn't really matter what he did. He ate a biscuit, and then another, which brought some of the colour back to his face.

He caught her looking at him. 'How do you do, mistress?' He left the briefest of pauses and added with a slight emphasis, 'Hakesby.'

The 'mistress' pleased her, however foolish of her that was. 'I do very well, thank you, sir.'

He turned to Hakesby. 'I don't wish to cause trouble. You don't mind being seen with me?'

'We've heard nothing to alarm us, sir,' Hakesby murmured. 'About the other matter.' They were quite alone but he shifted uneasily and leaned closer. 'I have no idea if Mr Alderley is still looking for Catherine Lovett.'

The men exchanged glances. The Alderleys were her cousins. She hated her cousin Edward more than anyone in the world.

'I've heard nothing either,' Marwood said. 'Nothing of any moment.'

'Catherine Lovett has become Jane Hakesby,' Hakesby said. 'Why, I almost believe it myself. She makes herself useful at the drawing office.'

'I am still myself, sir,' she said sharply. 'And I am here beside you. I do not forget who I am and what is owed me. Nor do I forget who has harmed me.' She glared impartially at them. 'In this company at least, I am Catherine Lovett.'

Hakesby shied away. 'Pray don't upset yourself.'

She saw the alarm in his face. 'You mustn't mind me, sir. When I was a child, they called me Cat. I have claws.'

Marwood said, 'Are you content?'

'I am a maidservant, sir. I assist Mr Hakesby in his business. I live a quiet life. What more could I possibly want?' She heard the bitterness in her voice and abruptly changed the subject. 'Who are you in mourning for?'

Marwood seemed to huddle into his black cloak like a tortoise retiring into his shell. Hakesby cleared his throat, filling the silence. Her abrupt, unwomanly behaviour made him uneasy. He had grown used to it in private, but he did not like it when she spoke so directly to others.

'My father. On Friday.' Marwood finished his second glass of wine. 'He was run over by a wagon in Fleet Street.'

'I'm sorry to hear it, sir,' Hakesby said.

'I mustn't bore you with my troubles. Tell me about the Court where these three judges sit. Why would they be listed together?'

'Because the Fire Court usually consists of three judges to hear each case,' Hakesby said, a little stiffly because Marwood had rebuffed his attempt at sympathy. 'Perhaps there was a particular case that came before these three. Or there will be.'

'Three judges for a trial?'

'Not a trial, sir. The Court exists to resolve disputes arising from the Fire. Parliament and the City are anxious that rebuilding should begin as soon as possible, and that the costs should be shared fairly among all the concerned parties. In many cases the tenants and so forth are still liable to pay rent for properties that no longer exist. Not only that, the terms of their leases make them responsible for the rebuilding. Often, of course, they lack the means to do so because they lost everything in the Fire. So Parliament set up the Fire Court, and gave it exceptional powers to settle such disputes and set its own precedents.'

'There must be a list of forthcoming cases,' Marwood said. 'If I knew which ones were coming up before those three . . .'

Hakesby said: 'It depends which judges are available.'

'Mr Chelling would know,' Cat said. 'As far as anyone does.'

'Yes, but the selection is not usually made public until the last moment. To prevent annoyance to the judges. They don't want to be pestered.'

Marwood hesitated. 'I'd rather not trouble Mr Chelling again.'

Hakesby smiled. 'He has a loose tongue. And your . . . your connections impressed him mightily. He will try to make use of you if he can. He will tell the world you're his friend.'

'But if you were to make the enquiries, sir,' Cat said to Hakesby, 'and in a fashion that suggested the matter had to do with something quite different, one of your own clients . . . '

'Would you, sir?' Marwood said, his face sharp and hungry.

Hakesby hesitated. 'I am pressed for business at present, and I—'

'He means, sir,' Cat interrupted, impatient with this unnecessary playacting, 'would you do something for us in return?'

'Jane!' Hakesby said. 'This is not polite.'

'I don't care much about being polite, sir.'

'What do you want?' Marwood said, returning bluntness for bluntness.

'Would you lend Mr Hakesby some money?'

'Jane!'

Cat and Marwood stared at each other. Perhaps, she thought, she had made him angry by asking him a favour at such a time. But he looked prosperous enough. And there was no room for sentiment. Didn't one good turn deserve another? This was a matter of business, after all, an exchange of services.

'Well,' Mr Hakesby said uncertainly. 'Taken all in all, I can't deny that a loan would be most welcome.'

After dinner, Hakesby and Cat took a hackney back to Henrietta Street.

To be Jane Hakesby in Henrietta Street was Cat's refuge, for the Government did not care for her. The reputation of her dead father and her dead uncle clung to her like a bad smell, and her living cousin wished her harm.

But Mr Hakesby's drawing office was more than a refuge: it was a place where, if she were fortunate, she could pursue the one occupation she preferred above all others: like the great Roman architect Vitruvius, she dreamed of designing buildings that would be solid, beautiful and useful, 'like the nests of birds and bees'.

The hackney meant more expense, Cat thought, but it could not be helped. They did not speak during the journey until the end, when Hakesby turned to Cat.

'I wish you had not asked Marwood for money. And so bluntly.'

'Do we have a choice, sir?'

As they climbed the stairs, Hakesby reached for Cat's arm. Floor after floor they climbed, and the higher they rose, the tighter his grip and the slower his step.

The drawing office was on the top floor. It was a converted attic that stretched the width of the house, with wide dormer windows to make the most of the light. Two drawing slopes were set up at an angle to the windows, each one separate from the others, so they could be turned individually to increase or occasionally reduce the light that fell on them from the windows.

As Mr Hakesby and Cat entered the room, Brennan laid down his pen, rose from his stool and bowed to his master.

'Any callers?' Hakesby said, making his way to his chair.

'No, master.' Brennan's eyes strayed towards Cat. 'I've finished inking the north elevation if you care to inspect it.'

Hakesby lowered himself into his chair. 'Good. Bring it here.' His finger flicked towards Cat. 'Then I shall dictate a note to my lord.'

Cat hung up her cloak. In this case, my lord was the freeholder for whom Hakesby had held a watching brief at the Fire Court this morning. While she gathered her writing materials together, she watched the two men studying the elevation. Or rather she watched Brennan. He watched her so she watched him.

Brennan had been working here for less than three weeks. He had come with a letter of recommendation from none other than Dr Wren himself, with whom Hakesby had worked on several projects. He had been one of the men working on the Sheldonian Theatre in Oxford, helping to adjust the designs after discussions with the masons employed on building the theatre. He was certainly a good draughtsman, Cat gave him that, and a fast worker too.

In this next hour, Cat took dictation from Mr Hakesby for the letters, wrote a fair copy for him to sign, and copied it again into the letter book as a record. It was not work she enjoyed but it was work she could do. Afterwards her reward came: she was allowed to work on the plans for a house and yard in Throgmorton Street – routine work, but with details she could make her own, subject to Mr Hakesby's approval.

Brennan was behind her, and she felt his eyes on her. Her skin crawled. She twisted on her stool, presenting him with a view of her shoulder. The afternoon was drawing towards its end, and the light was changing. She took her dividers and pricked first one hole in the paper before her and then another. She laid the steel rule between them and, frowning with concentration, pencilled a line, a mere shadow, on the paper.

There. The base of the architrave. And now, at an angle of twenty degrees—

Her irritation faded as the lines of the east façade spread across the paper. In her mind, the same lines sprang up, newly translated from two dimensions to three, acquiring solidity as well as depth, existing in space and time. The miracle was familiar but no less astonishing for that.

While the two of them worked at their slopes, Mr Hakesby sat by the fire, reading and occasionally making notes in his crabbed hand. At present he was checking accounts and invoices, and scribbling notes on the margins of letters. He had caused a carpenter to fix a board to each arm of his chair, and these he used as a desk. His handwriting was now almost illegible, because of the ague. On a bad day, even Cat found it hard to read.

Time passed. The light faded. The bells of surrounding churches chimed seven o'clock, though not quite at the same time.

Mr Hakesby dismissed Brennan for the day. The draughtsman was due an extra fee for a piece of work he had done at home. Hakesby found the money in his purse himself and told Cat to make a note of the payment. She added it to the current sheet of sundry expenses. Glancing back, she saw an alarming number of entries already. She drew up a rough total in her head, and the amount staggered her. There were two months to go until the quarterly rent on the drawing office was due at midsummer.

The draughtsman came over to where she was sitting so she could pay him the money and initial the entry as a receipt. At that moment, Mr Hakesby retired to his closet to answer a call of nature.

Brennan took his time. He stood very close to Cat's stool. He was fair complexioned, with pink cheeks and a sprinkling of freckles on his nose. He wore his own hair, which was sandy in colour. Cat saw two grey lice squatting among the roots where it fell into a parting on the left-hand side of his scalp.

He laid down the pen and blew on his initials to dry them. Cat felt his breath touch her cheek. Involuntarily, she turned her head. He took up the paper. He stared at her with pale eyes, neither blue nor grey, that made her think of pebbles on a shingle beach.

She held out her hand for the paper, anxious for him to be gone. His hand touched hers. She snatched it away.

'Less haste,' he said, smiling, 'more speed. What's the hurry?'

He leaned on the table, resting on his right hand. His left hand touched her neck in a caress which was as light as a feather. She seized her dividers and jabbed them between his index and middle fingers, missing them by a fraction of an inch on either side. He snatched his hand away. The points of the dividers had passed through the expenses sheet and dug into the wood of the table.

He raised his hand. 'God damn you, you could have stabbed me. My right hand, too.'

'Next time I will stab you.' Cat tugged the dividers free from the table and turned the points towards him. 'And it won't be your hand.'

'Ah.' He lowered his arm and grinned at her, exposing long, yellow canines. 'A vixen. I like a woman with spirit.'

The closet door opened. Brennan sauntered over to the peg where his cloak was hanging.

'Why are you still here, Brennan?' Hakesby said. 'I thought you'd be gone by now.'

The draughtsman had recovered his composure. 'Talking to Jane, sir.' He bowed low. 'I wish you goodnight.'

'He promises well,' Mr Hakesby said as his footsteps sounded on the stairs. 'Particularly on the fine detail. Dr Wren was right.'

Cat busied herself with throwing another shovel of coals on the fire, keeping her face averted to conceal her rising colour. The fire was a luxury at this time of year. More expense. Hakesby craved warmth, a symptom of his illness. His blood ran cold nowadays, he said. Colder and colder. She stood up and looked at him.

'Come here,' he said.

She put down the shovel and stood beside his chair.

'This damnable question of money,' he said. 'I wish I had not taken yours.'

'Sir, you had no choice in the matter. Neither of us did. If you hadn't taken it, both of us would have starved.'

Cat had lent him sixty pounds in gold on Lady Day, all the money she had in the world, taken from her dead father's body. Hakesby had been behindhand last quarter's rent and the wages for his employees. He had owed his own landlady for two months' board, and there had been

75

a host of other debts. The commissions were flowing in but few clients paid promptly for the work. With luck, most of the money would come in its own good time, and they would be more comfortable, but in the meantime they all had to live.

'Money confers an obligation,' he said. 'I'm worried I may not be able to discharge it.'

'Of course you will. But at present we need ready money. Which is why Marwood was a gift from heaven, sir. If you go to a moneylender, they would rob you.'

'I can't get reasonable terms.' Hakesby held up his right hand. The bony fingers fluttered. 'This grows worse.'

'It's been a hard winter, sir. Everyone says so. But now summer is here, the warmth will soon—'

'I have seen the doctors. This ague of mine will not get better. In time, it may touch the mind, as well as the body. With your help, and Brennan's, and perhaps another draughts-man's, we shall manage for a few months, perhaps a few years. But then . . . '

'We shall contrive somehow,' Cat said. 'If you rest more and worry less, the ague will progress more slowly.'

'And how will I pay you back if I cannot work? Or Marwood?'

'You give me shelter, sir, and you give me work. That is repayment. We'll manage with Marwood. He looks pros-perous enough to be kept waiting a little.'

After a pause, he said: 'What will become of you if I'm not here?'

A silence spread between them. Cat did not want to think about the possibility of Hakesby's death. It was not just the trembling that was growing worse, it was the depression of his spirits.

Hakesby straightened in his chair, squaring his shoulders as if for a fight. 'Fetch me the ledger, Jane. We shall reckon up the accounts. Let us find out how bad matters really are.'

CHAPTER NINE

'MY HUSBAND,' JEMIMA said, sitting at her dressing table in Pall Mall and staring sideways at her reflection in the mirror, 'is a fortunate man.'

And Mary, whose own reflection shimmered and shifted behind her mistress's, murmured like a mangled echo, 'Yes, my lady, the master is very fortunate. I'm sure he knows it too.'

Yes, Jemima thought, and when my father dies and Syre Place and everything else is mine, he will be even more fortunate. Because of me. When her father died, her husband would have the management of Syre Place and everything that went with it. Including herself — unless she could learn the art of managing him.

When she was ready, she descended the stairs, one hand on the rail of the bannisters, the other clutching Mary's arm. She wore her grey taffeta, sombre yet elegant, and a pendant with a diamond the size of a pigeon's egg. Mary had dressed her hair and applied the patches and powders to her face.

Rather than go directly to the dining room, where there

was already a murmur of voices, she went halfway down the stairs to the kitchen. The smells of their dinner came up to meet her, and made her feel queasy. For a moment her hand touched her belly. Was it possible she could be pregnant?

In the kitchen, the birds were turning on the spit over the fire, the fat sizzling as it dropped on to the hungry flames. The cook and the scullery maid curtsied, Hal the coachman doffed his hat and made his obedience, and the boy, Hal's son, tried to hide behind the scullery door until Hal dragged him into the open and cuffed him so hard he fell against the wall. The Limburys did not maintain a large establishment in London – all of their servants were in the kitchen, apart from Richard and Hester, who were serving at table upstairs, and the gardener.

Without speaking, Jemima stared at them. She had sent Mary down with her orders. But it was good to show oneself in the kitchen too, even if one didn't want to. Marriage was a contract, her father had told her, and she would fulfil her part of it, to the letter, even if her husband faltered in his.

Faltered. What a puny, insignificant, inadequate word.

'Well?' she said.

The cook curtsied again. 'Yes, my lady. Everything as it should be.'

She held the cook's eye for a moment, as her mother had taught her to do all those years ago at Syre Place, and then let her eyes drift over the other upturned faces, from one to the next.

'The guinea fowl will turn to cinders if you don't have a care.'

The cook gave a strangled yelp and dived towards the fireplace. Without a word, Jemima tightened her hold on

Mary's arm and turned. As they climbed the stairs to the hall, she felt as much as heard the rush of pent-up breaths escaping in the kitchen below.

In the hall, she hesitated. She had not seen Philip since he had come to her chamber the previous afternoon, though this morning he had sent up to make sure that she would dine with them today. She did not like meeting strangers, even in her own house. She did not want to see Philip, either.

As if sensing her mistress's anxiety, Mary touched her hand and murmured: 'You look very fine, my lady. I've never seen you look better.'

In the dining room, the gentlemen rose and bowed as she entered, and Richard moved forward at once to help her. Richard was Philip's servant, brought with him from his other life before their marriage. He wore his livery and had his teeth in, so he made a respectable show. Mary said he hated to wear his teeth because they hurt his gums.

Jemima curtsied to the gentlemen and allowed herself to be assisted to her chair.

'My wife has not been well these last few days,' Philip said, 'but she would not keep to her bed when she knew you would be dining with us, Sir Thomas. And our old friend Gromwell too.'

'What a charming diamond,' Gromwell said, staring admiringly but respectfully in the direction of Jemima's bosom. For all her dislike of him, she was forced to concede that he was a tall, fine-looking gentleman. He had once known great prosperity but his fortunes were now much reduced. 'My Lady Castlemaine was wearing one that was very like, only the other day, but it wasn't nearly so fine. Smaller, too.'

'It was my mother's,' Jemima said coolly, impervious to

80

his attempt to charm her. The last time they had met, at Clifford's Inn, his charm had been in short supply.

'Quite outstanding,' he murmured, leaving it discreetly ambiguous whether the compliment referred to her diamond or her bosom.

Sir Thomas cleared his throat and ventured into a complex and finely nuanced expression of opinion, which, though initially obscure, seemed to suggest that in this case the wearer adorned the diamond, rather than the other way round.

Philip smiled down the table at her, his brown eyes soft and adoring. It was a smile designed to melt the heart and during their courtship it had melted hers, against her better judgement. 'Lucius is right, my love,' he said, 'and Sir Thomas too – you look very well today, better than ever perhaps, if that can be possible.'

'How can one improve upon perfection?' Gromwell enquired; his manners were courtly though, like his yellow suit, they were a trifle old-fashioned. 'But my lady has. Behold, a double miracle, a miracle of both nature and logic.'

'You are pleased to jest, sir,' she said automatically, and twitched her lips into what could pass as a smile.

'I never jest on sacred matters, madam.'

You parasite, she thought, and smiled and nodded her head while the gentlemen laughed and toasted her. Duty done, they went back to their conversation.

'I had no idea you would be sitting on the Dragon Yard petition,' Philip said to Sir Thomas. 'What a coincidence.' As Jemima knew to her cost, he had the knack of speaking the clumsiest, crudest lie with such assurance that it became a self-evident truth. 'It is so truly admirable that you judges sit for love of country, and for the city, and not for gold. You will be a pattern for future generations.' He raised his glass. 'A toast. Good health and prosperity to our Fire Court judges.'

They drank solemnly, and Hester came to the door with the guinea fowl, now dressed for table in their sauce. Jemima tasted a morsel and found the dish perfectly cooked, which pleased her, for she had pride in the food served at her table, as in other matters that belonged to her.

'I sometimes attend these hearings myself, sir,' Gromwell said. 'Not that I have a pecuniary interest in them, you understand, but for the sheer quality of the judgements.'

'You're a lawyer, sir?' Sir Thomas asked. 'I don't think I've had the pleasure of seeing you in court.'

'I've never practised, sir. As a young man, however, I passed many profitable hours in the study of the law, and I believe I retain the ability to appreciate a well-argued case' – he bowed towards Sir Thomas – 'and a well-considered verdict.'

The gentlemen ate, and drank, and drank again. The room grew warmer. Sir Thomas was obliged to retire behind the screen to relieve himself. Jemima wanted to laugh at them, at their mockery of good fellowship, but instead she picked at her food and smiled at the compliments which were thrown her way like scraps to the bitch under the table; occasionally, as a well-bred hostess should, she threw in the sort of question designed less to elicit information than to allow the hearer to shine in his answer. But she said nothing to Gromwell.

Later – half an hour? an hour? – the conversation returned to the subject of the Fire Court. 'It is not a court of law,' Sir Thomas was saying, apparently to herself, 'though our judgements have the force of law, and have the ability to override such things that are usually considered sacrosanct. Leases, for example, and contracts relating to property.'

'And if I understand you correctly, sir,' Gromwell put in with the air of an eager student, 'your judgements do not set a precedent, but apply only to the petition under consideration.'

'Precisely.' Sir Thomas nodded vigorously and held out his glass for more. 'You have understood me perfectly, sir.' He beamed at Gromwell. 'If I may say so, it is the law's loss that you decided to apply your energies in other fields of knowledge. Our powers are intended simply to help London return to its former glory as soon as possible, for the good of the City and the Kingdom as a whole.' He hammered his fist on the table. 'And indeed the world. For does not our trade encircle the entire globe and enrich all it touches?'

This led to another toast, after which Philip said, smiling, 'And if all goes well, sir, with the wise help of the judges, we shall do more than restore London. We shall increase its glories for centuries to come.'

'I suppose Dragon Yard will be a case in point,' Gromwell said. 'Eh, Philip? If the decision next week goes in your favour, that is.'

Here we are, Jemima thought, we have come at last to the point of this tedious meal.

Gromwell turned to the judge. 'I've studied the plans. It's a most noble development, sir, with houses of the first class, laid out and built in a way that will make them proof against future fires. Safe, commodious and an ornament to the City. And also to the benefit of the public and of trade, I understand. It will provide another way to Cheapside, thereby easing the congestion of traffic there.'

Twisden's face became serious; he looked like a flushed owl. 'No doubt, sir, no doubt. Though all that would require considerable investment.'

'We must not weary Sir Thomas with talk of business.' Philip smiled round the table. 'Would you care for a hand or two of cards, sir?'

The judge brightened. 'If her ladyship would not object. And Gromwell too, of course.'

'I should like it above everything,' Gromwell said, smiling. 'What would you say to lanterloo? And perhaps a shilling or two on the outcome?'

'Why not? It adds a certain spice, does it not?'

'I think, sir,' Jemima said, 'if you would not object, and if Sir Thomas and Mr Gromwell would not think me discourteous, I shall leave you to your play.'

'Of course they will excuse you, my love,' Philip said. 'You are not fully yourself yet, and you must not overtire yourself. We can play with three as well as four. Richard? Send for Mary to help her mistress upstairs.'

A moment or two later, she withdrew. Sir Thomas bowed so deeply he stumbled against a chair and almost fell.

'All well, my lady?' Mary said softly as they climbed the stairs.

'Well enough.'

Jemima was tempted to add 'for your master', but held her peace. She would lay good money that Philip would have known beforehand of Twisden's taste for lanterloo, and that he would have arranged with Gromwell for the judge to win a pound or two from each of them.

When he was courting her, Sir Philip Limbury had seemed a creature of impulse, and his love for her had seemed as open and sincere as the sun itself. After their marriage, however, it had not taken her long to learn that he did little or nothing by chance. There was a purpose in almost everything he said and did. Sometimes more than one purpose.

When she was back in her chair by the window, and the chamber door was closed, she called Mary to her. 'The other matter. There's nothing? You're sure?'

'Yes, my lady.'

'The servants will know. They always do. Richard? Hal?'

'Hal Coachman would blab, madam. Richard, maybe.'

Jemima looked up at Mary. 'Talk to Richard. See if he will let slip anything about Thursday.'

'That one gives nothing for nothing, madam. He serves the master and himself. No one else.'

Jemima ran her tongue over her lips. 'Then make him desire you. See if that will open his toothless mouth. I must know who the woman was.'

Mary stared down at her mistress. 'Are you sure you want me to . . . ?'

Jemima stared back. 'Yes.'

CHAPTER TEN

AFTER DINNER AT the Lamb, I went to collect a small debt I was owed by a man I had helped to find a job distributing the *London Gazette*. He lived in Leadenhall Street, on the opposite side of the road from the market, in the small part of the walled City that had survived the Fire.

When I had the money, I turned to my right and walked west towards what was left of Cornhill. The streets through the ruins were almost entirely clear now, and much of the ground on either side was parcelled out into building sites. In the meantime, in this hiatus of the City's life, weeds were colonizing the rubble and making wild gardens in lost corners.

At this time of day the ruins were safe enough, clothed with a fragile, provisional normality. After sunset, everything changed among the ruins, and only fools ventured into the burned areas of the city without lights and protection. Now, however, there were workmen labouring among the shattered buildings, preparing for the City's resurrection. Citizens hurried to and fro, going about their business, as they had in these streets for centuries past and no doubt would for centuries to come. Street-sellers plied their trade, for everyone needed something, and the urge to buy and sell was as tenacious as life itself.

Beggars stood and sat at every corner, straining to clutch the sleeves of passers-by, many claiming to be former house-holders who had lost everything to the Fire. Here and there, faded notices appealed for the missing. In Poultry I paused to read a weathered slate on which someone had scratched in faded, just legible capitals: MARY COME TO MOORFIELDS WEST SIDE PRAY GOD YOU ARE ALIVE. There was still a scattering of tents and sheds in Moorfields, though far fewer than there had been. Most of the refugees had melted away like snow in spring: a few remained, huddled in smaller, unofficial encampments; others had found lodgings in the houses of families and friends; and many had drifted away in the hope of making new lives in other parts of the kingdom.

I followed the road to Poultry and Cheapside, where some householders had already begun to rebuild their houses in defiance of the regulations and had set up stalls in the ruins of their homes. From the stone carcase of St Paul's Cathedral I went west through the blackened arch of Ludgate and down to the bridge over the Fleet Ditch. In Fleet Street itself, I paused by the stalls that clung like chicks to a mother hen to the south side of St Dunstan-in-the-West.

At that moment, a wave of grief overwhelmed me. It took me entirely unawares. I stumbled, and steadied myself on the side of one of the bookstalls. My father had died here, only a few feet from where I stood, crushed under the wheels of a wagon. But I felt more than grief, more than guilt. There was also a hard edge of anger that cut into me like a blade.

It was the ant that had tipped the balance. That tiny creature, entombed in white paint, had finally convinced me that there had been sense in my father's story, the dreamlike account he had given me during our last conversation on the last evening of his life. Everything else had fallen into place: Clifford's Inn, the lawyers, the brick building by a garden. But it was the ant that proved to me it had not been his waking dream.

If the ant had been real, and those other circumstances, then was it not probable that the rest of it was real too? In other words, that he had followed a woman who resembled my dead mother, at least from behind. And by the same token, did that mean his account of what had lain behind Mr Gromwell's door was equally real?

To my amazement, I found myself believing that there really had been a luxurious chamber where there was now a scholar's study. The bright carpet, the sinful picture and the wanton woman on the couch had been as real as this stall beside me, as real as the battered, damp-stained and fire-damaged volumes it offered for sale.

The wanton woman whose blood was probably on his cuff, and on the scrap of paper in my pocket. The dead woman whose eyes he had closed. There was no other conclusion.

'Sir,' said a deep voice at the level of my elbow, 'I believe I have the pleasure of addressing Mr Marwood? I am indeed fortunate.'

I started. Immediately in front of me was a large black hat. Its broad rim tipped backwards, revealing a small nose set in a broad face, red as the evening sun, and two blue, bloodshot eyes looking up at me.

'Good day, Mr Chelling,' I said. 'Forgive me, sir, I was wool-gathering.'

'You are come from Whitehall, no doubt. Is there . . . is there perhaps news from the King?'

'Not yet, sir. In fact, I have not been there this afternoon.'

'When you do, you will remember our conversation?' Chelling put down the book he had been examining and took my sleeve. 'About the Fire Court, and our difficulties with our bills? Not to mention with the authorities at the Inn.'

'Of course.' It occurred to me that this could be a fortunate encounter. If I could persuade Chelling to tell me what I needed to find out, it would remove the need for me to ask for Hakesby's help – and, in return, to make him a loan that would leave me almost penniless. 'Perhaps you would care to drink the King's health with me?' I said. 'We might step over the way into the Devil.'

'By all means, sir.'

Chelling bowed, which was not a success as he chanced to put his back foot on an uneven stone, which made him stumble. I caught his arm and steadied him. We crossed the road together with some difficulty, partly because of the traffic and partly because he was tottering along on two-inch heels. At the Devil, we went upstairs to the taproom. I ordered wine and found us a space at the end of a table at the back. The room was noisy – four law students were raising their voices in a ballad at the other end of the table, and two soldiers were arguing with passionate intensity about the disposition of the dragoons at an unnamed battle.

'Have you known Mr Hakesby long?' Chelling asked.

'No, sir. Only since last year – the business at St Paul's he mentioned.'

'Of course — you told me earlier. What do you think of this so-called cousin of his, eh? Jane. Who did he say she was?' Chelling stabbed his finger into my arm. 'The sly old dog. Keeps him warm at night, I'll be bound.'

I smiled politely. 'It was civil of you to help me this morning,' I said, trying to steer the conversation away from Catherine Lovett. 'You mentioned this man Gromwell. I—'

'Gromwell!' Chelling burst out. 'Always a maggot in his head about something. I cannot abide a man like that. We've all had our disappointments in life, but he bears his less gracefully than some I might mention.'

'Have you known him long?'

'Too long, sir. Far too long. I don't want to be unchristian about any man, but I fear he gives himself airs, though with little justification. After all, we are both members. We are equals.'

'Members . . . ?'

'Of Clifford's Inn, sir.' He paused as if to give time for me to digest the importance of this. 'I was bred for the law, you see, though at present I assist them at the Fire Court. But I have lived in Clifford's Inn for nigh on thirty years. Why, the Principal was good enough to say to me the other day that the place would be very much altered without me. But of course Gromwell is a Rule now, and by God he makes the most of it and carries himself very high with everyone. This business of the Fire Court is the perfect example. It's not as if Staircase Thirteen is of any use to anyone else at — ah! Is that the wine?'

'Staircase . . . ?'

Chelling was watching the waiter. 'Staircase Thirteen,' he said absently. 'I told you about it earlier. It's not completely ruinous. The ground floor is perfectly weathertight, and the use of it would make it so much easier to store the Fire Court's furniture and supplies and so on. As it is, we have to empty the hall when the court is not in session, so the Inn may have the use of it again. And that means – Dear Christ!'

The waiter was clumsy. The bottle tipped too far, and drops of wine spattered on the table.

'Blockhead!' Chelling snapped. 'Numbskull!'

'Beg pardon, masters, beg pardon.' The waiter began to wipe the table.

'Should we not drink His Majesty's health at once, sir?' Chelling said, seizing the bottle. 'Loyalty to the throne demands no less. Allow me, sir.'

He poured the wine – hastily but without spilling a drop. We drank the King's health, and then that of the other members of the royal family.

I set down my glass when we had drenched the monarchy in wine. 'Are there many other gentlemen who are Rules?'

Chelling smiled, comfortably superior. 'Clearly you were not bred to the legal profession,' he said with a touch of pity. 'In this Inn, there are twelve Rules under the Principal. Sometimes we call them the Ancients. They form the council that administers the affairs of the Society according to our statutes, as laid down by our honoured Founder.'

'But your members are all lawyers, I take it – like those of the Temple, for example, or Lincoln's Inn.'

'The case is not quite identical, sir. We enjoy a different status. We are an Inn of Chancery, whereas such places as the Temple and Lincoln's Inn are Inns of Court. In times past, our members were attorneys and solicitors who followed the Courts of the King's Bench or Common Pleas. Or they were young gentlemen from the universities or from our grammar schools, who came here to gain a grounding in the law before moving to one of the Inns of Court. And it is the Rules who decide who shall enter our fellowship, and who shall be admitted to a set of chambers within the Inn. We—'

'So Mr Gromwell is a lawyer?' I cut in.

Chelling puffed out his cheeks. 'I should hardly call him a lawyer.' He paused to drink more wine. 'One can hardly call him anything that's worth the name. True, as a young man, he was admitted to the Society, so he may have some scraps of legal knowledge, but that's all . . . He's a man of fits and starts and idle fancies. He tried the law, and failed in that. He calls himself an antiquary, which means he fiddles about among dusty old papers and grubs about in ruined places and preys on the generosity of his friends.'

'If he's no lawyer, why is he here?'

'A good question, sir.' By now, Chelling was sweating profusely. 'In the last fifty years, Clifford's Inn has opened its doors to people our Founder would never have countenanced. Mr Gromwell's uncle was once a Rule, and he spent a great deal of money refurbishing his chambers, as a result of which he was granted the right to bestow them on an additional life after his own. He chose to bestow them on his nephew.'

'Number Three, on Staircase Fourteen.'

Chelling nodded but shot me a suspicious glance.

I said, 'It seems most unjust, sir, that such a man should benefit by his uncle's generosity, and in that way. And at the cost of others, too.'

'Precisely.' Chelling hammered his fist on the table, distracted from his suspicion. 'One could hardly have come up with a less appropriate choice.' He peered up at me, and wiped his brow with the trailing cuff of his shirt. 'We live in terrible times. Since the great rebellion against his late majesty, nothing has gone right for this unhappy country. Or for Clifford's Inn. We can't get the students now. Not in the numbers we used to before the war. They go elsewhere. Before the war, I tell you, the Ancients would never have sunk so low as to elect a man like Mr Gromwell as a Rule. It beggars belief! He claims to have influence at court, but he has no more influence than' – Chelling stamped hard on the floor – 'than my shoe.'

During this last speech, Mr Chelling's words had begun to take on a life of their own. They collided with one another. Consonants blurred, and vowels lengthened. Sentences proceeded by fits and starts.

My guest, I realized, was well on his way to becoming drunk on a mere bottle of wine. But perhaps this had not been the first bottle of the day. Or even the second. I doubted I would get anything useful about the Fire Court from him this afternoon. But at least he seemed happy enough to rant about Gromwell.

'My father called at Mr Gromwell's chambers last week,' I said, attempting to seize control of the conversation before it was too late.

'To see Gromwell? But why?'

'He called there by mistake. I'm not sure that he saw Mr Gromwell at all.'

Chelling drained his glass and looked mournfully at the empty bottle. I raised my hand to the waiter.

'Surely your father can inform you whether he did or not?'

'Unfortunately he died on Friday.'

'God bless us, sir!' Chelling seemed to take in my suit of mourning for the first time. 'How did it happen? It wasn't plague, I hope, or—'

I shook my head. 'An accident.'

'The poor gentleman. We . . . we must drink to his memory.'

The second bottle came, and Chelling accepted a glass. His interest in my father had departed as rapidly as it had come, however, and we did not drink to my father's memory. Instead, Chelling returned to the subject of Gromwell, and worried at it like a dog scratching a flea bite.

'The trouble with Gromwell,' he said, 'is that he believes he's a cut above the rest of us. He was born the heir of a fine estate in Gloucestershire. His father sent him up to Oxford but he frittered away his time and his money there. Then his father died, and the estate was found to be much embarrassed – every last acre mortgaged, I heard, and the land itself was in a poor state. To make matters worse, his brothers and sisters claimed their legacies by their father's will, but there was no money left to pay them, so they all went to law against their brother. Gromwell is a fool, and fought them all the way rather than settle the business out of court. As a result he has nothing left but worthless old books and papers and a great heap of debts. I tell you frankly, sir, he has no more idea of how to manage his affairs than my laundrywoman.'

'Then how does he afford to live?'

'I told you: he's a perfect parasite – he preys on his friends.' Mr Chelling was still capable of relatively coherent thought, but his speech had now acquired an other-worldly quality, as if spoken with care by a foreigner who did not fully understand the meaning of the words or how to pronounce them. 'Gentlemen he knew in his prosperity. He has friends at Court,

94

and one of his schoolfellows is even a Groom of the Bedchamber. They say he's quite a different man when he's with them. Ha! No one could be more affable or obliging.' He shrugged, a mighty convulsion of the upper body that almost dislodged him from the bench on which he sat. 'He can make himself good company if he wishes, and he makes himself useful to them, too. He will find out their pedigrees for them, or keep them entertained with his conversation. In return, they lend him money and invite him to stay and lay a place for him at their tables. For all his airs, Lucius Gromwell is no more than a lapdog.' Chelling glared at me and shook his fist. 'Let him beware, that's what I say. No man is invulnerable.'

'That is very true, sir.'

'Believe me, I shall make him laugh on the other side of his face before I'm done. I have the means to wound him.'

Chelling paused to take more wine. His face was very red and running with moisture.

I said, 'You know something that will do him—'

Chelling slammed the glass down on the table so forcefully that its shaft snapped.

'A lapdog!' he cried in his booming voice, so loudly that the taproom fell silent for a moment. 'You must be sure to tell His Majesty when you see him. Gromwell is a damned, mewling, puking, whining, shitting lapdog!' His face changed, and he looked at me with wide, panic-stricken eyes. 'Oh God, I am so weary of it all.'

His body crumpled. He folded his arms on the table and rested his head on them. He closed his eyes.

* * *

For a small man, Mr Chelling was surprisingly heavy.

Once I had paid our bill, a waiter helped me manhandle Chelling down the stairs to the street door, a perilous descent because he twice made an attempt to escape, insisting that he had always stood on his own two feet and had no intention of changing his policy in that regard.

I had to bribe the servant a second time to help us across Fleet Street. With the lawyer dangling between us, sometimes kicking at our shins, we carried him safely past St Dunstan's to the gate of Clifford's Inn. At this point a porter came to our assistance.

'Been at it again, has he?' he said. 'He's got no head for it, sir. On account of his size, I reckon. Stands to reason: if you put a quart in a pint pot, it's bound to overflow.'

'I have the heart of a lion,' Chelling mumbled. 'That is what matters.'

'Yes, sir.' The porter winked at me. 'I just hope the Principal don't hear you roar.'

'Take him to his chamber,' I said.

The porter patted Chelling's pockets until he found a bunch of keys. 'Sooner he's out of sight, the better.'

He left a boy to mind the gate. He and another of the Inn's servants half-carried, half-dragged Chelling across the court, watched by a small but appreciative crowd of spectators outside the hall, where the Fire Court was still in session. I paid off the waiter and followed them.

Chelling lived in chambers on Staircase V, part of a range on the eastern side of the court that butted up against the north of St Dunstan's churchyard. The building was one of the oldest parts of the Inn, dating back to its days as a private house, and the staircase was cramped and ill-lit. At each landing there were two doors, one on either side, just as there were in New Building, but there were few other resemblances. The air smelled of damp and decay, and the stone steps were uneven, worn by generations of feet.

As luck would have it, Chelling's chambers were on the attic floor, which had been added to the building as an after-thought. The porter unlocked the door. They dragged him into a study with sloping ceilings and a sloping floor. It was sparsely furnished with a table, a chest, an elbow chair and a single stool. A dormer window looked east towards the ruins of the City. There was a broken pipe in the hearth and the study smelled of stale tobacco.

The porter dropped the keys on the table and glanced at me for guidance. 'On the bed, master?'

I nodded.

The servant unlatched the inner door, and the pair of them manhandled Chelling into a chamber little larger than a cupboard. They dropped him on the unmade bed. His legs dangled over the side. One shoe fell with a clatter on to the floor. His round face was turned up to the ceiling, and his hair made a grey and ragged halo on the dirty pillow. His mouth was open. The lips were as pink and as delicate as a rosebud on a compost heap.

'Friend of his, sir?' the porter asked. 'Ain't seen you before, I think.'

'Yes.' I paused, and then, as the man was looking expect-antly at me, added: 'Mr Gromwell will vouch for me. My name's Marwood.'

The porter nodded, giving the impression that he had done everything and more that duty required him to do. 'Will that be all, then?'

I felt for my purse. 'Thank you, yes.'

I gave the men sixpence apiece. I went back into the study and listened to their footsteps on the stairs. Snoring came from the bedroom, gradually building in volume. I glanced around the cramped chamber. It was very warm up here, directly under the roof. The windows were closed and the air was fetid. There were few books in sight. An unwashed mug and platter of pewter stood on the table.

Chelling had fallen on hard times. Perhaps Gromwell was not the only man at Clifford's Inn who survived on the kindness of friends. Everywhere I looked, there seemed to be unanswered questions, large and small. After the efforts I had made, the time I had spent, the money I had paid, all I had to show was a cloud of uncertainties.

Suddenly I was angry, and anger drove me to act. I could at least make the most of my opportunities while I was here. There was a cupboard set into an alcove by the chimney breast. It was locked, but one of Chelling's keys soon dealt with that. When I opened its door, the hinges squealed for want of grease.

The smell of old leather and musty paper greeted me. The cupboard was shelved. In the bottom section were rows of books in a variety of bindings. The upper section held clothing, much of it frayed and well-worn. On the very top shelf, a leather flask rested on a pile of loose papers an inch thick, with writing materials beside them.

I uncorked the flask and sniffed its contents. The tang of spirituous liquor rose up from it, with a hint of something else, perhaps juniper. So Chelling had a taste for Dutch gin as well as for wine. As for the papers, they were notes, by the look of them, and written in a surprisingly fine hand, the letters well formed and delicately inscribed. I glanced at the top sheets. They were written in Latin. Every other word seemed to be an abbreviation.

I leafed further down the pile and found a page that was written in English. It was an unfinished letter, though its contents made no more sense than the others.

Sir,

It grieves me beyond Measure that my Conscience requires me to communicate this Distressing Information to you, not merely for the Good of our Fellowship and its Reputation in the World, but also to warn you of the Dangers of a too Generous and too Trusting Spirit. In Fetter Lane, by the Hal—

The last three words were smudged, suggesting the writer had pushed the letter into the pile of papers without troubling to blot it.

A door closed on one of the floors below me. I cocked my head. Someone was climbing the stairs. The footsteps drew steadily closer. I picked up the papers, returned them to the cupboard and put the flask on top. The hinges shrieked as I shut the door.

The steps were on the landing now. There was no time to relock the cupboard. The door of Chelling's study was still ajar. There was a tap on it. The door swung open.

Lucius Gromwell entered the room, stooping because the lintel was so low. Once inside he straightened up. The crown of his hat brushed the ceiling at its highest point. He was dressed in a fine suit of yellow broadcloth, though the effect was somewhat spoiled by a large red stain on the chest and a hint of grubbiness about his shirt. His face was flushed with wine.

He frowned. 'I know you . . . You're the man who came to my chambers this morning with a cock and bull story about your father. What are you doing here?'

I nodded towards the open door of the bedroom. The snores were louder than ever. 'Mr Chelling was unwell,' I said. 'I had him carried to his bed.'

'But who are you?' Gromwell demanded. 'What right have you—'

'Hush, sir, he's only just fallen asleep. It would be unkind to wake him.'

'So you're a physician, are you? And he your patient? A likely story.'

'No. A friend.'

Gromwell laughed. 'Chelling doesn't have friends. If you know him at all, you would know that.'

The words were offensive in themselves, but the man's manner was worse. This morning he had been at least superficially polite to me. Now, he radiated hostility.

Gromwell crossed the room and pushed the bedroom door fully open. He stared down at Chelling, his face twisting with distaste. He turned back to face me. He gestured to the outer door. 'After you, sir.'

I held his gaze, wondering why Gromwell had taken the trouble to come to call on a man he neither liked nor respected.

'You must leave,' Gromwell said. 'At once. I have authority in this place. Do not oblige me to exercise it.'

He left me no choice. I bowed and left the room. On the stairs, I paused to listen.

The building above was silent. Gromwell was still in Chelling's chambers. I heard, faint but unmistakable, the shriek of the cupboard door's hinges.

CHAPTER ELEVEN

A KNOCK AT THE door. Hakesby looked up sharply, and a sheaf of papers slid from his lap to the floor.

It was Wednesday, early in the afternoon: the sky was overcast, and so was the mood in the drawing office. The stationer's apprentice had delivered an unexpected bill a few hours earlier.

The boy downstairs had brought up a letter. Hakesby tore it open and scanned the contents. He passed it to Cat. 'Marwood cannot complain that we do not keep our side of the bargain.'

The letter was from Chelling, in answer to an enquiry that Hakesby had sent to Clifford's Inn the previous evening. The next Fire Court case that was due to be heard before Judges Twisden, Wyndham and Rainsford was a week today, on 15 May. According to Chelling's notes, the case concerned a property known as Dragon Yard, which occupied a site about halfway between Cheapside and what was left of the Guildhall. The petitioner was Sir Philip Limbury, the freeholder, and there were four defendants, whom Chelling had not named.

'DY,' she said quietly. 'Marwood asked about that. Dragon Yard.'

Hakesby nodded. 'That confirms it. Limbury? The name's familiar.'

'Sir Philip Limbury, sir?' Cat said, her memory providing an unwanted glimpse of her cousin Edward with one of his friends, a tall dark man. 'The courtier?'

'Very likely,' Hakesby said. 'Dragon Yard's a substantial plot, if I remember right. I wonder what he plans to do with it. We should look into it.'

His voice had sharpened, and he sounded younger. Hakesby had a nose for an opportunity, if not a head for balancing his accounts, and he was never slow to recognize an opening that might possibly lead to a commission.

Brennan put down his pen. 'It's off Cheapside. I could step over there, sir, if you wish. See what's what.'

Cat held her breath.

'I think I shall go myself,' Hakesby said. 'No harm, after all, the air will do me good. Summon a hackney, Jane.'

'Would you like me to attend you, sir?' Brennan asked. 'In case you need to take a measurement or dictate a note?'

For a moment the decision hung in the balance. Cat's nails dug into the palm of her hand. Why couldn't Mr Hakesby see what Brennan was about? The draughtsman was trying to ease himself into Hakesby's good offices, to make himself indispensable.

She was learning cunning. 'In that case, master, should I finish Brennan's work? It's the north elevation of the ware-house on Thames Street.'

Hakesby frowned at her. 'That would never do. It is a fair copy, and the difference between your two hands would be obvious. Besides, you don't have the experience.'

She lowered her head submissively.

'No,' he went on. 'Brennan had better stay here. I suppose you must come with me instead.'

'Dragon Yard, master? That's Dragon Yard.'

The beer-seller leaned over the side of his stall and pointed across Cheapside at a jagged line of ruins, marked out by a row of white posts with lengthening shadows on their eastern side. It was early evening, but two labourers were still working at one end of the site, shovelling rubble on to a barrow.

Hakesby slid a shilling on to the plank that served as a counter. 'Who owns it?'

'It used to be the Poultons – see, that's the old gentleman there.' The beer-seller nodded at a tall man wrapped in a cloak who was examining a blackened chimney stack at one end of the ruins. 'Lucky devil.'

'He doesn't look lucky,' Hakesby said.

The beer-seller leaned politely to his left and spat on the ground. 'Don't judge a book by its cover, master. Clothier. Rich as they come.'

Cat glanced in his direction. Poulton was a gaunt figure, stooping as if he had grown that way after a lifetime spent passing through low doorways. For a clothier, he was plainly, even shabbily dressed.

'Poulton – of course. I know him by reputation,' Hakesby said. 'He's a friend of Robert Hooke's. Indeed, I believe I may have met him once in Mr Hooke's company . . . You say he used to be the owner?'

'I suppose he still is, of what's left. But there's a gentleman from Whitehall who has the freehold. It's a sorry business, isn't it? Mr Poulton's been there nigh on forty years, over there: see, where he is now – that's where the big house was.

And his brother's family was in the house next door, and some cousins behind. A garden too, and a livery stable next to the paddock beyond. All gone now.' The man's eyes flickered towards Cat and back to Hakesby. He added the unconvincing piety, 'God has punished us all, high and low, for the sins of the City and the wickedness of the court.'

'What will they build there?'

'Houses for rich folk, that's for sure. Ask Mr Poulton if you want to know more. But I warn you, he'll bite your head off if you don't have a care. Or you could ask his niece if you can find her.' The beer-seller grinned. 'She's a widow. A merry one.'

Hakesby drained his beer. He seemed more vigorous than he had for days, if not weeks. Their expedition had acted as a tonic on him.

He took Cat's arm, and they crossed the flow of traffic on Cheapside. 'It's a big site,' he said as they reached the safety of the other side. 'Probably an inn at one time.' He led the way into what had once been a lane between two buildings.

'You! You there!'

Mr Poulton was brandishing his stick at them.

Hakesby let go of Cat's arm and picked his way towards the old man, navigating a zigzag course between a large heap of rubble and rows of blackened posts that might once have been a range of outbuildings.

'This is private property,' Poulton said. 'There is no right of way. I don't permit trespassers.'

Hakesby bowed. 'Of course not. Mr Poulton, I believe? My name is Hakesby. I think we met at my Lord Brouncker's two or three years ago.'

Instead of a wig and hat, Poulton wore a tight-fitting black cap which emphasized the shape of his skull. His eyes were sunk deep in their sockets. 'Perhaps we did. I don't recall it.' The words were abrupt but his tone was less aggressive. 'And what can I do for you, sir?'

'I'm a surveyor and a master draughtsman. I design buildings and oversee their construction. I'm a colleague of Dr Wren, who will speak for me, and of course Mr Hooke will too, and my Lord Brouncker. This is clearly a substantial site, and I wondered if my services might be of use to you.'

'I wish to God I knew.'

'Forgive me, sir – I don't understand your uncertainty.'

'Nor do I, sir, nor do I.' Poulton's bitterness forced its way to the surface. 'I tell you, sir, it's barbaric, unchristian. My family has lived here since my father's time. We've built our houses here, and managed our businesses, and brought up our families. My lease has five years to run, and I expected to renew it when it fell due. And on reasonable terms, too, for our losses from the Fire have been enough to melt a heart of stone. But the freeholder will have none of it: if he has his way, he will cast us all into the street.'

'Surely he must compensate you?' Hakesby said.

'He has made an offer. The amount was an insult, and he must have known it.'

'But you have a legal recourse, sir. The Fire Court is sitting. I have spoken for several clients there in the last month or so. The judges are not unreasonable, and their priority is to see the City rebuilt as soon as possible – and to give every man his due.'

'Do you think I don't know that?' Poulton sat down suddenly on a fragment of wall. 'Forgive me. I see you know what you're talking about.'

Uninvited, Hakesby sat down beside him. 'These questions are not easy to settle, sir. There are so many sources of disagreement. But all parties must agree that the rebuilding should go ahead as soon as possible. It would be wise to negotiate a compromise.'

'Sir Philip is not interested in compromise.' Poulton scowled. 'Nor am I, for that matter.' He raised his voice and shouted at the two labourers: 'I don't pay you to rest on your spades, you idle knaves. Dig!'

'Sir Philip is your freeholder, I assume?'

Poulton nodded. 'Unfortunately. He wants to build a street of new houses, eight, perhaps, or even ten. Three storeys high.'

Hakesby shook his head. 'That can't be right. Technically, that street over there would be classed as a yard or a lane. So new houses should have no more than two storeys, according to the Rebuilding Act. And they will insist on the regulations for a development of this type, I'm sure of that. They don't want another fire in the heart of the City.'

'That's the wicked part of it. Limbury wants to cut a street through the middle. To slice Dragon Yard in two. They say the Court of Aldermen likes the idea – another way into Cheapside from the north, thirty feet wide, and at no cost to them.'

'The first two storeys at ten feet high, the third at nine,' Hakesby murmured. 'Each house built of brick and fitted out for, say, three hundred pounds.' He raised his eyebrows. 'Two thousand, four hundred pounds to build eight houses. Plus fees and so on. A pretty little speculation. And perhaps more could be squeezed on to the site, if it were better laid out, particularly at the Cheapside end. A wide frontage – ample room for shops.'

'Sir Philip Limbury is an idle spendthrift,' Poulton said. 'Like so many of these Whitehall parasites. I cannot imagine how he would bear the cost of it all. Unless his wife's father helps him. But I hear there's no love lost there.'

'It wouldn't be hard for him to sell new leases,' Hakesby said. 'Or he could borrow on the security of them, even before the building starts. If done well, the scheme could attract much interest. Say thirty-year leases, with deposits of a hundred and fifty pounds apiece at the start of them, plus an annual rent of sixty or even seventy. In two or three years' time, Sir Philip would cover his costs and start to make a handsome profit. And he and his heirs would retain the free-hold.'

Cat, keeping her eyes lowered, murmured: 'And the existing tenancies, master?'

Poulton frowned at her.

Hakesby grunted. 'Always the difficulty.' He turned back to Poulton. 'You're not the only tenant, I think you said.'

'That's part of the problem.' Poulton's head drooped lower. 'There are two main tenancies, sir, including mine, and a number of subtenancies. The main leases were granted around twenty-five years ago. As I said, they've only about five years to run. I hold the larger, and my niece the other, so effectively it is mine, unless she remarries. But the other two leases have been subleased over the years to people who have only the slightest connection to the family, and some who have none at all. They are a different matter. Some of them lost everything in the Fire, and they can't afford the cost of rebuilding. And I fear they will be easy prey for a man like Sir Philip. But I hope we shall have a fair hearing from the judges, my niece and I.'

'You plan to rebuild yourself?'

'Of course. And so will my niece. I shall have her sign the necessary papers . . . ' A flicker of emotion passed swiftly over his face. 'When I next see her. Limbury will find that a man must get up very early if he wishes to get the better of me.' He pointed with his stick. 'My house stood here, with my niece's on the other side of the lane. The lane itself is over my land. So between us we can sink his entire scheme. Even if he redevelops the north part of the site, he can't put his road to Cheapside through if he doesn't have our land. He may have friends at Court but I have friends among the Aldermen.'

'What about your subtenants?' Cat said, as if to herself.

'They can be bought,' Poulton said, looking at Hakesby as if it were he who had spoken. 'Everyone can be bought. Limbury knows that, and so do I.'

CHAPTER TWELVE

I WAS EARLY FOR the meeting with Hakesby and Catherine Lovett. I had frittered away the day, partly because I had drunk deep the previous evening after my encounter with Theophilus Chelling, which meant that I had slept long and heavily, though with confused dreams of flames, falling buildings and despairing searches for something I never found.

I should have gone into the office, but somehow I could not bring myself to walk the familiar road to Whitehall. I risked Williamson's anger – he had given me the indulgence of Monday and Tuesday away from the office, in order to bury my father and settle his affairs. I had taken today without his leave, without even sending word that I was ill. At present his disapproval seemed unimportant. Grief turns everything topsy-turvy.

Instead I sat in my father's chamber and went through his meagre possessions again. I don't know why I did it, unless it was part of saying farewell to him. But part of him lingered in my mind, refusing to depart.

Later, after Margaret had made me eat something, I wandered along to Fleet Street and into Clifford's Inn. The Fire Court was in session. I stood in the body of the hall while three judges on the low dais heard a petition brought by a merchant who could not afford the rent on his destroyed house; a lawyer, defending the freeholder, the Dean and Chapter of St Paul's, methodically tied the poor man in knots. Mr Chelling was not there.

By the evening I felt more vigorous, and the internal fog that had filled my mind all day had dissipated. I set out for the Lamb. On a whim, I did not walk into Wych Street but passed under Temple Bar to the mouth of Fetter Lane. The fragmentary letter I had found yesterday in Chelling's cupboard was in my mind.

In Fetter Lane, by the Hal—

Fetter Lane ran north from Fleet Street towards Holborn and marked the western boundary of the Fire. To the east lay the ruins, with the blackened church towers where choirs no longer sang and prayers were no longer said. To the west, the buildings were largely undamaged, though here and there the flames had leapt across the road and devoured what they could before the wind had changed and driven them away.

The sun was out, but the shadows were lengthening. I walked slowly northwards, keeping to the western side. To the left was the square tower of St Dunstan-in-the-West and the roofs of Clifford's Inn. The Fire had reached a section of the buildings on this side, including part of the Inn. By this stage, however, its fury had been abating. Some of the damaged buildings had been made habitable after a fashion.

A beggar pursued me for a few yards until I shouted at him and waved my stick. The man fell back, grumbling. For all that, and against my better judgement, I felt a twinge of pity. I had known hunger myself, and the beggar was about my own age; the man had had the misfortune to lose an arm.

I came to the mouth of the lane leading from the east into Clifford's Inn. The gate was open. Black-clad figures moved in the court beyond, walking slowly as if in a dream world. To the right was the boarded-up ruin and the improbably green foliage of the trees in the garden. The tree trunks were dark with soot, like most of London's trees, but the spring leaves glinted where they caught the sunshine.

Time was passing. If I wasn't careful, I would be late. I walked on, drawing level with the long roofline of the brick building in Clifford's Inn. It rode like the side of a tall ship over the humbler buildings between it and Fetter Lane. These belonged to a rambling house set back from the road, its frontage damaged by the Fire, with a yard and outbuildings behind it. The house was still inhabited, and a post stood before the door, signifying that there was hospitality within. A sign hung from the jettied first floor, but it was so blackened by the heat that there was nothing to be made out on it.

Somewhere a church clock began to toll the hour. One, two, three . . . I was late already.

The beggar drew level again. 'For the love of God, your worship—'

I swung round to face him. The man cowered and raised his one arm to cover his face.

Four, five, six . . .

'You there,' I said. 'What's the name of that house?'

Seven. Damnation.

The beggar blinked, taken off guard. 'The Half Moon, master.'

'A tavern?'

'Yes. Good enough food, sir, if you can pay for it. For the love of God, sir . . . '

I felt in my pocket for a sixpence. It was a ridiculously generous amount for the service rendered. I dropped the coin into the man's palm and walked quickly away, ignoring two more beggars who were now moving towards us like wasps to a honeycomb. The one-armed man stayed put, calling down unwanted blessings on my head. I felt the familiar guilt: there, but for the grace of God, go I.

I turned into Fleet Street and set off in the direction of the Strand. The beggars dropped away, and with them went my guilt.

In Fetter Lane, by the Hal—

So did Chelling's unfinished letter refer to the Half Moon? Was the tavern connected to its promise of 'distressing information'?

Dear God, what murky business had my poor father strayed into?

After all that, I needn't have hurried.

'Mr Hakesby?' the landlord said. 'He's not here yet. Will you be wanting a private room, sir?'

'Yes. But I'll wait for him.'

I went back downstairs and stood in the doorway. The street was full of people – mostly men, mostly lawyers, who swaggered about the neighbourhood as if they owned it; which in a way they did.

Five minutes later, I caught sight of Hakesby and Cat approaching: the tall, thin man and small woman with the delicate features. They made an unlikely couple. Hakesby was slow and halting in his movements. Beside him, Cat was unnaturally stiff, as if fighting to contain the vitality that spilled out of her. I hardly knew her but in my mind she was always in motion, darting like a flame from one thing to another, her outline constantly shifting. Not like a woman at all. A sprite, perhaps, some creature from another world where they managed things differently.

The road was narrow, and it lacked the posts along the sides that gave some protection to the pedestrians in wider thoroughfares. Hakesby and Cat were forced to step into the roadway by a couple of law students, who were walking rapidly by in the opposite direction, and arguing as they went.

One of them jostled Cat, perhaps intentionally. He paused, turned and leered down at her. She spat at him, not at the ground. His face contorted with anger.

Swearing under my breath, I left the shelter of the doorway and ran towards them. Why did the little fool have to be so indiscreet? I had no stomach for a street brawl.

But I wasn't needed. The man wheeled suddenly away and set off down the street. I reached Cat just in time to see the dying sunlight glint on a blade. The knife vanished under her cloak.

'You mustn't do that again,' Hakesby said to her, his voice trembling. 'You're too rash. It will be the death of us all one day. What if that man lays information against you? What were you thinking of?'

She did not reply. Nor did she curtsy. If she had been a real cat, she probably would have spat at me.

'I've ordered a room,' I said.

'We were delayed,' Hakesby said. 'But we have news.'

At the Lamb, we were shown to our private room. As soon

as we were alone, I took out the leather pouch, secured with a drawstring. It chinked when I set it on the table, and the invisible contents shifted as if they were alive.

Hakesby sighed.

'Twenty pounds,' I said. 'Some gold, but mainly silver.'

'You will have it back within eight weeks,' Cat said.

'Jane!' Hakesby put his hand on her arm. 'You cannot say such things. It's not your place. Besides, you can't know whether we will be in a position to repay Mr Marwood so soon. Though of course I hope we will. What's your rate of interest?'

'I'm not charging interest. Just pay me back the principal.' I hesitated, reckoning up my more pressing debts and setting the total against my likely income in the next few months. 'Eight weeks would be most convenient.'

In that moment I was struck by an overwhelming sense of my own folly. I hardly knew these people. The service they were doing me was trifling. Yet I was lending them, without security, all the portable wealth I possessed. What in God's name was I doing? It was as if my father's death had removed something vital from me, something that had hitherto prevented me from acting like a credulous fool. Without it, I was as helpless as a child.

'I'm grateful for your kindness, sir.' Hakesby compressed his lips. 'And I wish the loan weren't necessary in the first place.'

'He doesn't do this for nothing, sir,' Cat said, flaring up. 'No doubt he has his reasons.'

I wanted to snap at her. Instead I said, 'You've heard from Chelling?' I didn't mention that I had seen him yesterday.

'Yes,' Cat said, even as Hakesby was opening his mouth

to reply. 'There's a Fire Court case next week that will come before those three judges.'

'It concerns Dragon Yard,' Hakesby said. 'I assume that is your DY. Strange, isn't it?' He cocked his head. The waiter's step was on the stairs. 'One way or another, everything comes back to the Fire Court.'

When I returned to Infirmary Close, Sam met me at the door of my house. Margaret hovered behind her husband. Neither met my eye.

'What's this?' I said. 'A committee?'

The furniture and the panelling had been freshly polished. I sniffed. A smell of cooking was wafting up from the kitchen. My mouth watered. I had eaten nothing at the Lamb. I realized that for the first time in days I felt hungry.

Sam, who was wearing a clean collar, drew himself up and rapped the tip of his crutch on the floor. 'I hope I see your worship in good health.'

'Why so formal? Yes, I'm perfectly well.'

'There's a letter for you, sir.' Sam cleared his throat. 'I chanced to notice it bears the seal of Mr Williamson's office.'

'Give it to me, then.'

Irritated, I took the letter and turned aside to open it. It contained nothing more than a line scribbled by a clerk.

Mr Williamson expects yr attendance by 8 tomorrow.

I crumpled the paper and stuffed it in my pocket. By his lights, Williamson had treated me indulgently in excusing me from attendance at the office since Saturday. It wasn't as if I could plead that settling my father's estate required time, because there was nothing of consequence to be settled.

It was infuriating. The strange business of the Fire Court and Clifford's Inn filled my mind so much that there was little room for anything else, let alone for the routines of gathering information for Williamson's private ear and disseminating selections of it, suitably presented for the public, in the *London Gazette*. Whatever I felt about my father's death, however, I could hardly risk my employment, my main source of income – especially now, when I had given almost all the ready money I possessed to Mr Hakesby.

'Begging your pardon, sir,' Sam said, implausibly obsequious, 'might I ask the honour of a word?'

'What the devil are you about, jackanapes?' I snapped, my irritation striking the nearest target like a bolt of lightning. 'Why are you talking like a gallant in a bad play?'

'It's this, sir,' Sam said, reverting to his normal voice, with an answering edge of irritation in his own. 'The wife and me are worried. And it's not right, you leaving us like this. Not knowing our arse from our elbow.'

'Sam!' Margaret whispered, her face filling with anguish.

'When you hired us,' Sam went on, scowling at me, 'it was because of your father needing us, Margaret especially. And that's why you took this house, so there'd be room for him and us all. You told me so yourself. So what's going to happen now, master? He's dead. He doesn't need us any more. Nor do you, for that matter, nor a house this size. For all we know, you're going to give up the lease come midsummer.'

I hadn't even thought about such things. But he was right. I no longer needed a house the size of Infirmary Close or two servants.

'I don't know what I'm going to do yet,' I said. 'Damn

your insolence,' I added, though without as much conviction as I should have done.

'We need to know if you're going to turn us out into the street, sir,' Sam said. 'That's all.'

Margaret sniffed. Her fingers plucked at her apron.

I understood now the reason for the gleaming woodwork and the smell of cooking, and for the care and patience that Sam and Margaret had lavished on my father, saving me from the burden of doing it myself. I also understood that by giving them employment and taking them into my family, I had somehow acquired an obligation as well as conferred one. I owed them a debt. Just as I owed my father a debt for not believing him on the last evening of his life.

'I don't know what I'm going to do,' I repeated, in a gentler voice. 'But — even if I move from the Savoy — I will not see you left without a roof over your head if I can help it.'

Margaret curtsied and said, as if this were an evening like any other, 'And when will you be wanting your supper, sir?'

'Later,' I said, coming suddenly to a decision. While I had loyal servants, I might as well make use of them. 'Sam, we're going out in a moment. Attend me.'

He followed me into the parlour and stood looking at me with his bright eyes. I heard Margaret retreating to the kitchen.

'Come armed,' I said softly, so Margaret wouldn't hear.

The light was ebbing from the sky, and the smoke from a thousand chimneys made a grey pall over London. I didn't need to adapt my pace to Sam's — he was extraordinarily agile, and with his stump and crutch he negotiated the streets as rapidly as most men did on two undamaged legs.

We walked along the Strand and passed under the Bar into Fleet Street.

Sam drew level with me. 'Clifford's Inn, sir?'

'Not exactly. Though it may have a bearing.'

I glanced at him. His face was alight with excitement. God's blood, I thought, he's enjoying this. When I had first met him, he had been surviving on his wits in Alsatia, the sanctuary in Whitefriars where thieves and debtors lived unmolested by the law. Sometimes I wondered if he was wearied by the respectability of his life at Infirmary Close.

We were on the north side of the street. As we drew level with St Dunstan-in-the-West, I threw a glance up the alley leading to the Inn. The gate was open. Beyond it was the stunted south court and the door of the hall. It seemed to me that there was something secretive about Clifford's Inn, about its untidy, close-packed huddle of buildings: it set itself apart from the world, drawing in its skirts like a prudish lady from the common crowds of Fleet Street.

We walked on and turned into Fetter Lane. Beggars have long memories, and two or three of them swarmed about us. Sam was ruthless and drove them away with his crutch and his sailor's vocabulary.

I paused outside the Half Moon. At the southern end of the building, towards Fleet Street, an alley little more than a yard wide wriggled between the gable wall of the inn and the side of the neighbouring building.

Sam glanced up at the sign over the door. His face brightened. 'You'll take a glass of wine, master?'

I lowered my voice. 'I've a fancy to see the back of the house. There must be a yard, outhouses perhaps. See that ruined building behind? And that long roof on the right? That's part of Clifford's Inn.'

He wrinkled his nose. 'Are we going up that alley?'

'You aren't. Stay here. If anyone asks what I'm up to, tell them I have a powerful need to shit. Try and keep them away.'

I left him there, leaning against the wall and picking his teeth. The unpaved alley wound between the buildings on either side. Judging from the smell of it, many people had already used it as a makeshift necessary house. By this time the light was fading, and I had to watch my step.

The buildings gave way to the walls of the Half Moon's yard, which were topped with spikes. The alley seemed to be going towards the back of the new building, where Gromwell's chambers were. Then it swung abruptly to the left. After a few yards the path ended at a heavy door banded with iron, set in an archway of blackened stone. There was an extensive collection of turds of various ages on and around the doorstep. But the refuse had recently been scraped away from the centre, leaving a clear path up the alley and on to the step.

I looked up. The door was an entrance to the ruined staircase at Clifford's Inn, the one that had aroused Chelling's passions. He had pointed it out when we first met. There was no sign of a latch or a keyhole. The threshold was worn to a deep curve, as if someone had taken a neat bite from it. I laid the palm of my hand on the door and pushed. It didn't move. That was when I heard the footsteps behind me.

Someone was coming up the alley. I heard men's voices, two of them. They appeared around the corner. One was a workman, wearing a stained leather apron over his breeches.

The other was a tall, slim man in a dark cloak and a broad-brimmed hat. He was carrying a staff shod with iron.

'What are you doing here?' he said. He sounded as if he had his mouth full.

I pointed at one of the fresher piles of turds. 'What does it look like?'

The hat shielded much of his face, and in the poor light the rest of his features were a blur.

'It's private here.' The hard consonants were indistinct, but not his meaning.

There were more footsteps in the alley, and I recognized their halting rhythm.

The tall man turned towards the corner, just as Sam appeared. 'You're trespassing. Both of you. Get out.'

Sam stopped, his hand flicking back the edge of his cloak. I knew he had a pistol in his belt on that side. There was a dagger on the other.

'As you please,' I said, as pleasantly as I could.

'And don't come back.' The tall man pointed his staff at Sam. 'Nor you, cripple.'

Because of the narrowness of the alley, he and the workman had to stand with their backs to the wall to let me pass. His head was bowed, the brim covering the upper part of the face. As I squeezed by, I glimpsed a small, compressed mouth overshadowed by the chin below and the nose above. That explained the articulation: he had lost all or most of his teeth.

As part of my mourning, there were black silk weepers attached to my hat, and they touched his shoulder as I passed. He brushed them away as if they were cobwebs.

I walked on, frowning at Sam to keep him from intervening.

One of the men followed, at a distance. He wanted to make sure we had really gone.

We reached the street. A large handcart was waiting near the end of the alley, with a small boy guarding it.

'Who's old sourface then?' Sam said. 'I don't think he likes us.'

The boy with the handcart glanced incuriously at me. I ducked back into the alley. I did not go far – a few paces would bring me back to the safety of the crowded street.

But a few paces was all it took to reduce the sound of traffic on Fetter Lane to a fraction of its volume on the street. I waited a moment.

I heard three knocks in the distance – first one, then a pause, then two in swift succession. After another pause, the sequence was repeated. In my mind's eye, I saw the tall man standing among the turds and knocking the head of his staff against the door to Clifford's Inn.

Sourface. As good a name as any.

CHAPTER THIRTEEN

THE SUN, DRAPED with fiery streamers of cloud, was sinking towards the horizon over Hyde Park. Jemima was in her bedchamber, sitting by the window overlooking the garden, with a novel by Mademoiselle de Scudéry lying unread on her lap.

The kitchen yard was to the side of their garden, divided from it by a fence. From her chair, she was able to look down slantwise into the strip running along its far wall, which also served as part of the boundary wall between the Limburys' house and the one next door in Pall Mall. The hut over the cesspool, which the servants used as their privy, was in the yard, along with the midden, the gardener's shed and the kennels for the dogs.

The house around her was still. Two hours or so before supper, there always came a lull in the routine, a time for the household to draw breath. In the bowels of the building, the cook and the kitchen maid were at work, but they were out of sight and did not count.

Richard was the first to come out. He was a thin man, older

than his employer by a good ten years, with the attenuated, overstated elegance of a greyhound. He dressed in dark clothes of good quality, as befitted his position as one who was seen in public with his master. But Philip was at Whitehall now, attending on the King, and his absence meant that his servant was at leisure.

In honour of the occasion, Richard was wearing his teeth. When he wore them, his face was passable, though no one would call him good-looking. Without the teeth, his face collapsed in on itself.

As Jemima watched, he took a turn about the yard, throwing glances in the direction of the door to the kitchen.

Mary glided outside. The girl looked well enough, Jemima supposed, quite a handsome creature in her way, and her green eyes would have adorned any woman's face. She appeared not to see Richard, but slipped between the kennel and privy. Here was a sort of alcove, framed by the side walls of the outbuildings and the boundary wall behind. He glanced back at the kitchen and followed her.

Jemima shifted her chair to the right, which gave her a clear view of most of the alcove. Though the window was open, she could not hear what the two servants were saying. But soon there was no need of words.

Richard's arms snaked out and tried to wrap themselves around Mary's waist. She sprang back. He hunched his shoulders and spread his hands in supplication.

Mary edged closer, extended her arm and let him take her hand. He raised it to those damp, mobile lips. He pulled her slowly towards him. She resisted at first, but allowed herself, step by step, to be drawn into his embrace.

Jemima leaned forward in her chair, trying to see more.

Her book, volume ten of *Le Grand Cyrus*, slid from her lap to the floor, but she did not notice.

Richard's hand slid over Mary's hips. He pushed his knee between her legs. He gripped her gown and tried to lift it.

Suddenly it was over. Mary was walking briskly towards the house. Richard turned aside, his back to Jemima at the window, and appeared to be adjusting his dress.

Jemima sat back, leaving the novel where it had fallen. She closed her eyes. She did not bother to answer when there was a light tap on the door.

Mary came in, shutting the door behind her and sliding the bolt across. She crossed the room and stood by Jemima's chair.

'Did Richard tell you anything?' Jemima asked without opening her eyes.

'Something, madam. Only a little.'

'Comb my hair.'

She felt Mary's arm brush against hers as the maid leaned forward and took up the silver-mounted comb from the dressing table. The comb's teeth tugged at Jemima's hair. Mary steadied her mistress's head with her other hand. The tips of the teeth scraped the skin of Jemima's scalp. She felt her muscles relax, first in her face, then in her neck and then lower down her body, a gentle tide of well-being.

If I were a cat, she thought, I should purr.

'He was ready enough,' Mary said. 'He wants me.'

'I saw,' Jemima said softly.

'His breath stinks.'

'Did he answer you?'

'I asked where he'd been,' Mary said. 'Why he was always out these days. He said it's the master's business. So I said, what about on Thursday, when he was gone all day and most of the evening. I pretended I'd been mad with passion for him then. He wouldn't answer at first, so I let him touch my breasts.'

'You wicked woman,' Jemima said.

'He said the master had a difficulty that he helped him deal with, and he'd been well paid.' The comb found a knot, and bit into it, tugging and pulling, loosening the strands of hair with delicious deliberation. 'A pound, he said.'

'A pound!'

'And in gold, mistress. He said he'd buy me a pair of gloves if I would grant him the last favour. That's what he wanted.'

'That's what men always want,' Jemima said. 'If they want you at all. It's either that or nothing.'

Mary snorted. 'He wanted it there and then, up against the wall. But I wouldn't let him. He wouldn't have told me, even if I had. He's hot for me, but he fears Sir Philip more.'

Jemima opened her eyes. 'Look at me.'

The comb stopped its work. Mary came to the side of her mistress and looked down at her.

'What do you think?' Jemima asked.

'About Richard? I think he's a bag of wind and piss.'

'No. About my husband's bitch in Clifford's Inn. Who is she?'

It was nearly midnight.

A single candle burned on the night table. Shadows crowded in the corners of the room. The mistress and maid were sitting in the bed, side by side, so close that their shoulders touched. They were both in their smocks. Jemima felt the warmth of Mary's body, seeping through the linen that separated their two skins. Their feet touched.

The bed curtains were tied back. Jemima thought they might be alone in the night in some far-off place – the Indies, perhaps, or Africa – sitting in their silken pavilion with the flaps raised. The candle was their campfire, its glow keeping them safe from the wild beasts that prowled about them, invisible in the darkness.

Mary turned her head. 'Why does master care so much?' she whispered, and her breath brushed Jemima's skin and made it tingle.

'About Dragon Yard? Because it's his, you foolish girl. Nothing else is. Only that freehold. His salary from the Bedchamber goes to pay the interest on his debts.'

'But why should he bother, mistress? He lives high, thanks to you and Sir George. He wants for nothing, and never will.'

'Except his own money in his purse.'

'So this is his chance then? To have money he can call his own?'

'Even the clothes on his back and the food on his table comes from me and my father. And he won't have the use of the property I bring him until my father dies. Perhaps not even then. Father means to tie up everything in knots if he possibly can, to make it safe for his grandson.'

There was a silence. Mary had come to Syre Place when she was thirteen. Jemima allowed her a latitude she allowed no one else. Talking to Mary was like talking to herself. Her mind veered to her husband, and jealousy twisted inside her. Not just jealousy. Oh, Jemima thought, I would give anything to be with his child. How was it possible to love someone and hate them at the same time?

She said abruptly, to divert herself: 'I believe that Dragon Yard is not merely a matter of money.'

'What is it then, dear madam?'

'My husband does not care to be idle. Since he came back from the navy, he has done nothing except fritter his life away at court, or wander about here, or see his friends. He has no occupation apart from warming the King's small clothes when it's his turn to serve him.'

Her father kept Philip on a tight leash like a distempered dog. Distempered dogs sometimes turned on those that fed them.

'But that's no reason for him—'

'Stop it, you foolish woman.' Jemima pulled away from Mary. She was tired of talking, tired of thinking bitterly familiar thoughts that led nowhere but endlessly back on themselves. 'Bring me my draught. I can't sleep properly at present.'

Mary laid her hand on her mistress's forearm. 'Madam,' she said softly, pleadingly. 'I know a better way than a sleeping draught.'

'Hush. Did you hear?'

Both women listened, hardly breathing. There were footsteps in the passage. Then a firm knock on the bedroom door, and the clack of the latch.

'Jemima. Are you awake?'

'Shall I say you're sleeping?' Mary whispered.

Jemima pushed her away. 'Open the door. Quickly.' She raised her voice. 'A moment, sir.'

Mary took up the candle and padded across the floor to the door. She drew back the bolt. The door opened sharply, banging into her.

'Be off with you,' Philip said to Mary.

Without looking at her, he pushed past and strode towards

the bed, his leather slippers slapping on the floorboards. He was carrying his own candle, and the flame danced like a wild thing, throwing shadows around the room. He was wearing his bedgown and looked, Jemima thought, like an Indian prince striding into his harem. She had given him the gown; it was made of scarlet and gold silk, ankle-length, trimmed with fur at the neck and wrists, and padded against the chill of the night. He wore a silk kerchief around his shaved head.

'Mistress?' Mary said. 'Shall I—'

'Go away,' Jemima said without looking at her. 'Don't bother me.'

Mary left the room quickly, taking her candle with her. She closed the door with unnecessary emphasis.

'I'm glad I find you awake,' Philip said. He sat down on the edge of the bed, on her left side, and took her hand. 'You look very fine, my love. And quite restored, thank God.'

Despite everything he had done, despite everything she knew about him, and everything she was, she felt herself respond to his voice. She looked at her small white hand as it lay defenceless in the palm of his. She pulled it away and turned her face away from him.

'Are you sleepy?' he said.

'Not in the least.'

'Come, then.' He stood up and pulled back the coverlet and sheet. He stared down at her. 'Let us while away the time by entertaining each other.'

She sat up sharply. 'How can you come to me like this?'

He raised his dark eyebrows and chose to misunderstand her. 'Who better than me? You're my wife. You would want no one else, I hope.'

She tried to pull the sheet over her, but he would not let

her. 'You come from another woman. I can smell your punk's stink on you. Your punk in Clifford's Inn.'

'What nonsense is this?'

'I know it all. I saw the woman's letter.' She spat out the name. 'This Celia.'

Philip stared at her. He forced a smile. 'You mean Gromwell's mistress?'

She stared at him. 'What? I thought—'

'Don't.' He pulled away from her. 'I should beat you for even thinking such slanders.'

'But the letter . . . '

Philip whistled. 'I remember now. Gromwell showed me the letter the other night. I left it on my desk when he and I walked over to watch the play at Whitehall. It named the time and the place of their meeting . . . So your little Mary was playing the spy?'

Jemima said, 'She – she has my best interests at heart. And as well someone has.'

'I'll have the jade whipped.'

'No, sir. You shall not.'

He held her eyes for a moment, and then shrugged. 'I'll let it pass this time.'

She tried to stand but he pulled her down. 'Let me go.'

'Full of passion, that letter, wasn't it? Full of my love this, and my love that. But think back – my name wasn't mentioned in it. You assumed that I must be the woman's lover because your jealous nature would have it so. But the letter was written to Gromwell, you goose, not to me. He brought it to show me. He was in raptures – she had agreed at last to meet him privately, in his chambers, and he thought he was as good as wed to her.'

'But – but that can't be true. I don't believe it.'

'Of course it's true.' He stroked her hand. 'Now, my dearest. Let us return to what matters.'

He straightened and pushed the bedgown from his shoulders. The wavering flame of the candle converted his body into a map of hills and shadowed valleys; in places, the skin glowed as if a fire was raging across it. He was running to fat but she didn't care about that.

She stretched out her finger and touched his leg. It was warm and rough. Completely unlike a woman's. Tonight, she thought, perhaps God will at last permit—

'My love,' Philip said, sliding into the bed beside her. 'Oh – by the way – I had almost forgot: there is a small matter of business to discuss as well.'

Her excitement shattered.

'I should find it a great convenience if I had a little ready money. Two hundred would be enough, I think, and I shall soon be in a position to repay it and more.' His hand slipped over her left breast. 'Do you think Sir George might see his way—'

'You know what my father said last time.' Her nipple hardened under the smock, treacherously ignoring its owner's feelings.

'Yes, but this is different. It's an investment that cannot fail to yield a rich profit. See, I'm talking like a plump alderman already . . . If my plans for Dragon Yard go ahead – and there's no reason why they shouldn't – I'll even be able to repay his last loan.' He untied the neck of her gown and slipped his hand inside. 'I could borrow the money elsewhere, I know, but the interest would not be agreeable.'

She forced herself to think clearly, just for a moment, to

float above the tide of sensation that was flowing through her. 'There's only one thing that will make him look kindly on you. You know what that is.'

He withdrew his hand abruptly. 'Yes, my love. An heir.' His voice had an edge to it. 'And we are doing what we can to achieve that most desirable aim at this very moment. But this other matter is important, too – not to him, perhaps, but to us. Now I think of it, we could avoid troubling your father entirely. You recall those earrings he gave you on your birthday before last? You never wear them – you told me they were too heavy, and ugly besides. And he wouldn't expect to see them on you, either, because he never leaves Syre Place now, and you would hardly wear such baubles in the country. So you wouldn't miss them, and nor would he.'

'How can you say this?' she said. 'Now, of all times?'

The room was almost silent around them. She listened to the sound of their breathing and a faint scratching near the chimney piece. Mice, perhaps rats. A distant owl screeched among the trees of the park.

Was it possible that he had lied to her after all, and that he, not Gromwell, was the woman's lover? Why should she trust him?

'Well, well,' Philip said, and his voice had changed again: it was warm now, and soft as a caress. 'It is only business, like Dragon Yard. What do such things matter, after all, as long as we have each other?'

The hand was back. Only this time it was raising the hem of her smock. His fingers touched her inner thigh and she could not restrain a sigh of pleasurable anticipation. Her body was treacherous, her body was his ally.

'And we have this, my love,' he whispered. 'Always.'

His mouth hovered over hers, his breath brushed her skin. 'Let us give your father a grandson, my love. A little Henry who will have Syre Place when he is gone.'

Somewhere on the far side of the curtain windows, a distant church clock began to strike the hour. Her husband's fingers moved in time with the chimes as one day passed into another.

CHAPTER FOURTEEN

'WILL YOU TAKE some warm wine, sir? With spices to heat the blood?'

Mr Hakesby shook his head. He was huddled over the fire with a blanket draped over his shoulders. The ague was bad today.

The office was already uncomfortably warm. The morning sun streamed through the big windows of the drawing office at the sign of the Rose in Henrietta Street. Brennan was in his shirt sleeves, and there were patches of sweat under his arms. Cat thought he stank like a fox.

'I must see Poulton this morning,' Hakesby said. 'Is that the half hour already?'

'Yes, sir,' Cat said. 'You're engaged to meet him at ten o'clock in Cheapside.'

'I know, I know.'

They listened to the chime of a distant church clock.

'I could hire a coach . . . ' Hakesby said. His deep voice quivered.

'You are not well enough to go abroad, master.'

He frowned at her and then looked away. A fit of shivering ran through him. 'I suppose I could send the boy downstairs with the plans . . . '

'Mr Poulton will have questions. The boy can't answer anything.'

'Or Brennan.'

She glanced at the draughtsman, who had his back to them and seemed absorbed in his work. 'But, sir, you need him here to finish the warehouse plans. That's as good as money in the hand.'

'Then it's hopeless.' Hakesby's eyes filled with tears; these sudden swings of mood were growing worse with the tremors. 'We've lost a possible commission. And Mr Poulton has the reputation of being a man who pays on the nail. He is exactly the sort of client we need.'

Cat wondered if Hakesby were right. Despite his wealth, Poulton might be the sort of client they didn't need. He was somehow mixed up in this dubious business that Marwood was concerned with. On the other hand, Hakesby might be right. Besides, they had already done the work.

'Send me instead,' she suggested.

'Think how it would look — sending a maid in my place. Mr Poulton would take it as a slight.'

'He would take it as a worse slight if you sent the boy, who knows nothing about anything. If you send me, at least I know the plans, which is more than Brennan does. I should do. I drew them for you. And I know what's in your mind too. I could answer at least some of his questions.'

'Very well. It appears I have no choice.' Hakesby sighed. 'To think it has come to this. Let us hope he won't be insulted that I sent you in my place . . . But you must take the boy with you. You cannot wander the streets alone, particularly among the ruins. And even so . . . '

Cat had no wish to take the porter's boy with her. He had damp hands that left smudges on the letters he brought up to them. Despite his youth, she suspected him of trying to peep at her through the cracks of the necessary house in the yard.

But the boy's company was a small price to pay. Before Hakesby could change his mind, she put on her cloak, found her pattens and gathered up the plans into a folder.

She left the house with the boy, the plans under her arm. The clock struck the three-quarters as they passed St Dunstan-in-the-West by Clifford's Inn. Cat quickened her pace, and the boy straggled behind her, whining when she urged him to hurry.

When they reached Cheapside, Poulton was already at Dragon Yard, pacing over the site with a servant who was taking notes at his dictation. A hackney coach was waiting nearby, the driver refreshing himself at the beer stall on the other side of the road, and the horse, its head lowered, standing perfectly motionless apart from his tail, which flicked from side to side in a vain attempt to remove the flies.

Though he must have seen them approaching on the path that snaked through the rubble, Poulton ignored them until they were almost at his shoulder. He continued to dictate in a low, monotonous voice. The porter's boy stared open-mouthed at him, as if at a prodigy of nature.

At last Poulton turned towards them. 'Well? What's this? Where's Mr Hakesby?'

Cat curtsied. 'He sends the most profound apologies, sir. He's unwell.'

'So there's an end to it.' Poulton turned away.

'But he has sent me in his stead with the designs, as he promised, and instructed me on the details.'

Poulton frowned down at her. He held out his hand. Cat gave him the folder. He took out the three sheets of paper and studied them – a sketch of Dragon Yard, marking the access roads and the locations of the houses, the front elevation of one of the terraced houses of three storeys, and plans of the principal floors.

'This is not unlike Limbury's design,' Poulton murmured, to himself rather than Cat.

'Mr Hakesby considered the matter and thought there was no reason why you should not follow a similar plan, with the new road to Cheapside. It would enhance the value, as you said yourself, and of course it would also be agreeable to both the Court of Aldermen and the Fire Court.'

His eyebrows shot up. He stared at her, Cat felt, in much the same way as he would have stared at the hackney coachman's horse if he had spoken.

'And did he say anything else?'

'Yes, sir. He begs you to consider that his scheme makes possible the building of twelve houses, rather than eight or ten, as Sir Philip intends.' She came closer and pointed at the plan. 'By inserting a crossroad there. And that would also make space – there – for a larger house at the south-west corner, which you might wish to reserve for yourself. All this is subject to a full survey, of course, as well as a favourable decision from the Fire Court. But if all goes well, it would increase your profits considerably.'

'You're Hakesby's maid, eh?'

Cat stared back at him. 'And his cousin, sir.'

Poulton grunted. 'Clearly he confides some of his business to you. I hope his work isn't conducted so eccentrically.' He paused. 'And what do you think about it all? You. Not your master.'

The question took Cat by surprise, and surprise made her answer with more honesty than tact: 'I think it all depends on the other leaseholders. I have watched other Fire Court petitions, and the judges try to act fairly to everyone. Or, failing that, to the majority of the interested parties.'

'So it will be which of us the others support that will decide the day – Limbury or me?'

'Perhaps. Assuming both of you either have or can borrow the necessary funds and can rebuild in roughly the same time. As Mr Hakesby said the other day, it shouldn't prove difficult to raise a loan if you need to.'

'Remarkable,' Poulton said, looking at her. 'Quite extra-ordinary.' His expression was grave but he did not speak unkindly. 'Tell Mr Hakesby that I have had a word with Dr Hooke as to his suitability for employment in a work of this nature. He was most complimentary, and Dr Hooke is usually sparing of his compliments.'

'Yes, sir. Thank you, sir.'

'And tell him—' He broke off, frowning. 'No matter. There will be time for that later, if necessary. And one other thing. I should like to prepare a set of full plans as soon as possible. The hearing is next week, on Wednesday, so speed is vital. I've an accurate survey of the ground at my house, as well as several copies. It shows Dragon Yard as it was, including the vaults, and the route of an underground stream that runs down to the river. Mr Hakesby will find it useful to have a sight of it before he continues. You had better come back with me now, and I will give you a copy. And I shall write him a note, concerning the fees.'

Cat curtsied. 'Will it take long, sir?'

'Half an hour or so. An hour at most. My house is in Clerkenwell.'

'Then I'll send the boy back, sir. So Mr Hakesby knows where I am.'

Poulton nodded. He walked away towards the coach, leaving his servant and Cat to trail after him and, last of all, the porter's boy to follow everyone else.

There was no conversation on the journey to Clerkenwell. The coach smelled like all hackneys, of sweat, horse manure, tobacco and stale perfume. Both Poulton and his servant were tall men, and the servant was fat as well. Cat felt surrounded by walls of masculine flesh.

The curtains were up, and she stared at the world as it jolted past. Cheapside was coming to life again – families were camping in shelters in the former cellars of their houses; make-shift stalls lined the street frontages; and there were even more permanent structures, built largely of wood, sprouting along the street in defiance of the new building regulations. You could not destroy a city merely by destroying its buildings.

Poulton's house was near the green in Clerkenwell. It occupied the wing of an old mansion. The porter admitted them to a hall that was open to the blackened roof timbers. He was big with news, his eyes bulging with excitement.

'Master,' he cried, 'it's Mistress Celia.'

For an instant, Poulton's chilly air of self-sufficiency faltered. 'Where is she? Is she here?'

'No, master, but – well, there's a Coroner's man to see you. In your study.'

139

'A Coroner's man?' Poulton's eyes widened. Then the self-sufficiency was back. 'Take this girl to Mistress Lee.' He glanced briefly at Cat. 'My housekeeper.'

He walked away. The servant opened a door for Cat but did not bother to bow to her.

The room was a parlour, sparsely furnished and hung with faded tapestries illustrating scenes from the Old Testament. An old lady sat in the only chair. Her head was turned away from Cat. She was doing nothing, though a pile of sewing lay on the table beside her. At first Cat thought she was asleep but, as Cat advanced slowly into the room, she turned her head. She was small and plump, with a face marked by time and smallpox.

'Who are you?'

Cat curtsied. 'Jane Hakesby, mistress. Mr Poulton brought me here about the Dragon Yard business.'

'He won't have time for that now.' Mistress Lee moved her head slightly, enough to catch the light from the single window. Her cheeks were wet with tears.

'Why?'

The housekeeper dabbed her cheeks with a handkerchief but didn't answer.

The door opened. Mistress Lee rose from her chair and flew to embrace Mr Poulton.

'My dear,' she said. 'Remember we don't know for sure.'

He was paler than ever, his face thinner, his shoulders more stooping.

'The foolish girl,' he said in a voice that did not seem wholly under his control. 'What was she about?'

'No, sir, you must not distress yourself. As I say, we must not jump to conclusions.'

'I cannot understand it. Among the ruins. Why would Celia go there?'

'Which is one reason why they may be mistaken.'

'And her clothes—'

Something in Mistress Lee's face stopped him in mid-sentence. A warning frown? A touch on his arm? A flick of the eyes towards the visitor?

Poulton stiffened, straightening his shoulders. He turned towards Cat, who was standing to one side of him and had been out of his line of sight.

'Ah – yes. I had forgotten . . . Hakesby's girl . . . Of course.' He swallowed. 'I can't attend to you now. Or to the Dragon Yard matter. Later, perhaps . . . We have had – well, it comes to this: you must go.'

'You can't turn the girl out, sir.'

He shook his head. 'We must go with the – the man. He has a coach waiting.'

'Where do you live, child?' Mistress Lee said.

'I am commanded to go to my cousin's drawing office, mistress. In Henrietta Street.'

'In that case we will take you up with us as far as Fetter Lane, and send you on in the coach. You'll never get a hackney here.'

'But, mistress – I can't cause you so much trouble. And at such a time—'

'I'm not letting you roam the streets by yourself.' The house-keeper was a foot shorter than Mr Poulton, but in her way she was as formidable as he was, perhaps more so. 'Especially now. When it seems there may be a monster roaming abroad.'

'A monster . . . ?' Cat said.

'I won't brook any argument.' Mistress Lee glanced from Cat to Mr Poulton. 'From anyone.'

CHAPTER FIFTEEN

O N THURSDAY MORNING, I was at Whitehall by half-past seven. Under-Secretary Williamson was not there, but he had left word I was to work at the Scotland Yard office, copying out his private newsletter to a score of his correspondents scattered the length and breadth of the three kingdoms. It was tedious work in the extreme, and made my wrist and fingers ache.

Williamson himself looked in between eight and nine but he said nothing to me. He seemed not to see me. I knew his methods. He intended me to feel his displeasure, to brood on it, to wonder when and how the storm would break on my head. He was an artist in his way.

He went away to spend the rest of the morning with my Lord Arlington. I was worried. Williamson was careful, calculating and controlled. He did not rage at his clerks or at anyone, to my knowledge. But he demanded obedience and he was capable of nursing a grudge.

A few months ago, I had been in good odour with him — and indeed with my other master, Mr Chiffinch, the Keeper of the King's Private Closet and a useful ally at court. The King himself had looked kindly on me. But memories are short at Whitehall, and I did not fool myself into thinking I was invulnerable.

The summons came an hour or so after dinner, in the middle of the afternoon, at a time when even in the best-regulated office diligence tends to be on the wane. Williamson sent a servant commanding me to attend him by the Holbein Gate.

I seized my cloak and ran out of the office and into Whitehall. There was no sign of Williamson by the Holbein Gate or anywhere else. He kept me waiting a good twenty minutes before he strolled out of the Great Court. He waved me over to him.

'I'm going to the Chancellor's. Walk with me through the Park.'

The Chancellor's new mansion was in Piccadilly. We walked side by side into St James's Park. Williamson did not say anything until we were skirting the canal. He stopped suddenly and for the first time looked directly at me.

'Well, Marwood. What have you been up to?'

I could hardly tell Williamson the truth, not least because I did not know what the truth was. 'Settling my father's affairs, sir.'

'Your father was a trouble to us all in life. So now he will be a trouble in death too?'

'My father—'

'You've work to do here. What have you been up to? Why didn't you come into the office? I should have known better than to rely on a man from such cross-grained stock.' He scowled at me. 'A rotten tree produces rotten fruit.'

'I was distressed, sir, and I knew not what I was about.'
My voice stumbled along, convincing neither of us. 'And
there were debts to be paid, and so forth, and I quite . . . '

Williamson stared at me, wrinkling his nose as if I were a
slug or a foul smell.

'Forgive me,' I said quickly, knowing that total abasement
was my only hope of salvation, 'especially after all your
kindness to me. It was . . . grief that prostrated me. I swear
I shall mend my ways.'

His expression did not soften, but the anger left it.
Williamson was a man who calculated everything in the most
economical manner, even his outbursts of rage. 'I have a task
for you now. Not an agreeable one.'

I bowed. 'Anything, master. Whatever you command.'

'A body has been found in the ruins. My lord is concerned
that there are disaffected elements abroad.'

In this context, my lord meant my Lord Arlington, the
King's Secretary of State and Williamson's superior. The
security of the kingdom was in his charge.

'It's a woman,' he said. 'And she was stabbed.'

'A whore?'

'The Coroner thinks she's probably a widow by the name
of Hampney. Perfectly respectable woman. Something of an
heiress, in fact.'

That explained Lord Arlington's interest in the death. It
was one thing for a woman of no account to turn up dead,
her body abandoned in the ruins. But it was quite another
for a wealthy widow to be found in a similar state. Wealthy
widows had friends.

'But he's not convinced it is her,' Williamson went on.
'They say this woman is dressed like a whore, or the next

best thing. Why would someone like Mistress Hampney dress like that?'

'Not a beauty,' the Coroner's clerk said. 'Though to be sure it's hard to tell.'

I said nothing. I was fighting the urge to vomit.

'She seems to have been well enough made if you like them on the skinny side. Me, I like my birds a little plumper.'

I turned aside, sickened. The clerk was hardly more than a boy, puffed up by his office and trying too hard to impress.

The woman had been placed on her side in a shallow grave. She was small and slight. Her body was lying in what had been the cellar of a house. It had originally been covered by a thin layer of rubble and ash. But it could not have lain completely hidden for long.

'See the calf of the leg, sir?' He was a ferret of a youth with a single eyebrow across his forehead. 'Looks like fox to me. What do you think?'

For a moment I lowered the cloth that covered my nostrils and mouth. 'Perhaps.'

'The jaw must have been quite a size. You see badgers sometimes at night, but I don't think the shape of the bite is right. Wild dog, perhaps? There's a good few of those out here. All it would need is one animal to get a sniff of her and start scraping away with its paws.'

'How did she die? Can you tell?'

'Stab wound under the left breast,' he said. 'Probably hit the heart. Stabbed in the neck, too, in the artery. A lot of blood.'

'She must have been buried in haste. By night?'

'They'd have been seen if they'd brought her here during

the day. Now look there, sir.' His fingers fluttered over the exposed forearm. 'It's not dog or fox did those. That's rat, and more than one of them. I'd put a crown on it.'

Unwillingly I stared down at the body. The horrors attending death have a dreadful allure. Black or very dark brown hair partly masked an unnaturally white cheek. Bled like a calf for veal.

'Someone found her before we did,' the clerk said. 'Someone with two legs, not four. See that hand?'

He pointed. My eyes followed. The woman had lost a finger from her right hand. Bone shone white at the stump.

'Probably a ring.' The clerk shrugged. 'Quicker to hack off the whole finger than work it loose, if it was a tight fit. As for the eye, I reckon a bird had that. A crow. They go for eyes, you know. They have a particular taste for them. My uncle keeps sheep, and the crows always go for the lambs' eyes. Living or dead, it's all the same to them. It's a delicacy, you might say.'

There was no sign of the woman's shoes. I stared at her feet. One was covered in a pale silk stocking, which had fallen to the ankle. The other was bare.

Somehow the worst thing was the loss of the eye. It made her look less than human. A velvet beauty patch clung to the corner of the empty socket, gaily mocking the bloody crater beside it. The patch was in the shape of a heart. You couldn't see the other eye, because she was lying on her side.

I said, 'How long has she been here? Can you tell?'

'Upwards of a week?' The clerk tapped his nose, to give himself a look of worldly wisdom: he looked like a smug little boy strutting through the kitchen with his grandfather's hat on his head. 'When you've seen a few, you can form an opinion. It's the smell, partly, and the way the skin goes.'

I climbed out of the cellar, partly to get away from the stink of putrefaction and partly to get away from the clerk. We were in a section of ruins to the east of Fetter Lane, in what had been a court off Shoe Lane. The thoroughfares had been cleared in this area, but many of the buildings remained choked with their own debris.

From where I was standing, the blackened remains of houses, shops and manufactories stretched down the slope to the polluted waters of the Fleet Ditch. Beyond it, Ludgate Hill rose to the City walls and the taller ruins behind it, dominated even now by the hulk of St Paul's Cathedral. I turned the other way. There was the familiar tower of St Dunstan-in-the-West, with the roofs of Clifford's Inn to the north.

The clerk and I were alone, though another of the Coroner's men was trying to dissuade a knot of people from approaching. The news of the body had not spread far yet. But it soon would.

Why did it have to be here – so close to Clifford's Inn, to the Fire Court and Fetter Lane? I looked back at the corpse. It had been buried, if that was the right word, in a large, dark-brown cloak originally made for a man. But where it had been pushed aside you could see what she was wearing beneath. Some thin material, probably silk and certainly expensive; yellow in colour, almost golden, but badly stained with blood. The blood was rust-coloured now, but when it was fresh the contrast with the yellow must have been dazzling.

Yellow as the sun, red as fire . . .

For a moment I heard my father's weary voice on the last evening of his life, as he recounted his strange, fantastic dream. The dream that had turned out to have so many unexpected correspondences with reality.

147

A sense of foreboding crept over me. Yellow as the sun, red as fire . . . Had he been trying to describe the dress the woman had been wearing? But how could he have seen this woman in the ruins? As far as I knew he hadn't come here.

Unless he had seen her in Clifford's Inn.

'Jackson says she's a widow,' the clerk said. 'And wealthy, too.'

'Jackson?'

'The Coroner's coachman. He used to work for the woman's uncle before he came to his worship. But he's wrong, if you ask me. I know an old whore when I see one. This wasn't one of your tuppenny knee-jerkers, mind. Soft hands. Handsome gown. She'd been one for the gentlemen, though you wouldn't think to look at her now.'

'Turn her head,' I said.

'What?'

'I want to see the other side of her face.'

He shrugged. 'If you say so.'

'I do say so. Put her on her back.'

He spat on his hands and crouched beside the body. He thrust his hands and forearms underneath the shoulders and the waist. He made a half-hearted attempt to heave the body over. He glanced up.

'Easier if you'd lend a hand, sir.'

'No.'

I stared at the clerk until he looked away. I had shown him my warrant from Williamson, countersigned by Lord Arlington, and he dared not oppose my authority.

He applied himself a little harder, or at least with a great appearance of effort. The trunk of the body flopped over. He dragged up the legs and, careless of decency, left them splayed, with the gown and the smock below hoisted above the knees. Finally he pushed up the head, bringing the face towards the sky.

The smell grew worse. I gagged.

Underneath the woman's left breast was another rust-coloured stain of dried blood. Her face and her dress were smeared with ash. The left eye was still there, thank God. The ground beneath the body must have protected it from predators. It was closed.

I closed her eyes, I owed her that at least.

My father's words filled my mind. They were a reproach. He had done his duty to the dead. But I had not done my duty to him. I had not even believed him.

Ignoring the smell, I jumped down to the cellar's floor and stooped beside the woman's head. That's when I noticed the second patch on her face: a miniature coach and horses galloping towards the left-hand corner of her mouth.

With a coach and horses too. Oh, vanity, vanity.

The shock of it hit me like a blow. My father had spoken nothing but the truth to me, and in my folly I had ignored it and condemned him as an old man in his dotage. Who was the fool now?

Oh, vanity, vanity.

Shock comes in waves, like the sea. While I braced myself against the impact, part of my mind ran on undisturbed, dealing with my appointed task.

'I'm told her name may have been Hampney,' I heard myself saying.

The clerk nodded. 'We've sent for her uncle. We'll soon know.' He pointed towards Fetter Lane. 'That could be him.'

A coach was drawing up by the side of the road. As I

watched, a tall, thin old man clambered out, followed by two women. A younger man came round from the other side of the coach.

'There's Thomas with them,' the clerk said. 'The Coroner's man.'

The elder woman stumbled. The younger took her arm. The two men and the two women advanced into the ruins. The older woman was limping; perhaps she had landed awkwardly as she descended from the coach and twisted her ankle. She leaned heavily on the younger woman.

'Leave the body on this side,' I ordered. 'If she's the old man's niece, he shouldn't see her like this, with an eye missing. Not at first. And cover her up with the cloak. Make her decent, as far as you can.'

The clerk scowled at me. But he shrugged and obeyed.

The urge to parade his knowledge triumphed over his truculence. 'He's rich as the devil,' he murmured, eyeing the little party picking their way through the ruins towards us. 'So they say.'

'The uncle? What's his name?'

'Poulton.'

'The cloth merchant? Late of Dragon Yard?'

'That's him.'

All lines converged on the Dragon Yard case and the Fire Court at Clifford's Inn.

Then came another shock to add to the others: the younger woman was Catherine Lovett.

CHAPTER SIXTEEN

THERE ARE LANGUAGES without words.

You may speak volumes with symbols, Cat knew, or gestures or hesitations or even silences. Your clothes may say what you cannot, and your eyes may plead, cajole or command.

These languages had never come naturally to her, but she had acquired a knowledge of them almost against her will in the days when she had lived in affluence and believed that her fate was to marry a courtier. Her Aunt Quincy had been a mistress of the sidelong glance or the twitch of a white, softly rounded shoulder.

'Patches,' said Mr Poulton. 'And paste. She looks like a woman of the court or those painted whores at the theatre. How could she have sunk so low?'

'And that gown . . . ' murmured Mistress Lee, clinging to his arm; it was not easy to say who was supporting whom. 'Her hair . . . '

Cat said nothing. What could you say to death? Besides, it was not her place to say anything. She was here against

Poulton's will, because Mistress Williams desired to lean on her arm as they came across the ruins; and perhaps the old woman had wanted the support of one of her own sex, too.

'Patches,' Poulton murmured. 'Badges of sin.'

They seemed not to realize, Cat thought, that patches had their meanings, as precise and finicky as the chop-logical definitions of a scholar.

'Oh my poor Celia . . . ' Mr Poulton sat down abruptly on the top of a wall. Tears coursed down his cheeks.

Mistress Lee sat and took his hand in both of hers. Cat stood to one side, watching, listening. The Coroner's clerk threw a glance at her and gave her a wink. Cat ignored him. At least the dead woman could no longer feel. Someone had valued her so little that they had dumped her here, carrion for the crows, a prey for the ghoulish. Even worse than death was the callousness of the living.

'Is that how she was found?' Mr Poulton asked.

'More or less, your honour,' the clerk said smugly. 'We made her look decent.'

'Decent?' said Mistress Lee in a faint voice. 'You call that decent?'

The clerk lowered his voice. 'There are . . . wounds, mistress. As I was telling Lord Arlington's man, the lady must have lain here for days.'

Mistress Lee whispered, 'No . . . ' and looked away.

Poulton's head snapped up. 'My Lord Arlington?' he rasped. 'What's this to do with him?'

'He sometimes sends for further information when we report a body in the ruins, sir.' The clerk pointed down the slope to Shoe Lane. 'His man's over there.'

Cat followed the direction of the finger. A man in a suit

152

of mourning stood with his back to them, talking to the Coroner's servant who had brought them from Mr Poulton's. She knew at a glance, and with a jolt of shock whose nature she did not care to analyse, that it was James Marwood.

CHAPTER SEVENTEEN

'MADAM,' I SAID, bowing to the elderly lady and the man beside her. 'Mr Poulton?'

Seated on the remains of the wall, they barely acknowledged my presence. I did not look at Catherine Lovett. She was standing to the side, watching me.

'Sir,' I persevered, 'my name's Marwood. I am come from my master, Lord Arlington.' I took a step forward, forcing the clerk to move aside. 'My lord commands me to convey his compliments of condolence.'

'Who did this?' Poulton said.

'I don't know, sir. The justices will spare no effort to find out, and nor will my lord.'

'What good will that do? Even if you find the monster who did it, it won't bring back my niece.'

The lady took Poulton's hand and squeezed it.

'How long has she lain here?' he burst out. 'Why is she dressed like a . . . like that?'

No one spoke.

'What was she doing?' he went on. 'Was she sleepwalking among the ruins when she was set upon? Was she alone?'

'Can we at least cover her face?' the old woman said.

'Of course,' I said, turning to the clerk.

He shrugged. His upper lip rose, increasing his resemblance to a ferret. 'What with?'

I took out my handkerchief, which was made of fine lawn edged with black; it was designed for display rather than use and, according to my tailor, it was absolutely indispensable for a decent appearance of mourning. I shook out the square and laid it over Mistress Hampney's head.

'Sir,' I said, 'forgive me, but may I ask a question? Had the lady been away from home? Had you seen her recently?'

Poulton's companion snorted. 'Chance would be a fine thing.'

He touched her arm and she fell silent. 'My niece didn't live with us. Until the Fire she lived in Dragon Yard, in the house she had shared with her husband. Afterwards, she found it convenient to lodge with a lady in Lincoln's Inn Fields. Mistress Grove.'

'You offered to take her into our house, sir,' the old woman said. 'You pleaded with her. But she was always headstrong. Ever since she was old enough to walk.'

'Elizabeth,' he said, his voice a low growl. 'Peace.'

'Then when did you see her last?' I asked.

'At church, the Sunday before last.'

'What will happen now?' the lady said, refusing to be repressed.

'There must be an inquest, mistress,' I said. 'And then the family may take away the body and bury it.'

'Indeed, sir,' said the Coroner's clerk, appearing at my

shoulder and trying to seize the initiative, 'if you will permit me to say so, that is my—'

'Men will see her,' Poulton said, stumbling over the words. 'They will see her like this. It is not seemly.'

'Sir, the Coroner will see that her body is treated with all respect.' I wondered how true that would be, especially if the character of the Coroner's clerk was any guide to his master's. 'It's best you leave us now. The body must be removed.'

'I should stay with her. I . . . I owe it to my sister, her poor mother.'

'You will distress yourself needlessly if you stay.'

'And me,' the lady put in, tugging Poulton's arm. 'You will distress me, too. You needn't think I will leave you here alone.'

Poulton looked about him, a dazed expression on his face. He detached the old woman's hand from his arm. With painful slowness he knelt by the body. He peeled back the handkerchief and kissed his niece's cheek, his lips brushing the skin just above the coach and horses. He rose, even more slowly, to his feet, ignoring my attempts to help him. He took the old woman's arm and they walked a few paces towards Fetter Lane. She was still limping, and this time Poulton noticed her lameness and supported her.

She stopped and looked back at Cat. 'Young woman,' she said to Cat. 'Thank you. You mustn't go back to your master alone. The streets are too dangerous.'

Cat curtsied. 'It's broad daylight, mistress, and the streets are crowded. I'll come to no harm.'

'No, no, no,' Poulton said, his voice cracking on the last syllable. 'I will not permit it. Look what happened to my poor niece.' He stared wildly about us. 'There may be a monster abroad. I shall give you something for a hackney.'

'May I help, sir?' I asked.

Mistress Lee said, 'This young woman needs to be conveyed to her master at . . . ?' She threw a glance at Cat.

'Mr Hakesby,' Cat said, staring straight ahead at Fetter Lane. 'In Henrietta Street, by Covent Garden.'

'I'll make sure she's escorted there, mistress,' I said. 'You have my word.'

I dropped a coin into the outstretched palm of the man who had escorted them from the coach. He hastened after them.

I turned to the clerk, who continued to hover at my elbow, his lips tightly compressed and his single eyebrow crinkled into a frown. 'Lord Arlington particularly wishes that the body should be treated with the utmost respect, as if it were that of his own sister.' I paused to let the words sink in. 'You will take care that it is so. What's your name?'

'Emming, sir. But the Coroner—'

'The Coroner will not want to disoblige Lord Arlington, any more than you do.' I held his gaze until he looked away. I turned to Cat. 'Come.'

She scowled at me but obeyed. We walked in silence through the ruins until we were out of earshot.

'I'm sorry,' I said quietly. 'It can't be easy for you to play the servant.'

'Better to play the servant than the whore,' she snapped. 'But whatever that poor woman did, she didn't deserve to die like that.' She hesitated. 'You were gentle with the old man and his housekeeper. That was well done.'

I looked at her. 'I haven't always been gentle with old men.'

'Your father?'

I let the question hang but of course she was right. 'Why

are you here? I could hardly believe my eyes when I saw you.'

'Thanks to you, Mr Hakesby saw an opportunity for work. Mr Poulton is a rich man, and Dragon Yard is a big site, and on Cheapside, too. I was at his house when he heard the news.'

'Who is the old woman?'

'Her name's Mistress Lee.'

'Poulton seems to depend on her. I thought at first—'

'That she was his wife?' Cat said. 'She carries herself like a wife. But their servant said she's his housekeeper. She's lived in his family for many years.'

We looked at each other. I dare say that Cat and I were thinking the same thought: that there was a certain irony in the old couple's disapproval of Celia Hampney's conduct.

'Did you examine the body before we came?' she said.

'I had the clerk turn the woman over before Mr Poulton saw her.' I hesitated, a sense of decorum affecting me at the last moment. But Catherine Lovett was such a strange creature that to talk to her was not like talking to a woman – or to a man, for that matter. 'The right-hand side of the woman's face had been mutilated after death. The eye was gone.'

'Crows?' she said, in a matter-of-fact way that was a thousand miles away from the clerk's prurience a few minutes earlier.

'Probably.'

Poulton and the housekeeper were clambering into the coach in Fetter Lane. Cat and I hung back, not wanting to catch up with them. There was a small crowd opposite the Half Moon tavern, staring at the activity around the corpse. Theophilus Chelling was among them. It looked as if he was bobbing up and down in his excitement.

'The patches upset them,' I said. 'Almost as much as anything else. "Badges of sin" — that's what the old man called them.'

'There were more than one?'

'On the other side of the face. A heart.'

'Where?'

'At the outer corner of the eye.'

'*Il y a une langue des mouches.*'

I stared at her. 'What?'

'It means the flies have a language. It's what my Aunt Quincy used to say.' Cat looked up at me, and I saw mockery in her eyes. 'Did she never say that to you? You talked a good deal with her, I think.'

I shrugged and felt the colour rising in my cheeks. 'Never about flies. Why flies? There were flies around the body.'

'Not real flies. My aunt lived in France at one time. *Les mouches* — it's what the French call beauty patches. The point is, sir, they have their meanings for those who can read what they say.'

'The shape of the patch?'

'And its position and its name. For example, a patch that masks a blemish is known as *la voleuse*, because it steals away a blemish, and perhaps steals truth away with it.'

'And this lady's patches?'

'A patch at the corner of the mouth is called *la coquette*. It invites compliment or even a kiss. Then she has the coach and horses there — and at a hand-gallop towards her lips. You do not need me to parse you the sense of that. As for *une mouche* at the corner of the eye, that is called *la passionée*. In the shape of a heart, too. All in all, I know what my aunt would say about such a woman and her intentions.'

She gave me another mocking glance. At one time, I had desired her Aunt Quincy beyond reason, beyond everything.

'What would my Lady Quincy say?' I said.

'She would say that there went a woman who was happy to give her lover everything.'

Fifty yards ahead, Poulton's coachman touched the horses with his whip and the coach wheels ground into motion, gradually picking up speed.

'I must go back to Mr Hakesby,' Cat said. 'You needn't trouble yourself to take me there. I'll manage perfectly well by myself.'

I laid my hand on Cat's arm. 'Wait.'

For a moment there had been a gap in the traffic passing to and fro. On the other side of the road were the sooty gables of the Half Moon, with the roofs of Clifford's Inn beyond. As Poulton's coach moved aside it revealed the entrance of the alley I had explored yesterday.

Standing on the edge of its shadows, by the corner of the inn, was a tall man in a dark cloak and a wide-brimmed hat. He was leaning on a staff. He was too far away for me to make out his face clearly, even under the hat, but I could see that he was looking into the ruins. I knew he was looking at me.

'What is it?' she said.

'That man over there.' Sourface. 'I think he knows me.'

'Which one?'

'On the far side of the road. Standing to the left of the tavern. The tall, thin man. Another man's just come up to him. A man with a cart.'

'Who is he?'

'It doesn't matter,' I said.

'Is that Clifford's Inn behind the tavern?' Her intelligence moved too quickly for comfort. 'Is this something to do with the Fire Court?'

I ignored the question. 'I don't want to meet him. We'd better go to Covent Garden another way. Back to Shoe Lane and down Harp Alley to the Fleet. We can cross the ditch and find a hackney on Ludgate Hill.'

'You won't meet him,' Cat said. 'He's gone now.'

I turned back to Fetter Lane. The carter was still there, but Sourface must have gone into the alley.

'Perhaps he didn't recognize you after all,' she said. 'Perhaps he was just looking past you at the place where the body is.'

I didn't reply. If Sourface had been watching me for any length of time, it was equally likely that he had no need to follow me. He would have seen me talking with the Coroner's men. He would just have to ask one of them who I was.

'Or,' Cat said, 'if I'm wrong and you're right, he can just ask the Coroner's men who you are.'

At Whitehall, I found Mr Williamson pacing arm-in-arm with Mr Chiffinch in Matted Gallery. That was both surprising and disturbing.

Neither man cared for the fact that I served the other as well as himself. It was an open secret that the two of them were not close friends. One served Lord Arlington and the other the King. They had few tastes in common.

Williamson caught sight of me first. 'Marwood,' he said, asserting a prior claim to me, 'are you come to tell me you've finished that copying at last? I hope you are, or by God, you shall pay for it.'

I bowed at the space between the two men, where their arms met. 'Yes, sir.'

I knew by this opening that the Shoe Lane murder was not something that Williamson wanted discussed in the hearing of Mr Chiffinch. For this I was grateful.

'I will look over the letters in a moment,' Williamson went on, 'and sign them. They must go down to the Post Office today.'

All the while, Chiffinch was looking at me, not directly but aslant, rubbing the great wart on his chin as if it were itching. His colour was always high, but his cheeks were more flushed than usual. I guessed that he had dined well. It was a curious fact that Chiffinch was capable of drinking steadily and in volume, yet he never seemed drunk.

Williamson flapped his hand at me. 'Go back to the office and wait for me.'

'To my lord's?' I asked, meaning Arlington's office overlooking the Privy Garden.

'No. Scotland Yard.'

I bowed to them and withdrew. Williamson did not keep me long. As he passed through the outer room where the clerks worked, he beckoned me to follow him into his closet.

'Is it the Widow Hampney?' he said.

I nodded. 'Her Uncle Poulton confirmed it. He came while I was there.'

Williamson sat down at his desk. 'And?'

I picked my words with care. 'It appears that Mistress Hampney had been lying in a cellar near Shoe Lane for some days. She had been covered in rubble.'

'Murder, then.'

'Yes. There was a stab wound below her left breast which

probably hit the heart. And an artery in her neck had been severed.'

'Was she killed where she was found?'

'Probably not. There wasn't much blood around the body.' I didn't want to bring my father into this, or Clifford's Inn. 'The body had been mutilated after death – by animals for sure, and probably by a thief as well. Someone had cut off a finger, perhaps to remove a ring.'

Williamson sat back in his chair. While I was speaking, he had taken up an ivory toothpick and was cleaning his teeth. He laid this aside and rubbed the bristles on his chin. 'And the rest of the report. Was that true as well?'

'Her gown, sir? Yes. And she was patched and painted as well.'

'And Poulton was quite sure of her?'

'Yes, sir. So was his housekeeper, who came with him. They were . . . distressed by the lady's clothing, as well as by her death. But they knew nothing of how she had come to be there, or of a lover, or any reason why anyone should wish her harm. She didn't live with them, but in lodgings in Lincoln's Inn Fields. They hadn't seen her since the Sunday before last.'

He grunted. 'So. Part of the matter is clear, at least. She was robbed, and that was probably why she was murdered, too. No doubt there were other things of value about her.'

He paused and stared at me. I had the sense he was testing me, though I did not know why or even how.

'Why,' he said, 'it's clear enough. A secret lover. And if we ever lay the man by the heels, we shall find that he killed her and robbed her corpse. Not a pretty tale.'

'Then my Lord Arlington believes that her murder was

merely a private crime? That it had nothing to do with affairs of state as he feared at first?'

'It's nothing to you what my lord believes, Marwood. As far as it touches you, you will bear in mind that this poor woman's death will bring much shame on her family and friends. No doubt the Coroner will deal with it as he thinks fit. As for us, we must do our best to ensure that there are no unseemly broadsheets and ballads on the subject. You must report any that you come across. I shall tell my lord that we will come down on the culprits very sharply.'

Everything printed in the country was subject to censorship. Both of us knew that tracing culprits and enforcing the law was often impossible, particularly for such things as ballads and broadsheets, which were here today and gone tomorrow. Still, his order was significant.

'Of course if you find any further intelligence about the murder,' he went on, 'make sure you bring it to me first. Don't spread it abroad.'

I bowed.

'Enough of that. Bring me the letters to sign.'

Williamson waved me from the room. Two things were now clear to me: he wanted to have sole control of any further information about the murder I might gather; and he was more concerned to quash publicity about it than to see the murderer on the gallows.

Which suggested that someone of considerable influence had put pressure on Williamson in the few hours since I had walked with him in St James's Park. And I could not help wondering whether that person had been William Chiffinch, the Keeper of the King's Private Closet.

CHAPTER EIGHTEEN

'YOU LOOK VERY fine tonight, my love. I could drown in your eyes.'

'You are pleased to make fun of me.' Jemima smiled across the table, wanting to believe in his love though she could not be sure of it. 'You're a wicked man, sir, indeed you are.'

'True, I'm a sinner,' Philip said. 'But only you can forgive me.'

He raised his glass to her and drank a silent toast. The Limburys were having supper in the parlour. They were sitting at a table pulled up to the fire. Jemima's body glowed – Mary had washed her this afternoon, and then rubbed her down with perfumed oils and dressed her hair with especial care.

Philip enquired about this with delightful solicitude, and then made her cheeks glow too by suggesting that one day they should wash each other in all their private places.

'Or, even better,' he said, leaning towards her, 'we shall have a bath built for us – a stone trough, big enough for us to lie side by side and pleasure each other as fishes do.'

'But the cost, sir . . . ' she protested, blushing all the more.

'What is money compared to love? Besides . . . '

She knew what his silence said. Besides, one day your father will be dead, his estate will come to us, and we may have a bath the size of a millpond if we should wish it, and fill it with milk and honey.

'Which reminds me,' he went on. 'You remember those earrings we talked of last night?'

Her happiness fell away, as she had feared it would. 'The ones from my father?'

'Yes. You offered to let me sell them or pawn them to assist me in our Dragon Yard venture.'

'You suggested I should, sir,' she said sharply. 'I did not offer.'

His smile did not falter. 'And you kindly agreed, from the sweetness of your heart. I know, my love. It must seem . . . What? Greedy of me? Unkind?' Philip's face was now so open, so frank, one could not imagine a devious thought could exist in his mind. 'But, as I explained, this is for us. And I have a particularly pressing need – an expense concerned with this business that I simply could not have foreseen.'

She delayed, for form's sake. But she knew from the start that she would give in, as in the end she generally did. When Philip had set his mind on something, who could resist his sugared words, his smiles and his caresses? In her limited experience, only her father: but her father was so obstinate he would argue with God Almighty at His judgement seat if he disagreed with God's verdict.

When at last she said yes, Philip rose from his seat, knelt beside her chair, took her hand and kissed it. She stroked his cheek.

'Tonight,' he whispered. 'May I come to you?'

'Yes,' she said. 'Oh yes.'

Then he leapt to his feet and, saying there was no time like the present, rang the bell. A few minutes later, Mary brought down the jewel box and set it on the table. Jemima unlocked it with her key and took out the earrings. She placed them on the table between them.

'I know you never cared for them, my love,' Philip said. 'They never pleased you. But what I do with them will please you. That I promise.' His hand closed over the earrings, drew them towards him and tucked them away. 'I told you of my new street, did I not? It will cut through Dragon Yard into Cheapside, with my fine new houses on either side. I shall call it Jemima Street, in your eternal honour.' He paused, his eyebrows rising in comical consternation. 'Unless you would prefer Syre Street, in honour of your father and your family as well? It is too momentous a decision for me to make. It must be yours alone.'

So, by degrees, he expunged the sour taste the transaction had left behind. He made her laugh with a long, involved tale involving a squabble between pages in the Bedchamber. Philip could make a nun laugh on Good Friday if he set his mind to it. She was still laughing when there was a hammering on the hall door.

Her mood shattered. 'Who's that? And so late?'

'Only old Gromwell,' Philip said.

'What in God's name is he doing here?'

'I told him to call. Didn't I say?'

'No, sir, you did not.'

They heard the front door slam and the rattle of the bolts and bars. She frowned at her husband across the table. 'Twice in one week? You do him too much kindness.'

'Friendship is like a vine, my love. A man must cultivate it to increase the harvest and improve the grape.'

'Some old vines are not worth the trouble. They are better grubbed up to make way for new ones.'

He wagged his finger at her as if indulging a child. 'You turn a pretty phrase.'

'I shall withdraw.'

'No,' he said, smiling, as if this was a conversation about something frivolous. 'You shall stay.'

Footsteps crossed the hall. The servant announced Mr Gromwell, who bowed so low to her that for a moment she thought he might topple over.

'I am rejoiced to see you looking so well, madam. I hope you will forgive me for disturbing you at supper.'

'Not at all, sir,' she was obliged to say, though her voice was chilly and she did not look at him.

He had already supped, he said when Philip pressed him to eat something, but he joined them at the table and took a glass or two of wine with them.

'You are quite recovered from your indisposition, I understand?' he said, peering at her across the flame of a candle. 'There is no sign of it at all – indeed, if I may say so, madam, I believe I have never seen you look so radiant. Philip, will you allow an old friend to toast your wife, to worship with profound respect at your hymenal altar? And join me in raising a glass to her beauty?'

Afterwards, Philip pushed back his chair and glanced at his guest. 'Well, we must not linger in my wife's company, much as we would wish to.'

'Where are you going?' She noticed Gromwell look sharply at her; he had never heard that tone in her voice.

'Whitehall, my love. Didn't I tell you? Gromwell and I will stroll across the park and watch them at cards.'

'And will you play yourself, sir?' she asked, her voice cold.

'No – I've long since put away such childish things. I shall be as sober as a Puritan at prayer.'

Gromwell had risen too. 'I wish we could remain, my dear lady, but I confess I have work to do there.'

'Work? Is that what you call it?' Philip laughed as if he had not a care in the world. 'He hopes to find more subscribers for his great book. You remember, madam? His *Natural Curiosities of Gloucestershire*. Those who win at cards are easy game. Their generosity knows no limits.'

A moment later the men were gone, leaving her to stare at the fire while the servants cleared away the remains of their supper. What did Philip expect her to do with herself now? He would pay for his discourtesy, she told herself. Preferring Gromwell to her, and at such a time, and with so little regard for her feelings – it beggared belief! She would not be trifled with. Did she love Philip any more? Did she hate him? She hardly knew. Her feelings swung erratically from one side to the other, like a drunk man staggering home in the dark.

After a while, Mary came into the room. She made her curtsy and waited in silence.

'Well,' Jemima said at last. 'Why are you here? I didn't call you.'

Mary bowed her head on its long white neck. 'Forgive me, my lady. It was something I heard in the kitchen. I thought you would wish to know.'

'Why would I wish to hear servants' prattle?' Jemima hesitated. 'What was it?'

'A boy called before supper with a letter. Hester took it

into the study and gave it to master. She said there were two letters, one sealed within the other. And he tore them open and swore as he read them. He kicked over a chair, he was so angry.'

'Who was it from?'

'She didn't know. He locked the letters away. Then he gave her sixpence and told her to pick up the chair and not to speak of what she'd seen.'

Coal shifted in the grate, and a flame spurted high, casting a flickering light into the room.

'There's something else, mistress. Hal heard it at the stables when he took the coach back. They've found a woman's body between Shoe Lane and Fetter Lane, somewhere in the ruins. She'd been stabbed . . . '

'Who was she?'

'I don't know. Perhaps a whore? But she was wearing a silk gown, they say, and so perhaps she was a lady.'

Celia, Jemima thought, could it be Celia?

The two women stared in silence at each other. By some trick of the light, Mary's green eyes reflected the glow and turned red.

CHAPTER NINETEEN

O N FRIDAY MORNING, Hakesby arrived late from his lodgings in Three Cocks Yard. He had hardly sat down before there was a knock on the door of the Drawing Office.

Mr Poulton was waiting outside, the crown of his hat brushing the low ceiling of the landing. His deep-sunk eyes were red-rimmed. He was already dressed in mourning, though his suit showed signs of wear. At his age, which Cat thought to be at least fifty-five if not sixty, she supposed that you must be hardly ever out of mourning.

'Mr Hakesby within?' Poulton demanded.

Cat curtsied and held the door wide. She began to murmur her condolences on the death of his niece, but he brushed past her. Hakesby rose to his feet, and bowed low. Brennan rose to his feet as well.

'I'm determined to build on Dragon Yard,' Poulton said loudly, ignoring Hakesby's attempt to speak. 'All the more so now. It will be a fitting memorial to my poor niece.' He shot a glance at Cat. 'We – that is, I – have decided to employ you about the business. If you are willing, and if you will press it forward as urgently and as swiftly as if it were your own.' He drew out a purse. 'You won't find me ungenerous.'

'I shall be honoured to give the matter my best attention,' Hakesby said.

'One question first. Forgive me, but I think you are not in the best of health.'

'It is but an ague, sir. It comes upon me sometimes, and then it goes away. It doesn't affect my ability to work, not where it matters.' Hakesby tapped his forehead. 'As for the rest, I employ a draughtsman to draw up my designs, and I hire others if I need them, while I remain, as it were, the presiding genius. But may I ask a question in my turn? What will happen to your niece's leasehold interest in Dragon Yard? The Fire Court petition may rise or fall because of that.'

'The leasehold comes to me. On my advice she made a will before her marriage. Had he lived, of course, her husband Hampney would have had everything. But he's dead, and there were no children. So, by the terms of her will, her estate falls to me.' He hesitated. 'Assuming that she did not make a later will.'

'You will need to make sure of that, sir.'

'Of course. But her lawyer is also mine – I saw him yesterday, and she hadn't asked him to draw up another will. But we must search her papers.' He paused, moistening his lips. 'I'm sending my housekeeper to my niece's lodgings after dinner, to pack up her things. If there's a later will, we shall find it there. Which reminds me, sir, I have a favour to ask.'

'Anything.' Hakesby spread out his trembling fingers. 'Anything within reason.'

'Reason? There's nothing reasonable about this business with my niece.' Poulton shifted his weight from one foot to the other. 'My favour is this: Mistress Lee is not as strong as she was, and she asks if you will allow your cousin to accompany her to my niece's lodgings this afternoon.' He glanced at Cat, who was pretending to busy herself with her work. 'She's taken a fancy to the girl, and it is good that she should have company at such a time.' His face looked gaunter than ever. 'I do not wish to go myself.'

Mistress Lee said barely a word in the coach that carried them to Lincoln's Inn Fields. They drew up outside the house where Celia Hampney had taken lodgings. The coachman jumped down to talk to the porter, a heavy fellow shaped like an egg and dressed in faded brown and silver livery.

'I didn't want our friends to see this place,' Mistress Lee said, turning to Cat. 'Or our servants. It would lower Celia even further in their estimation, and give them more to prattle about.'

'Why, mistress?'

'Mr Poulton does not care for Mistress Grove – the woman who lets out the apartments. He does not think she is quite . . . He and poor Celia had words about it, but he had no control over what she did. No one had, once she was a widow, with her own property. That's why I thought it better that he did not come with us. It would only distress him needlessly.' Mistress Lee looked older than she had the previous day, and more frail. 'I would manage everything myself, but these days I lack the strength. So I asked for you. I hope you're not shocked.'

'No,' Cat said. I am a nobody, she thought, but a nobody

she thinks she can rely on because of Mr Hakesby and the commission. On the whole, Cat liked being nobody. It was safer than being someone.

'Celia has a maid. Had, that is. Tabitha. A sly creature. I shall pay her what's due to her and send her away.'

The coachman let down the steps. The house was newly built and well-proportioned, with a façade of brick. The porter showed Cat and Mistress Lee into the hall. He summoned a servant and sent word of their arrival upstairs. While they waited, he watched the two women as if he suspected they might pilfer something.

When the servant eventually returned, he led them to a lofty parlour overlooking the Fields themselves. They waited in silence, examining their surroundings. The curtains and the furniture were new but there was dust on the floorboards and cobwebs on the cornice.

The door opened, and a stout, middle-aged woman entered the room. She greeted the visitors with a stately lack of enthusiasm.

'Mistress Hampney murdered,' she said, rising from a token curtsy. She patted her formidable bosom somewhere in the region of her heart. 'I was never so shocked in my life. *Effroyable!*'

Her voice was modelled on the leisurely tones of the court, but her vowels belonged further east.

'I could hardly close my eyes last night for fear of being attacked in my own house,' Mistress Grove went on, with all the excitement of a person describing the location of the necessary house. 'If I'd known this was going to happen, I'd never have let the apartments to her.'

Mistress Lee, formidable in black despite her short plump

figure, drew herself up to her full height. 'And if Mistress Hampney herself had known what would become of her, no doubt she would have made other plans as well.'

Mistress Grove's pink features were too large for her face. Her eyes and lips had a sheen to them, as if varnished. 'I'm told that when she was found, she was dressed like a whore. She was gone for nearly a week . . . where was she? Her maid says she knows nothing, but you can't believe a word Tabitha says . . . Was there a lover? Was it he who—'

'Have you had Mr Poulton's letter?' Mistress Lee interrupted.

'Ah, poor Mr Poulton.' The bulging eyes stared into Mistress Lee's face. 'The shame of it. He must be so distressed.'

'You need not trouble yourself about Mr Poulton.'

'If only she had taken another husband, this would never have happened. Do you know what she said to me?' Mistress Grove arched her eyebrows in a parody of surprise. 'She said she wouldn't marry again for all the money in the world. She would rather live and die a merry widow than be at the beck and call of a man. Her very words!' Her lips pouted in horror. 'I fancy she would change her mind now.'

'We have come to make arrangements about Mistress Hampney's possessions,' Mistress Lee said in a voice as thin as a knife blade. 'If it would be convenient, we shall pack up what we can now and take it away. Mr Poulton will send a cart for the rest in the morning.'

'A cart? You'll need a wagon.'

'By the way, Mr Poulton has an inventory of his niece's possessions. It was made after the death of her husband.'

There was a momentary silence. Cat found that she was

175

holding her breath. In her quiet way, Mistress Lee had told their hostess that she doubted her honesty.

'Mr Poulton must understand that I cannot repay the balance of the lease,' Mistress Grove said, returning to the offensive. 'It's true that our arrangement runs until Michaelmas, but I shall find it very hard to let the apartments after what has happened. Every kitchen maid in town is gossiping about this dreadful business.'

She conducted them upstairs to the apartments on the second floor where Celia Hampney had lodged.

'The whole house is newly furnished,' she told them on the stairs. 'Why, Sir Charles said to me only the other day, that he wished he had such things in his own house. Sir Charles Sedley? You know him? A great friend. He dined here only last month.'

Mistress Lee screwed up her lips as if to keep words from bursting out of her. She was climbing the stairs slowly, clinging to the rail and refusing to take Cat's arm. The whole world knew that Sir Charles Sedley was one of the most dissolute men at Court. He was not a man that a respectable woman would wish to see at her table, or indeed to have anything to do with.

'I suggested he bring his friend my Lord Rochester,' Mistress Grove was saying, 'but alas he was engaged. A most ingenious young man, don't you think? With quite a French twist to his wit as well. It's something I appreciate well – I lived in Paris for several years.'

Mistress Lee said she was not acquainted with his lordship, nor was she likely to be, so she was not in a position to judge his wit or its nationality.

Mistress Grove opened a door and led the way into an

apartment at the front of the house. Cat's first impression was of colour – too much of it; a deluge that drenched her eyes. She and Mistress Lee took a step into the room and stopped.

There were carpets, cushions, curtains and paintings, as well as a profusion of gilding on every surface that would take it. There was an empty wine glass on the table. There was also a smell in the air, a sour blend of perfume and spoiled food.

'Why hasn't Tabitha aired the room?' Mistress Lee said.

Mistress Grove shrugged her ample shoulders. 'I'm sure I can't tell, madam. I was in the country last week. My servants tell me that Mistress Hampney had an entertainment on Wednesday evening. Gentlemen were present, and there was a fiddler and dancing. They were at it until two or three of the morning.'

'Pray let us have some air in here.'

Mistress Grove did not move. Cat crossed the room and flung open the window.

'I do not like to speak ill of the dead,' Mistress Grove said, turning like a man of war to bring her majestic bosom broadside on to Mistress Lee, 'but she had proved a sad disappointment to me. There was a wildness about her that I could not approve. I had already made up my mind not to renew my arrangement with her.'

'Would you send her maid to me?'

'Willingly, madam. Pray remove Mistress Hampney's possessions as soon as possible. And then I must insist that the apartments are returned to the state in which they were when she took possession. I shall send my account for sundries to her uncle.'

Mistress Lee made no answer. She turned away as if struck by the prospect from the window. Mistress Grove sniffed audibly and left the room. Cat closed the door behind her.

Mistress Lee turned to face Cat. 'That dreadful woman.' She paused. 'I hardly know you. But may I trust you not to speak of this? It would wound Mr Poulton so deeply if he knew how his niece lived in this house.' She made as if to take out her purse but, seeing Cat's face, stopped. 'You are a good girl.'

She ran her finger over the table and frowned at the thin layer of dust on it. They set to work. The bedchamber was in a worse state than the sitting room. The dressing table was strewn with cosmetics. Mistress Lee put aside the jewel box to take away with her. She told Cat to bring her any papers that she found.

'Pray God we do not find a later will,' she said. 'But if there is, we must obey its provisions. Mr Poulton will insist on that.'

There was a tap on the door, and the maid entered. Tabitha was a slender young woman with bony shoulders. She wore a dress that was too large for her. She curtsied to Mistress Lee and glanced at Cat.

'The floorboards are sticky,' said Mistress Lee in a querulous voice. 'What is it? Honey? Punch? What is the meaning of this?'

'Mistress had a party the night before she went. You should have seen it after that. I've done what I can.'

'Nonsense. When did you last see your mistress?'

Tabitha's eyes were small and narrow, and they grew smaller and narrower still. 'The day before she went away. At dinner.'

'Why not later?'

'She said I could go and see my mother, and stay the night there. And I needn't come back till evening the next day. And when I did she wasn't there.'

'But why did she send you away? Because of her party?'

The maid shrugged. 'I don't know.'

Mistress Lee's lips tightened. 'Did gentlemen call to see her?'

'Sometimes.'

'One in particular, perhaps?'

Tabitha's eyes opened wide. 'I'm sure I wouldn't know, mistress. Besides, she often went out without me.'

'You are concealing something,' Mistress Lee said. 'You will find it's in your interest to be frank with me.'

The maid stared at the old woman and said nothing.

'Your mistress is dead. You'll leave this house within the hour. Do you hear me?'

Tabitha curtsied, twisting her face into the mockery of a smile. She threw another glance at Cat, who was standing silently by the dressing table.

'Go and pack your box.' Mistress Lee was trembling. 'And I shall tell Mr Poulton how you have behaved.'

'It's already packed. And I don't care what you tell the old miser. That's what she used to call him, you know. The old miser.'

'You hussy. I shall have you whipped for your insolence.'

'You can't, and I'll rouse the house if you try. You're not my mistress.'

Without waiting to be dismissed, Tabitha flounced from the bedroom. They heard her slamming the sitting room door.

'Call the servants,' Mistress Lee said, white-faced. 'I shall have that girl taken before a justice, I shall——'

Cat said softly, 'Madam Grove's servants won't obey you. And if you have Tabitha taken up, who knows what she'll tell the justice.'

The old woman sat down on the edge of the bed. After a moment she said in a calmer voice, 'But her insolence . . . How dare she?'

Cat held her peace. She would have liked the answer to a different question. Tabitha hadn't demanded her wages. Something or someone had changed her, had emboldened the girl to discard not only the respect she should show to her betters but also a servant's common prudence.

What? Or who?

CHAPTER TWENTY

M Y OTHER MASTER sent for me on Friday evening: William Chiffinch, the Keeper of the King's Private Closet. There was something about him that made it difficult to be comfortable in his company: perhaps it was the cheerful air of good living that failed to correspond to the watery gaze of his cold eyes; or his reputation for infinite corruptibility; or perhaps merely the unsettling knowledge that this man had the ear of the King in his most private moments and could whisper whatever he wished to his master.

The servant brought me through a maze of apartments, passages and staircases to a small, dark chamber near the Privy Stairs. The room was empty, and he left me to wait.

The barred window looked out on the river. The tide was low, exposing the foreshore, an expanse of dank mud stained with the outflow from the palace privies and dotted with the sort of refuse that even the scavengers disdained. The slimy supports of the Privy Stairs marched down to the water's edge, where a four-oared skiff was pulling alongside the steps on the downstream side.

It was a dreary scene, and it matched my mood. My eyes were sore from copying, and my fingers ached from holding a pen for so long. The drudgery had filled the forefront of my mind all day. But now I wanted to be at my house, and at my ease. I needed time to mourn. To think.

The death of someone you love is bad enough. It creates an absence in your life, and your awareness of it rises and falls; its peaks and troughs are as unpredictable and as dangerous as the waves of the sea, whose rhythms work beneath the surface according to their own mysterious logic.

But my father's death came with a host of unanswered questions, and now with another body. Was his death somehow connected with the murdered woman half-buried in the rubble between Fetter Lane and Shoe Lane? Had he seen her lying dead in Clifford's Inn the day before he died? And what had all this to do with the Fire Court and Dragon Yard?

A movement caught my eye. Two men were descending the steps, deep in conversation. One of them, a tall, dark man I didn't recognize, scrambled nimbly into the skiff, where he sat in the stern, under the awning, and settled his black cloak around him. The other man raised a hand in farewell as the boat pulled away. He tilted his head up and I glimpsed the familiar profile beneath the hat. It was Chiffinch.

Ten minutes or so later, the door opened. My master entered.

'Marwood,' he said without any preamble. 'Your duties as Clerk to the Board of Red Cloth have not been onerous, have they?'

'No, sir.'

Chiffinch and I both knew that the Board of Red Cloth

had no duties worth speaking of. Perhaps there had been duties when it had been instituted in the reign of Henry VIII. But now, more than a century later, it existed mainly to provide its commissioners, including Chiffinch, with generous salaries and its clerk with a much smaller one. The clerkship paid me about fifty pounds a year, and brought useful perquisites at Whitehall as well. I didn't want to lose it.

'Sometimes the Board requires its clerk to undertake commissions over and above his usual duties. Which is the case now.' He ran his eyes over me, from my feet to my head; it was an oddly humiliating inspection that made me feel I was of no more significance to him than a hog or a pony. 'I see you're in mourning. Perhaps a change of scene will be a distraction from your grief.'

'What do you wish me to do, sir?'

'The King has commanded me to send a letter privately by a trusted bearer. You will carry it to the gentleman, and wait for his answer. Though there's no great hurry about it, discretion is essential. But that, of course, is always essential for those of us employed about the King's business. Wherever we are, whomsoever we consort with, we must never forget the need to be discreet.' He paused. 'Wouldn't you agree, Marwood?'

'Yes, sir. When should I go?'

'Tomorrow morning. Wait on me at nine o'clock, and I'll have the letter for you and a warrant for the necessary funds.'

'And where does the gentleman live?'

'About twelve miles east of Inverness. You should take the road to Nairn.'

For a moment I was too surprised to speak. Scotland? Everyone knew that Scotland was a land of mountains and barbarians, where the men did not wear breeches and acquired the rudiments of witchcraft with their mothers' milk. The further north one went, they said, the more savage the Scotch became.

'But, sir, Inverness must be nigh on six hundred miles.'

'At least that, I should think,' Chiffinch agreed. 'You will travel on public coaches, by the way. We must economize. Though that may not be easy once you reach the Highlands – I'm not sure there are public coaches up there. But there will be carriers' wagons, I'm sure, or ponies, or something of that nature.'

'It will take weeks. Wouldn't it be faster to go by sea?'

'Indeed. But, as I said, discretion is important in this matter, not speed. Besides, there will be letters for you to deliver on the way as well – did I mention that? – so going by sea would be impractical.'

'But Mr Williamson—'

Chiffinch dismissed Williamson with a wave of his hand. 'You needn't concern yourself with that. I will speak to him. Call at my lodgings in the morning, and my clerk will give you the letters and your warrant.'

He paused and looked at me, expecting me to acknowledge his instructions. I said nothing.

'I wish you a safe journey. I'll send someone to show you out.' He turned to go, but stopped with his hand on the door. 'Don't disappoint me in this, Marwood. Discretion, eh? Discretion and obedience. Those are the virtues you should cultivate.'

I was full of rage.

First Williamson, now Chiffinch.

Astrologers find significance in the conjunctions of the stars. Those of us who work at Whitehall discover meanings in the conjunctions of great men. (And sometimes, in these changed times since the King's Restoration, the conjunctions of great women.)

Yesterday, I had seen Williamson and Chiffinch walking arm in arm in the Matted Gallery. That was unusual in itself. Then Williamson had questioned me at length about the dead woman: his curiosity had been unusual too, and so had been his desire that the murder should be viewed merely as the accidental consequence of a robbery, and also his decision that the matter required no enquiry on the Government's behalf. Which made it all the stranger that he had been concerned to stamp out any undue publicity about the crime.

Now Chiffinch had sent me from London on what was clearly a trumped-up mission. It would probably take the better part of a month to complete and would bring me considerable discomfort into the bargain.

The conclusion was obvious. Someone had brought their influence to bear. If not influence, then money. It was said that Chiffinch would do anything if the price were right. As for Williamson, he wanted power: to be Secretary of State in Lord Arlington's place. To do that he needed allies in high places. Who better than Chiffinch, the man who had the King's private ear, who ministered to his pleasures and assisted his intrigues?

There are no friends at Whitehall. Only allies and enemies. Among the great, power ebbs and flows according to their conjunctions and oppositions. And the rest of us are tossed about in the current, helpless to direct our course, let alone navigate our way to safety.

I walked swiftly down to Charing Cross. In the Strand, however, rather than turning down to the Savoy, where Margaret and Sam were waiting in Infirmary Close, I veered away north towards the piazza of Covent Garden.

In Henrietta Street I knocked on Hakesby's door and sent a message up to him. A few moments later I heard several sets of footsteps on the stairs.

The first to appear was a plainly dressed young man of about my own age with a narrow, freckled face. He cast a curious glance at me.

'Master's on his way down, sir,' he said.

'Brennan?' Hakesby called. 'Come earlier tomorrow, will you? There is a great deal to do.'

'Yes, master. Good night.'

The young man disappeared into the gathering dusk. Hakesby reached the hall, his feet dragging as if he hardly had the strength to lift them. Catherine Lovett was by his side.

'I didn't expect to see you here, sir,' he said quietly. 'You're fortunate to find us — we were working later than usual.'

'I have to talk to you. Have you time?'

'Very well. Shall we go to the Lamb? What's it about?'

'I'll tell you there, sir,' I said. 'In private.'

Catherine Lovett said nothing. I was aware of her eyes on me, and I sensed her disapproval of my recklessness in coming here so openly, and thereby revealing our acquaintance unnecessarily to others.

My anger briefly spilled on to her. Be damned to her. What Mistress Lovett can't cure, I told myself, she must endure. Yesterday afternoon, when we had met over Celia Hampney's body, she had seemed almost friendly. She had instructed me in the language of the flies, the meaning of face patches, and she had teased me for my attachment to her aunt. All that was gone.

Hakesby walked between us, and we slowed our pace to his. My impatience was such that it spilled out into an absurd irritation with him and his halting gait. To make matters worse, he would not stop talking, rambling on, as old men do, as my father had once done, as if we had all the time in the world.

'We have such a quantity of business at present,' he was saying as we passed through the piazza. 'It is pleasing, of course, but I believe I may have to hire a second draughtsman to cope with it. Did you hear that Master Poulton has asked me to look at his Dragon Yard scheme? Interesting, especially if he can carry it through, but it's proving more complicated than I expected. Sir Philip Limbury's scheme is impressive, and he's in a position of strength as the freeholder, so we must study how best to counter the arguments his side will bring out at the Fire Court . . . '

'No, sir,' Cat said, gently tugging his arm. 'This way. And take care not to step into the gutter . . . '

'And Jane has been absent for most of the day,' he said, turning his head towards her as if he had only just remembered her presence. 'Most inconvenient. Mr Poulton asked for her this morning, as a particular favour, and I could hardly say no.'

I was so surprised I stopped at the corner of the arcade, causing a gentleman behind me to swerve and curse me loudly for a clumsy dog. 'Why? What did he want?'

'It wasn't Mr Poulton who wanted me,' Cat said. 'It was his housekeeper, Mistress Lee.'

'To help her at the lodgings of Poulton's niece,' Hakesby said. 'That poor lady.'

That was when I made up my mind to tell them the truth: partly because I wanted to know more about Celia Hampney and how she had lived, but more because I knew I would burst if I left my anger to fester inside me.

They gave us the same room at the Lamb, and I ordered wine to be brought.

'I have not been entirely open with you about this Fire Court business,' I said.

'What do you mean?' Hakesby demanded.

Cat just looked at me. She showed no surprise. Her face was grave.

So I told them everything, or almost everything, about my father's wanderings and what he had said to me about them; about his death and the bloodstains on his person; and about the scrap of paper with the judges' names and 'DY' written on it, which I had found in his pocket.

'So I think Mistress Hampney was killed at Clifford's Inn,' I said. 'And later they brought her body out and left it in the ruins. There's a private door from the fire-damaged building – it leads to an alley that goes to Fetter Lane. I went there with my servant on Wednesday evening.' I glanced at Cat. 'You remember that man who was watching us on Wednesday? The tall thin man by the Half Moon? He caught me in the alley. If Sam hadn't been there, God knows what would have happened.'

Hakesby waved his hand, brushing away my words. 'What is this business? I thought it concerned your father's death.'

'I don't know what it is,' I said. 'I've just come from

Whitehall. They are sending me to Scotland on a fool's errand. It's to get me out of the way. It's to stop me asking questions that they don't want answered. There can be no other reason.'

'The dead woman your father saw,' Cat said. 'Was it Celia Hampney?'

'I think it must have been. Though God knows how it was done.'

Hakesby considered this. Then: 'So it's all connected. Does Mr Poulton know?'

'No. And he mustn't.'

'I tell you plainly, sir, I shall have nothing further to do with the intrigue. It's the sort of affair that leads to the gallows.' He began the slow process of standing up. 'Come,' Hakesby said to Cat. 'We're leaving.'

'Wait,' I said. 'I beg you. I understand – but, before you go, would you allow me to hear what Mistress Hakesby found in Lincoln's Inn Fields?'

'No.' He was on his feet now, wavering slightly like a tree in a still breeze. 'I'm sorry to hear about your father, of course, but there's an end to everything else. Come along, Jane.'

But Cat remained sitting on the bench. 'There's no harm in my telling Mr Marwood, sir.'

'No. We are going.'

'He helped me in the past,' she said. 'I should help him now. If only in this.'

'You must be quick,' Hakesby said harshly. 'I shall allow you a minute or two. No more.'

It was a surrender, but she was wise enough to allow him to cling to the appearance of victory.

'Yes, master,' she said, eyes cast down. 'Thank you.'

Hakesby sat down again. She turned to me and explained in a brisk voice that Mistress Lee had required a younger person to help her when she went to Celia Hampney's lodgings in Lincoln's Inn Fields. I heard traces of the old Catherine Lovett, secure in the arrogance that money and position bring:

'There was a most vulgar, greedy woman who called herself Madam Grove and gave herself the airs of a duchess. I wouldn't have her as my washerwoman.'

'Hush,' murmured Hakesby. 'You're too forward. And be quick about this.'

'The apartments were luxurious but disordered,' she said. 'And Mistress Hampney's maid was worse than insolent. Her name's Tabitha. She claimed to know nothing about her mistress's affairs or of any friendships with particular gentlemen. She also said that she'd been sent away on the day before her mistress disappeared, and told to come back the following evening.'

'By that time her mistress was dead,' I said.

Cat nodded. 'Celia Hampney held a party in her lodgings on the last evening of her life. For gentlemen. I suppose that's why she sent her maid away, to prevent her gossiping about what she saw. The Grove woman says she knows nothing, and in any case she was in the country all that week. She also said that Mistress Hampney desired to remain a widow, that she did not wish to lose her independence.'

I was watching Hakesby lifting his glass: it was cupped in his trembling hands and he guided it slowly towards his lips with a palpable effort of will. I said, 'So nobody knows anything?'

'Or if they do, they're not saying. Mistress Lee discharged Tabitha on the spot – the girl was asking for it, the way she behaved.' She moistened her lips. 'Tabitha didn't care.'

'Where did she go?' I asked.

'To her mother's. That's what she said. But I don't know where the mother lives.'

'Very well,' Hakesby said, setting down the glass and once more trying to rise. 'Let us leave, Jane. Now.'

Cat ignored him. 'Her impudence was strange . . . It was almost as if she had a protector, someone who made her invulnerable.'

'The Grove woman?'

She shook her head. 'There was no love lost there.'

'Do you think Tabitha knew about a lover? Do you think he bribed her?'

'As plain as day,' Hakesby said impatiently. 'Of course there was a lover. Jane – come with me. This instant.'

I had to admit that he was probably right – and indeed everything I had learned this evening supported Williamson's view of the murder: a lovers' tryst and a robbery that had gone wrong and led to murder.

But there had to be more than that. There must be. My father had seen the woman lying dead in Clifford's Inn, not in the ruins east of Fetter Lane. Gromwell and Chelling had some knowledge that touched on the murder. It was even possible that one or both had been accessories before or after the fact of it. What of Dragon Yard, which linked Celia Hampney and Poulton to the Fire Court?

And what of my father? My poor dead father.

Something snapped in my mind.

I stood up, pushing back my bench so violently that it fell

191

over. 'Stay here for a moment,' I said to Hakesby. 'Finish the bottle. I'm going.'

Hakesby sank into his chair. 'Have you considered, sir,' he said slowly, 'that sending you away might be a blessing in disguise?'

The wine I had taken on an empty stomach was loosening my tongue. 'Why in God's name?'

'Because sometimes it's better to let sleeping dogs lie.'

'Sleeping dogs be damned.'

'By sending you away, they have left you with no choice in the matter.' His voice was firmer now. 'Perhaps they have your best interests at heart.'

'They have no one's interests at heart but their own.' I had my hand on the latch. I looked back at them. 'I will not let this go.'

Hakesby said, 'Then it must be a matter for you alone. It is not my business.' He glanced at Cat. 'Nor hers. It is too dangerous. Remember, it doesn't concern you, and it concerns us even less.'

'That's plain-speaking,' I said, with an edge of anger in my voice, though I knew in my heart that Hakesby was right. 'I shall pursue this wherever it leads. And be damned to your cowardice.'

I flung out of the room. Even at the time, I knew I was being unreasonable, but I was so angry with the world I did not care.

I found the landlord and, with a lordliness I could ill afford, bought a bottle of Malmsey to take away with me and paid the score for what I had ordered already. I stormed down the stairs, half hoping that Hakesby would send Cat to call me back. But he didn't.

I emerged into the street. Night had fallen, and Wych Street was only dimly lit. There was a man on the other side of the road. As I appeared, he turned away and began to walk briskly westwards. By chance, he passed a lantern hanging over the doorway to a shop. For a second or two, I glimpsed the lower part of his face. He looked teasingly familiar.

Cradling the bottle under my cloak, I walked off in the opposite direction. It was only as I was turning up to the Fleet Street gate of Clifford's Inn that I realized why the face was familiar. For a moment, it had looked a little like the man I had passed in the hall at Henrietta Street: Brennan, Hakesby's draughtsman.

CHAPTER TWENTY-ONE

THE FLEET STREET gate was barred. A lantern swung above it, shedding a dim light on the path beneath. My anger vanished. I watched a tall gentleman approach the gate. The porter came out to let him in, and they exchanged a few words. Afterwards the porter barred the gate again. At this hour of the evening, I realized, it might not be easy for me to enter Clifford's Inn.

Then a party of revellers blundered by me as I stood in the shadows by St Dunstan-in-the-West. They were half a dozen young lawyers, drunk as lords, innocent as children: they staggered up the path by the church, swearing affectionately at each other and laughing loudly for no reason.

The last of the party stumbled as he passed me. Suddenly I saw my opportunity. I stepped forward, took his arm and steadied him. He turned his head away from me and vomited politely in the gutter.

'Your servant, sir,' he said. 'Truly you are a good – a Good Samaritan.'

'Careful, sir,' I said. 'The path is treacherous in this light. Pray lean on me.'

'God bless you. We shall sink a bottle between us, damned if we don't. We must toast our everlasting friendship.'

'We shall!' I cried.

'We shall be the Damon and Pythias of Clifford's Inn. I'll be Pythias, shall I, because I must pith soon or I shall burst.'

The joke caught me unawares, and I burst out laughing. So did he. Side by side, the two of us staggered after the rest of the party, roaring with laughter.

Pythias patted the bottle in my hand. 'Ah! A man with forethought as well as wit. That is a friend indeed.' His fingers tightened on my arm. 'But it is wine, I hope? It is not a chimera? I am not dreaming this?'

'No, sir – it's Malmsey, as God's my witness. You need not fear.'

Our leaders started singing, if that is the word. After a moment, I guessed that the song was probably 'Come, Come Pretty Wenches, More Nimbler Than Eels'. On this assumption, I joined in. There was some confusion about the different parts and their harmonies, as well as about the precise wording, but what we lacked in musicality we more than compensated for in enthusiasm and volume.

Our party bunched together as it passed under the archway and into the cramped court between the Fleet Street gate and the hall of Clifford's Inn. The porter on duty held up his lantern as we went through, but we must have seemed indistinguishable from one another in its feeble light – a wobbling, noisy cluster of dark hats and dark cloaks. Someone tossed him a few coins which sent him scrabbling to retrieve them on his hands and knees. He did not question my presence.

I disentangled myself from my new best friend and attached him to someone else. This was a success until they reached the hall doorway, where Pythias collided with one of the jambs and slithered to the ground. Two of his other friends tried to help him up.

Under cover of the excitement, I slipped away to the bottom of the staircase where Chelling lived. A faint light burned over the door, but otherwise the building on this side of the court was entirely in darkness.

If I didn't talk to Chelling now, it would be weeks before my next chance, and it might be too late. He knew something. I was sure of it. Perhaps something to do with Gromwell.

In Fetter Lane, by the Hal—

The scrap of a letter I had found in his cupboard must surely refer to the Half Moon tavern, with the alley up to the locked door into the ruins. For all its fine words, it could be interpreted as the beginning of an attempt at blackmail.

The door swung open at my touch. Air swirled around me, cooler than the air outside. Drawing my cloak around me, I stood at the foot of the stairs and peered into the darkness above.

The voices in the court outside and the distant clatter of the traffic in Fleet Street ebbed away. Old stone buildings have a special form of silence, cold and dense. Gradually the darkness became less absolute, resolving itself into delicately graduated shades of black. Then the faintest of outlines appeared – the merest suggestion of the archway that led to the landing above.

As far as I was concerned, my surroundings were largely hypothetical. Faced with a hypothesis, the gentlemen of the Royal Society put it to the test. I could do no better than follow their example. I inched forward until the toe of my right shoe touched the riser of the bottom stair. I climbed the worn stone steps one by one, running the fingertips of my left hand along the cold, damp wall to keep me on course.

In this way, slowly, by trial and error, I climbed from floor to floor. On the second landing there was an uncurtained window which made my task easier. Some of the shades of black became shades of grey. There was an odd smell in the air, a blend of unexpected ingredients – linseed oil? Sulphur?

Up and up I went. None of the doors I passed showed a line of light beneath. Chelling, I remembered, had told me that the Inn had found it hard to attract students since the Civil War. And no one would wish to live in this decaying building except from necessity.

The steps were of stone until the attic storey where Chelling lived. This was a later addition of timber and wattle, reached by a narrow wooden staircase. Up to now my slow footsteps had made little sound, apart from the occasional scrape of leather on stone and the patter of dislodged dust. But now the wood creaked under my weight.

A current of air brushed my cheeks. The stairs rounded a corner. A few steps more and I was on the landing.

Chelling occupied the set of chambers at the back of the building. The other set was empty. I inched my way towards his door. The draught increased in force.

The door was ajar. The hinges groaned as I pushed it open. The study beyond was in darkness but there was a line of light under the inner door to the bedchamber.

'Mr Chelling?' I called. 'Are you there, sir? It's Marwood.'

There was no answer. At the same time a new smell reached

my nostrils. Something was burning. The smell of sulphur was stronger.

'Chelling!' I cried.

In the near darkness I blundered across the outer room, jarring my thigh against the table. I threw open the door. A flickering orange light almost blinded me. For an instant I stopped. Fully clothed, Chelling was lying face down on the bed. On the floor lay a pewter candlestick. Beside it was a ball of fire, little larger than a tennis ball. The window was wide open. As I stood in the doorway, cradling the bottle, flames began to lick up the bed curtain.

I dropped the wine and lunged towards Chelling. I felt a tremendous blow on my skull. There was an explosion of blinding light. Somehow it managed to be both inside and outside my head.

The world fragmented. I was on my hands and knees. An acute pain stabbed my side. Another savaged the back of my head.

The air stank of burning and Malmsey. The ball of fire was much nearer now, its flames licking my face. Consciousness was sliding away from me. I curled up, as a babe in the womb.

The bang of a door. Heat, growing hotter and hotter. Footsteps thundering down the stairs. Rough wood grazing my cheek.

Hotter. Hotter.

An instinct for preservation cut in. I seized the nearest bedpost and hauled myself up. Coughing, I kicked the fireball aside. The room was thick with smoke. I stumbled through the fog towards Chelling. The flames were growing higher and higher, running up the bed hangings and along the sleeve of his coat.

I grabbed his ankle and tried to pull him on to the floor and through the doorway. He was a dead weight, and I couldn't shift him. I dived into the flames and pushed my hands under his armpits. I dragged him from the mattress and through the door.

The fire came with him.

Someone was screaming. Oh Christ.

The flames were dancing over me. I had long since lost my hat, the black silk streamers dissolving into fire. Chelling's hair had caught and so had mine. Our hair sparkled and shrivelled and blackened like a firework display. The stench made me cough even more. I noticed that my hands were dripping with blood.

Pulling my burden with a series of tugs, I staggered backwards across the study to the outer door. The flames followed us, filling the chamber with their gaudy, murderous light.

The outer door was closed, though I had left it open. I let Chelling fall to the floor and lifted the latch.

The door would not move, however hard I tugged. By now I was so desperate that I had almost forgotten poor Chelling. The air was now so hot it seared my lungs.

The door was a flimsy thing, a ledge-and-brace affair more suited to an outbuilding than a lawyer's chambers. I snatched up the elbow chair and swung it against the door with all my might. On the second blow, wood splintered and a gust of fresh air poured into the room, whipping up the flames like the blast from a pair of bellows.

After two more blows I charged at it with my shoulder. The first time I bounced back and tripped over Chelling's body, which reminded me that he was there. The second time, I plunged through splintering wood and sprawled on the floor, half inside and half outside the room. I tried to wriggle free, back to Chelling. I couldn't. I was trapped by the wreckage of the door, unable to go forward or backward. I couldn't even save my own skin.

So this, I thought, in a moment of clarity, is where it ends.

The last thing I remember was a flame that sent glowing tendrils dancing up to the landing. That and the screams. My screams.

CHAPTER TWENTY-TWO

WITH THE FIELDS on one side and the park on the other, Pall Mall by night was almost as quiet as the country.

Jemima turned over in the bed. After a while, Mary began to snore. The maid was lying on a mattress beside the bed. Jemima told her to be quiet, but the snoring continued. She parted the curtains, fumbled on the night table for her book, picked it up, and tossed it in the general direction of Mary's face. The snoring stopped.

Beyond the bed curtains, the room was in complete darkness. Philip was still not back. He had gone out after supper, just as he had the previous evening, saying he would not be late. She suspected that he was seeing Gromwell.

The snoring began again, building gradually in volume.

Jemima nursed her anger like a flame until it blazed up and made her swear aloud into the darkness. But then the fire died, leaving her cold and miserable. She wanted Philip back. She wanted Gromwell to go to the devil, along with his ill-omened name and his shabby finery.

Then it was three o'clock, announced by the watchman's hoarse voice in the street below and the sounds of distant church clocks. Dawn could not be far away.

Later, she heard footsteps in the street, which paused outside the house. Two people, she thought, Philip and a link boy to light his way. There was a knock at the street door, and soon another, louder one when the porter failed to stir.

Then came the rattle of bars and chains, and Philip's slow footsteps crossing the hall and climbing the stairs. He walked down the landing, passing her door without stopping, and went into his own room. He closed the door softly.

Time passed. The snoring stopped. Jemima tossed and turned. More time trickled painfully towards eternity, and suddenly she was seized by panic: soon she would be dead, and so would Philip; soon it would be too late for them all.

Jemima sat up abruptly. She dangled her legs over the side of the bed. She trod on Mary; the maid stirred in her sleep, whimpered softly and slept on.

The lantern that burned all night in the hall cast a faint outline around the doorframe. Jemima felt for her gown and wrapped it around her, drawing it tight against the chill of the night air. She pushed her feet into her slippers.

Jemima did not bother to light her candle. She made her way to the door, unlatched it and stood for a moment listening, while the draughts of the house swirled around her ankles.

She stepped on to the landing and closed the door. The house by night was dingy and unfamiliar. She padded along the passage to her husband's door. She did not knock. She raised the latch and went in.

Two candles burned on the mantle. Philip was sitting on the side of the bed. His wig lay like an untidy black spaniel beside him. He had thrown off his coat and waistcoat. A cap of short, black hair shadowed his scalp. He looked like a boy.

Something moved inside her, as if her heart twitched and twisted of its own volition. She closed the door and crossed the room towards her husband. She perched on the bed, sitting to his right, leaving a few inches between them. He did not stir.

'Philip,' she said. 'What ails you?'

He raised his head and looked at her. His eyes were black pools. The heavy lids drooped over them. Why was he so troubled? She had never seen him like this. It must be something to do with the letter that had come this afternoon, the letter that had sent him into a rage, and with the woman whose body had been found in the ruins, the woman in the yellow silk gown. Had it been Celia? And did his sorrow mean that he had loved her?

Neither spoke. He was breathing very slowly. Gradually her own breathing slowed until it matched his, breath for breath.

After a while, Jemima put her arms around him. He didn't pull away from her. Holding her breath, she drew him down on her breast. When all was said and done, he was her husband.

She stroked his head as if it were a small, hard animal in need of comfort. Philip's natural hair was surprisingly fine and soft. Like a little boy's.

CHAPTER TWENTY-THREE

B RENNAN WAS AS impossible to ignore as a bad smell. Cat couldn't see him but she heard his breathing. The hairs lifted on the back of her neck.

'Sunday tomorrow, isn't it?' he said.

'Yes.' Cat bent closer to her drawing board and hoped that he would take the hint.

'Thought I might take a boat on the river.'

She said nothing. With luck, Brennan would drown himself in the Thames. His footsteps drew nearer. She caught sight of him to the right, at the edge of her range of vision. He was closer than she liked.

'Old skin-and-bones gives you Sunday afternoon as a holiday, doesn't he?'

She glanced up, nodded and went back to her work.

He was directly in front of the window now, blocking her light. 'Want to come along with me? I know this tavern on the Surrey side. They have music there. Dancing, too. You'd like it.'

'No,' she said. 'I can't.' Besides, she didn't like music much, or dancing, though she had no intention of revealing that much of herself to him.

He came closer. He was head and shoulders taller than she was. She put down her pen and pushed her right hand into her pocket.

He stretched out his hand and picked up her dividers. He smiled and showed his teeth, not a pretty sight. 'The cat's claws.'

Cat. The word jolted her. Brennan couldn't know that in her old life she was Catherine, known as Cat from childhood, especially to herself. But was it possible the man was more than he seemed?

'Give them back to me,' she said, keeping her voice low. 'If you please.'

'All in good time. I don't want you scratching me again, do I? What about it then? The river. It's going to be a fine day.'

She said nothing. Had her cousin or even one of her dead father's friends sent him here to find her? Perhaps this lure of an outing on the river was nothing more than a ploy to kidnap her, or worse.

'You're trembling,' he said. 'Why would you tremble? If you're cold, I know a way to warm a maid.'

'Go away.'

'Or what?'

'I'll tell Mr Hakesby that you are pestering me.'

'And I'll say you were imagining it, as silly girls do, and in any case old skin-and-bones won't want to believe you. He can't afford to lose me just now. You know that's the truth.'

Cat glared at him. 'Then he'll lose me instead.'

Brennan smiled. 'That's what I like about you. Your spirit. Come on the river tomorrow. You know you want to. I know you want to.'

'Give me the dividers.'

He slipped his left hand over her wrist, and his right arm encircled her shoulders. He drew her towards him. She felt the tip of one of the dividers press through her clothes, and touch the surface of her skin.

'Come on, my little sweeting. One kiss, eh?'

There was only one thing left to do so Cat did it. She snatched her right hand from her pocket. She was holding the unsheathed knife, given her long ago by an old man who used to call her Cat when she was a child. She stabbed it into Brennan's left arm where the shirt cuff met the wrist. He howled and leapt backwards, knocking over her drawing board with a great clatter. He dropped the dividers and clamped his right hand over the wound. Blood appeared between his fingers.

'You bitch, you punk, you devilish little quean—'

Knife in hand, she advanced towards him. He backed away from her. She saw fear in his eyes. She was glad of it. 'Next time I'll slit your throat,' she said softly. 'Or cut off your manhood.'

'You wouldn't dare,' he said. His eyes darted about the drawing office, looking for a weapon. 'I'll make you suffer, God's breath I will.'

Without warning, the door opened. Hakesby was on the threshold. He stared at them as if they were a pair of ghosts.

Brennan's mouth fell open. Cat's drawing board was on the floor. The plan she had been working on, she now saw, had detached itself from its clips. She was standing on it.

Worse than that, she had a knife in her hand, and Brennan was bleeding, bright red splashes on the floorboards.

But Hakesby seemed not to notice. 'Chelling's dead,' he said in a voice that sounded like someone else's. 'It's all they could talk about in the coffee house. And Marwood will be dead soon too.'

Arm in arm, Hakesby and Cat followed the cobbled way from the Strand, passed under the archway where a porter sat dozing with a cat on his knee, and entered the precincts of the Savoy.

'It's not too late,' Hakesby said, tugging on her arm. 'We can turn back.'

Cat stopped. 'You may go back if you wish, sir.'

'This is folly. You know it is.'

'I don't care about that. I must know how he is. He may be dead.'

'In which case,' Hakesby said, scenting an opening, 'there's nothing we can do. So —'

'He saved my life once.' She looked up at him. 'I pay my debts.'

'Oh, be damned to it.' Hakesby rarely swore. 'You obstinate girl. Come then, but be quick about it. All we shall do is enquire after him.'

They walked on. Had she been by herself, Cat would have soon lost her way, for the old palace was a clutter of blind alleys, blank walls and dark courts. But Hakesby knew the place, as he seemed to know all of London, and he guided her into the winding lane near the foul-smelling graveyard, which led them eventually to Marwood's lodging in Infirmary Close.

Cat knocked. The door was opened by a wiry man with a weatherbeaten face and only one foot. He leaned on his crutch and scowled at them.

'We are come to enquire after Mr Marwood,' Hakesby said.

'He's not well.'

The man began to close the door. Cat put her foot in the way.

'Take it out,' he said. 'Or I'll squeeze it till you only have one foot worth mentioning. Like me.'

'Is he dying?' Hakesby said.

'You're Sam,' Cat said. 'He's mentioned you. You went to that alley by the tavern with him.'

His eyes widened. 'He told you that? You?'

'Why not? What's it to you?'

She held his eyes until the man shrugged and looked at Hakesby instead. But he relaxed the pressure of the door on the side of Cat's foot.

'We've been helping him in this matter,' she said. 'The alley off Fetter Lane? The tall thin man?'

He grunted. 'Sourface. That's what I call him.'

'Listen,' Cat said. 'Is that your master?'

The sound of screaming wasn't loud. But it was unmistakable.

'He's not dead yet.' Sam grimaced, and the lines deepened on his face. 'He's got a good voice on him, even now, after hours of it.'

He opened the door more widely and stepped back. He hadn't actually asked them to come in but Cat took it as an invitation.

'What happened?' Hakesby asked.

Sam closed the door. He said in a hoarse whisper: 'Don't

ask me. I don't know what's going on. We had a man down from Whitehall this morning, saying why wasn't master on his way to Scotland. To Scotland? What the devil was that about? And I said to the fellow, just you listen to him, that's why my master's not on the road to Scotland or anywhere else. He was howling even worse then. They could probably hear him the other side of the river.'

'What does the doctor say?' Cat said.

'We sent for him but he hasn't come yet. My wife's doing her best.'

Hakesby shivered. He sat down suddenly on a chest against the wall.

'Take me to your master,' Cat said.

Sam stared blankly at her.

'Now,' she snapped.

'Why?' Hakesby said, his voice querulous. 'What could you do?'

She rounded on him. 'I have some knowledge of how to treat burns.'

A door opened above them. A woman's voice called down the stairs, 'Sam? Is that the doctor?'

Before either of the men could say anything, Cat went quickly up the stairs, across the landing and into a small chamber whose door stood open. A figure swathed in white lay on the bed. For a second, she thought it was a corpse, because the face was covered.

But the figure was tossing from side to side. In the middle of the blank white head was the pink, open wound of the mouth. Dead men didn't moan, and this one did – continuously and loudly.

The servant by the bed was stout and red-faced, her skin

shiny with sweat. She threw a glance at Cat and scowled. 'Get out. I don't want a nurse, I want the doctor.'

'I'm not a nurse,' Cat said. 'How bad are the burns?'

The servant frowned at her, but something in Cat's tone made her answer. 'The left side of his face is the worst, then the left arm and the leg. They pulled him out before his clothes went up. He's lucky to be alive.'

The figure on the bed screamed again.

'Lucky?' Hakesby murmured from the doorway behind Cat.

'Go away,' the servant snapped.

'Beg pardon, master,' Sam said. 'Margaret doesn't know what she's saying. She's—'

'Those sheets won't do,' Cat interrupted. 'We need to wrap the burned skin in cerecloths.'

'None in the house,' Margaret said.

'Then send Sam out for them.'

'There's no money to pay for it.'

'We will pay,' Cat said.

Hakesby stirred. 'But—'

'Have you a salve?'

'No,' Margaret said. 'And how would I find time to make a salve now? God give me patience.'

Marwood was moaning now, the sound rising and falling.

'Poor devil,' Sam muttered to Hakesby behind Cat's back. 'And all for nothing. The other man died. You know – the one he tried to save.'

'The apothecary in Three Cocks Yard sells ready-made cakes of a salve,' Cat said.

Margaret threw a glance at her. 'What's in it?'

'Ground ivy simmered in deer suet. I've seen it used, applied with a feather. It helps.'

Margaret nodded. 'My mother used something like it.'

'Tell Sam what you need. What about rosewater? Honey?'

'I have both. We have houseleek as well. But he needs something for the pain.'

Cat said to Sam, 'See what the apothecary can offer. Your master needs opium, perhaps henbane as well. The apothecary will know.'

'Listen . . . ' Mr Hakesby drew Cat aside. 'Is this wise?' he said softly. 'We don't wish our presence here to become known. It may be dangerous to us – and to Marwood, for that matter. And as for the money . . . '

Cat stared up at him, without speaking. For a few seconds, they fought a silent battle. She would not back down. Even then, she knew the battle's outcome concerned more than whether or not to help Marwood. It was about herself and Mr Hakesby.

After a moment Hakesby lowered his eyes and felt for his purse. 'Very well,' he said uncertainly. 'But pray God send a happy outcome. And how we pay Brennan, I—'

Cat said: 'There won't be a happy outcome to anything if we don't get the salve and the cerecloths soon.'

'The pain!' Marwood cried suddenly from the bed, his voice unrecognizable. 'For Jesus' sake, I beg you. Something for the pain.'

CHAPTER TWENTY-FOUR

FOUR DAYS LATER: WEDNESDAY, 15 MAY

THE CASE UNDER consideration relates . . . Cat watched the shorthand symbols marching in a stately fashion across her page in the manner prescribed by Mr Shelton in his *Tachygraphy*. The woman next to her on the gallery was trying to read what Cat was writing, craning her head while humming loudly and discordantly, in an attempt to suggest that her mind was on other things.

. . . to the extensive freehold known as Dragon Yard, situated immediately to the north of Cheapside between Lawrence Lane to the west and Ironmongers' Lane to the east . . .

Cat angled the pad towards the woman, who jerked her head away. A red stain spread up the woman's neck and across her face. There was a pleasure in shorthand, Cat thought, independent of its usefulness for making a rapid record: the symbols had their own beauty, and so had the secrecy of them: it offered a private language, for private thoughts, for private people.

. . . and in the possession of Sir Philip Limbury . . .

She could see Sir Philip himself in the body of the court, standing with his man of business beside the dais where the three judges sat at their round table, with their clerks behind them and the ushers against the walls, one on each side.

Theophilus Chelling would have been on the dais too, if he had been alive, taking notes and fussing with his papers. But Chelling was dead, and his chambers were reduced to charred timbers and shattered roof tiles. According to Hakesby, the authorities who controlled Clifford's Inn, the Rules, were not unhappy to have a reason to rebuild his staircase as well as Staircase XIII, damaged in the Great Fire. Also, Hakesby had said to her before the hearing, perhaps they were glad to see the back of Chelling too.

Limbury was whispering to the man of business, an attorney named Browning. Professional representatives were the exception rather than the rule at the Fire Court hearings – most people argued their own cases as best they could, not least because of the expense. But the major freeholders with many properties, such as the Dean and Chapter of St Paul's and the Livery Companies, employed lawyers or surveyors to do the work. Dragon Yard was a large, complicated site, a patchwork of freeholds, leaseholds, covenants and rights of way, so expert advice was sensible.

Besides, a gentleman like Sir Philip Limbury, a Groom of the Bedchamber, could hardly be expected to represent himself in such a matter. His presence here was unusual in itself, and had attracted some curious glances, both in the hall below and from the women in the gallery.

Limbury was dressed in black, in a sombre but magnificent suit of velvet. Beside him, Browning was small and dumpy, apparently insignificant. According to Mr Hakesby, it wouldn't be wise to underestimate Browning. He had his fingers in many pies – and he also represented the London interests of Sir Philip's father-in-law, Sir George Syre, a man reputed to have a very long purse.

'And who speaks for the defendants?' asked Sir Wadham Wyndham, who was chairing the proceedings.

Mr Hakesby shuffled towards the dais. 'I do, my lord. At the behest of Mr Roger Poulton, who is one of the principal leaseholders.'

'But Mr Poulton is not the only defendant. Do you speak for the others?'

'Yes and no, my lord. There are many interests involved. It is a complicated matter to reconcile them all, which is why Mr Poulton begs the Court to defer the hearing for two weeks.'

Sir Philip stooped to Browning's level and murmured something in his ear. Browning approached the dais, bobbing up and down as if his irritation would not permit him to remain still.

'My lord, surely this is unreasonable? It is in no one's interest to delay the matter, let alone the City of London's. Here we have a well-thought-out scheme, providing a clear benefit to—'

Wyndham held up the palm of his hand. 'Enough, sir. You'll have your turn to speak in a moment.' He turned back to Hakesby. 'Sir, as you know, delay is the last thing that this court wants – we are here to speed things up, not slow them down. Why should we consider your request?'

'Because Mr Poulton and his family have an interest in Dragon Yard that stretches over three generations, as well as a smaller, adjacent freehold which he offers to merge with Dragon Yard. Their existing leaseholds still have years to run. And, on his behalf, I have drawn up plans for the site which will result in more houses than Sir Philip's development, without any loss of size, quality or amenities, and which will also allow better access to Cheapside. It is the City's preferred option – I have discussed the matter at length with one of their own surveyors, Mr Hooke, and I have a letter from him that—'

'But this is not to the point, my lord,' Mr Browning broke in. 'The truth of the matter is that the leaseholders cannot agree among themselves. Whereas Sir Philip is—'

'My lord, the reason for my client's request benefits Sir Philip as well. Indeed, a short delay may simplify the entire case in a way that will be in everyone's interest.'

Sir Thomas Twisden, sitting on Wyndham's left, leaned across the table and murmured something to his colleague. Wyndham nodded, and turned to the third judge, Sir Richard Rainsford, who shook his head.

Cat wrote in shorthand: *They can't agree among themselves?*

'After Sir Philip and Mr Poulton, my lord,' Hakesby went on, inexorable as death itself, 'the main interest in the Dragon Yard site is held by leaseholds in possession of the estate of Mr Poulton's niece, the late Mistress Celia Hampney.'

This led to a buzz of conversation below, that grew so loud that Hakesby was forced to stop. The clerk called for silence. The judges conferred among themselves. But it was not until Wyndham himself rapped his gavel on the table and threatened to clear the court that silence spread through the hall.

Wyndham beckoned Hakesby to approach the dais. 'Mistress

Hampney, you say? You mean the lady who was murdered in the ruins last week?'

'Yes, my lord. After her death, her uncle instituted a search for her will, for she had an absolute right to convey her wealth as she wished, apart from the jointure she received on her marriage to her late husband. There is indeed a will, but it's an old one that was made at the time of her marriage. Under its terms, Mr Poulton would be her principal heir, since her husband had predeceased her and there were no surviving children of the marriage. But now, Mr Poulton learned only yesterday, there is the possibility of a later will. If that is true, and if the will is valid, its provisions may alter the circumstances of the case.'

As Hakesby was speaking, a tall man pushed his way through the crowd and joined Limbury and Browning near the dais. He glanced up at the gallery, surveying who was here. He had strongly marked features set in a thin, handsome face. Limbury turned as he approached and muttered something, accompanying the words with a slashing movement of his right hand. The newcomer nodded.

Gromwell? she wrote.

Sir Thomas Twisden was whispering something in Wyndham's ear, and gesturing towards Limbury. Cat wrote: *Twisden doesn't want to defer.*

Wyndham raised his head. 'I'm not minded to grant this request, Mr Hakesby, unless you can make a better case for the delay.'

'Thank you, my lord,' Browning said. 'Then may we proceed to outline our proposals?'

Hakesby drew himself up to his full height. Cat knew he was drawing on diminishing reserves of strength; he would pay later for this prodigal outburst of energy, and so in a different way would she. 'My lord, before we continue, may I beg you to read the letter my client has received from the agent employed by the Hampney family? It may materially affect your decision.'

Wyndham nodded wearily and beckoned an usher. 'Hand it up, sir.'

An usher stepped down into the body of the hall, took the letter from Mr Poulton, and carried it to the judges. Wyndham unfolded it and scanned the contents. He made no comment but passed it first to Rainsford and then to Twisden, who shrugged and returned it to Wyndham.

The hall was full of whispers and shuffling feet. The Dragon Yard case was unusual, something to feed the gossips that hung around the Fire Court. The judges conferred in low voices. Again, Cat thought, if the language of their bodies was any guide, Twisden was not in agreement with Wyndham and Rainsford. At one point, Twisden looked and glanced down the hall in the direction of Sir Philip, Browning and the man who was probably Gromwell.

At last, Wyndham rapped on the table, and the hall fell silent. 'The late Mistress Hampney's leases lie on the Cheapside boundary, and are therefore most important to the development of the entire Dragon Yard site. It appears that, two months before her death she visited Lincolnshire, where she had a lifetime interest in a house and farm under the terms of her jointure. While she was there, according to this letter, she signed a new will, drawn up for her by a local attorney. It is in Lincoln, with various deeds and other documents relating to the marriage settlement that need the signatures of her heirs. The contents of the new will are unknown. So it is necessary for it to be brought down from Lincoln and inspected by this court before we can assess with any certainty who has an interest in Dragon Yard, and indeed the precise nature of these interests.'

'Thank you, my lord,' Mr Hakesby said. 'My client is—'

'I have not finished,' Wyndham said, frowning at the interruption. 'But we cannot allow this to hold up the work of the court indefinitely. Therefore we shall set a term on this: the will and any other relevant documents must be presented to us within seven days. I shall give you an order of the court for your client to send to Lincoln, requiring that the will be brought before us. At the end of that period, using the extraordinary powers vested in us, we shall determine the case in the light of whatever information is available.' He rapped the table with his gavel. 'It's time for dinner. The court will reconvene tomorrow.'

Cat found Hakesby outside the hall, leaning against a wall in the court between the hall and garden. His face was the colour of chalk. Despite his exhaustion, he was in a good humour.

'I didn't think we would do it,' he said. 'By God, it was close. If Rainsford or Wyndham had agreed with Twisden, it would have been all over in a moment. Limbury's plans are more advanced than ours, and everyone's wary of his Court influence, even if they pretend it doesn't matter here.'

'Do you think Twisden knows him?' Cat asked.

Hakesby's eyebrows shot up. 'Limbury? Why?'

'I thought I saw something between them.'

'Perhaps. Usually Twisden's a follower – he agrees with the other judges.'

A smell of roast meat drifted past them. A procession of

waiters crossed the courtyard, carrying the judges' dinner up to their chamber.

'There was another man with Limbury as well as Browning,' Cat said. 'A tall man. He came in late.'

'That was Gromwell,' Hakesby said. 'Limbury's creature.'

'Is that the Half Moon?' Cat said, pointing at a group of roofs which were just visible beyond the buildings of Clifford's Inn.

Hakesby looked puzzled at the abrupt change of subject. 'The tavern? Yes, it must be. Why do you ask?'

Before Cat could reply, Mr Poulton joined them, rubbing his bony hands together. 'A week. It's not long, but you did well, Mr Hakesby. I'll send a man to Lincoln immediately.'

'Will there be time?'

'God willing. At least the roads are drier now. But of course we don't know what we shall find at the end of it.'

'The contents of the new will?' Hakesby said.

'Nothing would surprise me, the way Celia was since she went to live at Mistress Grove's. She was as predictable as a butterfly. But in any event it is better to know than not to know. Will you dine with me? We must plan for both best and worst.'

'With pleasure.' Hakesby glanced at Cat. 'You should go back to Henrietta Street.'

'But not alone,' Poulton put in. 'What if the monster who killed Celia is about?'

'It's only a step from here, sir,' Cat said.

Hakesby coughed and said he thought it scarcely likely that Cat would be attacked in broad day.

Poulton pulled out his purse. 'I insist you take a hackney.'

He was obstinate as well as their client, so Cat took the money he offered her without argument.

'Come, Hakesby. Let us go across the way to the Devil. It's as near as anywhere, and I can get a coach in Fleet Street afterwards.'

Cat said to Hakesby, 'If you'll allow it, I'll correct my shorthand record before I go, while it's fresh in the memory.'

He nodded, his mind on Poulton and Dragon Yard. Cat stood in the sunshine and watched the two men moving towards the hall door on their way to the Fleet Street gate. It was true that it would be wise to check her shorthand as soon as possible. But her main reason for lingering in Clifford's Inn had more to do with the fact that Brennan was at Henrietta Street, and she had no desire to be alone with him in the drawing office.

The courtyard was now empty. The Fire Court was no longer in session. As for the remaining inhabitants of Clifford's Inn, it was time for dinner. The air in this sheltered place was as warm as summer. It was very quiet, as if the world were holding its breath.

On the other side of the courtyard was the green shade of the garden. It would harm no one if she sat on one of the benches for twenty minutes while she read back her short-hand. In normal circumstances, the use of the garden was probably restricted to members of the Inn, but now the Fire Court was here, the circumstances were no longer normal. If anyone objected, she would plead ignorance of the regu-lations. But at present there seemed no one about to object.

The garden was surrounded by railings, but the gate leading into it was unlocked. Once inside, Cat followed a gravel path that made a circuit of the enclosure. No one else was here.

She found a bench in the sunshine, which was sheltered by a hedge of yew. There was a narrow gap in the hedge, which gave her a view of part of the new building, with what was left of Staircase XIII beyond, and then the gate leading to the approach to Clifford's Inn from Fetter Lane.

Yawning, Cat read through her notes, pausing every few lines to make a correction or insert a clarification. She had already made the unhappy discovery that it was far easier to write shorthand than to read it back. Her eyelids grew heavy, and she let the notebook fall to her lap.

As her body quietened, her thoughts ranged free and latched themselves on to Marwood. She wondered how he was doing. She had called at Infirmary Close on Monday afternoon, but had not seen him. Fiercely protective of her master, Margaret had told her he was sleeping like the dead. Perhaps she should visit him this evening. If he was awake and in a lucid state of mind, he would want to hear what had happened this morning at the hearing.

Everything came back to the Fire Court, she thought, and Clifford's Inn. Gromwell lived here, and he was Limbury's ally and he had been Chelling's enemy. Chelling had lived here too, and he had been a clerk to the Fire Court. Limbury had a case before the Fire Court. Gromwell's chamber was where Marwood's father believed he had seen a dead woman reclining in sinful luxury. Celia Hampney was the woman, and Dragon Yard linked her with Limbury and Poulton – and then back to the Fire Court and Clifford's Inn.

The thoughts danced erratically in her mind, chaotic as a cloud of flies, buzzing and wheeling and ducking and diving. But even flies, she thought sleepily, must obey the regulations of their kind, must follow mysterious patterns of their own.

The sound of footsteps tugged her back to full consciousness. Someone was crossing the courtyard behind her. She glanced to her right and saw Gromwell striding along with his hands behind his back and his nose in the air.

She expected him to enter Staircase XIV in the new building, where his chambers were. Instead, he made for the fire-blackened door to Staircase XIII. He took a key from his pocket and looked over his shoulder, first to the left and then to the right.

In the silence, the scrape and click of the key in the lock were clearly audible in the garden. But just as Gromwell was about to open the door, there was an interruption.

'Sir! Sir!' Hurrying footsteps crossed the courtyard. 'Thank God you're not at dinner — there's a difficulty between Mr Jones and Mr Barker. They're like to come to blows if they're not stopped. And the Principal is looking for you too.'

It was one of the Inn's servants, a wrinkled man with a shock of white hair below his hat. Gromwell snatched the key from the lock and stormed across the court towards the hall door. The servant scurried after him.

Cat acted on impulse. She stood up and made her way to the garden gate. When Gromwell and the servant had gone, she walked quickly to the door leading to Staircase XIII. She lifted the latch. The door opened.

It was as easy, and as foolish, as that. Gromwell might return at any time. But it was such a golden opportunity — not just his absence and the temporarily unlocked door, but also the fact that it was the dinner hour and the open spaces of Clifford's Inn were as empty as they were ever likely to be in the hours of daylight.

She slipped inside and closed the door. A faint and musty smell of burning lingered from the Great Fire more than eight months ago.

This staircase was one of the older parts of Clifford's Inn. The ground-floor walls were three or four feet thick, pierced on either side of the door with pairs of mullioned windows in frames of dressed stone. These had lost their glass in the heat of the fire. The heavy shutters kept out all but a few cracks of light.

But it wasn't dark. Daylight filtered down from above, casting a hazy light that shifted and shimmered, as if underwater.

Cat looked up. The fire had gutted most of the interior, destroying floors and the partitions between the chambers. The charred remains of some joists were still there, as well as the brick chimney stack, a relatively modern addition, which was standing to full height.

Less than a third of the roof remained intact, the section surrounding the chimney stack. Sheets of patched canvas, old sails, had been stretched over the remainder of the space. The breeze made the material ripple and flap lethargically, but the makeshift arrangement worked, and the interior was surprisingly dry.

On the floor above, pairs of planks rested on the joists, lashed in place with rope. They made a ledge along the back wall of the building. Cat took a few steps forward, so she could see the entire length of the run.

The planks stretched from one corner to the other. Archways were set in the thickness of the walls, facing each other along the two rows. The one to the right led to a stone staircase, buried in the thickness of the masonry at the north-east corner of the building, which rose in a spiral to floors that no longer existed.

At the north-west corner was a similar archway. It was impossible to see where it led. But the west wall must butt against the back of the new building where Gromwell had his chambers on Staircase XIV.

Cat made her way towards the staircase, her footsteps crunching on the layer of debris covering the flagged floor, a mixture of blackened tiles, plaster dust and ashes. It was only when she reached the arched opening that she realized that it also led somewhere else: to a short flight of steps rising to the right, branching away from the main staircase. There was enough light to make out a short passage ending in a door.

She felt a stab of excitement, followed by a less welcome sense of apprehension. Marwood was right: there was a private route between Fetter Lane and Clifford's Inn. He had been on the other side of this door last week.

Was this the way the murdered woman had come on the day of her death? Perhaps she had come by hackney to Fetter Lane and someone had met her in the alley and conveyed her here.

Cat climbed the steps. The passage was about three yards long. It was very dark here. She fumbled her way to the end. There was a door set in the east wall of the building, towards Fetter Lane and the Half Moon. It seemed undamaged by the fire. She felt the outlines of heavy bars, as well as the shape of a lock encased in a large wooden box.

As she turned back, she stubbed her toe on something resting against the wall by the door: something rigid that moved under the impact of her foot, making a scraping sound on the flagstones. She crouched. Her fingers touched a piece of wood. She explored it rapidly with her fingers, angling it towards what little light there was. A rectangle of carved wood, perhaps eighteen inches by two feet, with what felt like canvas within it.

A picture in its frame.

She picked it up and took it down the steps and into the watery brightness of the main building. She turned over the frame to bring it the right way up. She found herself looking at a painting of a group of naked women in the countryside. The picture was so absurdly lewd that it made her want to laugh.

Marwood had talked of the room where his father fancied he had seen the murdered woman: . . . a picture that disgusted him over the mantel . . .

The dead woman had turned out to be real enough. And now it seemed as if the rest of it had been true as well. In which case—

There was a crack like a gunshot behind her.

Cat bolted back through the archway and into the welcoming gloom of the passage. Trembling, she set down the picture against the wall.

The sound had been the raising of the latch on the door. She heard the door closing. There were footsteps crunching over the dust and ashes and drawing closer. She cursed herself for showing no more sense than a startled rabbit: she had run into a trap. She felt in her pocket for the knife.

For a moment everything hung in the balance. The footsteps were at the bottom of the stairs. Then, slow and deliberate, they began to climb the stairs.

Cat let out her pent-up breath. She tiptoed towards the

staircase. The steps climbed higher and higher. She stepped down to the archway. The footsteps were different — hollower, and even slower — the sound of them was louder. It was now or never.

Cat picked up her skirt and ran across the floor. She zigzagged round heaps of rubble. She tripped over a fallen beam and fell. She scrambled to her feet, and as she did so glanced upwards.

Gromwell was looking down at her from the walkway of planks. For a moment he was as still as an artist's model, his arms flung out in a strangely graceful pose, as if he had been frozen in the middle of a dance. He turned and ran back towards the archway to the stairs.

Cat reached the door. She lifted the latch and pulled. The door did not move. Panic jolted through her. Gromwell had locked the door behind him when he came in. There was no escape.

She glanced back. Gromwell was stumbling through the archway at the bottom of the stairs.

In desperation she tugged at the door again. As she did so, she saw that Gromwell had thrown a bolt across when he came in. She slid it back and lifted the latch.

This time it opened, almost knocking her over. Then, God be praised, she was outside in the May sunshine and running across the courtyard towards the gate to Fetter Lane.

CHAPTER TWENTY-FIVE

IN THE AFTERNOON, Jemima, Lady Limbury, had one of her fits of restlessness. Usually she preferred to stay at home, seeing no one apart from the members of her own household. But sometimes the house in Pall Mall grew oppressive and she had a craving for different air in her lungs and even a different life for herself.

I am a caged bird, she told herself, revelling in the sorrow of her plight, and I keep the key to my cage close to my heart.

Besides, she had a curiosity to see something. Something in particular.

She ordered the coach to be brought to the door at three o'clock. She summoned Mary, who dressed her mistress in the black, unrevealing gown that she usually wore when she went out for a drive. Despite the warmth of the day, Jemima insisted on her travelling cloak with the hood, as well as her veil.

When Mary ventured to suggest she might find herself uncomfortably hot, Jemima hit her with the back of the hand across her cheek. It was not a hard blow but the diamond she wore on her middle finger grazed Mary's cheek. Mary gasped and jumped back.

Jemima stared in fascination at the drops of blood oozing on to the surface of Mary's pale skin. Mary's eyes – those green eyes, her best feature – looked larger and brighter than ever, because of the tears.

'Come,' Jemima said, and beckoned her to approach her chair. 'Let me see your cheek. Closer, girl, closer.'

Mary bent nearer her mistress. A tear fell on to Jemima's bare forearm.

'Closer,' Jemima whispered. 'Closer.'

When Mary's face was only inches away from her, Jemima inclined her own head towards her. She licked the blood on Mary's cheek.

'There,' she said. 'That's better.'

A little later they went down to the coach. Richard escorted her outside, and handed her into the vehicle. He said his master had ordered him to attend them on their outing. But Jemima said that she did not require him, that they would take the groom from the stables where the coach was kept. She gave orders that Hal should drive to Hyde Park, and that he was not to stop for anyone.

The coach slowly climbed the hill to Piccadilly. The vehicle was new, a gift from Sir George, and it had windows containing glass above the doors rather than the usual openings covered by leather curtains.

The road surface grew rougher as the houses dropped behind. They turned left towards the park. The clatter of the hooves, the rattle of wheels and the cries and shouts of passers-by created a bubble of privacy. Jemima did not order

Mary to lower the blinds to cover the windows. She liked to see the world outside, softened by the distortions of the glass and the material of the veil.

'I don't want to go to the park,' she said suddenly. 'I've changed my mind. Tell Hal to turn round.'

'Shall I tell him to take us home, my lady?' Mary said, her voice shaky from crying.

'No.'

Mary rapped on the roof. The coach slowed, and the groom riding behind drew level with the window to receive his mistress's orders.

'We shall go to Fetter Lane,' Jemima said.

Mary's head jerked round to look at her mistress.

'Tell them I want to see where the whore was found dead the other day. Tell them to drive as close as they can to the very spot.'

'Must we?' Mary whispered.

'Do it.'

Jemima stared out of the opposite window while Mary relayed the changed orders to the servants. She felt a thrill of excitement at her own daring. She had planned this outing carefully, ever since it had been confirmed that the murdered woman in the ruins was Celia Hampney. She had always intended to go to Fetter Lane, but she had not wished to alert anyone to this until they were well away from the house, in case Philip caught wind of it. He would have tried to stop her.

There was a good deal of traffic in Piccadilly, and it took an age to turn the coach round and set off eastwards. To avoid the crush at Temple Bar, they took the route that led up to Holborn and turned down Fetter Lane from the north.

As they neared Fleet Street, Jemima looked out of the left-hand window at the ruins that spread down to the Fleet Ditch and then rose to the blackened City wall, with the gaunt remains of St Paul's beyond it.

Hal Coachman paused to ask directions from an apprentice, who guided them into a narrow entry on the left. The coach jolted along, straddling the central gutter, at less than a walking pace. When it drew to a standstill, half a dozen beggars appeared around them, all of them no more than children. Jemima stared into the freckled face of a street urchin.

The groom kicked the boy away and bent down to the window. 'If your ladyship pleases, Hal can't get any closer.' He hesitated, his tongue flicking out to moisten his lips. 'If her ladyship perhaps cares to walk? It's only twenty paces or less.'

Jemima sucked in her breath. She didn't want to leave the coach. But she wanted to see the place where the whore had lain. The exact place where she had made her last bed above ground.

'Tell them to make the people go away. Mary, give the man some pennies for them.'

The groom bribed the largest of the boys to point out the exact place where the body had been found, and to keep the others away from the coach. Hal made one of the smaller children howl with a flick of the whip on the girl's bare forearm. When the beggars had learned to keep their distance, the groom escorted Jemima and Mary down a path that led off the lane, swinging a staff in a manner that was sufficiently threatening to deter the other beggars from approaching too closely.

They came to a court surrounded by the remains of small, tightly packed dwellings. The groom pointed to one of the exposed cellars.

'In there, my lady.'

One of the beggars drew level. 'She was buried,' the boy said, glancing nervously at the staff in the groom's hand. 'In the rubble there. I saw her. But she wasn't buried well enough. The foxes and the rats had her.'

Jemima laughed. 'Give the boy a penny,' she said. 'Quickly.'

The groom held out the coin. The boy snatched it from him.

He tried his luck once more. 'And a bird had pecked out her eye.'

'And another,' Jemima said. 'Then make him go away.'

'See there,' the lad said, pointing. 'That's her blood.'

For a moment, Jemima stood there, staring into the cellar where they had found Celia. There was a darker mark on a heap of earth in the corner. It might be blood or it might merely be the boy's attempt to enter into the spirit of the occasion in the hope of a third penny. When Jemima said nothing, the groom cuffed the lad, who retreated to a safe distance.

The court was sheltered. Despite her cloak and her veil, Jemima felt the warmth of the sun. Yes, it had been worth the effort of coming here. The dead didn't feel the sun. All that was left for them was the cold of the grave and attention of the worms.

Celia Hampney. Who had owned one of the leaseholds on Dragon Yard, which must explain a good deal. Who had been Gromwell's lover, if Jemima's husband had spoken the truth. But had Philip spoken the truth? She tried to ignore the possibility but the pain of it stabbed her like a stitch in her side.

'Tell them we shall go home now,' she said to Mary. 'The long way round. By Shoe Lane and up to Holborn.'

She did not speak again until the coach turned into Pall Mall. Then she glanced at Mary. Her maid was weeping silently. Why? What had she to weep about? Servants were so mysterious.

Jemima leaned forward and stroked Mary's cheek. 'You're a good girl,' she said. 'You serve me well.'

She knew the value of a kind word in season.

CHAPTER TWENTY-SIX

MY MOUTH WAS horribly dry and my tongue felt like a scrap of leather left by the heat of the fire. I lay for a moment, uncertain of why I was here or even where here might be. Some time later, and with a modest sense of achievement, I realized that I was in my own bedchamber in the Savoy.

I thought at first that it was early in the morning, for I would not be in bed when it was light outside. Sometime later, however, I realized that the window shutters were open, and the bed curtains were tied back. Nor did the light have the freshness of morning. Also, I could hear sounds that belonged to the other end of the day. Pans clattered below. A man was singing a ballad in the lane outside our lodgings in Infirmary Close. Children were shrieking, and someone was hammering something.

By degrees, I discovered that I was lying on my back, though tilted a little to the right with what felt like a narrow bolster running down the left side of my body. It was a strange and uncomfortable position to be in, though I lacked the energy to do anything about it. The skin on my face felt tight and hot. I touched my left leg with a finger and was rewarded with a stab of pain that briefly penetrated the clouds in my head, but then dissipated swiftly.

I tried to concentrate but my mind refused to cooperate. It drifted like a boat without oars or sails. I found myself thinking of my long-dead mother, remembering the cool touch of her fingers when I lay in bed with a childhood fever.

A new sound forced its way into my consciousness, a knocking below. Why did people have to make so much noise? There were footsteps, and voices raised in argument. Someone was coming up the stairs. The door of my chamber was flung open so violently that it collided with the side of the press.

'You can't do this, mistress.' Margaret's voice, loud and upset. 'I'll have Sam throw you out.'

'Peace, woman,' I said. Or rather that is what I intended to say. The words emerged in a soft mumble that even I could hardly hear. I closed my eyes.

'I'll do him no harm. Mr Marwood, are you awake?'

I knew the voice. Catherine Lovett's. My mind filled with a jumble of memories and impressions. Cat. Hakesby's hellcat. Long ago, she had bitten my hand and given me a wound that had not healed for days. Half woman, half child and wholly formidable: a person of many talents, whom I could not for the life of me understand.

'It's no use.' Margaret sounded resigned. 'He's been asleep since yesterday morning. Or having visions. He was talking to his father during the night. As if the old man was there beside him.'

'The laudanum?'

'It's a blessing.' The anger had left Margaret's voice, leaving tiredness and anxiety behind. 'God knows what we'd have done without it. That and the cerecloths – you were right about those.'

I tried to raise my right hand above the coverlet on which it lay. I made my fingers flutter. Then weariness overtook me.

'Look,' Cat said. 'He's awake.'

I opened my eyes. The two women were standing beside the bed, so close they were almost touching, and looking down at me. Cat covered her mouth with her hand, as if holding back words that were trying to escape.

'Master?' Margaret said, bending over me, her red face crinkled with worry. 'Master?'

'Margaret,' I said. 'Oh, Margaret, I've had such dreams.'

'I tried to keep her out,' she said. 'But she just ran up the stairs.'

I wanted to explain to her that it didn't matter, that nothing mattered. Instead I touched the left side of my face. Fabric of some sort covered the skin. But even that slight pressure from my fingers was enough to make me wince. That mattered.

'Help me raise him,' Margaret said. 'Might as well make yourself useful while you're here. But for God's sake be gentle.'

Cat went round to the other side of the bed. Between them, the two women lifted me in the bed so my head and shoulders were supported by pillows. The process was exquisitely painful. I cried out. My eyes filled with tears.

'Hush, now,' Margaret said, as if I were a whimpering child.

She turned aside and filled a mug from a jug on the night

table. She held it to my lips. I sucked greedily at the liquid it contained. Small beer dribbled down my chin. But some of it found its way into the parched desert of my mouth and trickled down my throat. I had never tasted anything so wonderful.

When I had drunk my fill, she wiped the dribbles from my face and neck.

'Thank God,' she said. 'I thought you'd sleep for ever.'

Memories pushed into my mind, jostling each other in their haste. Fear rose in me like vomit. My mouth tasted sour. Friday evening, I thought. I was going to Scotland in the morning.

'What day is this?' I said, suddenly anxious. 'Saturday? Sunday?'

'Wednesday,' Margaret said.

I struggled with the arithmetic. 'But that means . . .'

'You've been here in this bed for five days.'

I looked from Margaret to Cat. 'The fire. I remember the fire.' More memories forced their way to my attention: a ball of flames by Chelling's bed; footsteps running down the stairs; a pain in my head. I raised my hand and felt the bulge of a bruise above the right ear. 'But then . . . ? Is he all right?'

I saw a glance pass between them. Cat said rapidly, 'Yes, you went to see Chelling. Do you remember? Before that you drank wine with Mr Hakesby and me at the Lamb and told us why you were interested in the Fire Court. You were angry because they were sending you to Scotland on a fool's errand. Then you grew even angrier because we thought you should let the business alone.'

'They brought you back on a door that night,' Margaret said grimly. 'Shouting your head off.'

'But Chelling?' I said.

'He set fire to himself in bed,' Cat said. 'He was drunk — he overturned a candle probably, and the bed curtains went up. You tried to get him out, but it was too late. The top of his staircase was destroyed. They'll have to rebuild it.'

She fell silent. I remembered the dead weight of the man, small though he was. I remembered breaking open the locked door to the stairs. But the door had been unlocked when I had come up to Chelling's chambers — how else could I have got in? — and I had left it standing open. I remembered the pain in my head. And the fireball glowing malevolently by the bed, with the draught from the open window fanning the growing flames. And I remembered the footsteps running away down the stairs.

Cat went on, in a more hesitant voice, 'You've had opium for the pain. It gives you dreams, sometimes. Vivid dreams. Like visions.'

'But I didn't dream this. Chelling was murdered.' I looked up at their shocked faces. 'As Celia Hampney was.'

I was tired, and I closed my eyes. I heard the two women whispering to each other. I understood that they thought I had lost my wits, that the opium had so entangled me in my own dreams that they were more real to me than this living, breathing world with its rough edges and its hard corners. But I knew I had not imagined what I had seen. Opium brings dreams and visions; but it may also bring clarity of memory and precision of thought; if the angels have the capacity to think, they must think like this, always.

Something eluded me. Something I had seen. But when?

I opened my eyes. 'How badly am I hurt?'

Margaret's face appeared above me. 'There's a wound on

your head, master. It's healing, God be thanked. But the fire caught you . . . it's the left side.'

'How badly?'

Margaret's features crumpled, and she glanced away. Then Cat was where Margaret had been.

'You were burned from your face to your knee. The doctor says there will be scarring. So does Sam.'

I frowned at her, struggling to understand this strange world where Catherine Lovett talked familiarly of my servant.

Margaret misunderstood the reason for the frown, thinking I was dismissing Sam's opinion as worthless. She fired up – almost literally, because her face became even more flushed: 'He knows what he's talking about, master, and better than most. When he was in the navy, his frigate was caught by a Dutch fire ship. He's seen what fire can do to a man.'

She continued speaking, and then Cat said something too. But by that time their words had lost their hard edges; they were blurring into one another; they merged and became a soft, shifting susurration, like the humming of bees going about their business. The sounds rose and fell, mixing agreeably with the hammering and the cries of children, until I fell asleep.

'What are you doing here?' I said.

The bedroom was full of hard, clean light. I had already established that another night had slipped away, and now it was morning.

Cat said tartly, 'What does it look like?'

She poured the contents of the chamberpot into the slop bucket, her nose wrinkling. She rinsed the pot with water from the jug and covered the bucket with a cloth.

'Why are you in this house? Doesn't Mr Hakesby need you in Henrietta Street?'

She swung round to face me. 'Do you think I'd be here unless I had to be? Do you think I'd be doing this?'

'Then why?'

'Because I can't go back to Henrietta Street even if I wanted to,' Cat interrupted. 'People are looking for me.'

'Who?'

'I don't know who, exactly. But it's because I was foolish enough to let you drag me into your affairs.'

'What's happened?'

'I was at Clifford's Inn yesterday,' she said. She put down the pot at last and perched on the stool by the bed. 'The Dragon Yard case came up before the Fire Court. Mr Hakesby was speaking for Mr Poulton, and Sir Philip Limbury had his man of business there, as well as Gromwell.'

'Limbury?' The name was familiar.

She looked at me as if I were an idiot. 'You remember him, surely? The freeholder, who has his own scheme for the site – Mr Hakesby mentioned him to you on our way to the Lamb.'

I nodded with unwise vigour, and cried out with the pain. 'What did the judges decide?'

'A deferment, as Mr Hakesby hoped, but only for a week. There's a possibility that Mistress Hampney made a new will, which would affect her interest in Dragon Yard. But that's not the problem. Afterwards, I went into Staircase XIII.'

It took me a moment to catch up with her. 'The fire-damaged building?'

She nodded. 'Gromwell was going into it. But he was called away suddenly, and he left the door unlocked, and like a fool

239

I went inside.' She drew a deep breath. 'You were right about that door to the alley by the Half Moon. And on the floor above there's another archway that could well go into the back of the new building, to Staircase XIV.' She saw my dazed expression and added, 'Where Gromwell has his chambers.'

Fuddled by sleep and the lingering traces of opium, my mind needed a moment to grasp what she was saying. 'Do you think Mistress Hampney might have come in that way? And someone might have taken her body out by the same route?'

'I found the picture by the door to the alley,' Cat said.

'Picture? What picture?'

'The one you said your father saw. The one over the mantel when he found the body.' Again the nose wrinkled. 'Women disporting themselves with satyrs.'

I twitched in the bed and was rewarded by stabs of pain. This too. My father, as honest a man as had ever lived, had spoken no more than the truth, and nothing but the truth, even in his dotage. And I had been stupid enough, arrogant enough, not to know it for what it was.

The pain subsided, steadying to an ache that ran from my left cheek down to the thigh of my left leg. 'I need another dose,' I muttered.

'Not yet,' Cat said. 'If you have too much, you'll need more and more, and then you will never stop.'

'The picture. Why was it there?'

'That puzzled me at first. But it was leaning against the wall, just by the door to the alley. What if they had piled all the furnishings your father mentioned by the door before taking them away?'

I nodded, remembering the handcart I had seen in Fetter Lane when Sam and I had found the alley by the Half Moon, and when the tall, toothless man had warned us away before he rapped on the door. Sourface. 'Why leave the picture behind?'

'They probably didn't see it. It would have been concealed by the open door. It's not very big.'

'Did you bring it away?'

'No,' she said. 'Because Gromwell came back and he caught me there.'

My head snapped round. I forgot the pain for a moment, I forgot that I needed opium. Cat looked very small on the stool, huddling into herself like a child that fears chastisement. She stared at me.

'You fool,' I said, angry with her for putting herself in danger, and angrier with myself for dragging her into this business. 'You little fool.'

'I'm no fool, sir,' she snapped, 'though you are to call me one.'

There was a silence.

She said, 'I ran away. I was lucky. But he saw my face, and he'd seen me before with Mr Hakesby. That's why I've come here. To hide.'

Another day and another night drifted past me on a tide of sleep and fantastic dreams, coloured by the opium. It was not until Friday morning, all but a week since the fire that had killed Chelling, that I felt more like myself than I had for days. I was weak, partly from lack of food. But I was no longer possessed by that deathly tiredness.

For the first time, I refused the morning draught of

laudanum when Margaret offered it. The pain was bad, but I thought I could bear it now, or at least try to do so for an hour or two.

I ordered Margaret to send Sam to me. He hopped across the room and hissed softly through his teeth, as he did when he was worried or confronted by a problem.

'I shall rise,' I said.

'Margaret says you must lie in bed for longer.'

'Who is master here?'

Sam shrugged and said nothing. With my good arm, I threw my mug at him but misjudged my strength. The mug fell short.

'You need to heal,' he said. 'That's what they both say.'

Both? Margaret and Cat?

I said, 'Have you heard from Whitehall?'

'I sent a boy with a message to your master's office. Mistress Hakesby wrote it, in my name. So they'd know you wouldn't be going to Scotland.'

Mistress Hakesby. Cat, despite her youth and her lowly position, had earned Sam's respect. Or he was afraid of her, which came to the same thing.

I said: 'That was well done.'

'They sent a man on Tuesday to ask how you did. Margaret told him, and he went away.'

'They know about the fire?'

Sam nodded.

'But not . . . ?'

'No, master. Everyone thinks Chelling came back drunk as a lord and set fire to himself, and you were burned, trying to save him. That's what I hear, anyway.'

I pushed back the covers. I winced at the pain that even

this effort caused me. I touched my face. The right side was itchy with stubble, almost a beard. A bandage encircled my head, masking the left cheek entirely.

Sam started forward. 'Master—'

'I'm getting up. Help me.'

Involuntarily, both of us glanced at my body. I was wearing a shirt of my father's, patched and frayed but wonderfully soft and familiar. Underneath the shirt were invisible dressings. My left leg was wrapped in a loose bandage, whereas my right leg was white and hairy, its normal condition.

I made an immense effort and dragged the right leg off the bed. It dangled towards the floor.

'Come along. Help me with the other leg or I'll turn you out on the street.'

Sam grinned at me, recognizing that I was jesting. Probably. As jokes go, it wasn't amusing. But it lightened the mood.

He propped himself against one of the bedposts and helped me sit up. Ignoring my cries, he lifted my left leg off the bed. My bare feet touched the floor.

When the pain had subsided, I said, 'Now I shall stand.'

'You're a fool, master.'

I repeated, between gritted teeth, 'Now I shall stand.'

Sam crouched, and I put my good arm across his shoulders. Slowly he straightened up. I cried out, again and again. But afterwards the waves of pain moderated into ripples, and then at last diminished to the uncomfortable tranquillity of dull, steady agony.

I was standing upright, still supported by Sam. I had regained control over a tiny portion of my life. It was a small victory, and it might not last long, but it was a victory nonetheless.

'I will need the pot,' I said. 'Then tell Margaret I will take some soup.'

He stooped to fetch the pot from under the bed.

'First, though,' I said. 'Where's Mistress Hakesby?'

He stood up. 'In your father's bedchamber.'

'At this hour?'

'She was up half the night, master,' Sam said with a hint of belligerence in his voice, as if ready to spring to Cat's defence.

'Why?'

'Because it was her turn to watch over you.' He stared pityingly at me. 'You didn't know? Margaret and me, we've taken it in turns to watch over you at night. And since she came here, Mistress Hakesby does the same. Margaret tried to stop her, said it wasn't fitting. Might as well have saved her breath.'

CHAPTER TWENTY-SEVEN

'WHY SO MELANCHOLY?'

Jemima looked across the table. She and her husband were dining alone. The servants were out of the room. The door was closed.

'Melancholy?' Philip said, barely raising his head to look at her. 'I'm not melancholy at all. I'm in a very good humour.'

'Then you keep it to yourself.'

'Your pardon.' He gave her a tight-lipped smile. 'The Dragon's Yard business drags on and on. Thanks to those old fools at the Fire Court.'

'Can't Browning do all that for you? My father wouldn't mind if he spends more time on your affairs.'

'There are some things, my love, that even Browning cannot do.'

He spoke lightly but she was not fooled. Of late, Philip had lost his taste for society. He had kept within doors for days – in fact, now she thought about it, ever since he had come back to the house in the early hours of Saturday morning, almost a week ago. She smiled, not so much at

Philip now, sitting across the table from her, as at the memory of how she had gone to his chamber that night, and he had laid his head on her bosom. She remembered with particular tenderness the softness of the short, dark hair on his scalp. There had been no lice among them. He was fastidious about such things and summoned Mary to use the comb almost every morning.

She said, 'You mustn't trouble yourself so much. It's only money, after all.'

No longer smiling, he stared at her. 'Only money? It isn't always the money that matters.'

'No, sir.'

She shivered as memories crowded into her mind. Something cracked inside her, like an earthenware pot too close to the kitchen fire.

'You miss the whore, don't you?' she said. 'And now she's dead, and I'm glad of it.'

'What are you talking about?'

'I know it was you she was meeting all along. Not Gromwell. I was right all the time. You're sick with love for her, and you will never be cured.'

'You damned, stupid woman,' Philip shouted in the sort of voice he used for the servants. 'How can you talk such nonsense? Hold your peace or I'll thrash you till you bleed for a week.'

They stared at each other. He had never talked to her quite so harshly before. Law and custom allowed him to treat her just as he pleased, short of murder. God had ordained that, if Philip wished, he could beat her, he could shout at her, he could lock her up. But they were different, Jemima had thought, she and Philip were the exceptions to the general rule and they always had been. Her father had seen to that when he arranged the marriage settlement with the lawyers.

'But you love me a little, sir – don't you?' she whispered.

'Love?' he said. Then, more loudly, 'Love?' He pushed back his chair and stood up. 'What do you know of love? What do you know of anything? You hide yourself away in this house like a snail in its shell.'

He left the room. Jemima listened to his footsteps in the hall and, a moment later, heard the slam of the study door. Minutes passed, as sluggish as the snail she was meant to be. Tears trickled down her cheeks, cutting tracks through the Venetian ceruse that caked the surface of the skin. Snail tracks.

After a while she heard the study door open and Philip's voice calling angrily for Richard. Then movements and voices in the hall, and the chinking and banging of bolts, chains and locks as the front door was opened and then closed. Afterwards, a silence settled on the house, heavy as a nobleman's pall on his coffin.

In a while, Jemima rang the bell. Mary came almost at once, as if she had been waiting for the summons.

'Mend this for me.' Jemima touched her cheek and laughed, a dry bark whose sharpness surprised even her. 'What can be mended.'

CHAPTER TWENTY-EIGHT

C AT WAS SURPRISED to see Marwood out of bed. Not only that, but standing. A chair had been brought up to the bedchamber, and he was holding the back of it with his good hand and standing by the window. He was alone.

He turned to look at her as she came in. The gown he wore covered most of his body, though his body had few secrets from her now. But the bandages that obscured much of his face made him appear a stranger, or perhaps a corpse wrapped for the grave. What made him seem even odder was the absence of hair. The old Marwood had worn his own hair, and worn it long. But the fire had taken more than half of it, and Margaret had cut the rest while he slept one day to make him look less of a monstrosity. Cat wondered whether the hair would ever grow back on the left side of his head.

He said, 'I want a mirror.'

'Why?'

'When Margaret changes the bandages, I want to see what I've become.'

A sight for nurses to frighten children with. Or something

you pay a penny to see at Bartholomew Fair. She said, 'Give it time. It will heal. Though I'm not sure that Margaret will ever recover.'

He frowned. 'What?'

'From the shock of seeing you out of bed and on your feet. She told me she was so cross she wanted to slap you.'

The trouble with the bandages was that they concealed so much of Marwood's face that Cat could read nothing from it. He turned his head, very slowly as though even the slightest movement required careful monitoring to lessen the pain, and looked out of the window. It was a bright day and the sky was blue beyond the smudges of smoke rising from the south bank of the Thames. The river sent its smell into the room, where it mingled with the darker, more disagreeable odours from the Savoy's graveyard.

'Have you any word of what's happening?' he said. 'Is anyone looking for you?'

'I don't think so. Sam says he's heard nothing. I think Limbury and Cromwell wouldn't want to let the world know their business.'

'But privately? Have they made enquiries?'

'I don't know. Probably. They might send one of their creatures to Henrietta Street. But they can learn nothing there.'

'I'm sorry,' Marwood said. 'I have brought you and Hakesby into this affair, and now you cannot escape the consequences. Will they threaten him?'

'It's possible,' she said. 'But he's not alone in the house, and he has powerful friends. And they must fear publicity.'

'If I had known, I would—'

'You can't undo what is done,' Cat said. 'Besides . . . '

Besides, she thought, Marwood had helped her at the time of her father's death; she owed him for that, and she always would.

After a pause, he said, 'Does he know where you are?'

'Hakesby? No.' She imagined the distress that he must be feeling but did not allow herself to dwell on it. 'There was no time. Besides, it's better that he doesn't know. I didn't want to risk Brennan finding out where I was. I don't trust Brennan. He's up to something.'

Brennan, she thought. Who stinks like a fox. Who may be even worse than he seems.

'Brennan,' Marwood said. 'The draughtsman . . . Did I tell you that I saw him when I left you and Mr Hakesby? I can't remember.'

For a moment her courage failed her. 'No,' she said. 'When was this?'

'Last Friday. When I left you on my way to Clifford's Inn. He was waiting outside the Lamb.'

'So he followed us there,' Cat said. 'He saw us together that evening when you came to the Drawing Office. And he knows about the Fire Court case and Dragon Yard, of course, and Mr Poulton and Sir Philip Limbury. And God knows what else. Is he working for—'

'Limbury,' Marwood said. 'He must be the key to all this.'

'Yes,' she said. 'Who else could it be? Celia's lover . . . ' Cat paused, and out of nowhere came a bitter anger that filled her so completely she found it hard to breathe. 'The man she made herself beautiful for.'

'So.' Marwood's fingers tightened on the back of the chair, and the knuckles whitened. But when he next spoke his voice was level. 'Limbury needed Celia Hampney's support to ensure he gained the outcome he wanted for Dragon Yard. He sought out her acquaintance at Madam Grove's, and he wooed her. Did she even know who he is? Or that he's married? Perhaps she was so hot for him, she didn't care.'

'Of course she cared,' Cat said. 'Perhaps he gave her a verbal contract of betrothal. Who knows? Perhaps . . . '

He looked at her in silence, and she was aware that she had aroused his curiosity. Why did she care? She hardly knew the answer herself. Only that she did care.

'And then,' Marwood went on, 'did she refuse to do what Limbury wanted about her Dragon Yard leasehold?'

Cat stared at him, almost rejoicing in the vicarious anger that possessed her. 'So he flew into a passion and stabbed her.'

'In which case,' Marwood said, 'who was the other woman? The one my father followed? Did he have to die because he had seen a dead woman or a living one?'

'There's no one to ask,' Cat said. 'No one who will speak to us.'

Even as she was speaking, it occurred to her that there was someone who might talk, if she could be discovered.

'Speak to *us*?' He rubbed the bandage on his left hand. 'You must not do anything. I'll brook no argument. I've harmed you enough already.'

She curtsied, mocking his tone.

'I want a mirror,' he said.

When Cat went down to the kitchen, she found Sam at the table cleaning a pistol and whistling almost soundlessly between his teeth. Beside the pistol was a long, thin dagger, its blade recently silver-edged by the whetstone.

He was sitting on the bench with his back to the wall. Propped within easy reach was a heavy stick. Margaret was tending a pot over the fire. She had her back to the room. Backs cannot speak, but sometimes they may betray emotion: Margaret's showed fury.

Sam glanced up at Cat. 'How's master?'

'Out of bed.'

'More fool him,' Margaret said without turning round.

'He wants a mirror,' Cat said. 'He wants to see what he's become.'

'Better not. Not yet.'

Sam squinted down the barrel of the pistol. 'Be careful what you wish for. That's what I say.'

Margaret threw him a look. 'I wish you'd put that thing away. And the dagger.'

Cat said, 'I want to go out. Will you help me?'

Sam set down the pistol. 'How?'

'Hire a pair of oars to wait for me at the Savoy Stairs. And make sure that no one's watching out for me. I want to go into the City.'

'Does master know?' Margaret said bluntly.

'No.'

'Will you tell him?'

Cat thought of the poor apology for a man in the bedchamber upstairs, half desiring and half fearing to see his own face. 'No,' she said.

Long shadows danced among the ruins. Soon it would be midsummer, and there would be madness in the air, even more than there seemed to be now.

The boatman had dropped her at the stairs by the ruins of

Barnard's Castle. Cat walked up to St Paul's, skirted the fence around it and turned into Cheapside. She threaded her way through the crowd, heading east.

The street bustled with life, albeit life of a makeshift kind. People clustered round the booths and shanties, following the old rituals of buying and selling, looking and wanting. In the surrounding alleys and lanes, it was a different story. Life was scantier here, more furtive, more precarious. Few people went there after dark unless they had no choice in the matter.

To the north of Cheapside, the Dragon Yard site was in a happier condition. Since Cat had last been here, the posts on the site's boundary had been replaced with a whitewashed fence designed to mark out the extent of Poulton's territory beyond dispute. The pathways were wider than they had been when she was last here, and some of the chimney stacks remaining from the former buildings had been taken down.

Four labourers, working in pairs, were shovelling debris into barrows and wheeling them into the north-west corner of the site, where there was already a great heap of spoil – stone, ashes, fragments of tile and timber, and broken bricks. Among them were clumps of green, for the weeds were colonizing the ruins.

Mr Poulton's angular figure was propped against the side of a horse trough. He was still wearing his skullcap, and his clothes seemed shabbier than before. He was talking urgently to a fifth workman, older and better dressed than the others. But when he saw Cat approaching, he dismissed the man and beckoned her to approach.

'I had Mr Hakesby's letter this morning,' he said without preamble. His cheeks were flushed. His face was more haggard than before, and he spoke rapidly. 'He thinks I should stop the work until the Fire Court reconvenes. Tell him I will not wait. Why should I?'

'Sir, I haven't—'

Poulton cut her off. 'Why should I waste time because Limbury chooses to make a fool of himself? My foreman can't keep his men waiting indefinitely, unless I pay them for doing nothing. Good workmen can go where they please at present, there's such a demand for them. No, the sooner we start, the better for everyone. And we can't rebuild before the site is cleared.'

'But if the Fire Court decides for Sir Philip?'

'It won't. They are men of sense. He has Court connections, of course, and that's a worry, I won't deny it. But I have my own friends here in the City, and I have made sure they will speak for me in the right ears. Even in Whitehall.'

If the contents of Mistress Hampney's will went against Poulton, all this expense, all this effort, would be for nothing. But there was something admirable about Poulton's obstinacy. And something foolish too.

'Thank your master for his advice,' he went on, 'but say I will not let my men stand idle. Was this why he sent you? To see if I had heeded what he said?'

'I don't come from him, sir.'

Poulton overrode her, his mind running ahead with feverish speed. 'He promised me a copy of the plans for one of my subtenants, and I told him he would find me here. Have you got it?' He seemed to see her properly for the first time, to realize that she had come empty-handed. He frowned. 'Where is it?'

'I don't have it. I don't come from Mr Hakesby.'

That caught his attention at last. He glanced at Cat, and the skin tightened over his face. 'What is all this? Is something amiss? Have you run away from your master?'

'No, sir.' Cat hesitated, for she had in fact done precisely that. 'Pray, may I ask you something? About Mistress Hampney.'

He frowned at her, and in that moment she saw herself through his eyes: a maidservant betraying an impudent and inexplicable curiosity.

She hurried on, 'Forgive me, sir, it's your niece's maid I'm looking for. Tabitha.'

Poulton's lips twisted and his face puckered, as if he had eaten something bitter. 'If your master's looking for a servant, I wouldn't advise looking in that direction. She's a lying jade.'

'It's not for Mr Hakesby.'

'Then why?'

'For the sake of your niece's reputation, sir.' In for a penny, Cat thought, in for a pound. 'And to do you a service.'

'How can you help poor Celia now?'

'As you said yourself, master, Tabitha is a lying jade. What if she told Mistress Lee a pack of lies about her mistress?'

'If she wouldn't tell the truth to Mistress Lee,' the old man said, 'why should she talk to you? A stranger.'

'That's exactly the reason. I'm a stranger to her. She has no reason to fear me. More than that, I'm just a servant, as she is, and servants like nothing better than boasting about how they cheated their masters.'

Poulton snorted. 'True enough.'

'Then where may I find her, sir?'

He hesitated. One of the workmen dropped his shovel with a clatter. Cat looked towards the sound. In the distance, a man was walking towards Dragon Yard – not from Cheapside but from the west, through the ruins. He was too far away for Cat to see his face, but she was almost sure she recognized the shape of him, and the way he walked, head down, swinging from side to side as if sniffing for a scent.

Brennan. The eternal fox. He was carrying something under his arm, perhaps the folder containing the copy of the Dragon Yard plans.

'Your pardon, sir,' Cat said rapidly. 'Tabitha?'

'Eh? Yes. With her mother, I suppose. That's why the girl came to Celia. Her mother had been our laundry maid before she married.'

'Where does the mother live?'

'On the Surrey side. Lambeth? I remember Mistress Lee saying there was a tavern nearby called the Cardinal's Hat, because we wondered if it had once belonged to Cardinal Wolsey, or to some other Papist. I wouldn't put it past the girl to be a secret Papist herself. She would murder us all in our beds, given half a chance.'

Brennan was walking more quickly now. He was looking towards them, shading his eyes.

Poulton was frowning at her. 'What ails you now, girl?'

Brennan shouted something, perhaps Cat's name, but the word was snatched away by the wind blowing off the river. She turned and ran.

Brennan cornered her in a ruined bakehouse somewhere between Walbrook and St Swithin's Lane. Cat had tried to throw him off her scent by ducking and diving among the ruins, on the assumption that she must know London better than a man from Oxford would do. But she had reckoned without his determination, his longer legs and, most of all, the fact that the London she had known before the Fire was gone for ever. In this wasteland, among the ash heaps and broken buildings, she was as much a stranger as he was.

No one else was in sight. They were alone in the heart of the City. The bakehouse floor was three feet below the ground level, and its brick walls were still high enough to prevent a quick escape. Brennan had stopped in the doorless doorway. He was panting. His face was red with the effort of running. He had lost the portfolio in the chase, and his hat as well. His pale eyes darted to and fro, assessing the nature of the trap he had driven her into.

Cat's hand slipped through her skirt and into her pocket. Her heart was beating wildly. Her fingers wrapped themselves around the handle of the knife. She backed against the curving breast-work of the oven. She drew out the knife, holding it so he could see the blade. She readied herself to duck, to dive, to spring.

'Don't. Pray don't, Jane. I beg you.'

'Leave me alone,' she said, her voice as ragged as his with lack of breath. 'I – I'll kill you.'

'You don't understand,' he said – almost wailed. 'You don't understand.'

Her fingers tightened around the knife. 'Understand what?'

'I wish you no harm. I swear it on my mother's grave.'

'Liar.'

'Please,' he said. 'I've no skill with women. I thought you would like a man to be masterful—'

'You? Masterful?'

'I don't know how to say sweet words, how to court a girl. But I – I admire you. Truly. From the bottom of my heart. And now you will hate me for ever.'

Cat stared at him, temporarily robbed of words. She was small, and she made nothing of herself; she knew that, thank God, she lacked the voluptuous charms that made men lust after a woman; nor did she smile at them and flutter and seek to trap their attention: yet Brennan had tried to woo her. It was beyond understanding.

And it disgusted her. What he could not have known was that, however he had approached her, she would have hated him for the very fact of his trying to court her. The last time a man had spoken such words to her, he had ended by raping her. Then her only resource had been to use her knife on him. So naturally she had been prepared to use her knife on Brennan now. Or, to put it more plainly, she had wanted to use her knife on him.

Neither of them moved. The light was softening and fading. Slowly she lowered the blade.

'Why did you run away?' he said. 'Old Hakesby's beside himself with worry. Someone was asking for you at the drawing office this morning.'

'Who?'

'A man. Said he used to know you.'

Cat frowned. 'What was he like?'

'In his middle years.'

'You must have noticed more than that.'

Brennan shrugged. 'He was tall,' he said. 'No flesh on him, thin as a pole.' He paused for thought. 'Not many teeth in his mouth.'

Was that the man that Marwood had seen watching them from Fetter Lane when they were in the ruins with the body of Celia Hampney? Sourface, Sam called him.

'Looked as if he had a mouthful of vinegar?'

'Yes. He said he was in a hurry. He didn't leave a name.'

'What condition?'

'Respectable. Well-dressed, even. Could have been a clerk or a shopkeeper or even a servant – a servant like you, I mean.'

He coloured again, the blood beneath the skin drowning the freckles. It was in its way a compliment that Brennan thought of her as a superior sort of maid, the sort with accomplishments.

'Was it you who talked to him?'

Brennan nodded.

'What did you say about me?'

'I told him you were away, and I wasn't sure when you'd be back.' He came a step closer to her. 'What's happened? Why did you run away? I don't understand. Nor does the master.'

'There are men who wish me harm,' she said. 'That's all you need to know.'

'Are you with that man?' Brennan demanded, taking a step towards her. His voice had acquired a surly edge. 'Is that where you went? To him.'

It was her turn to colour. 'What man?'

'The one I saw you with last Friday. He came to the office, and then you and Hakesby went to the Lamb in Wych Street with him. What is he to you?'

'You followed us,' she snapped. 'How dare you?'

He took a step backwards. 'I wanted to know if I had a rival.'

'A rival? Dear God, you give yourself airs. You're nothing to me.' She saw Brennan's face crumple. 'That man saw Mr Hakesby on a matter of business, and I chanced to be there.'

'I followed him,' Brennan said. 'I know all about him. After he left the Lamb, he went to Clifford's Inn, where the Fire Court is. Did you know that? They had a fire that night and he was badly hurt in it. I was there – they were shouting in Fleet Street for volunteers to help put out the flames. Another man was killed, burned to death. It's to do with the Fire Court, isn't it? The Dragon Yard case? And Marwood's lending master money, isn't he?'

Her old suspicions revived. 'How do you know his name?'

'Marwood,' Brennan said, as if the name were a curse. 'Marwood. The Temple Bar crossing-sweeper recognized him. I made enquiries. Nice little clerkship at Whitehall, eh? All perquisites and fees, I'll be bound, and not much work. How did he get it? Did his father make interest with someone? I bet he can afford a wife if he wants one. Burns and all. Do you know they're after him too?'

She heard the pleasure in his voice. 'I don't know what you mean.'

'I followed them when they took him home that night, to his lodgings in the Savoy. I thought he was dead at first. I wasn't the only one who was following him, either. That man was as well. I saw him that night.'

'Who?'

'What did you call him? Sourface? The one who's trying to find you.'

Cat squeezed the handle of the knife. 'I must go now.'

'Listen, Jane, now we're friends, why don't you come out on the river with me this Sunday?' Hope flared in Brennan's face. 'It's different now, so can't we—'

'No,' Cat said. 'No, no, no.'

CHAPTER TWENTY-NINE

THE TIDE WAS on the turn, and the boatman had to pull hard to approach the shore. It was past ten o'clock in the evening when they approached the Savoy but the Thames was busy, with boats and barges moving in both directions. Most of them had their lanterns lit, and they bobbed like fireflies on the water.

Cat could be sure of this, if nothing else: it would be safer to approach from the river. Sourface had followed Marwood when they brought him back to the Savoy after the Clifford's Inn fire. He had also been to Henrietta Street to ask for her. Who was he? A hireling of Gromwell's? What scared her was the fact that he and perhaps others were looking for them both, for Marwood and herself, and they knew both where she worked and where he lived. They might well have seen her leave the house today.

She had left Brennan among the ruins, plodding back towards Dragon Yard and Mr Poulton, assuming the old man had not already left in anger. The knowledge that she had somehow attracted his – his what? his devotion? his lust? his love? — made her feel physically queasy. She did not want to be the object of anyone's affection. But it was a relief to know that Brennan's motives were not more sinister.

The Savoy's river gate was still open. The only people about were going home to their lodgings, their minds on their own business, many the worse for drink. The porter was an idle fellow who took little notice of their comings and goings. He did not even look up as Cat passed under the archway.

Once inside, Cat did not make her way directly to Marwood's lodging in Infirmary Close, which would have meant going down the narrow cul de sac. If anyone were watching Marwood's house, it would be there, near the mouth of the alley. Instead, she took the path leading to the burial ground by the chapel.

Its ground level was several feet higher than elsewhere in the Savoy, rising to an irregular mound towards the centre. The graveyard had been filled several times over during the year before the Fire, when the plague had killed so many thousands. They had buried the dead on top of each other, layer upon layer, bringing wagon-loads of earth and quicklime to cover them. But the ground could not digest so many bodies: Margaret had told her that it vomited out what it could not consume: dismembered limbs and skulls, scraps of skin, clothing and rotten flesh.

No one went there by choice, even those who had recently buried a loved one. The smell was insupportable. Even to look at it, Margaret said, was dangerous, because the stink of the dead was so pernicious it insinuated its poison into a person through his organs of sight.

At the back of Marwood's lodgings, two small mullioned windows overlooked the graveyard, one above the other.

Because of the smell, they were never opened, and the edges of casements were stuffed with rags and scraps of paper. The upper one belonged to the bedchamber where Cat slept, which had once belonged to Marwood's father. The lower window was in the kitchen, tucked into the alcove where Margaret kept pails and brooms.

The sky was not dark but a pale, luminous blue that shaded into grey. Cat paused to let her eyes adjust. Other windows overlooking the graveyard glowed with the murky flickering of rushlights.

She followed the line of the buildings around the grave-yard, ducking in and out of the shelter of the buttresses that propped them up. Occasionally she stumbled on something protruding from the ground, and once something crunched beneath the sole of her shoe, and the ground gave way under her weight.

Better not to think too much about what lay beneath her feet. Better not to look down, either. She tugged her foot free and forced herself to plod on until she reached the back of Marwood's house.

The sill of the lower window was less than a foot above ground level outside. Cat crouched by the lattice and rapped with her knuckle on one of the squares of glass. Nothing happened. She looked round, suddenly convinced that someone was at her shoulder. But there was no one there, only the restless dead. She took up a fragment of stone and knocked harder.

A fingertip flattened itself against the other side of the glass. It rubbed the square with a circular motion, scrubbing away some of the grime. Cat spat on her finger and did the same on her side.

The pane cleared. The finger inside disappeared, to be succeeded by a distorted eye. The glass was so impure that she could not hazard a guess to whom the eye belonged.

It vanished. Cat huddled in the angle between the nearest buttress and the wall. Time passed, long enough for her fears to breed furiously among themselves.

There were faint sounds – a stealthy scrape, a click, another scrape. With a creak, the casement swung outwards, but only by an inch.

'Margaret?' Cat whispered.

The window opened a little more. There was Margaret's face and shoulders. She was open-mouthed. Behind her, the familiar kitchen glowed like the promised land.

'What – what are you doing?'

'Let me in,' Cat whispered. 'Quickly.'

The window was less than two feet high, and the gap between the mullion and the side of the frame was narrower still. Cat tugged open the window as wide as it would go. She raised her arms above her head. Like a diver in slow motion, she inserted herself into the gap.

Her shoulders caught, and she wriggled on to her side, grazing her skin. Margaret seized her under the armpits and tugged. For a moment, their two straining faces were only inches away from each other. Margaret's cheeks were red and slicked with sweat. Her breath smelled of onions.

Suddenly Cat was through. Her left hip bumped painfully over the sill, and her legs and feet followed rapidly after her. The speed of it took Margaret by surprise, and she fell backwards on to the flagged floor, with Cat sprawling untidily on top of her.

They rolled apart from each other.

'For God's sake,' Margaret gasped. 'The smell. Close the window.'

Cat scrambled up and pulled the casement shut.

'You're lucky I heard you,' Margaret said. 'God in heaven, what are you about? Why can't you come in at the door like a Christian?'

'It may not be safe.'

Margaret shot her a glance but said nothing. She opened the other kitchen window, the one to the yard, and also the back door. She turned back towards Cat. The room was lit by a single candle on the table, guttering in the draught, four rushlights and the glow of the dying fire.

Margaret's face was blurred and shadowed. 'This can't go on, mistress,' she said.

'I know.' Cat shook out the folds of her cloak.

'The master flew into a passion when he'd heard you'd gone. Never seen him in such a rage.' Margaret sniffed. 'And him in the state he's in, too.'

'Is he worse?'

'No. But he's downstairs.' The words hissed with outrage. 'And that's your fault. I couldn't stop him. He's been in the parlour this last hour.'

'But the doctor said he shouldn't come down for at least a week. And not before he'd seen him again.'

'And master said the doctor's a fool who only wants to make another visit because it means another fee for him. And he says you're a fool, too.'

'I'll go to him,' Cat said. 'Try to make him see sense. About the doctor, anyway.'

She heard the weariness in her voice. The day had been a

succession of terrors and crises, and here was yet another; she had no time to think, nor time to rest or even to eat.

'He won't thank you,' Margaret said. 'Especially smelling like that.'

Cat climbed the stairs to the hall. She straightened her back and went into the parlour. Marwood was slumped in the chair by the empty fireplace. He was wearing only a bedgown and a pair of slippers; and his head was bare, apart from a loose bandage, which gave him the appearance of a slovenly Turk.

'What foolishness is this?' she said, more harshly than she had intended.

He winced. 'Where the devil have you been?'

'You should let us help you to bed. Have you taken your laudanum today?'

'No.'

'Then you shall have it now.'

'I shall not,' he said.

Suddenly she was furious with him and his obstinacy, and ready to blame him for everything that had gone wrong since their ill-fated meeting outside the Fire Court. 'Then you must look after yourself, you fool. I wish to God we'd never met. I shall go away. I shall leave you to your folly, I shall—'

'Peace, woman,' he snarled, without even looking at her.

'Don't you dare peace me!' Her voice was rising in volume, and she didn't care who heard her. 'Peace? I'll give you peace. I am not your servant or your sister, sir. You're nothing to me. Less than nothing.'

He raised his head and looked at her at last. They glared at each other. The bandage had slipped, exposing the left side of his skull and the livid skin that had been concealed by it. The nearest candle was on that side of him, and by its light she saw shades of mottled pink, from pale to angry red, shimmering with the movements of the flame. Pity, that treacherous emotion, ambushed her.

'Where have you been?' he said in a quieter voice. 'Why have you come back so befouled? And you stink like a dead thing.'

She answered the first question. 'I've seen Mr Poulton.'

'Where? Why?'

'At Dragon Yard. I want to find Tabitha, Celia Hampney's maid. I think she knows more than she's saying, and someone's bribed her to keep her mouth shut about her mistress's lover.'

'Who?'

'Why, the lover, of course. Poulton thinks the maid's mother lives over the river, near a tavern called the Cardinal's Hat, and the girl's probably there. I would have asked him more, but Brennan found me.'

'The draughtsman? He haunts us both.'

Cat's cheeks grew warm, but she hoped Marwood saw nothing. 'He was bringing plans to Mr Poulton. He told me a man asked for me at the drawing office. The one Sam calls Sourface. Not many teeth in his—'

Marwood made a sudden movement. He cried out.

She said quietly, 'Are you in much pain?'

He didn't reply. After a moment, he said, 'So. You mean the man I met in the alley by the Half Moon?'

'I think so. And there's worse. When they brought you back here after the fire in Chelling's rooms, Brennan followed. And he said that Sourface was there as well. He knows who you are, and where you live. And he must also know there is a connection between us. That's why I came back through the graveyard and in by the kitchen window. In case the house was watched.'

'Who's he working for?' Marwood said. 'If we—'

There was a hammering on the outer door to the lane.

'Who is it?' she whispered. 'At this hour?'

'Sam will send them away.'

They listened to men's voices rumbling in the hall. The parlour door was thick, and Cat could not distinguish the words. Then the door was suddenly flung open. Sam was on the threshold, propping himself on his crutch. Another, taller man stood in the shadows behind him, his hat on his head.

Sam drew himself up and announced in a loud voice, attempting to sound like a properly trained servant in a respectable household, 'Mr Williamson, master.' Then he spoiled it by adding when he saw Cat, 'Oh God, where did you spring from?' He glanced from her to Marwood and jerked his thumb in the direction of Williamson. 'He just marched in as if he owned the place. I couldn't stop him.'

CHAPTER THIRTY

JOSEPH WILLIAMSON. UNDER-SECRETARY of State. My master. The sight of him at my parlour door was like seeing a swallow in the depths of winter. It was against nature.

We stared at each other, and it would have been hard to say who was the more dismayed. He knew I had been injured in the fire at Clifford's Inn, but he had not seen what the fire had done to me. I was not a pretty sight, particularly without the protection of the bandage, and particularly to one taken unawares.

'Merciful God,' he blurted out, for once careless of his words. 'What have you done to yourself?'

Of all the many people I did not want to see at present, Williamson ranked high. My absence must have sorely inconvenienced him – and puzzled him, too, because of the business with Mr Chiffinch, my other master, and the plainly unnecessary journey to Scotland that only my injuries had prevented. Williamson had both the power and the intelligence to ask awkward questions about what I had been doing. Worst of all, he had now seen Cat.

She dropped him a curtsy, but it was the sort of curtsy that does not imply respect. Nor did she lower her eyes, as a maid should, to show becoming modesty. To compound the problem, her clothes were worse than shabby: they were filthy, as if she had dragged herself through a field of mud and ashes to be here. And then, of course, there was her graveyard smell.

'Jane,' I said sharply. 'Why are you dawdling there? Tell Margaret to send up a bottle of Rhenish and something to eat for our honoured guest. And put yourself under the pump.'

Cat sidled round Williamson and slipped out of the parlour.

I stood up. The effort made me cry out. Both Sam and Williamson started forwards. 'Sir,' I said between clenched teeth, 'pray do me the honour of taking the chair.'

'For God's sake, man,' Williamson said. 'Sit down.' He waved Sam forward. 'You. Help your master.'

Sam hobbled forward, took my right arm and made me sit. There was only one chair in the room and in normal circumstances Williamson would have taken it by right. We both knew that his very presence here in my house was an immense act of condescension, whatever the reason, and he had every right to expect it to be recognized. Why was he here? If he had wanted simply to know how I was, he could have sent someone to enquire.

He unclasped his cloak, dropped it on the bench by the table and sat down beside it. He was dressed with more care than usual in a dark-blue velvet suit, and he wore new gilt buckles on his shoes. I wondered whom he had been visiting. A clerk must notice such things about his superiors.

'Was that your maid?' he asked, wrinkling his nose.

'A new girl, sir.' I waved towards the flask of laudanum on the table, which Margaret had left at my elbow to tempt me. 'She fell in the gutter on the way back from the apothecary.'

Williamson shrugged, dismissing Cat from his mind. 'I chanced to be passing,' he said. 'And it wasn't out of my way to call to see how you do.'

'I'm very sensible of the honour, sir, and I'm truly sorry that I have been unable—'

He cut me off with a wave of his hand. 'I give you one thing, Marwood, you're not usually shy of work.' He tapped his fingertips on the table until the silence became uncomfortable. 'How badly were you burned?'

'It's my left side.' I swallowed, for my mouth had become unaccountably dry at the memory of the flames. 'My face and my hand are the worst. And the wrist. The burns are less on the rest of my body – my clothes gave some protection. I was lying on my right side and, thank God, that's barely touched.'

'You could very well have died,' he said flatly.

'I was fortunate. They were able to drag me out in time.'

Williamson looked down his nose at me. 'I heard the man who died was a clerk at the Fire Court.'

'Yes, sir.'

'How did the fire start?'

There was a knock at the door, and Margaret brought in wine and a dish of oysters. By now I was in worse pain, accentuated by every movement in the chair, and by the effort of talking. I was aware of a niggling desire to look at the apothecary's flask beside me, and perhaps uncork it and at least sniff the contents.

Margaret poured us each a glass of wine, curtsied and left the parlour. Neither of us drank.

'When will you be ready to return?' Williamson asked.

'I can't tell, sir.' I was terrified that I might lose my clerkship. 'I wish I could come back tomorrow. I will need a day or two, I think, perhaps three. Not a moment longer than—'

He held up his hand to stop me. 'You are no use to me unless you are well, Marwood.'

'No, sir. I will come as soon as—'

'I command you to make sure you are restored to health before you come back to Whitehall. However long that may be.' Williamson picked up his glass, held it to the candle flame as if examining the wine's colour, and set it down without drinking. 'I saw Mr Chiffinch in the Privy Garden today. He asked me how you did.'

I bowed my head, as if overwhelmed by such consideration.

'He said it was a pity you had not gone to Scotland after all. He said you were a rash young man, though you had abilities.'

'Sir – why did Mr Chiffinch want me to go to Scotland?'

For a moment I thought I had presumed too far. Williamson took an oyster from the dish, ate it, and tore off a piece of bread to ram it down. He swallowed a mouthful of wine.

'Have you heard of a man called Limbury?' he said.

'The courtier?'

Williamson nodded. 'Sir Philip Limbury. A Groom of the Bedchamber.'

Yes, I thought, and therefore a man with the King's ear. And therefore perhaps Chiffinch's ear too, for Chiffinch was rarely far from the King. Chiffinch who had wanted me in Scotland on a fool's errand, and who had told Williamson I was a rash young man.

'A good family, but impoverished by their support of the late King. Sir Philip served with courage against the Dutch – reckless courage, some would say – but he was nearly court-martialled when he came back. There was a scandal about the division of prize money. The King chose to let it go. They say Chiffinch had a word . . . and a month or two later Sir Philip was betrothed to Jemima Syre. The sole heir of her father, Sir George. He's worth eight or nine thousand a year, if it's a penny.'

I nodded, touching the left side of my face, which was stinging. I could not stop myself. Not that touching did any good.

'As it happens,' Williamson went on, 'Sir Philip is the petitioner in a case at present before the Fire Court.' He paused. 'Where that acquaintance of yours worked. Chelling.'

I took up my wine and emptied the glass in one.

'The principal defendant is a man named Poulton,' he continued in his steady, methodical way as if briefing a committee. 'A cloth merchant. A man of substance, and a good reputation in the City, I understand, where he has many friends. The dispute centres on a site near Cheapside known as Dragon Yard. Sir Philip owns the freehold, but the existing leaseholders restrict what he can do with it. Poulton's niece, Mistress Hampney, is another leaseholder – she's a widow, so she controls it absolutely. Strangely enough, she was found murdered the other day. As you know, because at my command you inspected the body where it was found: in the ruins to the east of Clifford's

Inn.' He paused again. 'Clifford's Inn is where the Fire Court sits. Where Mr Chelling, the court's clerk, lived and died. It is like a dance, is it not, Marwood? Round and round we go. And always back to the Fire Court and the Dragon Yard.'

He looked at me. He wanted me to say something, heaven knows what. His words were clear enough in themselves: but, like ripples on the surface of a pond, they also marked the presence of something beneath the surface.

'Something's going on here,' he said at last. 'We both know that, don't we? So does Mr Poulton.'

I began to understand. Poulton must have friends at Court as well as in the City. Including, perhaps, Mr Williamson.

'Will it heal?' he said.

The question took me by surprise, and I did not know how to reply.

He clicked his fingers. 'Your face, Marwood, your face. Will it always be badly scarred?'

For answer I took up a candle, holding it at arm's length because I was now afraid of fire. I turned my head so that Williamson could see the left side of my face by the light of the flame. He leaned closer, frowning, and then wrinkling up his nose when the smell of the apothecary's salve reached his nostrils. The inflamed skin was sticky with the thick paste, the preparation of ground ivy and God knew what else mixed into the deer suet. I pushed aside the loose bandage to show him what remained of my left ear.

'Good God,' he said, recoiling.

'This will not mend,' I said. 'As for the rest, the doctor thinks my cheek and neck will show the scars until the day I die. The question is, how badly . . . The hair may grow back on that side of the head, he says, or it may not.'

Williamson sat back on the bench. 'You must have a periwig. A good full one.'

'When I can afford it, sir.'

'You shall have it sooner than that. And you must live, too. I shall make an advance on your salary.'

I began to stammer my thanks.

'But the periwig,' he interrupted, frowning. 'That's another matter. If you are to be of any use to Lord Arlington in future, we cannot have you looking so monstrous.' He must have seen something in my expression, for he checked himself and then went on in a gentler voice. 'But we shall make the best of it. I shall advise his lordship that you should have a grant from the Special Fund. Five or six pounds should be ample. There's no point in wasting time – I'll send my perruquier to you. It's a pity you lost so much of your own hair in the fire but we shall see what the man can contrive.'

I thanked him. The kindness – if that's what it was – made my eyes fill with tears. I felt a great weariness and wished he would leave me. Instead, and to my surprise, he took another glass of wine and settled back, his elbow on the table, as if he had all the time in the world.

'And now, Marwood,' he said, 'let us talk confidentially.' He leaned towards me. 'But first you have to choose where your loyalties lie. No man can serve two masters, or not for—'

He broke off, for at that moment we both became aware of a commotion below, of raised voices and running footsteps. Margaret screamed.

Gripping the arms of the chair, I pulled myself to my feet. Williamson also stood up. For an instant, our eyes met, and I saw my own confusion mirrored in his face.

Then came the sound of a shot.

Leaning on Williamson's arm, I descended the stairs to the kitchen. Below us was the sound of Margaret shouting at Sam, upbraiding him, and his deeper voice making a quieter counterpoint to hers.

At the bottom of the stairs, I broke away from Williamson and flung open the kitchen door. Silence fell like a stone. Williamson held up the candle he had brought with him. The room smelled powerfully of gunpowder. Tendrils of smoke moved sluggishly, wreathing around Margaret and Sam. They were on either side of the table, their faces staring open-mouthed at me as if I were an apparition from the far side of the grave.

Cat appeared in the doorway to the larder, bringing more smoke with her. Her eyes widened when she saw me, with Williamson looming behind.

'You could have killed us!' Margaret said to her husband. 'You fool.'

'What would you have me do, woman?' Sam roared at her.

'Hold your tongue,' I shouted. 'Both of you.'

Williamson pushed past me. 'What's this?' he demanded. 'Are you all mad?'

Cat said, 'They were trying to burn the house down.'

I walked unsteadily to the table and lowered myself on to the bench. Sam's pistol lay before me. I touched the barrel. It was warm.

'I heard a noise in the larder.' Cat had changed her gown since I had last seen her. She was wearing what looked like an old gown of Margaret's, a patched and faded garment that hung on her shoulders like an overlarge sack and trailed on the floor. 'Someone forced the window.'

'A burglar?' I said. 'That window's hardly big enough for a cat.'

The larder was served by a north-facing window that looked on to the alley at the front of the house. It was less than twelve inches square and protected down the middle by a vertical iron bar the thickness of a man's thumb.

'Big enough for a firebomb,' she said.

Williamson strode across the room, pushed her aside and inspected the larder by the light of the candle. He prodded something on the larder floor with his foot. He stooped down to it.

'The girl's right,' he said, looking back at me.

'It was struggling to stay alight,' Cat said. 'I threw my apron over it. And then—'

'And then Samuel must seize his pistol and rush into the larder and fire in the darkness like a foolish, overgrown boy.' Margaret shook her fist in her husband's face. 'Scaring us out of our wits, and to no purpose.'

'Who did it?' I said.

They looked blankly at me. Cat said, 'I heard someone running away.'

Williamson returned to the kitchen, carrying a bundled apron. He set it on the table and carefully pulled back the scorched folds. There was a harmless-looking, dun-coloured ball with an acrid smell rising from it.

'Raise the alarm,' Williamson said to Sam.

'No, sir,' I said. 'It's too late.'

Whoever had done this was long gone. It was hopeless.

The Savoy was poorly lit. Although the gates were meant to be locked in the evening, there were so many people coming and going that the porters did not trouble themselves overmuch and left the wickets open for latecomers until midnight and sometimes beyond.

Williamson raised his eyebrows at me. 'Why would . . . ?'

'I don't know.'

Someone meant us harm. But it also occurred to me that there was no better way than a well-placed firebomb to force the inhabitants of a house to flee in a panic. Perhaps someone had wanted to flush me out, and bring me into the open. Or, if not me, then Cat.

'Well?' Williamson said, when he had made sure the parlour door was fastened.

I said nothing. We had left Sam and Margaret in the kitchen, and climbing the stairs had exhausted me.

Williamson took my right arm and helped me to sit. He bent down, and I felt his breath on the skin of my undamaged ear as he whispered, 'I told you, Marwood. No man can serve two masters. So which is it to be? Chiffinch or me?'

'I choose you, sir.'

It was not only that I earned money through my connection with him, or that he was here in person to ask me such a question. It was that Chiffinch served no one but himself. He even served the King his master because he knew it was in his interests to do so. He would lie, cheat and bribe if it served his purpose.

So would Mr Williamson, perhaps. But there was more to him than a man of ability and ambition: there was also something as hard and uncompromising as his northern vowels and bluntness of speech; something private to the man himself; something I thought I could trust. I didn't think he would willingly break his word, even to a clerk who served him.

'Good.' He waved his hand as if sweeping the matter aside. 'I've no doubt that Chiffinch gave you that fool's errand to go to Scotland because Sir Philip Limbury made it worth his while. I don't know what you've been up to, but Limbury must think you a threat to his case before the Fire Court. And I had no choice but to permit it – Chiffinch showed me the King's signature on the warrant. I doubt the King knew what he was signing. He trusts Chiffinch, and will oblige him if he can without trouble to himself. I don't like Chiffinch interfering with the work of my department. But he's made a mistake, Marwood – he's overreached himself. If the King hears what Chiffinch has been doing in his name, he won't be happy. He places a particular value on the Fire Court and the fairness of its judgements. He abhors anything that might harm its reputation, because that would lead to a rash of appeals against its verdicts. If the court loses public confidence, it affects the rebuilding of London.'

'What would you have me do, sir?'

Williamson didn't answer me directly. 'And there's more,' he whispered. 'As you know.'

I shivered. 'You mean Mistress Hampney?'

'Aye. So. If you wish to continue as my clerk, Marwood, now is the moment when you must speak frankly to me and conceal nothing. Agreed?'

I bowed my head. 'I think Limbury seduced Mistress Hampney in the hope she would side with him in the Fire Court. They met in Clifford's Inn, in the rooms of a friend, a man named Gromwell. He and Limbury had been intimate friends since their schooldays. There is a private way to go unseen into his building from Fetter Lane. I think she refused to do as he wished, and perhaps threatened to expose him when she realized what he really wanted. They quarrelled, and it ended in him killing her. Later her body was moved out and left among the ruins where it was found, in the hope that no one would connect it to Limbury or Clifford's Inn.'

'And the Fire Court clerk who was killed in the fire?' Williamson interrupted. 'What was his name?'

'Chelling, sir,' I reminded him. 'He knew something of this. He hated Limbury's friend, Gromwell. I believe he tried to turn the affair to his advantage, and Limbury decided that it was safer to kill than pay him off.'

'Can you prove it?'

'No.' My concentration was waning. 'I saw a letter in his room. It could have been an attempt at blackmail.'

'I need more than a theory, Marwood.'

'There was a fireball burning his bedchamber where I found him.'

'Another fireball? Why didn't you mention it earlier?'

'And when I tried to drag him out, someone hit me on the head and locked the door from the outside. I heard footsteps running down the stairs.'

Williamson let out his breath in a long sigh. 'Ah,' he said softly, a smile of unexpected sweetness spreading over his face. 'So Chiffinch may be an accessory to murder twice over. An accessory after the fact of the Widow Hampney's murder. And quite possibly before the fact of Chelling's.'

He looked at me, as if expecting a comment on what he had said, or further information that touched on it. That was the moment when I might have said it: that I believed that another death was connected to this: my father's. If he had not fallen under a wagon, I should not have been here, now, scarred for life, and trading secrets like a conspirator with Mr Williamson.

The smile vanished abruptly. 'But we can't prove it, Marwood. It all rests on your word. And what is your word worth against Sir Philip Limbury's? Besides, you didn't see his face when Chelling died. We can't prove he killed Mistress Hampney, either. It's all speculation.'

I said, almost pleading with him, 'You saw what happened this evening, sir, with your own eyes. Someone tried to burn my house down. If it wasn't something to do with Limbury, who else could it have been?'

'That's the question. Who else?'

A thought struck me. 'What manner of man is Limbury, sir? Tall, short – fat, thin?'

'He's tall and dark,' Williamson said. 'Not a handsome man, but vigorous. He has a taste for wearing black that sets him a little apart at Court. Why?'

'I saw such a man in conversation with Mr Chiffinch last Friday.'

'Where was this?

'On the Privy Stairs. Mr Chiffinch escorted him into a boat and then came back to see me. That was when he told me I must go to Inverness.'

'Then you must see Limbury, and as soon as possible. If he is the man, it is another scrap of circumstantial evidence. But it is still not enough. If you are to be truly useful to me, you must find evidence that Limbury is a murderer and Chiffinch is his accessory. Can you do that for me?'

I was on the verge of saying that no one could promise to do that and be sure of keeping his word. But Williamson's face was as unyielding as one of his northern mountains.

'I will do whatever I can, sir. I swear it.'

It wasn't good enough, and we both knew it. He tapped me on the right knee and said, 'You had two masters, Marwood. Now you have one. Take care you do not end up with none.'

CHAPTER THIRTY-ONE

FAITH MOVES MOUNTAINS. So do money and hatred.

Sam kept watch throughout the night, dozing for an hour or two in the kitchen and then patrolling the house. He had a sailor's ability to slip in and out of sleep and wake, cat-like, to the slightest sound that deviated from the ordinary.

I summoned him in the morning. 'Do you know a tavern called the Cardinal's Hat?'

He scratched the stubble on his chin. 'There's one over the river. Lambeth way – but not near the palace. Further upstream.'

'Have you been there?'

'I've drunk everywhere, master,' he said, with quiet pride.

'Everywhere?'

'As near as gets no difference. Cardinal's Hat used to get its main business in the summer. Not much of a place, but you can sit outside and watch the river.'

We were interrupted by a knock at the door. A messenger from Williamson's office had brought me the promised money. Later, after dinner, the perruquier called with his boy and showed me his samples. He was a Frenchman with a lined face. He darted about like a monkey and stroked his wigs as though they were living things in need of comfort. His hands were gentle on my head, and he caused me hardly any pain.

Nor did he refer to my injuries, except indirectly when he advised me to choose one of the fuller, longer wigs he had in stock, and when he advised that softer, finer hair would be less of an irritant to the skin. Then he and his boy bowed themselves out of the room, promising to return on Monday with the wig ready for the final fitting.

After they had gone, Cat came to me with a letter in her hand. 'Will you send Sam out with this, sir? It's for Mr Hakesby.'

'What have you told him?'

'Nothing. Only that I am safe and will return.'

'He may guess where you are.'

Her lips twisted, and for a moment her face looked years older than it was. 'He probably does. But guessing isn't the same as knowing.'

I gave her money for Sam. Rather than leaving me, she hovered by my chair.

'What did Mr Williamson mean last night? When he said no man can serve two masters.'

So she had heard his whisper in the kitchen. I was tempted to tell her to mind her own business. But of course I had made it her business, which was the reason why she was obliged to hide in my house, quite possibly at risk of her life.

I told her the gist of what Williamson had said on Friday night, and how I had thrown in my lot with him and undertaken the impossible task of finding proof of Limbury's guilt and Chiffinch's collusion with him.

'The King would not ignore that,' I said. 'He could not. Particularly because it touches on the Fire Court and could harm its reputation.'

'But how can you prove anything?' Cat said, glancing at me. She didn't mean to be unkind, but her look was almost contemptuous. You, it said, a man in your pitiable condition.

I should not have believed it possible that on Monday, a mere three days after Williamson's visit, I should be walking up and down my own parlour – slowly, it is true, and with great caution.

For the first time I was wearing my new purchase – a fine, full wig of lustrous brown hair that flowed down to my shoulders and masked my ears and much of my face from prying eyes. Its weight felt warm and unfamiliar on my head. It was also painful, despite the dressings that protected the burns on my scalp and face. But I was vain enough to think that a little more suffering was a price worth paying.

The perruquier stood back to admire his handiwork, flinging out his arms in wonder. '*Ah, monsieur,*' he said, '*que vous êtes beau!* The ladies will flock to you, sir.'

The boy mirrored his master's gestures exactly, and I swear his lips moved, as though he were silently echoing his master's words. Not in mockery, for his face was serious: he was learning his trade. Sam was standing behind me, near the door. I distinctly heard him smother a laugh.

When the perruquier and his boy had gone, I told Sam to bring my old cloak and hat. My new ones – made to show I was in mourning for my father – had been ruined by the fire.

'You're not going out,' he said.

'I am.'

'Then you're stark raving mad,' he muttered.

'And I'll whip you if you don't mend your manners.'

Sam glared at me. We both knew I was in no condition to whip anyone. But he could not stop me from doing as I pleased, though he attempted to enlist both Margaret and Cat to support him. I overrode them all. Margaret was particularly furious. I ordered her back to the kitchen with a passable imitation of anger.

Cat was harder to dismiss. She lingered in the parlour when the others had gone. 'Where do you want to go?'

'To find Mistress Hampney's maid. Tabitha.'

'It suits you,' she said.

I stared at her, unsettled by the change of subject. 'What does?'

'The wig. It makes you look older.'

I turned away. 'As long as it conceals at least part of my face. That's what matters.'

'It does. You may rest easy on that score.'

I swung back, thinking that Cat might be on the verge of laughing at me. But her face was as grave as a nun's on Good Friday.

'But you shouldn't go out,' she said. 'You're not well enough yet.'

'You will not tell me what I should do.'

She stared at me. My anger deflated like a punctured pig's bladder.

'I want you to come with me,' I said. 'You know what the woman looks like.'

'If they catch me outside—'

286

'I know.' She had not left the house since she had returned, foul-smelling and filthy, by way of the graveyard on Friday evening. 'But they can't be watching all the time. And in broad daylight there's not much they can do.'

'Do you want to get rid of me?' she said.

'Of course not. You can't go back to Henrietta Street because they will be looking for you there. But you can stay here as long as you need.'

'And how long will that be?'

'We know this,' I said. 'There have been two murders. And the Dragon Yard petition comes up before the Fire Court on Wednesday. In two days' time. That will bring matters to a head.'

We knew something else: that the murders and the Fire Court case interested my two masters, which suggested that in some way they affected the constant manoeuvring for power at Whitehall.

'But what can you do about it? You?' There was a world of scorn in Cat's voice, though I do not think that she meant to speak unkindly.

I said, 'I want to find out what happened to my father. I don't care about the rest.'

I was lying, of course. I did care about the rest. I cared about Cat's safety, because I was the one who had put her in danger. I cared about my Whitehall clerkships and feared to lose them. And I cared most bitterly that the fire had turned me into a spectacle that would sour milk and frighten babies in their cradles, into a terrified apology for a man who dared not show his face in public.

That's why I had to leave the house now. Because otherwise I feared I would never have the courage to venture out into the world again.

* * *

287

We took a boat from the Savoy Stairs. I found it exquisitely painful, particularly when, with the combined help of Cat and one of the boatmen, I crossed from the dry land into the swaying craft. What made it worse was a squall of rain that chose to come scudding down the river, making the boat's timbers slippery and soaking our cloaks in minutes.

We huddled under the awning in the stern, and the boatmen pulled away. I didn't envy their task. True, the tide was on the ebb, and we were going upriver as well as across it. But the gusts of the west wind fought us, making the water choppy. Sometimes I could not prevent a whimper from escaping me as I was jolted against the side of the boat or Cat's arm.

Neither of us spoke. We watched the clusters of wherries and barges, gigs and light horsemen that bobbed about the surface of the Thames, their oars twitching and rising and falling like the legs of insects. It was cold for May, especially on the water, and I wished I had worn my winter cloak. My hands were cold, and I could not warm them. The seat of my breeches grew damper and damper until I could not pretend it was anything other than wet.

Slowly the untidy huddle of Whitehall slid away from us, then the Palace of Westminster. The boatmen pulled across the river to Lambeth, towards the brick buildings of the archbishop's palace, with the tower of St Mary's church close by. To the south lay the settlement that had grown up in their shelter. Beyond it, orchards and gardens were scattered along the bank of the Thames, interspersed with dilapidated houses and other buildings. There were marshes here as well, and patches of waste ground. The area had a ragged, untended appearance.

Our boat was making for the stairs beside the palace. I

leaned forward and directed the rower who owned the boat towards a landing place nearly a mile further south.

As I moved, the wind caught the periwig, and the hair lifted on the left side, exposing some of my face, and perhaps what remained of my ear. The man's expression changed, just for a moment. I thought I saw surprise, swiftly followed by disgust.

The moment passed. Upstream from Westminster, the river was much less busy. The men rowed on. I leaned against the back of the seat. No one spoke. Cat swayed towards me, and her left arm briefly touched my right arm. I knew that I would have to become used to this: to seeing my injuries reflected in the expressions on other people's faces, or at least imagining that I did, which in some ways was worse.

The boat's hull grated on the bottom. The tide had not yet covered the upper part of the foreshore. I paid the exorbitant fare the boatmen asked and told them not to wait. I did not want to see their faces again. Besides, the less they knew about us and our movements the better.

A walkway of old timbers stretched up the glistening mud of the foreshore to a small jetty, where there was a narrow flight of steps. There was room to walk abreast, and Cat took my arm, as if she needed my support; though God knows it was the other way round.

On the jetty a small crowd watched our approach. Perhaps it was the weather, perhaps it was my state of mind, but Lambeth seemed dreary beyond belief. There were beggars, scavengers and those who picked over the exposed mud in search of oysters and other delicacies. Their clothes were the same colour as the foreshore itself. At the top of the steps, they parted to allow us to pass among them, though three beggars, a woman with two children clinging to her filthy skirts, held out their palms.

The beggars followed us along the path, with the woman whining monotonously for alms. When we were clear of the jetty, I stopped and waited for them to draw closer.

'I beg you, master,' she said. 'A penny or two to get us across the river. My sister's there, she'll help us.'

'Do you know a tavern called the Cardinal's Hat?' I asked.

She pointed a finger that lacked a nail at a group of buildings a hundred yards away. I dropped two pennies into her hand. They vanished into the folds of her dress, and then her outstretched palm returned.

'And a young woman named Tabitha, who lives nearby with her mother?'

'Not now she don't, master. The old one died. Mean old bitch.'

'But Tabitha's here still?'

'Came back a week or two ago. That's her cottage.'

The beggar pointed to a house on the very edge of the hamlet. It lay on a parcel of waste ground, separated from its neighbours, including the tavern, by a shallow stream. It was little more than a wooden shed with a roof of rotting shingles. Shutters covered the only window. There was a brick chimney but no smoke was rising from it.

I gave the woman two more pennies and they vanished as rapidly as their predecessor.

We walked away, with the beggars trailing after us. I glanced back after a few yards, and they had stopped, but remained standing there in the rain, staring after us as if hoping against reason and experience that we might turn back and give them more money.

Cat said, 'How are you, sir?'

'I manage,' I said. 'It's easier on land.'

It was true that the damp discomfort of the boat had been harder to bear. Now I was walking, the exercise seemed slightly to moderate the nagging pain. Even the rain felt refreshing on my face. It was good to remind myself that I was not entirely helpless now, that my limbs would obey my commands.

As we neared the cottage, a cur staggered from the shelter of a water butt beneath an overhanging eave. He circled us slowly, barking and showing his yellow teeth. His coat was matted with blood, and it had a wound on its side that oozed pus. I fended off the brute with my stick and it slunk away to the side of the house.

We made our way across water-filled cart-ruts to the door. I knocked three times. There was no answer. I gave another knock, then tried the door. The latch lifted. The door opened into the room beyond, scraping on the mud floor.

As the door opened, light poured into the single room of the cottage, picking out a pile of clothes, a blackened cooking pot, a straw mattress strewn with blankets, a servant's box, a partly broken-up barrel, and a pile of ashes in the grate.

Something moved in the corner beyond the door, where the light barely reached.

Cat pushed past me and stepped inside. 'God have mercy,' she whispered.

I opened the door as widely as it would go and followed her into the cottage. A tie beam ran across the building, preventing it from collapsing under its own weight. A large bundle dangled from it. It stirred slightly in the draught from the door. My first thought was that someone had hung it there to keep it clear of the rats.

And then I saw that it was a young woman. Her head was uncovered. Her neck was at an angle to the body, pulled there by the noose around her neck and her own weight. She was bare-footed. On the floor beneath her feet was an overturned stool and a wine bottle lying on its side.

The face was suffused with blood. The tongue poked out of the mouth. It looked blackened, as though charred by fire.

'Tabitha,' Cat said. She turned away and vomited on the floor. She went outside.

I fought a desire to do the same. I made myself examine her more closely. The arms hung at the side. I touched one and tried to raise it, but it resisted me. The stiffness that follows death had already seized her limbs. But my efforts made the body rotate slightly, bringing her face to face with me. I shuddered, and left her to death.

I tried the lid of the box. It wasn't locked. Inside was a clutter of clothes and shoes. I stooped, wincing, and poked at them. It was too painful for me to bend so low and examine them properly. The clothes seemed well-worn but many were of good quality, perhaps cast-offs from Tabitha's mistress. They were worth good money on a second-hand clothing stall.

Cat returned and joined me. She knelt by the box and explored it more thoroughly. She fished out a darned woollen stocking with something hard in its toe. She pushed her hand inside and found a gold piece and a handful of silver.

I glanced back at the body, at the stool on the floor. 'Whatever happened here, it wasn't robbery.'

'Did she kill herself?' Cat said.

'It might have been designed to look like it. We should go before someone finds us.'

Cat looked up at me; she had a pair of women's shoes in her hand. 'And leave her hanging here?'

'She won't mind. Not now.' I felt callous for saying it, but it was true.

'Shouldn't we find a justice? We could ask at the tavern.'

'If we do that, there will be questions. Who we are. Why we came here.'

'But they will search for us after they find Tabitha.'

'It's only the beggar who knows we were looking for her, and she was waiting for a boat. With luck they'll never find her, even if they try. It's a risk worth running.'

'It can't be right to leave her like this,' Cat said.

'Right or wrong be damned,' I snapped. 'What choice do we have?'

She shook her head but said nothing more about it. She was examining the shoes. They were of yellow leather, with blue embroidery, with high red heels, perhaps a cast-off from Tabitha's mistress, for the leather was scuffed and stained. While we were speaking, Cat had been extracting balls of paper which had been stuffed inside the shoes to keep their shape. Methodically, she smoothed them out.

There were perhaps half a dozen sheets. I looked over her shoulder at them. They looked crudely printed, some with woodcuts at the head. Ballads and broadsheets, I thought, nothing of interest. But something had caught her attention.

'What's that you have there?' I asked, hoping to divert her from uncomfortable questions of right and wrong.

She held up a sheet of paper. 'Look. This one was folded, not made into a ball. As if she was hiding it. A clever girl. She made the money easier to find than this.'

The first thing I noticed, with the printer's eye I owed to

my father's training, was the quality of the paper, which was far removed from the cheap, coarse stuff they used for ballads and such. There were a few lines of handwriting on it. And, at the bottom right-hand corner, a large, curling capital L.

'Limbury?' Cat said.

There was no time to waste. We went back outside. The dog greeted us like old enemies and this time I hit him so hard that I stunned him. He fell on his side and for a moment lay there, panting, his eyes open and fixed on me.

It was then that I saw the wound on his side clearly. It was a small, neat puncture, flat and symmetrical, though the flesh around it was swollen with infection.

With painful slowness, the dog rose to his feet. He stared balefully at me. I raised my stick. He backed away. Weaving like a drunk, he slunk into the doorway of the cottage.

We dared not go back to the place where we had landed. Instead we followed a lane protected with high hedges, which ran north in the direction of the palace and the church. We did not speak of what we had seen. I was in considerable pain, and I could hardly drag one foot after the other. I leaned heavily on Cat as I walked. The lane was narrow and very muddy and the rain fell incessantly. But we met no one.

Near Lambeth Palace, the houses increased, and we met other people, passing to and fro. Few of them gave us a second glance. There was a little crowd waiting at the palace stairs for the common barge which with every tide passed up and down the river between London and Windsor. There were people of all sorts, many of them strangers to each other, and Cat and I lost ourselves among them.

We were fortunate – there was also a tilt boat taking

passengers aboard to cross the river to Westminster Stairs. I paid our fares and we crossed to the other side. We were more exposed to the rain on the water, and the sudden gusts of wind made the boat sway and buck like a wild thing, throwing us to and fro and driving gouts of spray on board.

I felt more dead than alive by the time we reached Westminster. There was a cab stand in Palace Yard, but I was in acute pain and we were both cold, wet, weary and miserable. I could not face the prospect of the jolting hackney ride to the Savoy.

'Come, sir,' she said. 'We must find shelter for a while.'

I no longer cared what we did. Cat took my arm and steered me towards the Dog, a vast tavern on the north side of the yard, near the gate to King's Street. The noise of the place almost overwhelmed me – since Chelling's murder, I had lost the habit of moving freely in the world. The great barroom was crowded but Cat found us places on a bench at the end of one of the common tables. I called for aqua vitae and she, more wisely, ordered us soup, bread and a jug of ale. The waiter gave me a curious look. I turned my head away.

We ate and drank in silence. The spirit made me cough violently but its fire slid down to my belly. The soup gradually warmed and revived me. I had not realized how hungry I was.

Afterwards Cat fumbled with her dress while I poured the last of the ale. She took from her pocket the paper she had found among Tabitha's clothes. It was now crumpled and damp. She smoothed it out on the table before us. In places the rain had smudged the ink but the tall, slanting handwriting was perfectly legible.

Whenas in Silks My CELIA goes
Then, then (methinks) how sweetly flowes
That Liquefaction of her Clothes.

Next, when I cast mine Eyes and see
That brave Vibration each way free;
O how that glittering taketh me!

L

'Verses,' I said softly, though there was little risk of our being overheard in this crowded place. 'A love poem written by Limbury to Mistress Hampney in her silks. Her yellow silk gown?'

'He didn't even write it,' Cat said. 'He copied it, and changed the lady's name to hers.'

'How do you know?'

'The lines are by Mr Herrick. My Aunt Quincy set them to music once.' She glanced at me. 'You wouldn't think it,' she went on, 'but he's a clergyman.'

'If we match the writing to Limbury's, then—'

'Then we have him. Only as Celia's lover, true, but that's a great deal.'

'Tabitha must have taken the verses from her mistress's papers,' I said. 'After her murder, to use as a tool for extorting money. Which means she knew her mistress had a lover.'

'And Tabitha knew who he was, too,' Cat said. 'The way she behaved to Mistress Lee shows it, and her lack of interest in finding another position. She believed that Limbury would keep her, to ensure her silence.'

'Then he decided it was wiser to shut her mouth permanently.'

'But perhaps she did kill herself,' Cat said. 'When she's found, they may think that her mind was disordered – perhaps with grief from her mother's death – and that is why she did it. And you and I can't be sure that it wasn't like that. After all, there's nothing to show that Limbury was there.'

I stirred on the bench. 'Nothing?' I dug my nails into the palm of my right hand to distract myself from the pain. 'Not quite. Someone was there. A man, very possibly a gentleman.'

'What makes you think that?'

'The dog. I think it had been stabbed with a rapier and left for dead.'

CHAPTER THIRTY-TWO

FILLED WITH JOY, Jemima sat in her private parlour with a silver pencil in her hand. She was alone.

Flurries of rain tapped on the window pane. The sky was grey, streaked with the darker charcoal plumes of smoking chimneys. It was colder than it had been, and she had ordered a fire to be lit.

She had not been sure until this morning, though she had suspected it for more than a week. But, after discussing it with Mary, she believed that she could not be mistaken. Her courses were late this month, and the plain fact was that she was never late. The only explanation must be that she was with child.

She had tried numerous methods guaranteed to lead to conception and done everything the physicians advised. One of the methods must have worked. Had it been the fern roots and steel shavings warmed in wine? Or perhaps the poultice of ram's dung applied to the belly?

No matter. She spread the palm of her left hand over her belly. Already she felt life stirring and twitching within her. She was sure of it.

Beside her was a list of names, arranged in two columns, one for boys and one for girls. Coming to a sudden decision, she scribbled out the girls' names, digging the pencil deep into the paper to erase even a hint of them remaining.

It was a boy. It must be a boy. Her father wanted him to be christened George Syre Limbury. She had no objection to the Syre — after all, the boy would sooner or later own Syre Place — but she had never cared for the name George. She had little doubt that she could bend her father to her will. As for Philip, she was confident that he would agree with whatever she wanted. If she gave him a son, he would allow her anything in his power.

Jemima wrote: Valentine; she laid down her pencil, folded her hands over her belly and sat back to consider the name. She picked up the pencil again and wrote: Christopher.

She had barely exchanged a word with Philip since their quarrel on Friday. But now she had the means to make all well between them — indeed, to make all better than it had ever been before.

She rose carefully from her chair. Her closet was on the first floor, next to her bedroom but overlooking Pall Mall at the front of the house, not the garden at the back and the fields beyond. She went on to the landing.

The house was silent. It was the hour after dinner. The servants were somewhere downstairs, living their mysterious lives and doing whatever servants did when they were not serving their masters. Mary would come if she rang for her. But she did not want Mary. She wanted Philip.

Somewhere below, a door closed. Footsteps ran lightly down the hall, and then down the stairs to the kitchen. She waited a moment until everything was quiet. Then she slowly descended the stairs, step by step, clinging to the broad bannister rail. She walked down the landing to the door of Philip's study. She tapped on the door, and entered.

He was at his desk, with a mass of papers before him – including, she noted, what looked like plans of houses. That wretched Dragon Yard.

Frowning, he rose and bowed. 'Madam,' he said. 'This is unexpected.'

He set a chair for her. She found the study an oppressive room, though it overlooked the garden. It was small and square, dark and masculine. The walls were panelled with stained oak. There was a desk by the window and a book press within reach. On the opposite wall stood a tall cabinet richly carved with satyrs' heads. Only a turkey carpet lent it colour.

Joy bubbled up inside her. 'I'm with child.'

She had meant to lead up to it, to tease his curiosity, to prolong the enjoyment of it. But she could not restrain herself.

'I am with child,' she repeated. 'It's a boy. I know it.'

And all our troubles will be smoothed away, she thought. God be thanked.

'Again? Haven't we had enough of this foolery?'

She covered her ears with her hands, pressing them tightly against the side of her head. But she could not shut away his voice.

'Is this the fourth time you've told me this? Or the fifth? I lose count. And always these children of yours melt away like snow in spring. They are but fantasies, madam, the imaginings of a disordered understanding.'

There was a knock at the front door.

'It's not true!' She tore her hands away. 'How can you say

such things? I've been unlucky. Why, I think I lost them before because I was cursed. It was the old woman, remember, the one who used to stand on the corner outside the house. She was a witch, Philip – you agreed with me, you know you did. In any case, she's gone now – Richard sent her away, though I wished she could have been burned – but all is well now.' She hugged herself. There were voices in the hall, and then footsteps. 'And I am bearing your son.'

He did not smile with joy. He did not take her in his arms. Instead he sat down at his desk and rubbed his eyes.

'Jemima, my love,' he said sadly. 'If this were true, no one would rejoice more than I.'

There was a tap on the door. Richard entered. He glanced slyly at Jemima, and she guessed he had heard something of what had been said.

'Mr Gromwell, sir,' he said.

Gromwell swept into the room in his shabby finery. His face lit up when he saw Jemima. 'Madam,' he said, 'you adorn this room as an angel adorns paradise.'

CHAPTER THIRTY-THREE

A S THE HACKNEY approached the southern end of Bedford Street, Cat raised the leather curtain above the door. She had taken a risk in coming here. As far as she knew, no one had followed her from the Savoy to the cabstand, but she couldn't be sure.

At first she thought Mr Hakesby wasn't there. Then a rider urged his horse forward, and she saw the old man's tall, angular figure on the corner. He had propped himself against one of the posts that protected pedestrians from the flow of traffic in the Strand.

Cat knocked twice on the panel that separated her from the driver. He drew up at the side of the road a few yards beyond the post. She felt a rush of relief as she watched him walk unsteadily towards them, leaning on his stick. Not just relief – affection, too. She had missed him, she realized, and missed the work of the drawing office as well. Infirmary Close was a refuge, but it was also a prison.

He opened the door. 'My dear—'

'Tell the driver to go on, sir.'

'Where?'

'It doesn't matter. Let him drive up to Holborn.'

When Hakesby climbed into the hackney, she took his arm and helped him to sit. It gave her a pang to see that he was frailer than ever.

With a jerk, the coach moved off, pulling into the traffic. Someone swore at them, and their driver swore back. Now the door was closed and the blind was down, the interior was lit only by the cracks of light between the curtains and the frames around them. Barely a yard away, Hakesby's face was a pale blur, the features smudged into shapelessness beneath his broad-brimmed hat.

'Thank you for coming. I thought perhaps you might not wish to . . .'

'I've been worried,' he said in a faltering voice that was barely audible above the clopping of hooves and the din of iron-rimmed wheels on the roadway. 'I don't understand why you went away. Brennan said he saw you with Mr Poulton the other day, but you ran off. It's something to do with the Fire Court, isn't it? It's Dragon Yard and Mr Marwood's business, whatever that really is. How I wish I'd—'

'Sir,' she interrupted. 'You must not worry yourself about me.'

'It's been most inconvenient. We have such a press of work at present. Where have you been? You didn't say in your letter.'

She ignored the question. 'I am perfectly safe, and I hope to be with you again soon.'

'I should turn you off,' he said, suddenly petulant. 'You are my servant, after all – what right have you to leave me unless I send you away?'

'Forgive me, sir. I wish it were not so.' She leaned forward. 'Tell me, have you brought it?'

'And there's another thing! Why in God's name do you want this?' He was working himself into a passion. 'A specimen of Sir Philip's handwriting. I never heard of such a thing. No explanation – no reason – barely even a by-your-leave.'

The hackney swayed as it rounded a corner, and a wheel scraped against a kerbstone. The jolt threw Hakesby against her.

'That fool of a driver,' he snapped, his anger diverted. 'I shall have his licence taken away.'

Cat helped him back to his seat. 'No harm is done, sir.'

'Did I hurt you?' he enquired, his rage evaporating as suddenly as it had come. 'I'm such a clumsy brute and so much heavier than you.'

'Not in the slightest.'

There was a pause. Hakesby fumbled in his coat.

'I have it here . . . ' He held out a folded paper. 'A letter from Sir Philip – it's very short . . . I shall need it back.'

She took the letter from his shaking fingers and slipped it through her skirt and into the pocket beneath. 'Thank you, sir. Tell me, has Mr Poulton heard anything from Lincoln?'

Hakesby shook his head. 'Not unless something came in these last few hours. There's so little time – we'll be before the Fire Court in two days. And I dread hearing from Lincoln in case it's bad news, and there's a new will, leaving Mistress Hampney's leases away from her uncle.'

'Pray don't be anxious.' She leaned forward and rapped on the panel. 'Forgive me – I must leave you now.'

'What? Where are you going?'

The hackney slowed. Cat took a couple of shillings from her pocket and pressed them into the palm of Hakesby's hand. It was shaking so much she had to hold it steady and fold the fingers over the coins.

'What's this? Money? Why are you giving me money?'

'For the fare. Mr Marwood said I must be sure to pay it, as he would not have you out of pocket. I'll tell the driver to take you back to Henrietta Street.'

The coach stopped and she opened the door and jumped down. She looked back at his creased, bewildered face.

'I will come back, sir,' she said. 'I swear it. Everything will be as it was before.'

Cat closed the door and told the driver where to go. She waited, watching the hackney rattling up Drury Lane. It was still raining. The roadway was filthy with mud and horse droppings. The sky was dingy and drab. But the coach had been newly cleaned and its yellow cab and red wheels made a splash of colour in the street. It turned left into Long Acre and disappeared from her sight.

The alley to Infirmary Close was gloomy and slippery with rain. It was empty. If people were spying on the comings and goings at Marwood's house, Cat saw no sign of them.

Sam opened the door to her knock. He had a pistol in his belt and an iron-shod staff in his hand. Cat slipped into the house, unfastening her cloak. He slammed the door, drove the bolts home and put the bar across. As he was securing it, Margaret ran red-faced through the hall with a tankard in her hand, throwing Cat a glance and then ignoring her. She thundered up the stairs.

'Is he bad?' Cat said.

Sam turned to her. 'It started soon after you left. He's moaning away like a baby.'

'Has he had any laudanum?' Cat asked.

'He won't. He's as stubborn as his father. If he wasn't my master, I'd call him a fool.'

Cat followed Margaret upstairs and into Marwood's bedchamber. He was lying on the bed, on his right side. The moaning had subsided to the occasional whimper.

Margaret looked old and tired. 'He'll not let me dress the burns,' she whispered. 'When it's really bad, he acts like one possessed.'

'Has he taken anything at all?'

'He called for beer to quench his thirst, but he'll not touch it now it's here.'

'Let me stay with him for a while.'

Cat went over to the bed. Marwood was lying on his right side with his eyes open. His expression didn't change when he saw her. His head was bare – even the loose bandage was gone. The skin was livid and shiny. There was no sign that the hair was growing back. For the first time she saw clearly the wreckage of his left ear, reduced to a pink, misshapen thing, unfamiliar and strangely unsettling.

'I saw Mr Hakesby,' she said.

Marwood took a deep breath but said nothing. She sensed that he was willing himself to concentrate on what she was saying.

'He gave me a letter from Sir Philip. Where did you put the verses?'

'In the Bible there.' His voice was faint and hoarse.

The book was on the night table by the bed, along with the beer and the laudanum. It was a small, shabby volume whose binding was in poor condition. She riffled through the pages until she found the folded sheet of paper.

'Put them side by side,' he said. 'The letter and the verses. Oh Christ, have mercy. I am a sinner.'

'You need to take a dose, sir.'

'No,' he shouted. 'No, no, no.'

She carried the verses to the window and laid them on the sill. She took the letter from her pocket, unfolded it and placed it next to them.

'Well?' he said. 'Well?'

The letter was brief, curt and clearly written in haste. It was addressed to Mr Poulton. The contents informed him that Mr Browning of Gray's Inn was acting for Sir Philip Limbury in the matter of Dragon Yard, and should be allowed full access to the site at any time as the accredited representative of the freeholder.

'The verses are written carefully, and in a fine neat hand,' Cat said. 'The letter is a scrawl. But they look as if they were written by the same person.'

'Then we have him. It's Limbury who was Celia Hampney's lover. And more than likely worse. Her murderer too, and Tabitha's. Put both papers back in the Bible. I shall show them to Williamson. I shall – ah, dear God, stop it and—'

The words lost their shape and faded to a whimper.

Cat picked up the laudanum. 'Why won't you take this?'

'It will make me its slave. And there are bad dreams . . .'

'Better that than be a slave to your pain.'

'No. When I show Williamson—'

'You'll show him nothing at all unless you take some of this.'

'I shall not—'

She stamped her foot, driving him into silence. 'You shall, sir. Or you will be no use to any of us, least of all yourself.'

His face was contorted. He was sweating. 'I – say – I – will – not.'

'And I say you will.'

'Leave me, you witch,' he shouted, his voice high and jagged. 'Leave me.'

'If you make me,' she said, 'I shall call Sam and Margaret to hold you down while I force it into you. The more you struggle, the more you will suffer.'

For a moment Marwood said nothing. She stared down at him. He bit his lip. A drop of blood appeared, reminding her of the dog they had seen in Lambeth. Tears filled his eyes and overflowed.

'By God,' he said. 'You're a devil. I believe you would do it and not think twice about it.'

'Take it,' she said, and picked up the flask.

The double knock on the door came after the candles had been lit. Cat was sitting upstairs with Marwood, who was now sleeping so deeply it seemed he might never wake. Perhaps, she thought more than once, it might be kinder if he didn't. Strange to think that before the fire at Clifford's Inn, she had envied his good fortune.

The chamber door was open. She heard Sam's footsteps downstairs, and the click of the door shutter opening, allowing him to inspect who was waiting outside. For a moment she held her breath. Then came the rattle of bolts and the grating sound the bar made when it was removed from its sockets.

She took up the candle and went on to the landing. Williamson's harsh voice filled the shadowy space below, demanding to be taken to Marwood. She glanced back at the man on the bed. He was still dead to the world and its pains, his breathing as regular as before. She left him and went downstairs.

'Master's not well,' Sam was saying. 'He's sleeping, sir, and mustn't be wakened.'

'You'll let me decide that. Where is he? Upstairs?'

'Sir,' Cat said, taking the last few stairs at a run. 'May I speak to you first?'

Williamson frowned down at her. 'Who are you?'

'Jane, sir. You saw me the last time you were here.'

He ran his eyes over her. There was nothing lascivious in his stare. She might have been a column of figures to be added up or a horse to be assessed for its suitability for a task. 'Did I?'

'Yes, sir. In the parlour. I had fallen in the gutter on my way back from the apothecary's.'

'Ah. I remember.' His expression was different now: he was comparing his memory of that filthy, dishevelled creature with the demure, neatly dressed young woman before him. 'The maid.'

'Yes, sir. Mr Marwood asked me to speak to you if you called.'

A puddle of rainwater was forming around him. He took off his cloak and tossed it to Sam. 'About what?'

The words were curt but his manner had subtly changed. He had adjusted his assumptions about her, if only by a trifle. There were maidservants of all conditions in London, some of whom had been gently bred. There were men who employed their unmarried sisters or cousins to serve them, often for little more than the cost of their board and lodging.

'There are two papers he wished you to see, sir.'

His eyebrows shot up. 'Where are they?'

'In the chamber where he's asleep. Would you come with me?'

Sam cleared his throat noisily but said nothing.

'But pray don't wake him,' she went on. 'He has had a large dose of laudanum. He went out today on your business, and now the pain is particularly bad.'

She led the way upstairs, with Williamson's heavy steps behind her, and took him into Marwood's room. Their shadows swooped drunkenly before them, thrown by the candle she had left burning on the chest by the door.

Cat went to the bed and held up her candle so the light fell on Marwood's face. He was snoring gently.

Williamson stared at him for a long moment. He nodded at the periwig on its stand at the foot of the bed. 'Has he worn that?'

'Yes, sir. When he went out today. With the wig and a hat on his head, you hardly notice the burns . . . most of the time, at least.'

He grunted. 'That's something, I suppose. Where are these papers?'

She took up the Bible on the night table, and removed the poem. She passed it to Williamson, who angled them to the light of the candle.

'What's this? Verses? Why did he want me to see this?'

'He found them in the possession of a woman called Tabitha, who was living in Lambeth.'

'He told you this?' Surprise battled with outrage in his voice.

'In case he could not talk to you if you called.'

'Very well. Who is this Tabitha?'

'Mistress Hampney's maid. But now she is dead.'

'How?'

'She hanged herself in her own cottage. Or someone did it for her.'

Williamson peered at the paper in his hand. 'Who wrote this?' he said sharply. 'Who is this "L"?'

'I don't know.' Cat turned the pages of the Bible and took out the letter that Hakesby had given her. 'He commanded me to show you this as well.'

Williamson read the letter, muttered something under his breath and then read it again. 'Addressed to Mr Hakesby, I see. The name's familiar.'

'He is the surveyor acting for Poulton.'

'How did your master get this?'

'I can't say.'

He took up the verses and compared them to the letter. 'By God, I believe they're in the same hand.' His eyes went back to the figure on the bed, still snoring. 'I must talk to him.'

'No, sir.'

He stared down at her. 'What did you say?'

'Pray don't wake him. He needs this sleep more than anything.'

Williamson shook his head and took a step towards the bed. He laid a hand on Marwood's shoulder.

'Stop,' Cat said, more loudly than she had intended.

He swung back, his eyebrows shooting up.

'If you wake him, you'll get no sense from him. You'll distress him to no purpose.'

'What makes you so sure?'

311

'I've helped nurse him these last few days. I know the pattern of it.'

Williamson shrugged. 'Perhaps you're right.' He folded the two papers and slipped them in his pocket. 'When he wakes, tell him I came, and that I wish to see him as soon as possible. If he's too ill to come to Whitehall, then send word to my office.'

She bowed her head.

'Can you write?'

'Yes, sir.'

'Then, if he cannot come himself, or write to me, you must write on his behalf. Or at least give me a report on how he does.'

He gestured to her to light him downstairs.

Sam was waiting for them in the hall. As he was unbarring the door, Williamson turned back to her. 'What did you say your name was?'

'Jane, sir.'

'And your surname?'

'Hakesby, sir.'

'Like the surveyor?'

'I am his cousin, sir. He took me in when my father died. He sent me here to help with nursing Mr Marwood.'

Williamson clicked his fingers. 'Curious. Are they intimate friends?'

'I can't say, sir.'

To her relief, he did not probe further. He said goodnight and left the house.

'Thank Christ for that,' Sam muttered piously as he barred the door.

Cat went back upstairs. On the landing outside Marwood's

room, there was a small, unshuttered window. Shielding her candle with the palm of her hand, she looked down into the alley below. A light burned on the corner at the end. She was in time to see Williamson marching slowly towards it, his outline wavering and indeterminate because of the lack of light and the distortion of the glass.

CHAPTER THIRTY-FOUR

'BRING ME THE box,' Jemima said. 'The one in the chest.'

Without a word, Mary curtsied and went away. The chest had a drawer with a false back, and it was behind this that the box was kept. It was a pretty thing made of ebony inlaid with silver.

At this hour, approaching midnight, the house was quiet. The other servants were in the kitchen or in bed, apart from Richard, who was attending his master at Whitehall; or so he said.

Jemima unlocked the box with a key she kept in her pocket. Among the litter inside were more keys, held together on a ring.

Mary did not need to be told what to do. She picked up a candle, opened the door for her mistress and followed her down the stairs, along the hall and into the study. Once inside, Mary closed the door behind them and stood with her back to it.

'Light another candle,' Jemima said. 'I don't want to be

poking about in the gloom. Put it on the desk and then hold a light for me over here.'

Jemima had commissioned the cabinet with satyrs' heads for Philip, as a wedding present. Most of the woods used for the inlays and the veneers had come from the East Indies. It was probably the most expensive piece of furniture in the entire house – it had cost even more than her own bed.

She unlocked and opened its outer doors. Inside were three drawers above a cupboard. The top drawer had its own lock, but Jemima had a key for it too – that was the advantage of commissioning the cabinet-maker and the locksmith yourself.

The majority of the contents were familiar from earlier inspections. There was a small bag of gold and a few trinkets that had survived the shipwreck of the Limburys' fortunes during the Commonwealth when Philip had been abroad with the King and the court in exile. Beside these was a bundle of documents relating to the Pall Mall house, and another bundle dealing with the Dragon Yard property and the Fire Court case.

Underneath them all was a folder of letters and notes, most of them about Philip's debts and his attempts to pay them. Until the last few weeks, Jemima would have said that gambling, not women, was his weakness. Now she was not so sure.

All this was familiar, though at a quick glance the debts amounted to almost twice as much as they had before, despite the earrings she had given him to sell. One of the new bills was for thirty pounds owed to a printer, the Widow Vereker at the sign of the Three Bibles on London Bridge. That puzzled her for a moment – her husband was not a man who cared for the printed word, by and large – until she remembered Gromwell's book of Gloucestershire antiquities. Whatever the favour that Gromwell had done Philip, it was an important one, and he desired to keep his side of the bargain.

Another thing was new since her last inspection: a letter at the very bottom of the drawer. Or rather two letters, for the outer one had another folded inside it.

She carried them over to the desk. The first letter had a broken seal (an anonymous smudge of wax with nothing imprinted on it) and Philip's name on the outside, but no address. She took it to the desk and examined it by the light of the candle. It contained a few words scrawled in pencil. It was unsigned.

This under my door by night. I will call on you at supper.

Jemima unfolded the second letter. It was much longer, and written in a fine, clerkly hand.

Sir,

It grieves me beyond Measure that my Conscience requires me to communicate this Distressing Information to you, not merely for the Good of our Fellowship and its Reputation in the World, but also to warn you of the Dangers of a too Generous and too Trusting Spirit. In Fetter Lane, by the Half Moon tavern, an alley leads to our Inn, to the Remains of Staircase XIII. I have had the Misfortune to learn that it is possible to pass between the two, and that it has been the means of conducting an Intrigue that will bring Shame upon our Fellowship.

Pray advise me. Should I lay the Matter before the Principal and Rules

at their next Meeting? Or would it be more prudent for us to deal with it

privately, to preserve the good Repute of the Inn?

    T.C.

Was this the letter that Mary had told her about the week before last? The one the boy had brought, which had thrown Philip into a rage? Underneath the fine words there was an unmistakable hint of a threat. The letter must have been sent to Gromwell – who else did Philip know at Clifford's Inn – who had indeed called at Pall Mall that evening and taken Philip away from her. She did not know who 'T.C.' might be, though he was obviously a member of the Inn as well.

. . . the means of conducting an Intrigue . . .

Jemima knew what the intrigue was, if nothing else. No wonder Philip had flown into such a passion. A bubble of pain burst inside her, and she cried out.

'Madam,' Mary said. 'Oh madam.'

Jemima glanced at her. For a moment, she wondered whether to show her the letter – Mary could read quite well, though writing was another matter. Then she read it again, thinking about its implications, and decided not to.

The letter had been delivered to the house on Thursday evening, eleven days ago. On Friday night – or rather in the darkest hour before dawn on Saturday morning – Philip had returned to the house and gone to his bedchamber; she had gone to him there and found him distraught; she had never seen him so distressed; and she had comforted him. Her heart

317

melted within her bosom at the sweet memory of it. She found consolation there, at least: in his time of trouble, he had not turned her away.

A triple knock echoed through the house.

Both Jemima and Mary gasped. It could not be Philip at the street door – he had his own knock, which the porter knew as his master's. This was a stranger's knock. An uninvited caller at this hour was unheard of.

The knock would bring the servants into the hall. They could hardly help noticing that their mistress was in the study. There was no reason why she should not be here. On the other hand, there was no reason why she should.

Jemima folded the letters. She glided back to the cabinet. Already there were footsteps outside, and the sound of voices. She put the letters back in the drawer, locked it, closed the cabinet doors and locked them.

'What do we do, mistress?' whispered Mary.

Jemima dropped her keys in her pocket. 'Do?' She did not lower her voice. 'Why, we shall go back upstairs. Snuff that candle and open the door.'

Mary obeyed. She replaced the study candlestick on the mantle shelf and lighted Jemima into the hall. Hester glanced at them, and so did Hal Coachman, who was standing in the shadows near the stairs to the kitchen. He was not supposed to come up into the house, but it was a sensible precaution when there was an unexpected caller at this time of the evening. Besides, according to Mary, he lusted after Hester, though Jemima found this hard to believe. Still, you could never tell with servants.

'Who is it?' Jemima said.

'The porter says it's a gentleman called Mr Chiffinch, mistress.'

'Let him in.'

Jemima had never met Mr Chiffinch, but she knew that Philip counted him as a friend. Hester bobbed an awkward curtsy to her mistress while the door was opening. Hal edged further into the shadows. They must already have seen the candlelight around the study door.

Cold air rushed into the house. The bulky figure of a man came into the hall, brushing raindrops from his cloak.

'Damn me,' he said. 'God rot this weather. Where's your master, girl?'

'He's out, sir.'

'Where the devil is he?'

Jemima advanced down the hall with Mary a step or two behind with the candle. 'My husband isn't at home,' she said. 'May I help you?'

The man turned to her, removing his hat, which sent a gout of water to the floor. His eyes ran swiftly over her, taking in the fur-trimmed gown and the maid at her elbow. He bowed. 'Madam, your pardon for disturbing you. My name is Chiffinch. William Chiffinch.'

'My husband has talked of you, sir. He's at Whitehall. He may be there still.'

'I couldn't find him there.'

'Then he's probably supping with friends. Will you leave a message?'

Chiffinch hesitated. 'I wonder, madam, if I might have a word in your private ear?'

'Of course, sir. In my closet, I think.'

He declined refreshment. Jemima went upstairs, with Mary padding almost silently behind her, and Chiffinch last of all, his steps heavy and deliberate. In the closet, she sent Mary away and sat down, waving Chiffinch to the sofa. His face was shiny with moisture, though it was hard to know whether it was rain or perspiration.

He did not sit. 'Forgive me if I go straight to the point – I'm pressed for time. Your ladyship knows who I am, I think?'

She inclined her head. 'Indeed, sir.' All the world knew of Mr Chiffinch, the Keeper of the King's Private Closet. All the world that mattered.

'I've the honour to serve the King in his private affairs, which means that I cannot always explain the reasons for my words and actions as frankly as I should wish to do. But, believe me, madam, I'm here to do your husband a kindness. Tell him that I strongly advise him to beg leave of His Majesty to withdraw from Court for a month or so. My advice would be for him to take you down to Syre Court as soon as you can contrive it – after all, what could be more natural than for you than to pay a visit to your father? His health would furnish you with an excuse.'

She registered the fact that he knew so much about her family's circumstances. She said, 'I must give my husband some reason, sir, surely? He would be most reluctant to leave London just at present. He has a case before the Fire Court, for example—'

'My lady, hear me out,' Chiffinch said. His voice remained soft but he spoke with more deliberation than before, which gave his words an edge. 'You may tell Sir Philip this: that the reason has to do with the Fire Court. He'll understand me.'

Jemima shivered.

'Forgive me, madam,' Chiffinch said. 'I've kept you talking in a room without a fire. Let me ring for your maid. I'll leave you in peace now.' He took a step towards her and loomed over her. His voice dropped. 'Be sure to tell your husband what I've said as soon as he comes in. Tell him I will do what I can, but you two must go down to the country as soon as possible. Otherwise I can't answer for the consequences.'

He left the room without another word. She listened to his tread on the stairs. Then Mary was with her, urging her to retire to her bedchamber, where there was a fire.

Jemima allowed herself to be taken to her bedroom. But she would not get into bed, though it had already been warmed for her.

'Light more candles,' she said. 'Build up the fire and bring me a posset. I shall wait up for your master.'

Mary left her alone. Jemima hugged her belly. Was it larger than before? So it came back to the Fire Court. Chiffinch's warning must have to do with Clifford's Inn and Philip's intrigue, with the letters in the cabinet and the murder of the widow Hampney. The ugly whore was dead. But even now she had power to haunt them.

Jemima hugged herself, hugged her son. Now though, Mr Chiffinch had changed the rules of the game. If she played the cards she had in her hand with skill, she could have everything she wanted. At Syre Court, with her father standing by, Philip would be entirely hers and for ever. She would make him love her once more. And—

My son, she thought, my son. I do all this for you.

CHAPTER THIRTY-FIVE

LAUDANUM. A SOLUTION of alcohol infused with
the juice of the poppy, to which the apothecary adds the
ingredients that his skill and his judgement suggest.

To know what composes a thing is not to know the nature
of that thing.

A body is a prison, within which the spirit dashes itself
against bars of bone and walls of flesh until death unlocks
the door and sets the spirit free.

Even in prison, a man may have visions that make him an
emperor of time and space.

These thoughts, and others of a like nature, marched
through my mind in a stately procession organized according
to some logic of its own. I knew each of them was of
profound importance. But when I tried to contemplate a
thought, the next arrived and shouldered its predecessor out
of the way.

Indeed, my mind was a lively place, busy but orderly in
its organization and its transactions – not unlike, it occurred
to me, a hive of bees. The metaphor pleased me, and I seemed

to see the outer forms of my thoughts take the appearance of bees.

While this was going on, a part of me was aware that I was lying on my left side in my own bed in my chamber in Infirmary Close. My eyes were shut, not that it mattered because I appeared to be able to see perfectly well with them closed. My body was immobile. I thought it possible that this condition would be permanent. The prospect did not trouble me unduly. I noticed without surprise that I was not in pain. Or, if I was, the pain was somewhere remote from me.

While I had been thinking of this, the bees had begun to misbehave. Their yellow had become red and they were forming patterns, which I discovered were letters of the alphabet. In another moment they were combining into words. Four words to be precise, written in scarlet letters and repeated over and over again.

The mark of Cain. The mark of Cain. The mark of Cain.

'I think he's awake,' Margaret said. 'God be thanked.'

'His eyes are open. But that don't mean a thing.'

'Aren't they blue, Sam? I never noticed how blue they were.'

'His eyes are the same as they always were, you foolish woman. It's the opium. Makes the pupils smaller. I've seen it a hundred times.'

I tried to say, 'Of course I'm awake.'

My father was sitting beside me now. He was smiling.

On Tuesday morning, Sam brought me the letter. I was downstairs, though in my bedgown.

By this time the effect of the medicine had passed its peak. I had emerged strangely refreshed from the trance-like state which had paralysed me a few hours earlier. I was alert and capable of movement. I felt some discomfort, though the laudanum masked the worst of it. The pain was a sleeping tiger, its claws unsheathed and resting on my skin, but not as yet digging deep into it.

'It come by hand, master,' he said. 'Messenger's waiting for an answer in the kitchen.' Unable to contain himself, he spat in the empty fireplace. 'Proud as a cock on his own dunghill.'

The seal told me who had sent the letter. I unfolded it.

Call at my lodging before midday. WC

There was a tap on the door, and Cat entered the room. Without a word, I handed her the letter.

She glanced at it, and then at me. 'Will you go?'

'I have to see him sooner or later. And the sooner the better. Tomorrow the Fire Court will meet, and they will settle Dragon Yard, one way or the other.'

'They say Chiffinch has the King's ear, and can make him do whatever he wants.'

'He has the King's ear,' I said. 'But the King isn't a fool, and Chiffinch won't want to tell him what he's been doing. I saw him with Limbury just before he tried to send me off to Scotland. I think he's been taking bribes from him.'

'Are you well enough to go anywhere?' she said. 'You should see yourself.'

Sam helped me dress. Despite his rough manner, he was deft and gentle in his movements. He hissed through his teeth as he brushed my coat.

'It's filthy,' he said. 'What were you doing with Mistress Hakesby yesterday? Rolling in the mud?'

'Hold your tongue.' I saw the leer on his face and I would have thrown something at him if I had had the energy. 'Fetch a hackney. You'd better come with me to Whitehall.'

We were on our way in half an hour. The pain was worse – I had taken a second, though smaller, dose of laudanum but it didn't protect me from the jolting of the hackney. I didn't like leaving Cat and Margaret alone in Infirmary Close but I needed Sam in case my condition worsened – or in case I was attacked.

At Whitehall, I left him to wait for me in the Great Court. Chiffinch's lodgings were close to the Privy Stairs and the King's private apartments. I found him in his study, making up his accounts. When the servant announced me, he closed the book and beckoned me to stand before him.

He studied me. 'A periwig, eh? You are becoming quite the gentleman, Marwood. I suppose you'll soon be strutting about Whitehall with a sword at your side.'

'I lost most of my own hair in the fire, sir.'

'Ah. At Clifford's Inn. So I'm to understand that your injuries prevented you from going to Scotland?'

'Yes, sir.'

'You've failed me, then. And failed the King, too.'

'I'm sorry for it, sir,' I said. 'But what could I do? I was in such—'

'What could you do?' he interrupted, banging the palm of his hand on the desk. 'You could have done nothing! But you chose, from your own wilfulness, to poke your nose into affairs that don't concern you. And this is the price you pay.'

I stared at him.

'Enough of your insolence!' he roared, as if I had said something to contradict him. 'Well?'

'Forgive me, sir, but I don't understand what you want of me.'

'You understand well enough.' Chiffinch leaned forward and said in a soft, insinuating voice, 'Listen to me. I am a reasonable man, Marwood. Here is what we shall do. You will tell me everything you know, everything you have done, everything you suspect, that touches on this affair of the Fire Court and Clifford's Inn. I want know about the death of that clerk you tried to save, and about the murder of Mistress Hampney. You'll tell me what Mr Williamson has been doing, too. Yes? And then you will do nothing more in the matter – you will put it entirely from your mind. And, in return, we shall say no more about your derelictions of duty. You will recover from your injuries, you will remain as clerk to the Board of Red Cloth, and all will go on happily as before.' He hesitated, fixing me with his watery, bloodshot eyes, and went on, 'And perhaps we may find other emoluments for you, in the fullness of time. One thing leads to another for those who are obliging, and know how to fit in.'

He waited for me to reply. 'Well? Well?'

'You are very good, sir,' I said, fixing my eyes on a spot on the wall six inches above his head.

He sighed. 'You have to choose, Marwood.' His voice had lost its unnatural softness. 'Either you do as I wish, and take the consequences. Or you don't do as I wish, and you take the consequences of that. Remember, your clerkship at the Board of Red Cloth is not yours absolutely. You can lose it tomorrow, and all that goes with it.' He clicked thumb and finger. 'Like that. In the twinkling of an eye.'

To lose the clerkship and its perquisites would be bad enough. But there was worse: Mr Chiffinch had been my patron, and at a stroke he would become my enemy.

'You have to choose, Marwood,' he repeated. 'So be wise as the serpent.'

Williamson had told me that I had to choose as well, and it was the same choice: a man cannot serve two masters, so which was mine to be?

But I would not say the word to Chiffinch, any word.

In the end, he lost patience. 'God rot you, you son of a whore,' he said. 'Get out of my sight before I have them throw you out.'

By and large Williamson's face was not a useful guide to his feelings. Most of the time it was rather less expressive than a block of wood. But I had studied him for almost a year, trying to discover what lay behind the blank expression, the curt words and the many silences. I was almost certain that he was pleased with me.

I had gone to him at Scotland Yard immediately after I had seen Chiffinch, though I wanted nothing more than to go back to Infirmary Close and take another dose of laudanum. I stood before him in his private room, trembling slightly, and told him what had passed with my other master.

Williamson seemed unaware of my discomfort. 'Poor Mr Chiffinch,' he said. 'A man could almost feel sorry for him. I know it cannot please you to lose your employment at the Board of Red Cloth, but you will find it's for the best.'

It might be for the best as far as Williamson was concerned. It was different for me. No man feels unalloyed pleasure at being forced to resign almost half his income and acquiring a powerful enemy in the process.

'Nevertheless,' he went on, 'I don't quite see our way clear yet.'

'But Limbury must be behind the murders, sir.'

'Of course.' Williamson held up his right hand and counted off the points on the fingers. 'One, we have the verses in his handwriting, which show he was Mistress Hampney's lover. Two, the Dragon Yard case at the Fire Court was clearly his reason for courting her. Three, she rejects him – or more probably his wish for her support – and they quarrel. Four, he kills her to keep her quiet; it would not do for his wife to hear about it, for a start – they say he depends on her father's assistance to live in the manner he does. Perhaps, in her anger, she threatened to expose him. She had friends. She was not some tuppenny drab he could afford to ignore.'

I stretched out a hand and rested it on the back of the settle by the fireplace. I was afraid I would faint.

Williamson's eyes flickered. He said: 'Then the Fire Court clerk – Chelling, was it? – threatens to expose Limbury's assignation with Mistress Hampney in Clifford's Inn, and so he must be killed as well. We might have thought his death an accident, if you had not been there. Limbury knows this, and he persuades Chiffinch to manufacture a reason for you to be sent away. A bribe is usually the only argument that convinces Chiffinch. Then there's the attempt to burn down your house, which could have killed you all.' He paused, compressing his lips. 'And indeed myself, as it happened. It smacked of desperation. Finally, he kills Mistress Hampney's maid, the one person who knew him as her mistress's lover, to shut her mouth. Or perhaps he has her killed – it's all one.'

'There was a dog at the maid's cottage. It had been stabbed with a sword, I think.'

'Sit down, you fool,' Williamson said, standing up suddenly and taking my arm. 'Before you fall down.'

He helped me to the settle. 'The trouble is,' he went on, 'there's a world of difference between what we know and what we can prove. Chiffinch and Limbury are not common people. We have nothing we could lay before the King – or before a justice, come to that.'

'Dragon Yard comes up before the Fire Court tomorrow,' I said. 'If I were there . . . '

'You can do nothing in your present condition.'

'I will be better tomorrow, if I rest today. I'm sure Sir Philip Limbury will be at Clifford's Inn. I should like to see him, sir. And to have him see me.'

He raised his eyebrows. 'To test his nerve?'

I nodded.

'It can't harm, I suppose, in the want of anything better. If you are well enough. And it would be useful to have a report of what passes when the case is heard.' Williamson was still standing, and he moved a little to improve his view of the damaged side of my face. 'And it would show Sir Philip someone suspects what he's done.'

'There's also Mr Gromwell,' I said. 'The gentleman at Clifford's Inn, whose room was used for Limbury's assignation with Mistress Hampney. If he sees my face, it might unsettle him . . . he might even be persuaded to give evidence against Sir Philip.'

'A long shot,' Williamson said.

'As you said yourself, sir. For want of anything better.'

'Be with people at all times. Take your servant with you.

The cripple. Better than nothing. When's the case due to be heard?'

'In the morning.'

'Then you'd better come and find me afterwards and tell me what passes. I'll be at the Middle Temple. Ask at the lodge for Mr Robarts.'

Williamson sent me away. As I left, he offered to send someone to fetch me a hackney, another uncharacteristic kindness. I told him Sam was waiting and would do what was needed.

Clinging to the balustrade, I went downstairs, step by painful step. I wished I could sleep for ever. It was not just the pain that made me long for oblivion. My spirits were depressed. Since my father's death, nothing had gone right for me, and I could not see how matters could ever improve.

Sam was in the yard below. I saw him glance at me. Only a glance. He did not raise a hand in greeting or move towards me. Instead he turned his head and stared at the archway that led into the court where the Guard House was.

I followed the direction of his gaze. A tall, thin man was standing there. He looked up for a moment, perhaps catching sight of me, and I saw his face. It seemed to have collapsed in on itself, so that the tip of the nose almost touched the chin.

It was Sourface, the man I had seen at Clifford's Inn, guarding the private door to Staircase XIII from the alley beside the Half Moon tavern. I had also seen him in Fetter Lane, watching me when I had been into the ruins to see Mistress Hampney's body. According to Hakesby's draughtsman, he had also followed me back to the Savoy after the fire in Chelling's chambers.

Sam hobbled away to the gate leading to Whitehall, where the hackneys and the sedan chairs were waiting for hire. I waited a moment and then followed him, pretending to be oblivious of the watcher behind me.

I passed through the gate. The street was busy – people were always coming and going in Whitehall – but Sam had already brought up a hackney, which was waiting twenty yards away. He helped me up the steps and then scrambled in beside me.

The driver cracked his whip and we set off at a decorous pace in the direction of Charing Cross. For a moment, Sam put his eye to the crack of light between the blind and the opening it covered. With a grunt, he sat back in the gloom and rested his crutch against the seat.

'He followed us out of the gate,' he said. 'He's looking around. Not sure where we are.'

'Sourface,' I said. 'You remember?'

Sam nodded. 'He was talking to someone before you came out. A courtier.'

'What was he like?'

'A tall dark gentleman, in black. I asked the guard on the gate if he knew him. His name's—'

'Limbury,' I said. 'Sir Philip Limbury.'

CHAPTER THIRTY-SIX

JEMIMA WAITED ALL day for Philip to return. She had not seen him since their last bitter encounter in the afternoon of the previous day. He did not come. He did not even send word.

In the evening, Mary made her ready for bed as usual. She wanted to stay with her mistress – she was as shamelessly devoted as a puppy, and sometimes just as irritating – but Jemima told her to build up the fire and leave her.

She tried to read. But Mademoiselle de Scudéry failed to hold her attention, and after a few minutes she flung the novel in the corner and gave herself up to the unsatisfactory pleasures of brooding.

Just after midnight, she heard Philip's knock on the street door below. This time she did not wait for him to go to his room. Wrapping the bedgown around her, she took up a candle and padded to the door of her chamber. She was waiting in the doorway when he came slowly up the stairs. Richard was beside him, lighting his way.

'Madam,' Philip said coldly as he reached the landing. 'Your servant.'

'I wish to speak to you, sir.'

'I'm not in the humour. I'm tired. Tomorrow.'

'It won't wait. Mr Chiffinch has been here. I have a message from him.'

Philip sighed. 'Go to my chamber,' he said to Richard. 'I won't be long.'

He followed Jemima into her bedroom. She sat by the dying fire. He stood on the other side of the chimney piece, looking at her.

'Chiffinch?' His voice was low. 'What the devil was he doing here?'

'Where have you been all this time? He said he couldn't find you at Whitehall.'

'I had business with Gromwell,' Philip snapped. 'Chiffinch. Tell me about Chiffinch.'

'He says that you must take me to the country to stay with my father. As soon as you can manage.'

'I've no wish to go to Syre.'

'But you must. Chiffinch says you must apply to leave Court for a while.'

'It is impossible. I have my duties at the Bedchamber.'

'You're to say it is my father's health that is the reason. Or mine, I suppose. In any case, we must leave London.'

Philip scowled at her. 'If Chiffinch wanted to say this to me, he could have written a letter. Is this some nonsense of yours?'

'Ask the servants if you don't believe me. Chiffinch was here.'

'But what possible purpose would be served by our going away?'

'I don't know.' She watched him closely. 'But perhaps you do. He told me to say that the reason has to do with the Fire Court. Does that give you a clue?'

He winced. 'My case is coming up before the court tomorrow.'

'I know that. So does he.' She hesitated, and then decided that there was no need to skirt around the matter. 'I imagine this has to do with the scrawny old whore who was murdered. Whose mistress was she? Yours or Gromwell's?'

It happened so fast that she didn't see it coming. His right hand whipped out from his side. He slapped her cheek so hard that the force of it threw her against the arm of her chair, winding her. Her head snapped over, wrenching her neck. The pain of it was so sudden, and so acute, that she shrieked.

He turned and left the room without a word.

It was the first time in their marriage that he had hit her. All that she had wanted was for him to say that he loved her, only her, and that he was true to her. And this was his reply.

Jemima stood up, picked up her candle and walked unsteadily to the dressing table. She heard movement above her head and Mary's feet stumbling down the stairs from the attic where the maids slept.

Jemima sat down before her mirror. She was breathing rapidly, but she could not fill her lungs with enough air. She stared at her face in the glass.

At the marks on the left cheek and the marks on the right. Her face was all of a piece now.

CHAPTER THIRTY-SEVEN

AFTER THE RAIN, the morning was bright with sun and unexpectedly warm under a cloudless sky. Clifford's Inn looked newly washed, though this was not to its advantage as the hard, unforgiving light revealed the shabbiness of the place, and left it nowhere to hide.

Cat arrived when the Fire Court was already in session. She climbed the steps to the gallery. She made her way to one end of a bench near the back.

Marwood had wanted her to stay in the safety of the Savoy, but she had argued forcefully that the Fire Court was such a public place that she would be as safe there as anywhere – and so, for that matter, would he. There was a risk that Gromwell would recognize her, but her cloak shielded her face and it was gloomy at the back of the gallery. Besides, she could use her shorthand to make a record of the proceedings for Mr Williamson. And what if poor Mr Hakesby should have need of her?

Cat peered over the balustrade and down to the hall below. Hakesby was standing with Poulton, with Brennan nearby.

335

They were looking towards the dais where the three judges were sitting at their table.

Marwood was further back; he was leaning against the wall with Sam by his side. He was watching Sir Philip Limbury, who was standing close to the dais, flanked by his attorney and the tall figure of Mr Gromwell.

Cat wrote in her notebook, the shorthand symbols recording what was passing around her. The same three judges as last week – Wyndham, Twisden and Rainsford.

The first case, which involved a messuage called the Artichoke, three lawyers, an irascible alderman and an aggrieved linen draper, wound its way to a conclusion that was, on the whole, in the latter's favour. The judges retired for a break. Many people left the hall. The dais remained empty, apart from a servant of the court who was laying out fresh paper on the judges' table and checking inkwells and shakers of sand.

There was a great bustle outside, and the sound of raised voices. The noise drew closer. Cat heard feet on the stairs. A man appeared in the doorway, and called back over his shoulder, 'Plenty of room, mistress. But we can clear it completely if you want.'

A maid appeared, and looked about her. Ignoring Cat and the other women, she looked out over the hall. Two women were sitting on the bench at the very front of the gallery.

'Move back,' the maid said to them. 'Both of you. My lady needs this.' She glanced at the rest of the women. 'You can stay where you are. But keep your distance.'

The women she had displaced muttered angrily. But the manservant came to stand beside the maid. He was a burly, silent man, one of the porters at Clifford's Inn. His presence was enough to reinforce the maid's orders. A boy appeared with an armful of cushions and shawls, which he arranged according to the maid's directions on the bench at the front.

While he was doing this, the judges returned to the dais, and the hall rapidly filled up again. This time there were more people than before.

A lady was ushered on to the gallery. She was heavily veiled, and wore a wide hat and a fine travelling cloak. Her arrival made a considerable commotion. The maid escorted her mistress to the bench at the front with as much care as if she were as frangible as glass.

Limbury's lady? Cat scribbled, the pencil travelling rapidly across the paper, less for Williamson than for herself. *Come to gloat with her cartload of monkeys?*

The judges had sat down, but one of them, seeing the lady's arrival, rose to his feet and bowed. The veiled lady inclined her head in reply.

Sir Thomas Twisden bows to her. Limbury looks up, then Gromwell, but both look away, and they mutter together.

Marwood had seen what was going on, too. But Poulton and Hakesby were still deep in conversation.

The clerk called the court to order, and Judge Wyndham reopened the Dragon Yard hearing by ordering those concerned to approach the dais.

Poor Mr Hakesby is so unsteady. Why doesn't Poulton or Brennan offer him their arm?

Browning, Limbury's lawyer, brushed Hakesby's shoulder as he passed, which made the old man clutch at Poulton's sleeve. Poulton, his face pale and haggard, glanced at Hakesby's hand as if he could not understand what it was doing there, or even what it was.

Limbury and Twisden seem to nod to each other.

'This matter should not detain us long,' Wyndham said. 'We have already heard the main points of the case, and the arguments on both sides. The Court wants to strike a balance between the interested parties. On the one hand, the freeholder, Sir Philip Limbury, wishes to cancel the outstanding leases on the site and rebuild over the entire ground on a new design. He offers compensation to the leaseholders. A minority of the leaseholders would accept the compensation. But many of the other leaseholders, notably Mr Poulton, desire to rebuild themselves and renegotiate the leases for longer terms and at lower rents, to take account of their investment in the property, which would be substantial. Both schemes have merits and can be put into action almost immediately.'

He paused, which gave Cat time to scribble *A fair summary, though Hakesby's scheme is more extensive and—*

'The decision now rests on a single point,' the judge continued. 'First we need to establish who now owns the leases formerly possessed by the late Mistress Hampney. They are long leases, which cover a substantial part of the Dragon Yard site along Cheapside. The support of their new owner will shift the balance of our verdict to one side or the other, though of course we shall consult the interests of all parties in our settlement. The question turns on whether the lady transferred ownership of the leases before her death or altered the terms of the will she made at the time of her wedding to the late Mr Hampney. If neither of these is the case, then the old will applies. When we have established this, we shall be able to make our decision. Who speaks for Mr Poulton?'

'I do, my lord.' Hakesby shuffled closer to the judges' table, forcing Gromwell to step aside. He straightened himself and faced them. *It's not possible. He looks taller, broader and younger.* 'Mr Hakesby, sir, the surveyor.'

'I know who you are, sir. Continue.'

'My lords, my client Mr Poulton has caused his late niece's papers to be searched at her London lodgings.' Hakesby's voice was firmer than usual, and clear enough to be heard even in the gallery. 'There is no sign of a new will, or any mention of her Dragon Yard leaseholds. He has sent to Lincoln, as the court ordered last week, and I have here the letter from the attorney with whom she dealt about her late husband's estate. If you remember, it was suggested that Mistress Hampney might have taken the opportunity to make another will while she was there. No evidence has come to light that she made a more recent will. Nor was there any evidence that she transferred ownership or control of her Dragon Yard leaseholds.'

'You can't prove that,' Gromwell shouted.

'Hold your tongue, sir,' Wyndham snapped, 'or I'll have you ejected from the court.'

'I have an affidavit from the attorney here confirming what I have told you,' Hakesby went on.

'Hand it up.'

An usher stepped forward to take the letter from Brennan.

'As you will see, my lord, the attorney writes that he asked Mistress Hampney if she would like him to draw up a new will for her, taking account of her husband's death and any other testamentary changes she might want, but she said there was no need for the expense and trouble of a new will as the old one would do perfectly well.'

'When will it be proved?'

Hakesby looked at Poulton, who gave him a sheaf of papers. 'As soon as possible – but I have here letters from two lawyers who deal mainly in probate giving as their opinion that the will is straightforward in its terms, and that on the face of it there is no reason to believe it could be successfully contested. So the fact of the matter, my lord, is that my client, Mr Poulton, has every reason to believe he controls the head leases for most of Dragon Yard. And – as we heard last week – many of those with an interest in the subleases will be glad to support him. As you know, he also owns an adjacent free-hold, so his plans cover a larger area than Sir Philip's.'

Poulton turns his head – he's smiling, though he looks like death . . . he stares at Limbury.

Without waiting for an order, Brennan handed the letters to the usher, who carried them to the judges.

Wyndham reads the letters one by one and passes them to the others. Twisden writes something on a piece of paper and slides it to Wyndham. They put their heads together and whisper. Why are they so slow?

On the gallery, the porter was blocking the door to the stairs, preventing others from coming up. The maid and the boy were standing to one side. As for the lady herself—

Sitting bolt upright in the middle of the bench at the front. As if she's sitting under a preacher in church, and daren't move an inch in case God strikes her dead. All alone. The maid keeps glancing at the rest of us.

Judge Wyndham signalled to his clerk, who called the court to order. Silence settled over the body of the hall.

'We are in agreement –' his eyes flicked towards Twisden and then back to the hall '– that, for the good of the City and in the best interests of the majority of those concerned in this case, Dragon Yard should be rebuilt according to Mr Poulton's plans, and at his cost, with newly drawn-up leaseholds of forty-two years, with rents to be fixed at—'

'By God, my lord, this will not do,' Limbury burst out.

Wyndham looked coolly at him. 'Sir Philip,' he said with cold courtesy, 'you may of course appeal, but not at this moment or in this way. As Mr Browning will tell you, you must set down your grounds for appeal in writing within seven days, as required by Section X of the Rebuilding Act. But I must warn you that we do not look kindly on appeals, any more than we look kindly on interruptions. They delay the work of the court. Costs may well be awarded against the appellants.'

Hakesby swayed on his feet. This time Poulton noticed, and gestured to Brennan, who at last came forward to help his master.

Browning tugged Limbury's sleeve and whispered something in his ear.

Wyndham glanced at his notes and opened his mouth to continue, but

—the veiled lady rises to her feet so sharply that she knocks over the bench behind. The noise makes everyone stare up at her. And she stares down at them, as if she's in a box at the theatre. She starts to laugh—

Once more, the usher called for silence. The lady stopped laughing. Her maid and the boy restored the bench to its position behind her. She gave no sign of noticing. She was standing almost motionless. Sitting behind her, Cat thought the border of the veil was trembling.

Judge Wyndham read out the terms of the verdict, itemizing the costs of the new leases, in an uninflected voice that made dull listening unless you were directly affected.

Cat continued her shorthand record, but she stopped when a movement distracted her. The lady had raised her right hand. The maid hurried to her mistress's side. There was an exchange of whispers. The maid gestured to the porter.

The lady drew her cloak around her. She walked in a slow and stately fashion towards the door to the stairs, with the maid attending her. The boy gathered up her belongings from the bench.

Though the party did not make a great deal of noise, their departure aroused considerable interest in the hall below. Even Wyndham hesitated in his reading, his eyes rising to the gallery, though his face remained expressionless. Preceded by her maid, the lady began to descend the stairs.

Limbury turned abruptly and pushed his way through the crowd towards the door to the passage. Gromwell murmured something to Browning and then followed Limbury.

The judge resumed his reading. The porter and the boy left the gallery. Cat heard raised voices below. She closed her notebook and slipped on to the stairs.

'Well, madam,' Limbury was saying below, 'you've made a spectacle of yourself before the world. I hope you're satisfied.'

'Take your hands off me.'

'You are my wife. I shall lay my hands where I please.'

Cat went down the stairs. She hesitated in the archway at the bottom. Apart from herself, the Limburys and their servants were alone in the passage. Sir Philip had grasped his wife by the wrist; he towered over her, his back to Cat. Gromwell stood between them and the maid and the boy. The porter had vanished.

'You make a fool of me at your peril,' Limbury went on, his voice low but hard.

'You do that yourself, without any help from me.' Lady Limbury's veil trembled. 'You and that whore.' She waved her free hand at the servants. 'Take me to the coach.'

The maid started forward. Gromwell blocked her path. The maid caught sight of Cat standing in the archway, and her eyes widened. Gromwell caught the movement and glanced in the same direction.

In the split second that followed, Cat registered the fact that there was a bandage wrapped around the palm of Gromwell's right hand.

Recognition spread over his face when he saw her. 'By God! It's the little thief—'

He broke off and plunged towards her. Lady Limbury's maid took advantage of the distraction and ran to her mistress. Cat darted past Lady Limbury to escape from Gromwell. She slipped her free hand into her pocket. Her fingers closed around the handle of the knife. She ripped the blade from its sheath.

'Philip,' Gromwell said urgently. 'It's that wench I caught prying the other day.'

But Limbury was still talking to his wife. 'I've had enough. Enough of your clinging ways, your play-acting, your lies, your schemes' – his voice rose slightly – 'and most of all your damned ugliness.'

He let go of her suddenly. She slumped against the wall, her head drooping. Limbury snatched at the veil and tugged. The veil fluttered to the ground, along with the hat that had helped to hold it in place. His wife crouched, covering the side of her face with her hands.

'You'll hide no more.' Limbury pulled her hands away. 'Let the world see what you are.'

343

Cat was not aware of making a decision. Had she thought rationally, she would have run away from Gromwell, who was making his way towards her. But she was in a place beyond calculation, beyond thought even, where only action existed. Which was why, quite of its own volition, her right hand shot forward and lunged with the knife towards Sir Philip's thigh. The blade slipped through the black velvet of his wide breeches. The tip met the resistance of skin. Cat pressed harder.

It was little more than a pinprick, not even half an inch deep. Limbury screamed with pain. He released his wife and swung to face Cat, one hand dropping to his sword, the other to the wound in his leg.

Cat backed away. Lady Limbury ran to her maid. The door to the hall opened. Marwood was on the threshold. Behind him was the crowded hall.

For an instant, no one spoke or moved in the passage.

'Mr Gromwell!' Marwood said. 'How do you do?'

He moved smoothly between Cat and Gromwell. 'You remember me, sir, I hope? We met the other day when I knocked on your door to ask if my father had called on you.'

Sam followed his master through the door. 'Your pardon, sir. Not in your way, am I? Since the damned Dutch took off my foot, I've been as clumsy as a baby.'

The Fire Court session had finished. Others were now pressing to leave the hall. Cat swerved round Gromwell and escaped into the narrow court.

The lady and her maid had already left. They were almost at the Fleet Street gate, with the boy trotting after them, burdened with his mistress's cushions and rugs. They passed through the archway with Cat hard at their heels.

Lady Limbury looked back. She had her gloved hands clamped to the side of her face. The hands were too small to cover all that was marred. A claret-coloured birthmark stretched from the hairline to the neck, covering most of the right-hand side of the face. The left-hand side was untouched, the face of a plain, unremarkable woman with small eyes and a long, thin nose.

In Fleet Street, a coach-and-four was drawn up near the bookstalls by the church, half blocking the narrow roadway before Temple Bar. It had a gentleman's coat of arms painted on the door and a large coachman on the box, with a whip in his hand.

Lady Limbury climbed into the coach. She sat down facing the horses, presenting her left cheek to the world. She looked past the maid to Cat, who was standing irresolute on the pavement. 'You'd better come with us for now. God knows what they'll do to you if they catch you.'

The maid sat down beside her mistress. Cat scrambled inside and sat opposite them. Lady Limbury draped an Indian shawl over her head, masking most of her face. The maid looked blankly at Cat. The boy closed the door.

The whip cracked, and with a jerk the coach moved off. The blinds were down over the glass windows. None of the three women spoke. Around them was the raucous, familiar din of London.

In the distance, a man was shouting, but the sound grew steadily fainter as the coach picked up speed. They were travelling east into the ruins of the City.

CHAPTER THIRTY-EIGHT

'WHERE IS SHE?' Mr Hakesby said. 'Brennan says he saw her on the gallery.' He clutched Brennan's arm. 'You're sure it was her?'

'Sure as the coat on my back.'

'She went towards Fleet Street, sir,' I said. 'She was in a hurry. I doubt you'll catch her now.'

'Why would she run away? She must have seen me, and heard me speak.'

Mr Poulton came out of the hall behind them. He was smiling and looked ten years younger. 'Have you found your cousin yet, Hakesby?'

'No, sir. Mr Marwood saw her.'

Their words washed over me like water. Perhaps it was the opium, but I felt entirely removed from what was going on. I was more than happy to stay where I was, doing nothing except lean against the wall of the passage, while Poulton and Hakesby talked. The hall was now empty apart from a solitary clerk clearing the papers and writing materials from the judges' table.

Gromwell and Limbury had gone. I had sent Sam to talk to the porter on the Fleet Street gate.

'It is most satisfactory,' Poulton was saying. 'Hakesby, you argued my case as well as any lawyer. And to be granted such long leases, and on such generous terms! There's nothing to prevent us starting tomorrow. You'll need ready money, of course, when you start in earnest. I shall arrange it in the morning.' He rubbed his hands. 'I can't wait to tell Mistress Lee.'

I noticed that the three of them – Poulton, Hakesby and Brennan – were looking strangely at me. 'What is it?' I said.

Mr Hakesby coughed. 'Your wig, sir, I – ah . . . '

I raised my hand. In the recent excitement, the left side of the periwig had been pushed back over the shoulder, exposing some of the fire-scarred tissue beneath. I rearranged it. 'Forgive me, sir,' Hakesby said. 'I – I had forgot. Poor Chelling – and you.'

'There's a difference,' I said sourly. 'Chelling's dead. I'm alive.'

'Yes, but I did not realize that—' He broke off. 'You poor fellow.'

Poulton asked Hakesby a question about the drainage at Dragon Yard, perhaps as a kindly attempt to distract the conversation from my injuries.

I should be grateful to be alive, I reminded myself, unlike poor Chelling. A man who was prodigal with gossip. My unruly memory turned a somersault, and I remembered a crumb of information he had let fall while he was drinking himself into a stupor that day in the Devil.

'Marwood?' Hakesby said. 'Marwood?'

A crumb? Memory turned another somersault. No. Two.

I heard the tapping of Sam's crutch before I saw him. 'What news?' I said, turning away from Hakesby and lowering my voice.

'The porter's lad followed them into Fleet Street, in case he could earn something from them,' he murmured. 'But he was out of luck. Mistress Hakesby went off in a glass coach with the lady.'

'Which way?'

'East. Into the City. Shall I find us a hackney, master?'

'No. I want you to find someone first.'

'It was laden,' Sam said. 'The coach, I mean. And four horses. The lad said it looked like they were going on a journey.'

She was a snaggletoothed woman with a freckled face and a fringe of greasy curls escaping from under her cap. She could have been any age from twenty-five to fifty-five. She rose from a curtsy, smoothing a patched brown skirt with grubby hands, and casting a longing glance at the pot of beer on the table.

'Miriam, sir,' Sam said, gesturing towards her with the air of a showman. 'As your worship desired.'

Miriam squinted up at me, trying to make out my features beneath the brim of my hat. We were in a yard behind the Half Moon, where the tavern's poorer customers could buy their drinks at a hatch in the wall.

I nodded at the beer. 'You'd rather drink good, strong ale, I'll be bound.'

She grinned unexpectedly. 'Who wouldn't, master?'

'Then you shall.' I turned to Sam, feeling for my purse. 'Fetch a jug of ale.' I saw his face and took pity on him. 'And a pot for yourself.'

He joined the knot of people at the hatch. I leaned against the wall. Miriam shifted uneasily under my gaze.

'Drink your beer. Don't let it go to waste.'

She seized the pot and swallowed what was in it as fast as she could.

I jerked a thumb in the direction of the roof of New Building. 'I hear you work there.'

'Yes, master. Clifford's Inn.'

Sam was already returning towards us, dextrously managing his crutch, the jug of ale and a pot.

I said, 'Who do you work for?'

Her eyes were on Sam. 'Some of the gentlemen, sir. Staircase Fourteen.'

'What do you do?'

'Clean the chambers, make the beds.'

'What else?'

'I used to help with the staircase next door too. Thirteen. But that was before the Fire.'

That set my mind on another track. 'Is there a connecting door between the staircases?'

She nodded vigorously. 'It's in the servant's closet on Mr Gromwell's landing. Between his door and Mr Gorvin's.' Alarm spread across her grubby face. 'Is there something wrong? I never stole a—'

'Nothing's wrong. And here's the ale.' I motioned Sam to pour it. 'What else do you do there?'

'I empty the pots in the morning, and do the fires, and I bring up coals. I'm only there till dinnertime.'

I watched her bury her face in the pot of ale. I said, 'And who are these gentlemen?'

I already knew the answers to this and earlier questions.

Sam had bought the information at the cost of sixpence from the aged and infinitely corruptible porter at the Fetter Lane gate, including Miriam's name and where to find her.

'There's Mr Moran, sir, and Mr Drury and Mr Bews. Mr Gromwell, Mr Gorvin and Mr Harrison.'

'Are the gentlemen kind to you?'

'I don't see much of them, sir. They're either asleep or out when I'm there. They all keep a man to serve them and look after their clothes, and give me my orders.'

'What about Mr Gromwell? Be open with me. You won't regret it.'

She glanced about her as if fearing we were overheard. She lowered her voice. 'He's rough in manner, sir. And he's not a generous gentleman. He goes weeks without paying, sometimes. He's got a temper, too. But he's one of the governors of the Inn, so we have to mind our step with him.'

'Tell me, about three weeks ago, when you cleaned his chambers, were they in any way unusual?'

Miriam looked blankly at me.

'I mean anything about them that was out of the common way.'

She smiled. 'Oh – you mean the day when the furniture was all arsey-turvey? Is that it?'

I smiled and nodded to Sam, who refilled her pot and then his own. 'When was this?'

'Three weeks ago, maybe?' Miriam stared at me over the rim of her pot. 'It was a day I had orders to go in early, make everything especially neat and clean. He had some new furniture coming, they told me. But when I came in next morning there was nothing new there. All the old stuff was still there – but all out of place – huddled against one wall. I reckon he must have got merry with his friends, and they fancied a change, and then they thought they'd have another bottle instead when they were halfway through. Or they were playing a game that needed the space. God knows what they get up to when they're in their cups.'

'Was there a brightly coloured carpet there? Or a couch?'

'No. He never had anything like that.' Miriam's face brightened and she smacked her lips. 'But I found a couple of sweetmeats in the hearth that morning. He must have thrown them away. Nothing wrong with them. I rinsed the ash off and had them for breakfast.'

'Can you read?'

Miriam shook her head. 'I leave that to the gentlemen.'

'You see, I need a piece of Mr Gromwell's handwriting. Anything will do.'

A doubtful expression crossed her face. 'I couldn't take anything from his room, master. More than the job's worth . . . And it would be wrong, wouldn't it?'

'No, no.' I smiled at her, fighting an urge to scratch the savage itching of healing skin under my periwig. 'I don't want you to take anything. I just want to see what his handwriting looks like. Perhaps you could borrow something. Or bring me a paper he's thrown away or left to use as a spill for the fire. Anything at all, as long as it has his writing on.' I took a shilling from my purse. 'Such a small service. And it will earn you this.'

'Why do you need it, master?'

'It's a wager,' I said. 'That's all. My friend and I have a wager about who wrote something, and when I know what Mr Gromwell's hand is like, I'll win.'

Her expression cleared. 'Will this do then?' She dug her

hand into her skirt and took out a crumpled sheet of paper. Panic flared in her face. 'But I can't let you take it away.'

'Of course you'll have it back. I only want a sight of it. Just for a moment.'

The reassurance satisfied her. She smoothed out the paper and passed it to me.

'Mr Gromwell's man give it me so the porters let me in and out. It says I work for him and the other gentlemen. Like I said, he's one of the governors, and you need to have a paper from one of them or they won't let you pass through.'

I examined the pass while she drank, her eyes following my movements over the brim of her pot. It permitted her to come and go at Clifford's Inn when serving the occupants of Staircase XIV. It was signed by Lucius Gromwell in his capacity as one of the Rules, the men who directed the affairs of Clifford's Inn.

Gromwell. Lucius Gromwell.

I looked carefully at the writing. For a moment, the pain, the itching and the tiredness dropped away from me. Mr Williamson had kept both Sir Philip Limbury's note to Hakesby and the poem that Cat and I had found among the belongings of Tabitha, Mistress Hampney's maid. But their appearance was fresh in my memory. The three pieces of writing had been written at different times and in different circumstances. Nevertheless, they looked as if the same person could have been responsible for them all – though I knew for a fact that that was not the case: Limbury had written the note to Hakesby, and Gromwell had written Miriam's pass.

Was it so very strange that their handwriting should be similar? The two men had been instructed from childhood by the same teachers: they had grown up together and they had been intimate friends at school and the university. They had probably learned their letters from the same teacher.

In that case, the handwriting of the poem stolen from Herrick – 'Whenas in Silks My CELIA goes' – could belong to either of them. As for the 'L' at the bottom of the poem, that might signify Limbury, as we had assumed until now, or – just as easily – Lucius.

I returned the pass to Miriam. Sam gave her the rest of the ale. It was strong stuff, and her face had grown flushed and her breathing more rapid. I held up the shilling. Her eyes fixed on it, like a cat's on a mouse.

'I'd prefer Mr Gromwell not to hear that we've talked together.'

She shook her head violently. 'I won't tell, I swear it. He's got such a temper, sir. He'll beat a servant as soon as look at her. Why, yesterday he struck the man that serves him, knocked a tooth out, and all because he was in a passion about the pain in his hand and the mad dog, so he—'

'What?' I snapped.

At the harshness of my voice, she cowered like a dog herself.

I softened my tone. 'I didn't mean to speak so loudly, Miriam. What's this about a dog? Tell me.'

'The one that bit him on the hand. Down to the bone it was, his man said, and he bled like a stuck pig.'

'When did this happen?'

'The day before yesterday. Mr Gromwell feared the dog was mad, and he'd soon be mad too, and he'd run through the streets foaming at the mouth.' She shivered with a sort of pleasure. 'And he'd be screaming curses at respectable folks and biting them and making them mad too . . .'

The pleasure seeped away from Miriam's face. 'But he's not gone mad yet, so maybe the dog wasn't mad in the first place. Maybe it just hated him.'

Prudence was better than pointless self-denial, I decided, for everyone's sake, not just my own.

So, to be on the safe side, I stopped briefly at an apothecary's in Fleet Street and took a modest and carefully calculated dose of laudanum. Sam looked askance at me, or I thought he did. I snapped at him, telling him to keep his eyes and thoughts to himself, and left the shop in a cloud of righteous indignation.

I ran Williamson to earth in the Middle Temple. He was dining privately with Mr Robarts, a man he often met on private business. He excused himself to his host and came out into the passage.

He led me to a deep window embrasure where we could talk unheard and largely unseen. I believe I made my report lucidly enough. I had measured the dose with great care: in moderation, I believed, the apothecary's mixture sharpened my mental faculties as well as eased the pain to a point where it was generally tolerable.

'Sir, this morning I recalled two facts that had slipped my memory. First, Gromwell's Christian name is Lucius. Secondly, Chelling told me that one of his schoolfellows is a Groom of the Bedchamber. That must mean Limbury, surely.'

Williamson frowned at me. 'Get to the point.'

'We assumed that the "L" on the poem to Celia stood for Limbury. But perhaps it stood for Lucius. And two men with the same schooling may well write a similar hand. Gromwell and Limbury do – I've just put it to the test. And then today

I heard that Gromwell has a dog bite on his hand, which could connect him to the wounded cur at the dead maidservant's cottage in Lambeth. The dog with a stab wound in his side.'

'What are you saying?' Williamson said. 'That Gromwell is the rogue in this affair? That he was Mistress Hampney's lover all along?'

'Why not, sir? He's better suited for the part. And it would make sense for Limbury to keep his distance from Mistress Hampney. Gromwell was acting for him, of course, though perhaps he had no objection to marrying her, if he could contrive it, thereby killing two birds with one stone. After all, she had money, he needs it.'

'And then he killed her when she would not do as he wished, and then killed Chelling when he threatened to unmask him. And the maidservant in Lambeth too – perhaps she tried to extort money from him as she knew he had been her mistress's lover. The poem could be taken as evidence of that.' Williamson hesitated, considering. 'You may be right, but what use is all this to me? You've given me nothing my Lord Arlington can take to the King. Chiffinch is in a strong position – as strong as any man's, because he knows the King's secrets. So if I am to hurt him, the evidence against him must be as strong as steel.'

I had expected praise from Williamson. I should have known that was almost always a vain hope. Besides, men who devote their lives to the strange, skewed world of Whitehall are not like the rest of us. They live by different rules. Williamson was less interested in finding the murderer than in gathering ammunition with which to attack Chiffinch.

I tried another line: 'Lady Limbury was at the Fire Court when the case was heard.'

'I thought she hardly stirred from her house.'

'There's no love lost between her and her husband. She came solely to mock him when he lost his case. And afterwards they met outside the hall, and the quarrel went beyond all bounds.'

'His passions outweigh both his understanding and his manners.' Williamson himself was a man who never let his own passions outweigh anything. As for his manners, they knew their place in his scheme of things and, like a good servant, appeared only when required.

'There's more,' I said. 'My lady has a large birthmark on her cheek. She covers it with a veil, but Sir Philip was so angry he tore it away from her face.' Even the memory of that scene made me uncomfortable.

'A birthmark? That's it, is it? I'd heard she was ugly as sin. Limbury wouldn't have had her if she hadn't been her father's heir. Come to that, if she'd been unblemished, Sir George Syre wouldn't have let her marry a poor man like Limbury, especially one with his reputation. But beggars can't be choosers. Did she go back to Pall Mall afterwards?'

'I don't know for sure. She went off with her servants. The porter on the Fleet Street gate at Clifford's Inn said she had a glass coach waiting for her, and she drove away as fast as she could. Four horses, and the coach was laden with luggage. They were going east. Towards the ruins.'

'If she and Limbury have quarrelled, she's probably going to her father's. Where else can she go? He lives in Kent – Syre Place is beyond Seven Oaks, on the road to Tunbridge Wells.'

Williamson paused a moment to think. I watched the lawyers criss-crossing the paths below the window. I had come a long and uncertain way from my father's death to the shabby Court intrigues of Williamson and Chiffinch.

'Talk to her, Marwood,' he said at last. 'That's the best thing to do. And do it soon, while the lady's passions run high against her husband. Tell her Lord Arlington desires to help her. Fan the flames in any way you can and she may blurt out what she knows of this affair. Does she know of an intrigue between Chiffinch and her husband? Try to persuade her to talk to me. I can be her friend in this.'

'She may be miles away by now.'

'I think not. If she continues in her own coach, they must go by the bridge. The traffic is so bad in the ruins, and it will take them an age to reach it. Once they get there, it will take at least an hour to cross to Southwark at this time of day, probably longer. If you don't catch her on the bridge, hire a horse at the Bear on the other side and go after her.'

'Sir, we can't be sure she is going to her father's house. Surely we should—'

He waved my objections aside. 'There's no time to be lost, and this is the best chance we have. You must go at once.' He found his purse. 'I shall advance you five pounds in case you have to follow her into Kent. Spare no expense to find her.' He blinked, and his familiar caution reasserted itself. 'I shall need an account of what you disburse, of course, and to whom and where.'

I nodded, wondering where I could buy laudanum on London Bridge. There must be an apothecary there or in the neighbourhood. I didn't need another dose now, but I would need more if I were riding down to Kent.

Williamson beckoned me closer. 'If we have her on our side,' he murmured, 'and if she knows something of her

357

husband's scheming with Gromwell and Chiffinch, we may be able to persuade her to appeal to the King. If she could be persuaded to write a letter to him – a memorial about the business, petitioning him to intervene – that would carry real weight. Let her make the most of Limbury's cruelty to her. The King is tender-hearted – he doesn't like to see a woman cruelly used.' He gave me a thin smile. 'Even an ill-favoured one.'

CHAPTER THIRTY-NINE

'OLD SWAN STAIRS,' I told the older of the two watermen. 'As fast as you can.'

I scrambled to the stern and sat down. Sam followed me, surprisingly agile despite his crutch. As an old sailor, he was comfortable in small boats. The two watermen pushed the boat out from Temple Stairs and began to row, swiftly picking up their rhythm.

The tide was behind us, ebbing fast, and we made good time downriver. The ruins of the city glided past us. At this hour there was plenty of activity, particularly along the wharves where gangs of labourers were clearing the rubble. Their shouts drifted across the water.

London Bridge grew steadily closer. Seen broadside from the water, the scale of it was even more impressive than it was from the land. It was about a hundred yards long, a straight, narrow street floating above the water. Though a fire – not last year's but an earlier one – had destroyed the houses at the northern end, most of its length was covered with towering buildings, distributed into three irregularly

359

shaped blocks. In the middle, a drawbridge crossed the central arch. It was occasionally raised for tall vessels when the water was calm enough to admit them. Houses and shops lined both sides, and over the centuries they had sprouted higher and higher, and wider and wider, so they now seemed impossibly tall and unstable, like plants run to seed.

The backs of the buildings overhung the river, just as their fronts overhung the roadway along the bridge. They were encrusted with closets and balconies and bay windows, many of them a series of afterthoughts added over the years.

The sun came out. The river stretched around us, a glittering and swaying monster, panting with the effort of trying to squeeze itself through the nineteen arches of the bridge. The massive piers blocked almost half the width of the river. Here at water level you felt the power of the tide, especially at times like this when, twice a day, it raged at the manmade obstruction of the bridge.

When the tide was ebbing or flowing hard, the river backed up against the partial obstacle of the bridge. With their splayed bases, the arches were narrow enough in the first place. To make matters worse, wooden starlings had been built out around them to protect the stonework from the impact of the water, which had the effect of constricting the flow still further, as did the waterwheels at either end.

Our boat was low on the water, the gunwale less than a foot above the surface. The wind was blowing briskly and the curls of my periwig were flying about my neck. I turned my head so the scars would not be visible to the others and pulled up the collar of my cloak.

The river was creaming through the arches and the water gave off a steady, rustling roar as it poured down the lower level beyond, several feet down. There were some boatmen who, if you paid enough, would take you through an arch when the tide was in flood and bring you, soaked and shaking, to the calmer waters beyond. Every year, however, the river exacted its tribute of shattered boats and drowned men.

Sam nudged me. 'Master,' he whispered in my ear. 'Over there. Starboard.'

He was pointing to another boat with two pairs of oars, this one nearer the south bank. There were three passengers, two in the stern and one perched in the bows. I squinted at the little figures, finding it hard to see them clearly because of the sway and glare of the river.

'It's Limbury,' Sam muttered. His eyes were keener than mine. 'With his friend beside him. Don't know who's in the bows.'

I guessed that Limbury and Gromwell were on the same errand as I was, trying to intercept Lady Limbury's coach. They had made the same calculations as Williamson and I. Wiser than myself, perhaps, they were making for the south end of the bridge.

It was possible that the Limburys' coach had already crossed. But Williamson had been right: at this time of day, the lumbering vehicle would not have made good time. Four horses were a hindrance, not an advantage, in the crowded streets of a city. If I were a gambling man I would have put money on the coach still being on the bridge, especially if the traffic hadn't been moving for a while.

I came to a swift decision and leaned forward. 'I've changed my mind,' I said. 'Take us to Pepper Stairs.'

'Across the river with the tide running like this?' said the

361

waterman, turning to spit over the side; a streak of silver whipped past my face, missing me by inches.

'Yes,' I said. 'And a double fare if you hurry.'

Our oars dug into the water, bringing the bow of the boat round towards the south bank. Pepper Stairs was the nearest landing stage to the bridge on the Surrey side. The rowers pulled hard, fighting the current pushing us downstream. The roar of the water was louder now, as it surged through between the piers of the bridge and plunged down to the lower level downstream.

Limbury's boat reached Pepper Stairs. I watched them disembarking and paying the boatmen. I recognized the third man now: Sourface, Limbury's servant, the man who looked as if he had a lemon in his mouth.

Sam nudged my arm again in the unmannerly way that he ought not to use to his master. He pointed up at the bridge.

'What?'

'The traffic, master. It's not moving.'

I followed the line of his finger. It was impossible to see what was going on among the buildings as they were packed so closely together, but in the clear spaces between the three blocks were stationary lines of wagons and coaches, head to tail. Even horsemen and sedan chairs had been brought to a halt.

'The stop's near the gatehouse,' Sam said.

The Great Stone Gate was at the southern end of the bridge, marking the end of the city's jurisdiction. A clump of buildings was attached to it, a hotchpotch of rooflines, turrets, balconies and windows. The queue of vehicles stretched along the visible sections of the bridge in one direction, from north to south. Traffic travelling in the other direction had been able to leave the bridge, but no more was coming on to it from the Surrey side of the river.

'There are always stops on the bridge,' the older waterman said with obvious satisfaction. 'Two or three times a day sometimes. Good for business. It's an ill wind, eh?'

Pepper Stairs was packed with people trying to hire a boat to get across. We landed there and left our boatmen holding an impromptu auction for their services.

The tower of St Mary Overie loomed over us as we followed Pepper Alley round to Borough High Street. A noisy queue of wagons and coaches stretched down the road. The Bear Tavern at Bridge Foot was packed, and its customers had spilled out on to the roadway. Tempers were souring as the queues grew longer and the crowd thickened. It wouldn't take much for people to start throwing things at each other.

I caught sight of Limbury and Gromwell, standing at Bridge Foot, the approach to the Great Stone Gate, and staring through the archway that led to the bridge. There was no sign of Sourface. I pulled Sam into the shelter of a stall selling old clothes.

We waited, watching the archway. Above the gatehouse were the long poles holding the heads of traitors – no more than skulls now, picked clean by time and birds. No new ones had been added for years, but no one had cared to remove the old ones.

In a moment or two, Sourface came out of the yard of the Bear Tavern and joined his master and Gromwell. They held a quick conference and then passed through the gateway to the bridge beyond.

I guessed that Limbury had done what I would have done – sent his servant to ask at the Bear's stables if the Limbury coach had come through. Ostlers noticed everything that went to and fro, especially if it involved horseflesh. A glass coach with four horses was not exactly inconspicuous.

Sam and I walked up to the gatehouse. One of the traitors' heads above the battlements was loose on its pole, and the wind was playing with it. The skull nodded at me. I took that as an omen, a dead man's agreement that I was doing the right thing.

Beyond the gatehouse was the street running high above the river over the bridge. The traffic kept to the left in both directions. Each carriageway was barely six feet wide. The houses on either side were jettied outwards, so the upper storeys were within an arm's reach of their neighbours opposite.

Because there was so little natural light, the street was perpetually gloomy, a fetid, slippery tunnel full of horseshit and disgruntled people. Usually there were sweepers who sluiced the dirt into the river, but they were not in evidence today.

Among such a press of people and vehicles it was difficult to keep our quarry in sight without drawing attention to ourselves. It was hard enough even to push our way through.

Only the shopkeepers were cheerful. They were doing a brisk trade, enticing people who had too much time on their hands to spend money while they waited. We passed an alehouse so packed that people could scarcely raise their pots to their lips. Next door to it was a pastry cook's whose shelves were almost empty.

A few moments later, we passed out of this block of buildings and into the open air. The wind from the river buffeted me, but I was glad of it after the stench of the street. We hung back, taking shelter behind a portly merchant and his equally portly lady.

We went into the next block of buildings. The cause of the blockage was here – a wagon and a coach going in opposite directions had locked wheels, and then the horses had panicked. A gang of labourers was now working with axes and saws and ropes, trying to deal with the mess.

By the time we had negotiated this obstacle, I thought we must have lost Limbury and Gromwell. With relief, I caught sight of Gromwell perhaps sixty yards away. He was standing before a shop talking to a large, middle-aged woman in its doorway. There was no sign of Limbury or Sourface. As I watched, Gromwell followed the woman inside.

I told Sam to wait and advanced cautiously up the street. As I drew nearer I saw that the shop was a stationer's and bookseller's. In front of it was a row of red posts to which were nailed sheets advertising new publications.

It was a substantial establishment by the standards of the bridge. It occupied the entire ground floor of an ornate house whose upper storeys billowed over the street. Above the door was a sign displaying three Bibles.

I realized that I had been here before, when I was an apprentice printer. I paused beside the shop as if by chance, as if drawn to examine the pamphlets and sermons displayed on the shelf at the front. There were no ballads or cheap broadsheets among them. This establishment was reaching for a different class of customer. Inside, there were some large, finely bound volumes, as well as folders of engravings.

Two apprentices were attending to the customers – like everywhere else, the place was packed – but there was no sign of Sourface or the woman he had been talking to. I sauntered inside and pretended to admire an engraving of my Lady Castlemaine which hung on the wall in a prominent position to tempt the gentlemen.

No one bothered me. The shop was well lit, with a bay window overlooking the river on the upstream side. Behind the counter was a doorway. Gromwell must have gone through it. Did that suggest he was known here?

The Widow Vereker had inherited the shop and business at the sign of the Three Bibles from her husband. Their customers came from Whitehall, the Law Courts, and the wealthy families of the City . . . Fine presswork, I gave her that, and prices to match.

I heard footsteps on the stairs, and Gromwell's tall figure filled the doorway. He was smiling. The middle-aged woman followed him.

'It's no trouble at all, sir,' she was saying, 'though the apartments are hardly fit for you. But I'll have them light a fire in there at least.'

He turned back to her. 'Madam, you are kindness itself. A veritable good Samaritan. We shan't trouble you for long, and I promise you won't be the poorer for it.'

'Oh – I almost forgot.' The woman was girlishly flustered by his attentions. 'The key for the outside door – going by the entry at the side of the house will save you the trouble of coming through the shop.'

He bowed and took the key she held out. Then he turned and strode towards the street door.

I had no time to escape. I examined Lady Castlemaine more closely, as if immersed like the King in the generous pleasures of her bosom, and prayed that Gromwell wouldn't look closely at me. He had seen me in my new periwig this morning, but not for long. I stooped closer and closer to my lady.

Gromwell's cloak brushed my arm as he left the shop. I let out my breath in a long sigh. I gave him a moment and then followed him outside.

There was no sign of him. I hesitated, wondering what to do. I cast my eyes up and down the street. When I stepped away from the shop, I felt a tug on my cloak. I turned, alarmed, fearing that Gromwell had noticed me in the shop after all.

The hem of my cloak had caught on a nail in one of the red posts outside the shop. The nail held in place one of Vereker's handbills. I glanced down at it, and a name leapt out at me. Thanks to my father's training, I knew that it was finely printed in a modern variant of Garamond, probably one of the new Dutch typefaces.

Lucius Gromwell, Esquire,
Master of Arts in the University of Oxford.

CHAPTER FORTY

THE INSIDE OF the coach was hot and airless. Jemima grew increasingly impatient, increasingly worried by the delay.

'How long will this last?' she burst out. 'Why can't Hal find out? Let me see outside.'

Mary raised the blind. Jemima found herself staring into a shoemaker's shop. If the coach window had been down, she could have stretched out a hand and touched the hinged shelf at the front of it, on which was displayed an array of samples. Beyond the shelf was the front room, with a shopman bowing low to her.

'Tell the man to approach. Ask him what's keeping us.'

Mary lowered the window and put her head out. The shoemaker's man told her that a wagon and a coach had entangled themselves ahead, blocking the traffic in both directions.

'Could be another half hour, mistress,' the man said, smiling invitingly and craning his head to gain a better idea of who was in the coach; Jemima shrank back from his gaze. 'Perhaps your ladyship would care to while away the time by inspecting some of our shoes. I have imported examples of the latest Paris fashions, brought over at great expense—'

'Shut the window,' Jemima ordered.

'—which are the delight of many ladies of the Court, and—'

Mary obeyed, cutting off the man in mid-sentence.

'Lower the blind.'

Then they were in the stuffy gloom of the coach once more. Jemima peered at the strange young woman who had helped her at Clifford's Inn. The girl was sitting opposite Mary, their skirts touching.

'Who are you?' Jemima demanded. 'Who's your master?'

'Mr Hakesby, madam.'

'Who is he?'

'The surveyor employed by Mr Poulton at the Dragon Yard hearing.'

'Of course.' Jemima remembered the thin old man who had made such a fool of Philip. 'Why did you come to help me?'

'Because . . .' The girl's voice acquired an edge. 'Because a man shouldn't treat a dog so, let alone his wife.'

Jemima warmed to her, though the words could have been taken as impertinent. She leaned forward and tapped her on the knee. 'You won't be the loser for it. I shall see you are rewarded.'

'Thank you, madam.' The girl sounded uninterested in the prospect of a reward, which irritated Jemima slightly.

'What's your name, girl?'

'Jane Hakesby.'

'The same surname as your master?'

'He's my cousin, madam. That's why he took me in.'

'We don't know her from Adam, mistress,' Mary interrupted. 'She could be a spy.'

Jemima knew, with the certainty of long and intimate acquaintance, that her maid was furiously jealous of the attention paid to the young stranger. 'How would you like to come to me instead?' she said, partly in gratitude and partly because she could not resist the temptation to torment Mary. 'I'll pay you more than Mr Hakesby. The work will be more fitting for you. I shall give you prettier clothes, too.'

Mary sucked in her breath. She twitched her skirt away from the stranger's.

The strange girl said nothing for a moment. Then: 'Thank you, madam. I—'

At that moment, there was a tapping on the right-hand window.

'What is it?' Jemima said. 'The fool will break the glass if he doesn't have a care.'

Mary leaned across and lowered the blind.

Philip's face was on the other side of the window. He took off his hat when he saw them and ducked his head in a parody of respect.

'Why don't they stop him?' Jemima wailed, shrinking back against the side of the coach. 'What's Hal doing? Why didn't he warn us my husband was here?'

Philip opened the door. His eyes glanced at Mary, then Cat. His eyes widened as he recognized her from the Fire Court.

Jemima wrapped the shawl around most of her face and neck. 'Go away, sir. I shall scream if you don't. I shall send for a constable. Where's Hal? I demand you send him to me.'

'Directly, madam. When Richard has finished giving him my orders.'

Jemima felt the ground sliding away beneath her feet. 'Why are you here?'

'I couldn't let my wife go unescorted to the country.' His voice was casual, as if their meeting here were no more unexpected than their chancing to pass on the stairs in the Pall Mall house. The anger he had shown at Clifford's Inn seemed to have evaporated. 'They won't clear the bridge for a while. But you can't stay here. I hoped we could hire a private room at the Bear, but they're all taken. Lucius is asking his stationer if she will let us use her parlour. If not, we may have to walk a little further.'

'Lucius . . . ? I don't want to see Lucius.'

'You can't stay in here. It's so stuffy.'

'I – I am quite comfortable as I am, thank you, sir.'

'No,' he said, his eyes moving from Jemima to Cat, and then back again. 'You are not. You must let me be the best judge of where you will be comfortable.'

For a moment, no one spoke. It was one thing for Jemima to slip away from her husband without telling him that she was going to her father's house. It was quite another to disobey what was clearly his command in public, and to his face as well. Things might have been different at Syre Place, with her father to throw his weight into the scales. But here – on London Bridge, in front of the servants and God knew how many strangers – his authority overwhelmed her. She guessed that Hal would obey his master if he had to choose between them.

'Ah – and here's Lucius coming up.' Philip turned his head. 'What luck!'

Gromwell appeared at the window, lifting his hat and smiling. 'It couldn't be better. Madam, your servant. Mistress Vereker's parlour would not be convenient – her aged mother is there. But there are apartments above that we can use – rather shabby, I'm afraid, but private and overlooking the river. They have lit a fire for us. We can send out for anything we need.'

'Admirable.' Philip held out his hand to Jemima. 'Madam. Pray let me hand you down.' He glanced at Gromwell. 'We have an unexpected guest. Look.' He nodded towards Jane Hakesby in her corner.

Gromwell's face changed. 'What's she doing here?'

'Perhaps my wife has taken a fancy to her.'

There was a flurry of movement. The girl flung herself at the opposite door, trying to open it, her hands desperately scrabbling for purchase on the handle.

'Stop her,' Gromwell snapped.

Mary's arm shot out and hooked itself around the girl's neck, dragging her back against Jemima's legs. Gromwell pushed the upper part of his body into the coach and wrapped the fingers of his left hand around the girl's thin wrist. This brought his face within inches of Jemima's. She smelled sour wine on his breath and turned her head away.

'Forgive me for incommoding you, madam,' he said to her. 'But this girl is a dangerous thief. She tried to stab your husband. We must take her before a magistrate.'

At this point, the Hakesby girl craned her head and bit Mr Gromwell's hand until he screamed like a girl.

CHAPTER FORTY-ONE

*T*HE *NATURAL CURIOSITIES of Gloucestershire.* The handbill outside Mistress Vercker's shop extolled the marvels of this forthcoming publication. It would be the first truly comprehensive account of the geography, history, antiquities and natural wonders of the county from the time of the Flood. The splendid, lavishly illustrated folio volumes would adorn any gentleman's library. The author, from a distinguished family long-settled in the county—

The clack of a latch made me look up. There was a door at the far end of the building, beyond the shop's frontage. As it opened I glimpsed a passage on the other side. Gromwell appeared, turning to lock the door behind him, which meant that he had his back to me. So that was how he had vanished so quickly when he left the shop.

He set off up the street, his sword swinging by his side. I stared after him. He was going in the direction of the City, towards the Limburys' coach probably, snarled up in the traffic. The handbill had given me an unexpected glimpse of a Gromwell I didn't know. I knew enough of antiquarians and their activities to know that such pursuits required dedication and scholarship – and, if they were to produce a book as handsome as the handbill promised – a good deal of money from someone. Was this strange obsession what had driven Gromwell to help Limbury in the first place? Underwriting the costs of a book like this would need several hundred pounds.

I walked back to Sam, who was where I had left him, loitering some fifty yards away.

'It looks like the coach is up ahead somewhere. Limbury's probably already there, and Gromwell's just gone up to join him. He went into the stationer's there, at the sign of the Three Bibles. I think they're going to let him use one of their chambers upstairs.'

'What for?'

'That's the question.'

'So what do we do?'

'We wait for the answer.'

In truth there was nothing else we could do. If I was to do what Williamson wished, I needed to talk to Lady Limbury when she was by herself. Sooner or later, I hoped, the chance would come, but it wouldn't while Gromwell and Limbury were here. If they went back to Pall Mall with Lady Limbury, I would have to give up. But if they let her travel on, or left her here, there might be an opportunity to reach her.

We didn't have long to wait – no more than ten or twelve minutes. Sam touched my arm. Further up the street, a knot of people was forcing a passage. They were tightly bunched together, despite the obstacles in their way. Two men of the party were wearing swords.

I recognized most of them. The small figure of Lady

Limbury, her face almost entirely covered by a shawl, was hanging on the arm of her husband, Sir Philip. Supporting her on the other side was the maid who had attended her at the Fire Court.

Behind them was Lucius Gromwell with his arm locked around a small woman whose head and shoulders were covered by a blanket. She was flanked on her other side by Sourface, who was gripping her arm. Her wrists were roped together in front of her.

The woman was kicking impotently at the men on either side, though it was obvious she could not see them because of the blanket over her head. She had lost one of her shoes.

The crowd parted before them but one man, braver than the rest, asked what the prisoner had done.

Gromwell scowled at him, his hand dropping to the hilt of his sword. 'A thief caught in the very act of her crime.'

The man backed away, raising his hands as if to say that he meant no harm by the question.

I didn't need to see the woman's face to know who she was. Oh God, I thought, this is all I need.

CHAPTER FORTY-TWO

WHEN THEY PULLED the blanket away, the light blinded her. A figure loomed over her, its outline wavering as if the light were eating away at its darkness.

The blanket had been thick and stuffy, smelling of horses. Cat sucked in lungfuls of air. Water roared continuously, and the very air seemed to vibrate with its restless force.

'Tell Mary to find me something to bandage my hand.' It was Gromwell's voice, harsh and assured, speaking to someone she couldn't see. 'The hellcat bit me.'

Cat's eyes were adjusting rapidly to the light. She was in a tiny room with a big window criss-crossed with bars. She was huddled on the floor in front of a box. Her arms were bound tightly, the cord biting into the skin just above the wrists. There was a draught coming from somewhere and also the smell of the river: salt and sewage, mud and seaweed.

Gromwell was standing in the doorway, scowling at her and nursing his left hand. His right hand already had a bandage on it.

Gradually her breathing subsided to its normal rate. Her wrists were painful from the rope, and she knew there would soon be bruises on her arms and on her right cheek. He had hit her as he was dragging her from the coach.

To be fair, though, she thought he would probably have hit her anyway, even if she hadn't bitten him. This, she reminded herself, was the man who had almost certainly killed two women already, Celia Hampney and her maid, Tabitha, as well as Mr Chelling. She wished she had been able to bite him harder.

'Who are you?' he said.

She moistened her lips. 'Jane Hakesby, sir.'

He snorted. 'Kin to Mr Hakesby, by any chance?'

'His cousin, sir.'

Gromwell leaned against the jamb of the door. His hat brushed the lintel. 'That's frankness, at least.'

Cat said nothing. He wasn't to know it was in fact a lie, and that she was really Catherine Lovett, daughter of the notorious Regicide. That was a small mercy.

'But it doesn't explain anything,' Gromwell went on. 'I can believe that Hakesby sent you to spy on us, but it can't be the whole story. The way you went for me. Look at that.'

He held up his left hand: her teeth had made two punctures; the wounds were rimmed with dried blood. She had bitten James Marwood once, in the heat of the moment, and drawn blood; but that had been different. Even at the time she had regretted the necessity for it.

'You broke into property belonging to Clifford's Inn and you ran off when challenged. You attacked me and drew blood. You attacked Sir Philip Limbury outside the Fire Court

– dear God, you stabbed him with a naked blade, and for no shadow of a reason. What's a justice going to make of all that? It'll be the gallows for you, my girl. Unless they show mercy and send you to Bedlam instead. But you wouldn't survive there long. Not on the common ward.'

There was a relish in his voice that made her shiver, however hard she tried not to show fear. The Bethlehem Hospital was in Bishopsgate, and viewing the miserable and often violent antics of the lunatics was a popular spectacle to the public and a lucrative source of income to the keepers. If you weren't insane when you were committed there, it wouldn't be long before you were.

'I was afraid, sir. I didn't know what I did in my fear. But I'm heartily sorry for it.'

'You take me for a fool?' He took her chin in his hand, squeezed it and raised it, forcing her to look at him. 'What is between you and Marwood?'

'I . . . I don't know him, sir.'

The timbers of the building creaked loudly, as if proclaiming the fact she was lying. She glanced over her shoulder. It wasn't a chest behind her. It was a bench with a hole cut in it. A privy.

'Of course you know him,' Gromwell said. 'You were acting together outside the Fire Court this morning. You were seen talking to each other a fortnight ago. Let me remind you. It was in the ruins, where they found a woman's body. You're working for him, aren't you? So is your cousin, I imagine, so far as he can, the state he's in. You're living in Marwood's house, aren't you? Is he your lover?'

Cat said nothing. He squeezed her chin more tightly. She tried to jerk it away. But he was too strong. The building groaned, and this time Cat felt it move slightly, as if twitching in its sleep.

Gromwell released her and stepped back into the doorway. 'Pray be careful. I'd avoid sudden movements if I were you.'

She cleared her throat. 'Why?'

'This privy projects over the water, so the waste falls directly into the river.' He spoke with exaggerated patience, as though explaining something to a slow-witted child. 'But the house is old, and the timbers supporting the closet have rotted.' He smiled at her. 'I'm standing in the main house. I'm quite safe, in case you were concerned. But the people of the house don't use this privy now, because it's too dangerous.'

She wondered if he was speaking the truth or merely trying to terrify her more. Directly below her was the river. At this moment the tide was ebbing rapidly under the arches, pouring downstream with violent, noisy urgency. Suppose Gromwell spoke the truth: even if she wasn't battered to death in the torrent under the bridge, she couldn't swim.

She heard footsteps in an adjacent room and the soft, slushy voice of Sourface: 'Sir? My master would speak with you.'

Gromwell stepped aside. 'What do you think of our prisoner?'

Sourface appeared at his shoulder. 'Skinny little thing, sir.'

'Could she please you? Do you think she's pretty?'

The servant smiled. 'Well enough, sir. If she was willing.'

'And if she wasn't?'

'Well enough again. Even if she weren't.'

Gromwell laughed. 'Stolen apples taste sweeter.' He turned back to Cat. 'I'll be back soon. Think over what I said. Tell me the truth, and you will find I can be kind. Richard will stay with you while I'm gone.'

'Shall I put a gag on her?'

'In a moment. I haven't finished questioning her. If you stand in the doorway, she can't go anywhere, except to you. And if she screams, well – who is there to hear on this side of the house except us?'

Gromwell left. Cat heard his footsteps on bare boards. Sourface came to stand in his place.

In the distance was the sound of voices, including a woman's. Lady Limbury's, presumably, or perhaps her maid's. Sir Philip must be there too.

She heard heavy breathing a yard or two away from her, and a rustling, creaking sound.

They must be on an upper storey of one of the higher buildings of the bridge. On the way here, they had pushed and pulled her up several flights of stairs. Unable to see, she had tripped and fallen twice. At the top of the stairs, they had walked across bare boards. How far? Ten yards? More than one room perhaps – the sound had changed. Then they had pushed her into the privy and on to her knees.

'Look at me,' Sourface whispered. 'You crafty slut.'

She squinted through her lashes. He was staring at her and rubbing himself, not so much for the pleasure of the thing itself as for the pleasure of seeing Cat's face as he did it.

She shut out the sight of him and fought harder to distract herself. Sourface was Limbury's servant. He had not been at the Fire Court this morning. Perhaps he had been at the Limburys' house, instead, and he had seen enough to realize that his mistress intended to leave for her father's house.

The rhythmical rustling in the doorway continued, just audible above the roar of the water beneath. Sourface must have warned his master about his mistress's plans, so Limbury and Gromwell could reach the coach in time, before it crossed the bridge.

'Oh, you doxy!' The whisper was soft as slurry. 'Oh, you dirty doxy.'

The truth was, there was no one who could help her now. No one knew she was here. Even if Marwood learned that she had boarded the coach with Lady Limbury, he would think that either she was still there, with the lady in the coach, and therefore relatively safe, or she had left, in which case he would expect her to return to the Savoy, or possibly to Henrietta Street.

If Cat wanted help, the only person who could provide it was herself.

'Look at me,' Sourface said. 'Look at me.'

Instead she spat in the direction of his whisper.

CHAPTER FORTY-THREE

H OW DARED THEY leave her like this, without even a servant to attend her, and amid such squalor?

Philip and Gromwell were whispering on the landing beyond the door to the stairs. Jemima had called for Mary, but no one had come. She was angry, miserable and afraid, all at the same time. Only pride stopped her from weeping.

At last the door opened and Philip came back. She heard Gromwell's heavy footsteps going downstairs.

'Why have you brought me here?' Jemima demanded.

'I told you,' Philip said calmly as if this were a conversation over their dinner table at Pall Mall. 'To rest and refresh yourself.'

'But it's so strange here. So dirty and old-fashioned.' She found it hard to breathe suddenly. Did they mean to murder her? 'Why am I here?'

He turned away and stared out of the window at the river. 'We must look after you, madam,' he said. 'You were distraught – exhausted – this morning. You didn't know what you were doing or saying. And then rushing off to your father's without any warning. Perhaps you're feverish?'

Jemima was scared – not so much of Philip, who was after all her husband and had an interest in her survival, but of Lucius Gromwell. She had always underestimated him, she realized, mocking his shabby finery and his elaborate manners, and disliking him purely because Philip liked him. But Gromwell was formidable, despite his handicaps. It was he who had brought them here, and he who seemed to be in command.

'Where is he?' she asked. 'Your – your friend.' She could not bear to say the man's name.

'He went back to deal with Hal and the coach. He won't be long.'

The air was dank and chilly. She glanced about her. They had brought her to a long, narrow chamber, almost a gallery, on the top floor of the building. There was another, smaller room beyond it, though the door to it was now closed. They had put the girl somewhere in there, with first Gromwell, then Richard to watch over her.

The walls were panelled in dark wood, splintered and cracked, and on the river side grey with mould. Plaster had flaked from the sagging ceiling, which was moulded with an old-fashioned pattern of roses and straps, and stained with the smoke of candles; damp was spreading from one corner. There was a tall, carved chimney piece, but the fireplace beneath was choked with a heap of soot and ash that had spilled out from the hearth. The only furniture consisted of three stools, a crudely built cupboard and the high-backed settle on which she sat.

'I'm cold,' she said pettishly.

Philip nodded towards the door of the second room. 'The chimney's clear in there – they've lit the fire, but we'll let it draw. It's smoking a little.'

'I don't want to see them. Richard or Gromwell.'

'Then you shan't. Or only in passing.'

'I want to go to Syre,' she said, trying to inject an imperious note into her voice. 'I want to see my father. Have them bring up the coach.'

'That's quite impossible at present.' He spoke patiently, as if to a child. 'You know that. Nothing's moving on the bridge. We shall go down there later if you wish, if the King will give me permission for a leave of absence from my duties. Perhaps at the end of the week.'

'Why's Mary so long? I need her.'

'She'll be back presently. I've sent her to buy food and wine. The shops on the bridge are picked clean, so she may be a while. In any case, I must talk to you first.'

Philip sat down beside her on the settle and lifted her hand from her lap. She let it lie in his, as unresponsive as a dead fish. She turned her head and stared through the window at the river, allowing her eyes to be drawn across the water towards the blackened stump of St Paul's tower.

'You must forgive me, my sweet,' he said, his voice low and gentle. 'I spoke to you most unkindly outside the Fire Court. I was in such a passion I didn't know what I was saying. I shall never forgive myself.'

'You were cruel, sir,' she said, feeling the itch of tears about her eyes. 'You insulted me before the servants, before strangers. You—'

'My love, it was that damned unjust verdict. Poulton must have bribed the judges. It overturned my reason – it let loose a devil inside me – my anger made such lies pour out of me.' Suddenly he raised her hand to his lips. 'Be my priest,' he said. 'I've confessed my sins to you, terrible though they are. I beg you, give me my absolution.'

His words were a caress. But she could not speak the words of forgiveness. He sensed her softening, however, and he covered her hand with kisses. She tried to delay her capitulation.

'What about that girl?' she said. 'What have you done with her?'

'She's quite unharmed. She's in a closet beyond the bedchamber where the fire is. Richard's keeping an eye on her.'

'He must be kind. She helped me.' She paused and then added pointedly, 'When others were unkind.'

Philip squeezed her hand. 'Your goodness does you credit. But I'm afraid the girl's a spy. She's Hakesby's cousin, which means she's in Poulton's pay.'

She shook her head. 'I don't care. She was kind.'

'She didn't help you from the goodness of her heart – it was from calculation.'

'I don't believe it, Philip. Even if it's true, you mustn't harm her.'

'We'll see. Lucius will get the truth out of her.'

'Lucius,' she said, seizing on another reason for complaint. 'Why is it always him?'

Philip's grip relaxed, and he pulled back from her as if to see her face more clearly. 'He's a brave fellow. Fortune hasn't dealt kindly with him, but you wouldn't want a better friend when matters go awry.'

'A better pander, you mean,' she snapped. Pain flared up in her belly at the very thought of it. 'He pimps for you,

Philip, and you call it friendship. Why, he even lent you his chamber in Clifford's Inn so you could meet your lover there.' She spat out the last words. She stood up, brushing away his hand. She backed across the room from him, holding up her hands as if to push him back. 'Your lover,' she repeated. 'You foul thing. Stay away from me.'

Philip was smiling, as if she had made the most excellent jest in the world. 'I told you, Jemima. Celia Hampney? That awful woman wasn't my lover. She was Lucius's.'

Her mouth opened, but no words came.

'I admit I had a hand in the business. If anyone acted the pander, I fear I did. I was trying to do Lucius a favour, and myself one at the same time. He's always known how to play the lover, even when we were lads. I asked him to try his luck with the Hampney woman. I lent him some money so he could make his chamber fit for an assignation. Why not? She looked like a half-starved horse but she was a rich widow, and she wanted amusement. If Lucius married her, he would restore his fortunes at a stroke. I hoped that he could at least persuade her to support me over Dragon Yard, even if she wouldn't wed him. It would have made all the difference. You heard what they were saying at the Fire Court today.'

'I – I don't believe you.'

'Nevertheless, it's no more than the truth.' He leaned back, still smiling. 'So he scraped an acquaintance with her—'

'Did you ever meet that whore yourself?'

'No, of course not. Why should I? Besides . . . ' He stood up and approached her. He stopped within arm's length but made no attempt to touch her. 'How could I even look at another woman when I have you?'

His brown eyes were like a dog's, melting with devotion.

'Lucius won her affections easily enough,' he went on. 'But it turned out she didn't want a husband. She wanted a man to amuse her, to take her to bed. And when she began to think that he was only making up to her because of Dragon Yard and her money, that angered her. It was no more than the truth, of course, but she should have known that no one's motives are wholly pure.'

'And then,' Jemima said, 'and then . . . '

He wasn't smiling now. 'Then someone stabbed her to death.'

CHAPTER FORTY-FOUR

G OD WAS MERCIFUL, in a small way at least.
Limbury called Sourface away to fetch more fuel for
the fire.

'We're in the next chamber,' Limbury said to Cat.
'Remember that. No one will hear you if you call, no one
but us. You have nowhere to go.' His lips twisted. 'I'd try
not to move, if I were you, in case you end up in the river
without meaning to.'

She stared up at him but said nothing. He shut her in. She
heard the click of the latch, and then the scrape of a wedge
driven in to secure it.

Her wrists were burning from the tightness of the rope
that bound them. She tried in vain to move her arms. The
rope had passed over her right-hand sleeve. She bent her
head and tugged at the material with her teeth. In less than
a minute she worked it free from the rope.

The pressure on her wrists instantly slackened. Only a
little, but it gave her hope. It also meant that she could move
her wrists slightly, one against the other. She tried in vain to

reach the pocket hanging at her waist beneath her skirt. They had not searched her, so she still had her knife. But she could not reach it, however much her fingers strained towards it.

There were footsteps in the room next door over the rushing of the water. She tensed. In a moment there was a bang that made the floor shudder, as if someone had thrown down a heavy weight. Then came the familiar scrape of a poker riddling ashes from a grate.

Behind her, on the seat of the privy, there was a flap of wood that had once covered the hole. Its hinges had rusted, and the flap was now detached and lay on the bench. The rusting halves of its hinges were fixed on the planking of the seat.

Cat knelt in front of the privy, with the water rushing below her, and rested her bound wrists on the jagged stump of the hinge on the left. She rubbed the rope to and fro, to and fro, over the rough edge of the metal.

The friction made heat, and the heat burned her chafed skin. Tiredness made her clumsy. The rusty iron dug into the soft skin above her inner wrist. She caught her breath, forced back a cry of pain and continued to work the rope to and fro over the hinge.

A strand parted. Spots of blood appeared on the seat of the privy. Then another strand separated. Her shoulders and arms ached but she dared not rest. Her throat was so dry she could no longer swallow.

A third strand broke, and the rope gave for the first time, slackening its hold.

She sat back on her heels, panting. Sourface might be back at any moment or – even worse, perhaps – Limbury or Gromwell. The sounds from the neighbouring room had faded away. All she could hear was the endless surge of the water below.

She set to work once more. Her muscles had stiffened already. She had been sweating hard, too, and the brief rest had given the moisture a chance to cool on her skin. She transferred her wrists to the remains of the second hinge, which was smaller than the first but unblunted by her rubbing of the rope.

Five minutes later she was free. She stared with something approaching disbelief at her two wrists. She raised her arms above her head and stretched. She swept the rope from the seat and into the hole. It writhed as it fell to the foaming water and disappeared under the surface.

Cat's knees shrieked with pain as she leaned against the seat of the privy and pushed herself into a standing position. She flexed her fingers. Both her forearms were smeared with blood.

She took out her knife. The familiar feel of it in her hand comforted her. She went to the door and listened. She heard nothing moving, though now — mingling with the noises of the river — there were muffled sounds that might have been voices. But not, she thought, from the room next door.

There were only two ways to leave the privy: through the window and into the river, or through the door and into a building full of enemies. As gently as she could, she tried the latch. It wouldn't move. She stopped to listen. Then she pushed the door outward. It shifted a little in the frame.

Cat took out her knife and poked experimentally at the jamb of the door, close to the latch. The tip dug itself into the wood, which was softer than it looked, perhaps rotting from the damp.

She didn't want to risk snapping the knife blade by using it as a lever. Instead, she picked up the flap of wood from the privy and worked it into the gap between the door and the jamb.

She leaned her weight against the flap and pushed as hard as she could. The door creaked and moved slowly away from her. The jamb splintered. Suddenly the door gave altogether. There was the sound of something falling to the floor. The door swung outwards.

'What was that?' a man's voice said.

She was in a square chamber hung with tapestries that sagged from their original fixings and in places trailed along the floor. They were so filthy and faded that their design was almost entirely gone. The room was empty, apart from a plain bedstead without either curtains or bedding. A newly lit fire blazed in the grate, throwing flames up the back of the chimney. The door opposite the privy was ajar.

'You make me the unhappiest woman in the world,' Lady Limbury wailed, her voice high and edged with hysteria. 'I'm your wife, sir. Promise me you'll never see that man again.'

Footsteps crossed the room beyond. Sir Philip Limbury paused in the doorway. He saw Cat. The logs settled in the grate, dislodging one of them, which rolled from the fire basket into the hearth.

'You cunning little bitch,' he said to Cat, his hand dropping to the hilt of the sword.

'What is it?' Lady Limbury called. 'What's happening?'

He ripped the blade from the scabbard and advanced slowly into the room, with the tip of the sword dancing in front of him at the level of her eyes. Cat's knife was useless against a sword. She darted to the fireplace and took up the poker.

'Don't be a fool, girl. Put that down.' The blade swung briefly towards the privy. 'Get back in there.'

There was movement behind him and the dishevelled figure of Lady Limbury appeared in the doorway. Her birthmark was uncovered, glowing a deep, angry red.

'Drop your sword, sir,' she cried. 'I told you, you mustn't hurt that poor girl. I command you.'

Cat backed into the corner of the room.

'Put down the poker,' Limbury said to her, ignoring his wife. 'And that knife. Or I'll spit you like a pigeon.'

Lady Limbury screamed with frustration. She darted into the room, seized the tongs and took up the burning log from the hearth. 'Listen to me, sir.' She waved the log at him, and acrid smoke curled around them both. 'You shall listen to me, just this once. I will not be ignored!'

Limbury swung the sword towards his wife. She shied away, her face contorting with fear. The blade swept the tongs aside. She lost her grip on them and they fell to the floor. The log rolled towards the wall.

He waved the sword towards the privy. 'In there,' he said to Cat. 'N—'

He broke off as his wife flung herself at him, wrapping her arms around his neck, so for a second or two he was bearing her full weight. Her feet kicked at his legs. Her body hung over his sword arm. She was howling at him.

Cat leapt forward and lunged, driving the tip of the poker towards Limbury's eye. It missed by a fraction of an inch and jarred against the bony socket. He shouted and staggered back, half-carrying, half-dragging his wife with him. But he did not fall, and he kept hold of his sword. Cat threw herself between him and the wall, keeping Lady Limbury between them. He tried to block her but his wife impeded his movements so much that all he managed was a sideways stagger that nearly overbalanced him.

Cat stopped abruptly, knees flexed, poker in one hand and knife in the other. Gromwell was standing in the doorway to the room beyond. Behind her, Lady Limbury coughed. Then so did her husband.

The air was full of smoke. Her eyes stinging, Cat retreated towards the privy. The log from the tongs had skittered across the floor to the foot of the wall. Still smouldering, it had come to rest against the bottom of one of the tapestries. They were as dry as tinder. The flames were streaking up the material with astonishing speed, bringing the tapestries briefly and glowingly alive in the moment of their destruction.

For an instant, only the flames and the thickening smoke moved. Then Limbury dropped his sword, tugged apart his wife's arms and dropped her on the floor.

She fell awkwardly, missed her footing and sprawled on her back, her arms waving, where she lay helpless as an upturned turtle. She cried out. Her hands clutched her belly.

The flames were spreading around the walls. 'Stamp it out,' Limbury called. 'Stamp out the flames.'

'Too late for that.' Covering his mouth and nose with his cloak, Gromwell lugged out his sword. He beckoned to Limbury. 'Quick – pull her out.'

Limbury scooped up his own sword and dragged his wife towards the further door. Gromwell waited by the doorway, sword in hand, his eyes on Cat.

'What about the girl?' Limbury gasped, coughing.

Gromwell stood aside to let them pass. He said – as much to Cat as to Limbury, 'Let her take her chances.'

Then he too left the room. He slammed the door. Cat heard the sound of a bolt driven home on the other side.

There was now so much smoke that the opposite door was invisible. Her ears were full of the familiar, dreadful crackling roar of the fire. Flames tore up the chimney; they danced along the old, dry wood of the bedstead; sparks rained on the mattress.

Cat ran back to the privy, pulling the door closed after her, though it would not latch. At least it was a barrier: it might grant her a few minutes' grace from the fire and the smoke.

Below her, the river roared between the piers of the bridge, pouring downstream towards the sea. She was caught between two roaring lions, the fire and the water, seeking whom they might devour.

The smoke leaked into the privy. She slashed the poker at the window repeatedly, poking out lozenges of glass and breaking down the lattice of lead. Air swept into the little room. A draught, she thought, suddenly realizing her mistake: a draught fans a fire.

The privy creaked on its supporting timbers. The floor shifted beneath her feet.

CHAPTER FORTY-FIVE

THE LAUDANUM DULLED the edge of the pain, but I wasn't comfortable standing still. Movement was a distraction. Sometimes I walked fifty yards or so away in one direction or the other, always keeping the stationer's building in sight. I didn't stand out – other people were doing much the same, moving aimlessly to and fro, trying to alleviate the tedium of waiting until the blockage was cleared.

I sent Sam into the alehouse we had passed earlier to see if he could pick up any information about the stationer's house and its layout. With hindsight, that was a mistake: it was a long shot at best, and giving Sam leave to go into an alehouse was asking for trouble.

But I was growing desperate. Everything had changed. I did not care about having a quiet word with Lady Limbury on Williamson's behalf. Gathering evidence against the murderer of the Widow Hampney, her maidservant and Chelling no longer seemed as urgent as it had. The only thing that mattered was Cat.

Somewhere in that house she was a prisoner, trussed like

a turkey for the oven. It was my fault that she was there. I had to do something but I didn't know what. If I banged on the door beside the shop until somebody came, how would that help? Limbury and Gromwell were in the house as the lawful guests of Mistress Vereker.

I would need a magistrate's warrant to search the place for Cat. It would take hours even to apply for one, and there was no guarantee of success. A magistrate would demand to see strong evidence before he risked alienating a senior courtier like Limbury. As for Williamson, the last thing he would want was to draw publicity to himself. Why should he care about a young woman of no importance?

Early on, Sourface and Lady Limbury's maidservant came out. She had a basket over her arm. They set off up the road towards the Great Stone Gate. I would have tried to talk to the maid if she had been alone.

I watched them until they were blocked from my view by a hackney coach. Shortly afterwards, Sourface came back alone, carrying a wicker scuttle full of coals. I cursed myself for sending Sam away – I could have sent him after the maid.

Sourface let himself in the house. After a while, I went into the baker's shop over the road. A woman came to serve me, wiping floury hands on her apron. I had missed dinner so I knew I must be hungry, though I didn't feel it. The laudanum played the devil with my appetite. Besides, there wasn't much to buy. The rush of unexpected customers had bought most of the stock.

I asked for a roll and she offered me a misshapen thing, slightly charred at one end. 'All I got left, master. Take it or leave it.'

I said I would take it, despite its flaws. As she took my

money, I said, 'Where does that door lead?' I pointed over the road. 'The one beside the stationer's shop. I think I saw a friend going in.'

'Widow Vereker's lodgings,' she said, handing me the roll. 'Her husband's aunt used to live up there. Dead now.'

The roll was so hard and heavy that it might have been fired from a cannon. The crust was as hard as plate armour. 'Who lives there now?'

'No one.' The woman's eyes looked past me. 'Look,' she said.

Both of us stared out into the road. The traffic was moving at last, albeit slowly. Someone applauded. A donkey plodded by, drawing a cart laden with someone's furniture.

'Shame,' the woman said. She shrugged. 'It was good while it lasted.'

I went outside. I waited, pressed against the wall of the baker's. Ten minutes later, the Limburys' coach rumbled along the road. The coachman was up on the box, and there was a boy beside him.

The coach stopped outside the stationer's. I tensed my muscles, ready to do something, though I had no idea what. There were angry shouts from the drivers behind, infuriated by yet another stop. The coachman pointed with his whip at the door of the lodgings. The boy jumped down. The coachman shook the horses' reins and the coach lumbered on.

The boy hammered on the door with the heel of his hand. No one answered. He looked around him for help, his face desperate. When he found none, he ran after the coach.

I lost track of time. Traffic moved sluggishly along the bridge in both directions. The pain was getting worse. I discovered that I was gripping the roll in my hand so tightly that my fingertips had made holes in the crust.

A throaty voice murmured in my ear, 'There you are, master. Thought I'd lost you for ever.'

Sam was at my shoulder, grinning at me.

I swung round. 'Where the devil have you been? You've been gone an age.'

'What could I do, master?' Sam put on an injured expression that didn't suit him. 'You get nothing for nothing, so I had to have a drink. But I learned something about the place.' He jerked a thumb at the sign of the Three Bibles. 'The tapster said the lease is running out and the building's falling apart. The word is that Mistress Vereker's moving off the bridge.'

'What use is that to me?' I snapped, taking my irritation out on him.

'I don't know. You said to find out anything I could about the place, so I did.' Sam stared over the roadway at the building opposite, running his eyes up the ornate but decaying façade. 'Mind you, anyone with a pair of eyes in their head can see it needs repairing.'

'You know I needed you here. You deserve a—'

'Master,' he interrupted. 'Look up there.'

He pointed at the top of the building. Smoke was drifting into the air above it. Not a disciplined thread from a chimney, but a dark and riotous cloud, growing larger and denser even as we watched. I heard, faintly, far above the street noises and the muted roar of the river, the sound of broken glass.

Others had seen the smoke too, including the baker's wife, who was standing in the doorway of the shop.

'Fire!' she screamed. 'Fire!'

CHAPTER FORTY-SIX

J EMIMA LOST ONE of her shoes on the stairs. Philip wouldn't let her stop for it. He held her arm – almost wrenching it from its socket – and dragged her down flight after flight. In his other hand was his naked sword.

She lacked the strength even to cry out. She had a pain within her.

Richard was running ahead and Gromwell's footsteps thundered after theirs.

Gromwell. If this was hell, there was the devil himself. Why in God's name didn't Philip protect her?

At the bottom, Richard fumbled with the door, his hands scrabbling in his haste at the bolts and the bar. He swung the door open just before they reached it, and slipped into the street in front of them.

There were cries of 'Fire! Fire!' People were everywhere, pouring out of houses and shops, abandoning their vehicles and struggling to escape from the bridge.

The door to the stationer's was open, and apprentices and journeymen and servants milled around the entrance.

A middle-aged woman was in the doorway, shrieking at them to come back and carry out the stock.

'This way,' Philip said, waving with his sword towards the south end of the bridge. 'The Bear.'

'But the girl, sir,' she gasped, recoiling from Gromwell, who had joined them. 'The girl's inside.'

She saw a face she knew on the other side of the road, not five yards away. It was the man who had accosted Gromwell outside the Fire Court when Philip had been attacking her. Beside him was the man with the crutch who had lost part of his leg, who had also been there.

'Save her,' she cried to them, to anyone. 'For the love of God. Save her.'

Gromwell took her other arm. In a dream, she saw the man raise his arm and pitch a small dark object across the street. It caught Gromwell in the face and made him recoil slightly. But he kept his grip on her arm. The object fell to the ground. Automatically she glanced down at it. It was a charred roll.

He and Philip dragged her away. The crowd fell back from their drawn swords. Behind them came Richard. Then her pain returned, worse than before.

CHAPTER FORTY-SEVEN

'FOLLOW THEM,' I ordered Sam.
'But, master, what—'
'Go,' I roared, suddenly furious with him. 'Or go to the devil. It's all one.'

I pushed past him, forced my way through the crowd outside the stationer's and went into the building. Once inside, I glanced back. To my relief, I couldn't see Sam. With luck, he had obeyed me for once. A cripple couldn't run upstairs. I didn't want to be responsible for killing him as well as Cat.

The covered passage led to a staircase and a doorway beyond to a bookbinder's workshop. I ignored the workshop and climbed the first flight as quickly as I could. The pain from my burn and the stiffness of my limbs slowed me down.

There was smoke in the air, but not too much to make breathing difficult. The higher I went, however, the worse both the smoke and the heat became.

But no flames. Not yet. I can't face a fire, I thought, and then Chelling's face floated into my mind: as he had been in death, when I had last seen him, bathed in flames.

I wrapped my cloak over my mouth and nose. I climbed higher and higher until I could climb no more. On the top landing, there was a single door, closed. It was a stout affair, in its way, but it couldn't hold back the fire for ever. There was already an orange glow around the frame.

I touched the latch. The iron was so hot I had to wrap a fold of my cloak around my hand in order to lift it.

It opened into a tunnel of fire. Smoke billowed towards me. There was no sign of Cat. An almighty cracking sound filled my ears, and one of the windows burst outwards. The flames licked through the opening towards the sky.

Fear gripped me, squeezing my bowels. On one level, I thought that history was repeating itself, and I was back in Chelling's room, and this time the fire would do even worse things to me.

But on another level there was no time to think at all. My actions seemed to have little or nothing to do with the part of me that was terrified. With the cloak clamped over my face, I staggered across the floor of a long room, making for a door at the opposite end. God be thanked, the floorboards supported my weight. The door was bolted. When I drew the bolt back, I forgot to pad it with my cloak, and metal burned my hand. I screamed with the pain of it, losing what was left of the air in my lungs.

I smelled burning hair. The right-hand side of my wig was on fire, the hair frizzling and blackening in the heat. I tore it off my head, along with my hat, and tossed them to the flames.

This chamber was smaller than the first, with another door opposite me. The air was clearer here. The windows had gone and so had part of the ceiling. In one corner was the blackened skeleton of a bedstead. The beams above had caught fire, as had some of the floorboards. Looking up, I glimpsed the sky. Roof tiles cracked in the heat and showered down on to the wreckage of the bed. Lines of fire were streaking along the remaining rafters.

I drew the cloak over my bare head, trying to protect the damaged skin from the intense heat. The joists below, which had supported the floor, remained intact, though two near the fireplace were smouldering and charring. I took in another breath, coughed most of it out, and skipped from one joist to the next. The door at the end had lost its latch. I tugged it open.

There was Cat at last, turned away from me, leaning on the window sill. Relief surged through me. In my heart I had feared she must be dead already.

I said her name, as I crossed the threshold, drawing the door shut behind me. The flames hadn't reached here yet. The room was a privy. Cat had punched a jagged hole through the glass and lead of the lattice. Her head and shoulders were poking outside.

She was unaware that she was no longer alone. I touched her side. She spun round instantly. I saw the glint of the knife in her hand. She didn't look like herself any more. Her face was white, the skin stretched tightly over the skull, the teeth bared.

I heard a crash of falling timbers and tiles behind me, and the roar of the fire increased.

'The river,' I said, trying to keep my voice gentle, as one would to a frightened child or a nervous animal. 'It's the only way now.'

'No,' she whispered. 'I'd rather stay here.'

'We must jump.' I dropped the cloak, tore off my coat and let it fall to the floor. 'Kick off your shoes.'

She made as if to lunge at me with the knife.

I stepped back as far as I could in the cramped space. I felt the warmth of the fire on my back and heard the hungry crackle of the flames.

'Cat—'

'I can't do it,' she said. 'You go.'

'Don't be foolish.'

'I won't.' She stamped her foot, reduced to a child in a temper. 'I can't swim. And I hate water.'

I seized her right arm and twisted it. She tried to bite me. She kicked at my legs. But I kept up the pressure until she dropped the knife. I clamped my arms around her and forced her back to the window opening.

The privy groaned. With a snapping and a cracking of timber, it swung outwards over the river until it was hanging at an angle of nearly forty-five degrees. It threw the two of us against the outer wall beside the window. The wall sagged and creaked.

Hand over hand, Cat pulled herself along the bench until she could cling to the hole of the privy. I clambered around her. My hand appeared beside hers, our skin touching. We stared at each other, as close as lovers or mortal enemies. I watched our knuckles whitening.

The privy sighed. It broke asunder like a cracked walnut. It crumbled out into the river in a shower of debris.

I closed my eyes as we fell.

The fire, the river, the falling building wrapped me in their sounds. There was a smack as my body hit the water. Hard objects buffeted me. Someone screamed. The cold was vicious: it paralysed me. The river sucked me underwater and rolled me over and then—

Something struck my shoulder. The force of it drove me under the surface, where the current played with me like a boy torturing a cat, or a cat torturing a mouse. It turned me round and dashed me against the starlings. I curled myself into a ball, trying to protect my head with my arms. The current tossed and twisted me over and over. It let me free for a second and then threw me over the weir tumbling downstream from the bridge.

The water was so cold that it made me gasp. I took in a mouthful of it and tried to spit it out before it reached my lungs. I couldn't reach the surface. I couldn't breathe.

I felt a sharp pain in my right thigh, the one the fire hadn't scarred, slicing down the leg to the knee. A stabbing agony blossomed in my chest. There was another hammer blow, worse than the others, on my curved spine. The river was killing me slowly.

Then – with miraculous suddenness – it was over. I was bobbing about in calmer water, downstream from the bridge. I broke the surface and sucked fresh air in my lungs. The current was bearing me with it, but much more slowly than before. I rolled on my back. Over my head was the grey dome of the sky.

Where was Cat? I flipped over and turned my head this way and that. I was nearer the north bank of the river than the south. The houses of the bridge rose above me like a jagged cliff. People were pointing down at me, their mouths silently opening and closing. But I couldn't see Cat.

With growing desperation, I swam to and fro. I called her name. My chest was heaving, forcing me to rest. I trod water and drew in mouthfuls of air. The pain in my chest slowly subsided, but not the despair I felt. I had killed her. I had let her drown. If it hadn't been for me, she would not have been here in the first place.

Thank God. A boat was putting out from Billingsgate Stairs. A man in the stern was pointing in my direction.

The swell of the water briefly lifted me higher. I saw a small hand poking above the surface. It vanished almost immediately.

With a sudden surge of energy, I swam towards the place where she had been. I dived. The water was murky, for the turbulence of its passage through the bridge made it cloudier and filthier than it was upstream. I waved my arms under the water, stretching my fingers out. I couldn't see her or touch her. I surfaced, filled my lungs and dived again.

My left hand found something. I swam further down. I touched what felt like an arm. It was sliding away from me. Before it could escape, I gripped it with my left hand, wincing as the tightening muscles increased the pain from the burns. I pulled it closer, and felt the outline of Cat's body with my other hand.

I kicked my legs and dragged her to the surface. Gasping for breath, I lay on my back in the water, kicking my feet. She floated inert beside me. I tried to pull her on to my chest.

Her eyes were closed. Her skin was broken on one shoulder, and there was a gash on the other arm. Her hair was floating free and bedraggled.

I shook her gently. I might have been shaking a wet mattress for all the response I had.

Desolation swept over me. Oh Christ, I thought, after all that she's dead.

CHAPTER FORTY-EIGHT

JEMIMA'S PAIN GREW worse as Philip and Gromwell dragged her along the street.

She was dimly aware of the crowd parting as they approached, of the murmur of voices, and people asking who they were and where was the constable. But no one was willing to interfere with two gentlemen with drawn swords.

They emerged from the gate passage at Bridge Foot. The approach of a fire pump forced them to stop. Men with buckets and hoses were running beside it towards the fire, caught up in their own drama. They had no eyes for hers.

Her legs collapsed beneath her. The pain was worse than ever. Philip glanced at her. He kept his grip on her arm. She saw the shock in his face before the pain distracted her even from him.

The pump and the firemen were gone.

'Come on,' Gromwell said. 'We'll have to carry her.'

'No,' Philip said. 'Wait. She's ill.'

Gromwell would have none of it. He tugged at Jemima's arm.

She saw someone running towards them. 'Mary,' she cried, 'Mary. Help me.'

'Let her go,' Mary cried.

Gromwell barged into Mary with his shoulder, sending her flying. She dropped the basket she had been carrying. It toppled over and the contents cascaded over the slippery cobbles.

But not all of them. When Mary straightened up, she was gripping a wine bottle by the neck.

Gromwell was already moving away. He took Jemima's arm. Mary swung the bottle at him in a rising backhanded blow that slammed into the bridge of his nose.

He recoiled with a roar of pain. Blood spurted down his face. His wig was askew, covering one eye. He tried to bring up his sword, but the wheel of a cart was in his way.

Before he could recover, Mary hit him on his blind side. This time, the bottle caught him just in front of his exposed ear. His body crumpled. The bottle broke with the impact and showered him with wine and broken glass.

Mary turned to her mistress, stretching out her hand to her. Jemima stared at her.

It was then that Philip released Jemima's arm. She saw the point of his sword leap forward and upward, catching Mary under the chin. It pierced the skin and slid smoothly into the soft matter beneath. Blood appeared between Mary's lips. Her green eyes opened wide and fixed on her mistress.

Jemima closed her own eyes, squeezing the lids together to shut the world out, and surrendered entirely to her own pain.

CHAPTER FORTY-NINE

I T WAS SAM, Cat discovered later, who had taken charge of matters.

He had heard the cries of 'Man in the water' further up the bridge, and had rushed towards them. He had been in time to see Marwood in the water, and the boats rowing out from Billingsgate Stairs.

He reached them there, shortly after they had been dragged like large inert fish from the boats and laid on the tarred planking of the landing stage. Cat had been lying on her side, Sam told her later, bleeding like a pig, and puking the Thames out of her belly. She had been freezing cold and someone had wrapped a blanket around her.

As for Marwood, Sam said, he had been crouching over her, clutching her and crying like a baby, and shivering worse than poor Mr Hakesby when one of his fits was upon him.

'Thought the master had lost his wits,' Sam said, seeming to find this possibility very amusing.

A little later, she and Marwood were still at the landing place, now sitting apart and wrapped in blankets. They were both conscious by this time, but they hadn't said a word to anyone – even each other. Neither of them had breath for words.

By his own account, at least, Sam had dealt with everything with speed and exemplary efficiency. By talking airy nothings about his master's lofty connections at Whitehall, he had persuaded the people of a nearby tavern to help. They had carried Cat and Marwood to a private room, set them before a fire, and swathed them in yet more blankets.

When Cat had stopped trembling, the landlady took her away to bathe her wounds and dress her in a cast-off shift, her maid's winter waistcoat and a thick cloak. The clothes were twice as large as she was and enveloped her like a tent.

Time must have passed, and a good deal of it, because when she came back to the room with the fire, Mr Hakesby had been there, holding his hands towards the warmth. But Marwood and Sam had gone.

Hakesby's skin was grey. His hair was uncombed. He had spilled gravy down his best coat. He looked ten years older than when she had last seen him, in the Fire Court this morning.

'How could you?' he demanded as she came into the room. 'You foolish, wicked child. Come and sit by the fire.' He waved a long, thin hand at the landlady, who was watching the proceedings with interest from the doorway. 'Bring broth for her. And wine . . . mulled wine? With ginger in it? Whatever you think will best revive her. But hurry, hurry, hurry.'

The landlady curtsied and left them alone. Cat sat on the bench beside him and stared at the fire.

'Is this Marwood's doing?' he asked. 'I thought he had more sense.'

She shook her head wearily. 'It no longer matters.'

'Of course it matters. You could have drowned. Or burned to death like poor Chelling.'

She said nothing. She was warmer, and beginning to feel drowsy.

'Has he dragged you into government business? Or is this just his mad folly about his father and the way he died?'

'I can't say, sir. I don't know the whole of it, and I don't want to.'

'They're saying downstairs that someone was killed on the bridge,' he said. 'A woman. Run through with a sword. Was that part of it?'

'I tell you I don't know.'

He said nothing. Slowly his hand crept along the bench and laid itself over hers. She glanced at it. She wanted to snatch her hand away; she didn't care to be touched. Instead, she forced herself not to move.

Her mind drifted. It was an old man's skin, wrinkled like a lizard's and speckled with liver spots. His fingers trembled slightly. The nails needed trimming. She must do something about that. But not now.

Food and a long night's sleep repaired at least some of the damage. The following day, Thursday, she rose late. Hakesby fussed over her and tried to make her rest, but she resisted him. She felt perfectly well, she said. In fact, her bruises were painful, and her cuts would take weeks to heal, but she was desperate for distraction.

Towards the end of the day, when the light was going and it was becoming harder to work, there was a knock at the door of the drawing office.

411

Brennan went to answer it. Mr Poulton's portly manservant was waiting on the threshold. He was clasping a very small package to his chest.

Brennan made as if to take it. The servant stepped back. 'I'm to put this in your master's hands. And wait for a receipt.'

'Come in then,' Hakesby called. 'Bring it here.'

He was sitting in his usual chair by the fire. After dinner, Cat had refused to return to her closet and rest as he had wanted. For the last hour, she had been taking his dictation in shorthand, hoping that she would be able to read it back in the morning. He was in a strange humour, bright-eyed and full of feverish energy.

Poulton's servant brought the package to him. Hakesby weighed it in his palm. He broke the seals – there were three – and unfolded the paper. Inside was a leather pouch with a letter rolled around it. He read it and handed it to Cat.

To Mr Hakesby

By the hand of my servant I send you forty-five pounds in gold, in payment for your services to date in connection with Dragon Yard and as an advance on future payments, as itemized in the Memorandum of Agreement. Pray sign and date this letter to confirm your receipt, and return it by the hand of my servant.

Roger Poulton

At a signal from Hakesby, she took the pouch, poured the coins into her hand and counted them. Brennan watched, his mouth slightly open, his eyes on Cat's face. He turned his head away when he saw that she had noticed him.

After Poulton's servant had gone, and the money had been locked away in the strongbox, Hakesby dismissed Brennan for the day.

'Will you pay back Marwood?' she asked when they were alone.

'We shall give him ten pounds at least.'

'Not more?'

'We must hold the rest of it back for ourselves. You can take the money to his house tomorrow, if you're well enough.'

'Of course I shall be well enough, sir,' she said. 'What about the rest we owe him?'

'Tell him he must wait a little. He gave us eight weeks, didn't he? After what he's done to you, the least he can do is be patient. And I have not forgotten the money I owe to you, either.'

Cat tried to change the subject. 'Talking of hackneys, you'll need one this evening when you go back to Three Cocks Yard. Shall I send the porter for one?'

'Wait — not yet. There is something I wish to say.' He stopped, and glanced furtively around the room, as if to make sure they were really alone. 'Something that concerns you. Sit here where I can see you.'

She obeyed. 'I am perfectly well, sir. I am quite capable of returning to my drawing board tomorrow. I—'

'It's not that,' he said. 'I've been uneasy in my mind about you.'

'There's no need, sir.'

He held up his hand, and they watched the tiny tremors that rippled through it. 'This doesn't get better,' he said. 'I don't think it will. What will you do when I'm gone?'

'That won't be for—'

'Or when I grow too ill to work? Indeed, what shall I do when I reach that point? How shall I keep body and soul together?'

'I shall find a way to support us both. Perhaps Dr Wren—'

'I've been turning this over, and I've come to a decision.'

Cat glanced sharply at him. His voice was sterner than usual.

'I wish to offer you a contract,' he went on. 'Purely as a matter of business, and with clear benefits, rights and responsibilities on both sides. An agreement, governed by law.'

'Why? We do very well as we are.'

'What I propose is that you marry me.'

'Marry you?' She stood up, knocking over her stool, and backed away from him. 'Marry you? Dear God, sir, have you gone mad?'

CHAPTER FIFTY

'MISTRESS?'

The voice insinuated itself into Jemima's dream, a desperate confusion of flames and screams and tumbling buildings.

Glad to be wakened, she opened her eyes. Hester's plain face, shiny with sweat, hovered above hers. She was frowning and biting her lip with anxiety. For a moment Jemima wondered where Mary was. Even as she was opening her mouth to ask, the memory of yesterday flooded back.

'Please, mistress, there's a gentleman below. You said to wake you.'

Jemima knew by the light that it was evening now – not late, for it wasn't dark: the colours were beginning to leach away, the outlines were softening.

'Who is it?'

'Mr Chiffinch. He's with master in the study.'

'Bring my gown. Sit me up.'

Hester was willing but stupid, and the fear of doing wrong made her even clumsier than usual. The pain in Jemima's belly grew suddenly worse. Her bandages were wet. They needed changing, and probably the sheets as well.

At the thought of all that this signified, her grief overwhelmed her, and her eyes filled with tears. Can you mourn the loss of someone who has not been born? Of course you can.

And of course she mourned Mary, too. But that was different.

Hester poked Jemima's arms into the armholes of the gown. Jemima bore the girl's clumsiness with patience she thought of as saintly. What did it matter now?

The midwife and the physician had separately examined her yesterday evening. Both of them had said in their different ways how sad her loss was, but neither could see any reason why she should not carry a healthy child to full term. The physician recommended he prescribe another course of treatment. The midwife, perhaps more usefully, promised to pray for her.

When Jemima was settled, her face washed with a sponge, the cosmetics applied and her book to hand, she sent Hester away with instructions to bring her a cup of chocolate.

'Make sure they tell my husband that I am awake, and I should like to see him.'

She waited, wondering why Chiffinch had come here, and turning over in her mind what she wanted to say to Philip. In the event she did not have long to wait before there were footsteps below and the sound of men's voices. The front door opened and closed. She heard Philip climbing the stairs. He walked more slowly than usual, and paused every few steps, as her father did, to rest and draw breath.

He tapped on the door and entered. He asked how she did.

As well as could be expected, she said, given what happened to her yesterday. He nodded and went to stand by the window.

'Well, sir. What did Chiffinch want with you?'

Philip swung round. She couldn't see his face clearly because the light was behind him. 'He came to warn me that the King is angry.'

She stared blankly at him. 'What about?'

'Me. I am dismissed – I'm no longer a Groom of the Bedchamber. Which means I'm five hundred a year poorer, too. As well as everything else.'

She knew at least part of what 'everything else' meant: the position at Court; access to the King; the power to whisper words in the ears of influential people; the little presents from less influential ones; the ability to dazzle tradesmen into providing infinite credit.

'They will all start dunning me in a day or two,' he went on in a dull voice. 'I shall have to sell the freehold of Dragon Yard for what I can get. Unless your father . . . ?'

'I'm sorry for it, of course,' she said, sidestepping the question. 'But at least we will no longer be tied to the Court.'

'There's more. The King has banished me. I'm forbidden to come within twenty miles of London.' He walked from the window to the bed and glowered at her. 'It's this damned business with Dragon Yard,' he burst out. 'Poulton has been spreading poison at Court about me. Arlington and his creature Williamson are using it to undermine Chiffinch. Do you know what the gossips are saying? That I bribed Lucius to woo Mistress Hampney to get her support, and he killed her when she would not do as he wanted.'

Her fingers plucked at the embroidery on the coverlet. She kept her voice light. 'But isn't it true? That you asked

Gromwell to woo her? Wasn't that why you were willing to pay the costs of his book and heaven knows what else? And have him here, in this house, at my table?'

'Well, yes – in a manner of speaking. I explained all this to you the other day, on the Bridge.' The confidence seeped away from his voice. 'But killing her? Why would he do that? He swore to me that he never laid a finger on her. Not in that way. Besides . . . '

Jemima studied his face. 'Besides what, sir?'

He swallowed. 'You can't still think that I was making love to her, can you? I—'

There was a knock on the door. Philip swore, stormed across the room and opened it. Hester was outside, carrying a tray. He picked up the jug of chocolate and threw it down the stairs. Hester scurried away, leaving her sobs in the air behind her.

He slammed the door and pushed the bolt across.

'I don't know what to believe,' she said coldly. In fact she was inclined to believe him now, but it was wiser not to tell him that. Not yet.

Philip made an effort to control his anger. 'I swear it was Gromwell who was Celia's lover, not me.'

'And what else did he do for you?'

'He helped Richard move her body, and bury it in the ruins. If he'd left her where she was, he was afraid of being taken up for murder, and then the whole business about Dragon Yard would have come out.' He sat down on the bed. 'There's worse about Gromwell. You'd better know the whole of it. People have been whispering about the little clerk who died in a fire in his chambers at Clifford's Inn. He worked at the Fire Court, you know, so he must have known about Dragon

418

Yard. People say he knew something about the widow's murder and tried to blackmail Gromwell about it.'

That was true enough, Jemima thought, about the black-mail at least: she had seen the proof of it locked away in Philip's cabinet, the blackmail letter that 'T.C.' had sent to Gromwell. And so, of course, had Philip. So he was not being entirely frank with her.

'And . . . and there was also some other folly about the widow's maid. It appears that the foolish girl hanged herself in Lambeth – from grief after her mother's death or perhaps her mistress's. But now they are saying that Gromwell killed her too, to stop her mouth about his wooing of the mistress.'

'Of course he killed the girl,' she said. 'And the clerk. And the whore.'

He shrugged. 'The King is persuaded that all this is my fault. That I used Lucius as the monkey did the cat's paw, to scrape the nuts from the fire.'

'Gromwell's dead,' she pointed out, hoping she did not sound triumphant. 'They can't prove anything, and nor can he. Nor can the King. He can't blame you for what Gromwell might or might not have done.'

He shook his head. 'It's not a matter of proof. The thing that matters is what the King believes. According to Chiffinch, he thinks I tried to interfere with the running of the Fire Court, and that enrages him even more, because he wants the court to be seen as impartial. And the affray yesterday on London Bridge . . . '

'Affray?' she said. 'Is that what you call it? Gromwell is dead, killed by Mary, who was trying to help me. And you yourself killed my poor Mary.'

He reared away from her. 'I ran her through in self-defence, madam. I swear it. Even Chiffinch agrees with me there. What else could I have done? She lost her wits and ran mad. She could have killed you next.'

She almost laughed at such a ridiculous suggestion. She leaned forward and pointed at him. 'Why, sir, all this happened because of you and your friend Gromwell. I was only there because the pair of you snatched me from my coach and held me in that dreadful place where I was nearly burned alive. As for your behaviour to me at the Fire Court—'

'Lucius thought—'

'Can't you think for yourself for once? You'll have to, now Gromwell is dead. He would have killed me if there had been any advantage in it to him. Between you, you made me miscarry our son. And so there's another murder to lay at Gromwell's door and yours. Your own child's.'

Exhausted, she sank back against the pillows. After a moment, and to her surprise, he sat down on the bed. He tried to take her hand, but she pulled hers away.

'I intended none of this,' he said gently. 'Not the first, not the last.'

'The murders, you mean?' she said. She felt the pain deep inside her, the absence. 'Our child's death?'

'I didn't want anyone to die.' Then Philip added, so quietly she had to strain to hear him, 'If I could live these last few weeks again . . .'

She watched the assurance flaking away from her husband like the shell from a hard-boiled egg, exposing something white and flabby beneath. How different from this was the hero whom she had sworn to love, honour and obey in the church at Syre.

'And I – I'm sorry about the other thing,' he went on. 'I'm

sorry that I didn't believe you when you said you were with child, and I'm sorry that you lost it.'

She turned her head away from him.

'Perhaps you're right – perhaps Gromwell killed Chelling and the maidservant in Lambeth,' Philip whispered. 'Indeed, he hinted as much to me . . . You remember that night when you comforted me?'

She nodded. Despite herself, her heart softened towards him. 'Was that the night when Chelling died?'

'Yes. They said it was an accident, but in my heart I knew it wasn't. I could see it in Gromwell's face when he told me of it, and I smelled burning on his clothes. He only meant to frighten the little man into keeping his mouth shut, not to kill him. It was an accident . . . But did he kill Celia Hampney, too? He swore that he didn't.' Philip looked at her, his face unhappy. 'Jemima, will you tell me what happened that day when Celia was murdered? What you did that afternoon? What you saw?'

The silence settled around them. Jemima stared at the blue and silver embroidery of the bed hangings. It was time to abandon the convenient fiction that fever had purged her memory of that afternoon when the Widow Hampney had died and all this had begun.

'Mary found me a hackney,' she said at last. 'I was angry with you – I own it. I thought you had gone to see that woman. I'd seen her letter, remember, and I knew where the meeting was, in Gromwell's chambers at Clifford's Inn. We went for a drive to Whitehall. It was hot and I had a fancy to go on the river because it was cooler.' She hesitated. 'And later we came ashore at the Savoy.' There was no reason to make this easy for him.

421

He persevered. 'Gromwell told me you went to Clifford's Inn. By yourself.'

'Then let us say that I did,' she said. 'I was distressed, of course, and it was on the spur of the moment. What did he tell you about me?'

'He said he saw you from the window when he was with Celia, and you came up his staircase, but he went out on the landing and stopped you from entering his chamber. He was half-undressed . . . He heard footsteps below so he bundled you out another way, by the fire-damaged staircase next door, to avoid scandal. You – you did not make it easy for him. When he came back, Celia was dead. Lying in her own blood.'

She stared at her husband. She had the measure of him now. For better or for worse, as the vows said. 'Gromwell told more lies than the devil, sir. He lied to you as he lied to everyone else. When the widow wouldn't do as he wanted, he fell into a rage and killed her as he did the others. Perhaps she threatened to betray your shabby little plot to the world. That's the long and the short of it. Whether he killed her after I went there or before is neither here nor there.'

He bowed his head. 'Perhaps you are right.'

After a moment, she surprised them both by taking his hand. 'What is done is done. We must make the best of it, sir. I suppose we shall give up the lease on this house and go to Syre. After all, we can afford to live nowhere else. We shall live very quietly, I expect, and perhaps our prayers for a child will at last be answered. My father will be pleased.'

CHAPTER FIFTY-ONE

S O THERE WAS more laudanum, and another expensive
visit from the physician.

Margaret nursed me when I allowed it, and Sam strutted
about the house as if he were its master. In his own mind, he
figured as the hero of the affair on London Bridge, on the
grounds that he had rescued Cat and myself, and brought us
to safety.

My patience ran out with him on Thursday. In practice, I
told him, all he had done was spend money that wasn't his
in the alehouse on the bridge, and spend more money at the
tavern near Billingsgate, and bring me home in a hackney.
And if he thought I hadn't noticed that he was more than
half drunk by the end of it, he was even more of a fool than
I thought he was.

By this time I had rebelled against Margaret's tyranny and
come downstairs to the parlour. As a compromise, I wore a
velvet cap on my head, as well as a gown and slippers. I also
permitted Margaret to drape me with blankets. But at least I
was no longer in bed. The laudanum kept the pain at bay,

though it plugged up my bowels and gave me bad dreams. Still, the price was worth paying, at least for now.

I sent Sam to Whitehall with a letter for Mr Williamson. I gave him a brief and strictly factual account of what had happened, both at the Fire Court and on London Bridge, with certain omissions, particularly in relation to Cat. I did not receive a reply.

I also gave Sam orders to call at Henrietta Street and enquire after her. Hakesby told him that she was in her closet and he could not see her. According to Hakesby, she appeared very little hurt, apart from cuts and bruising, but no thanks were due to me, who had led her quite unnecessarily into the dangers that had nearly cost her her life.

'Tough as an old boot, that one,' Sam said when he passed on the message to me. 'Mark my words, sir, she'll outlive the lot of us.'

He also told me the news: that Lady Limbury's maid, the one I had seen at the Fire Court yesterday, had run amok on London Bridge and killed Gromwell with a blow to the head, and that Limbury had run her through with his sword before she could turn on himself and his wife. He had also heard that Lady Limbury had been in great pain, so probably the maid had attacked her as well.

I chewed over the information in my mind. From what I had seen of Lady Limbury's maid at the Fire Court yesterday morning, she had seemed devoted to her mistress, to the extent of risking her master's anger by trying to help her. Why would she attack her mistress? It was surely more likely that the maid had been trying to protect her from Gromwell and Limbury.

Not that it mattered. The dead cannot defend themselves.

Besides, a gentleman's word weighs more heavily in the scales of justice than a servant's.

No more bad dreams, I promised myself in the small hours of Friday morning, no more laudanum, despite the pain from my burns and bruises.

I lay awake in the darkness. I heard the cocks crowing over the middens of London, and then the relentless chattering of the birds. I pulled back the bed curtains and watched the light, grey and dirty like the river on a cloudy day, returning to my chamber. I told myself over and over that I could bear the pain if I set my mind to it.

The sounds of the Savoy coming slowly to life gradually surrounded me. I heard Margaret crossing the hall and the rattle of the bolts on the door to the yard. I fell asleep. There were no more dreams, thank God, or not that I noticed.

When I woke, it was broad day. I lay there a moment or two, relishing the absence of pain all the more because I knew it would not last. I was at peace with myself for the first time in days, if not weeks. My mind was empty of clutter. Perhaps that was why those three words chose to float serenely through my mind like leaves on a stream, just as they had on Tuesday.

The mark of Cain.

My father's words, from the last time I had seen him, the last time we talked. Everything went back to there: to the day he had gone to Clifford's Inn and then, that evening, rambled on and on to me about what he had seen, until I was sick of his childish nonsense, and perhaps ashamed to own such a man as my father. If he was looking down on me from Paradise, perhaps my father was ashamed of me.

I swung my legs out of bed, ignoring the stabs of pain,

and found my gown and slippers. I took up my father's Bible from the night table and went slowly downstairs, one step at a time. Sam and Margaret were arguing about something in the kitchen. I went into the parlour.

There was an old press cupboard in the corner. The open box containing my father's possessions was on the top shelf. I took it down and put it on the table, with the Bible beside it. I sat in the chair and picked through the contents. I was slow and clumsy. Both my hands were bandaged now.

Here was all that remained of a life. The pieces of type, the scarred folding knife and the rag looked smaller and shabbier than before. So did the Bible. I took up the book and it opened at the end to show me my mother's hair pinned to the back cover. I turned to the beginning.

In the beginning God created the heaven and the earth.

Genesis, chapter one, verse one. My father had read his Bible every day of his life, apart from his last weeks when he could no longer decode the black marks on the paper let alone find any meaning in them. Even then, though, he would hold the book open on his lap and turn the pages mechanically, as a Papist tells the beads of his rosary. He had known his Bible as intimately as a man knows the body of his lover. He had found comfort in touching it.

Genesis, chapter four. Cain kills his brother Abel. God condemns him to wander the earth as a fugitive and a vagabond. That is Cain's punishment for murdering his brother. God forbids anyone to shorten his punishment by killing him, by granting him the easier fate of a swift death.

And the Lord set a mark upon Cain lest any finding him should kill him.

Yes, I thought, I see what my father meant at last, and the

knowledge shocked me. I closed the book, went to the door and shouted for Sam.

Sam and I took another jolting, painful ride in a hackney. With a heroic effort, he said nothing in the gloom of the coach's interior, but he stared reproachfully at me, and that was words enough. I was meant to be lying in my own bed, with Margaret fussing over me and Sam guarding me.

At Whitehall, I gave him money to pay off the driver and let him help me out of the coach. People stared at us as we made our slow way past the guards at the gate. One soldier made as if to stop us, but his sergeant knew me, and laid a hand on the man's arm to restrain him.

It was worse in the Great Court. People pointed at us. I heard someone tittering. Sam and I made a moving tableau of infirmity – the cripple with only one leg and his crutch, and a man with a maimed face, shabby clothes and the gait of an old man. It must have been hard for them to tell who was supporting whom.

I sent Sam to enquire for Mr Williamson. We were directed to Lord Arlington's office. I waited in the yard, propped against a mounting block, while Sam took my message to Williamson, begging the favour of a word with him. I didn't think that Williamson would appreciate my calling at my lord's office. Those of us who worked for him at Scotland Yard rarely ventured to my lord's unless our master commanded us to wait on him there.

It was a fine morning, and the mounting block was in the sun. While I waited, I closed my eyes and let tiredness roll over me. I don't know how long I was there. I felt something poke my shoulder and opened my eyes with a start.

Williamson was in front of me, his back to the sun so his face was little more than a shadow under his hat. Sam hovered behind him, keeping a discreet distance.

'Forgive me, sir,' I said, trying to rise. 'I must have—'

'Sit down,' he said, running his eyes over me. 'God's wounds, you look even worse than before. Where's your periwig?'

'In the Thames, sir. Thank you for—'

'I might have known. You'll have to get another. You'll pay for this one yourself.'

I wondered how I would manage that.

Williamson sniffed. 'I don't know what you did on Wednesday, but it's the talk of the town. And the Court. Half the bridge burned down. A gentleman stabbed to death by a servant maid, who is then killed in her turn by a Groom of the Stool. Lady Limbury made to look a fool in public. Or worse. Good God, what a mess.'

'Yes, sir,' I said.

'And that business at the Fire Court earlier in the day. I hate to think what her ladyship's father will say when he hears the whole story. Sir George Syre has many friends at Court, and he dotes on his daughter.' Williamson made a noise in the back of his throat which was the next best thing to a dog's growl. 'The only mercy is that no one seems to have realized that you were my man. You're mentioned in two reports of what happened, but not by name.'

He paused. My eyes were adjusting to the light. To my amazement I saw that he was smiling.

'So,' he went on. 'God willing, it has worked out well, or it should do. Limbury is disgraced, and out of the Bedchamber. He and his wife have already left London. The King isn't at all pleased with Chiffinch. It won't last, but my Lord Arlington finds it particularly convenient at present.'

I felt a rush of anger. For Williamson, all this – the killings, the sufferings of the living – had been reduced to a squabble for power and influence over the King in the back stairs of Whitehall. 'But, sir,' I said, 'there are also the murders.'

'You said Gromwell was responsible for them. In that case, it's fortunate that he's dead. For all of us. The maidservant did us a favour.'

'It is possible that he didn't kill Celia Hampney.'

He scowled. 'You said she was killed in his chamber.'

'Yes, but—'

'Then who else could have done it?'

I opened my mouth and paused. The mark of Cain. But what did that amount to? And did I really want to explain about my father's part in this, which I had concealed for so long? I said, 'I'm not sure, sir. It's just that we have no actual proof that he did. I'm sure he helped to move the body but—'

'Of course we have proof,' Williamson interrupted. 'You tell me she was killed in Gromwell's chamber. You also say that he was responsible for moving the corpse and leaving it for carrion among the ruins. You surely don't dispute that the threat of exposure led him to kill Chelling and the maid-servant?'

He paused, and that was my last chance. I didn't take it.

'Of course Gromwell killed her as well as the others,' he said. 'The evidence we have would convince a judge and jury.'

I bowed my head.

'Go away, Marwood,' Williamson said, not unkindly. 'By the way, the King declined to sign the warrant that Chiffinch gave him.'

I looked up. 'What warrant, sir?'

'The one to remove you from your clerkship to the Board of the Red Cloth. Either he wanted to cross Chiffinch or he has a kindness for you. Though I can't think why that should be. Either way, the post is still yours.'

I stared stupidly at him, gradually absorbing the meaning of his words.

'Go home,' Williamson said. 'I'll see your salary is paid as usual. Restore yourself to health and make yourself look respectable. Then come back to work.'

He strode away without a backward glance.

CHAPTER FIFTY-TWO

T O A TAVERN with Sam, for the poor man deserved something for his service and for my bad temper, and then home by water.

Cat Lovett was waiting for me in the parlour. She was talking to Margaret, and the smells of dinner rose from the kitchen.

I was glad to sit down, though I felt better than I had expected. Perhaps the ale I had taken in King Street numbed some of the pain. It helped with the craving, too. I wanted laudanum, but so far I had kept to my resolution during the night.

'Mr Hakesby has sent me with some money,' Cat said. 'Not all of it, but something on account.'

She laid a small paper packet on the table. I let it lie there. I was glad to have it. Though Williamson had promised to pay my salary, I was running short of ready money.

'Ten pounds,' she said. 'He wants a receipt.' She added quickly, as if defending herself from an accusation I hadn't thought of making, 'That's why I waited for your return.'

'I need paper and pen.'

But Margaret said that dinner would be spoiled if she did not bring it now, so I told her to serve it. Without my saying a word, she assumed both that Cat would dine with me and that Cat was no longer to be considered merely as another servant.

When the food was on the table, she and Sam left us alone. Cat and I sat opposite each other. At first we ate and drank in silence, seeking refuge in food. The bandages on my hand made eating slow and messy. She studiously avoided watching me. She seemed more restless than usual, shifting on her stool and glancing about the room. I knew she must blame me for what had happened to her on Wednesday, and indeed for dragging her into the Fire Court affair in the first place.

When we had run out of silence, we talked like polite strangers, enquiring at length about each other's health. That didn't last long.

'Margaret said you went to Whitehall this morning,' she said, breaking the second silence, which had grown even more uncomfortable than the first.

I told her what Williamson had said.

'It's over?' Cat said. 'All of it?'

'I think so.' Without my intending it, my hand touched the scars on my cheek. 'For Williamson and Chiffinch, at any rate. And the rest of them at Court.'

'It's all to the good, sir, surely? You'll get another wig, and we may go on with the rest of our lives.'

'But what about my father?'

'What about him?' Cat was not a woman to mince words and make palatable nothings out of them. 'You can't bring him back to life.'

'There's something I didn't tell you. After the wagon went over him, as he lay dying, the crossing-sweeper told me he asked where the rook was.'

'"Rook"?' She stared blankly at me. 'The bird? Or the piece in chess? Or did he mean to cheat?'

'It was his word for lawyers. From their black plumage, I suppose, and because he felt they'd cheated him out of his liberty and life. He said Clifford's Inn was a rookery. A place of rooks.'

'And therefore you think one of them killed him?'

I shook my head. 'Not killed. Caused his death. There's a difference.'

'You're chopping words and meanings, sir. What's the profit in that?' Cat glanced at the unopened packet of money on the table. 'I must go. Shall we finish our business?'

'In a moment. The sweeper thought that someone was chasing after my father. A rook, I think, if his last words meant anything. One of the lawyers, one of the people he had seen in Clifford's Inn.' I shrugged, which made me wince. 'It could have been Gromwell, who came from the rookery. You see, Gromwell wouldn't have realized my father's wits were wandering – he would have thought him a potential witness, someone who had seen the body of Celia Hampney in his chamber. But in his hurry my father stumbled and fell under the wagon. And then he wasn't a problem for Gromwell any more.'

'Let it go,' she said. 'This is madness. You're like a dog with a bone, except there's some purpose to that.'

'And there's another thing. The woman my father followed into Clifford's Inn. I told you. You remember? He thought she was my mother when she was young. But he told me that

433

she bore the mark of Cain, and that confused him. Why would my mother have borne the mark of Cain?'

'What did he mean by it?'

I shrugged, and wished I hadn't because of the pain it caused. 'What does it mean to you?'

Cat said slowly, 'The Lord set the mark on Cain so no one would kill him. He was condemned to live and wander the face of the earth for ever.'

'You saw Lady Limbury's birthmark. Was that my father's mark of Cain? If there's any meaning at all to what my father said, it must surely be that he followed Lady Limbury into Clifford's Inn about the time of the murder.'

'Are you really saying that this means Lady Limbury killed Celia Hampney?' She laid down her knife and lowered her voice. 'And Gromwell committed two more murders to protect her? For God's sake, sir. If you say that abroad, they'll throw you into Bedlam. Or worse.'

'But don't you see? Even if it was Lady Limbury who killed Mistress Hampney, Gromwell faced ruin, and perhaps the gallows as her accessory. And if he saw my father following her to his chambers around the time of the murder, that explains why he chased after him the next day – to stop him talking, or at least find out who he was, what he had seen. My father fled from him, as he fled from anyone he thought was a lawyer, and Gromwell pursued – and then came that cursed wagon.'

A church clock was striking the hour.

'It's one o'clock,' Cat said. 'Mr Hakesby will be worried.'

'I can't prove anything,' I said. 'So it doesn't matter. I can't tell anyone, except you.'

'And I shall do my best to forget it. So should you. We'll

434

never know which of them killed that poor woman. And it doesn't matter now, not to you, not to me. Will you count the money?'

Her voice was hard and brisk. I pushed aside my plate. The little parcel of coins was secured with string. Hindered by the bandages, I fumbled at the knot.

'Let me do it.'

I shook my head. I was cross with her for the way she had brushed aside my confidence. Besides, I thought I heard in her voice the note of pity that she sometimes used to Hakesby. I could not bear her pity.

The knot resisted me. I stretched out my hand to the box of my father's possessions and drew it towards me. I took out his knife. After a struggle, I managed to open it.

The blade and the corresponding slot in the handle were caked with a powdery substance. I scraped part of it with my nail, dislodging a shower of tiny rust spots. There was something else there, too, caught between the handle and the blade, just above the hinge that kept them together.

Yellow threads.

I stared at them, my mouth open, my face pricking with sweat. Perhaps Lady Limbury hadn't killed Celia Hampney, after all. Nor had Gromwell.

I looked up. Cat was watching me. I knew how fast her mind worked. Very slowly, I began to close the knife.

Perhaps Gromwell had chased after my father for another reason. Yellow silk, from a woman's gown?

'Stop,' she said. 'Let me see.'

The moment trembled in the balance. Perhaps I should have closed the knife and slipped it in my pocket. Perhaps I should have taken the money, signed the receipt and ordered

Cat to leave the house. Instead I passed the knife across the table.

She examined it. 'Whose is this? Where did you find it?'

I could have lied. I could have tried to bluster it out. But I owed her something for all that had happened, and the truth was better than nothing. 'It was my father's. It was in his pocket when he died.'

Cat frowned. 'I don't understand. Why?'

I knew what she was asking: why would my father have stabbed Celia Hampney? 'Because his straying wits took him to strange places. Because he believed that she was a whore. She was a sinner, and he was punishing her for her sins. To prevent her leading men to sin. Because he felt it was God's will. His God was very terrible.'

God the father. We never really know our fathers. We think we do, but we don't.

'For God's sake, sir,' Cat said, closing the knife and pushing it across the table towards me. 'Throw it in the river and be done with it.'

After Cat had gone, I stayed in my chair with the box of my father's pitifully few possessions before me. The afternoon passed slowly. I tried not to think about laudanum. Margaret came to clear the table. I shouted at her, and she went away. Two flies buzzed among the remains of our dinner. Something scratched behind the wainscot.

Had I ever really known Nathaniel Marwood? I used to think so. First there had been the giant of my childhood, the next best thing to God, whose word was law and whose powers were limitless. When I was young, I had never entertained the idea that my father, or indeed his God, might be wrong. My father could be stern, even cruel – I bore scars on my back to attest to that – and he had often been as tyrannical and capricious as Jehovah. When he had seen sin in me, or in anyone else, he had been savage in his efforts to root it out, whatever the cost to the sinner.

Then came the broken man who had emerged from prison last year, drifting through his second childhood towards its inevitable end. During the years of his imprisonment our roles had imperceptibly reversed themselves, and it had become my duty to care for him. He had seemed greatly softened by his tribulations – almost a different man, capable of a sweetness I had never known before. At the same time, he had been a burden. He had irritated me. But I had loved him. I mourned his passing.

But a few threads of yellow silk changed all that, together with the shower of rust spots, dried blood. Yellow as the sun, red as fire . . .

Now, for the first time, I realized there had been no division between the two men in the same body, between the tyrant of my childhood and the gentle, decayed fool of his last years. When my father had stumbled into Gromwell's chamber, he had found sin in the person of Mistress Hampney, waiting for her lover, displayed on a couch in all her lewdness.

Celia Hampney had been a small woman. She had been taken by surprise. My father had been large and still vigorous in body. Had she tried to stand up? Had he thrown her back on the sofa? Had he held her down in her death throes, clamped his hand over her mouth?

Dear God, I thought, the ugliness of it, the horror, the sadness.

He had told me what had happened, just as he had told me

437

everything else. *The poor, abandoned wretch. Her sins found her out, and she suffered the punishment for them.* He had taken out his knife and rooted out the sin. We had found blood on his shirt cuff that last evening, but no sign of a wound on him.

As so often in my childhood, my father had appointed himself God's agent and meted out the punishment to the sinner. Perhaps he desired the punishment of whores because he desired them too much. He had been a man of strong appetites. He punished his own lusts.

They say it's a wise father that knows his own child. Yes, and the contrary is also true.

CHAPTER FIFTY-THREE

WHEN SHE LEFT Marwood, Cat walked along the Strand with the receipt for the money in her pocket. She didn't hurry back to the drawing office, though it was perfectly true that Hakesby would be worrying about her.

The affair was over and done with, at last. Let the dead bury the dead. Marwood was probably right but, if he had any sense, he would forget what he knew and what he suspected. He would cover the more visible of his injuries with a new wig and go back to Whitehall to earn his living. What else was there for him to do?

For the moment, life went on. She would try to forget what Marwood had told her. She would push her own injuries deep inside her to join the others that lay there in the darkness. For most of the time, it was a simple matter to pretend that they weren't there.

As she waited to cross the road, she forced her mind into a different direction. She thought with satisfaction of the plan for a set of stables at Dragon Yard that Hakesby had entrusted to her. If he would permit it, she would start work this afternoon.

Cat turned up towards Henrietta Street and Covent Garden. For a moment, another thought crossed her mind like a cloud drifting over the sun. She hadn't told Marwood her news, that she had agreed to marry Hakesby.

There had been other, more pressing things to talk about. If she saw Marwood again, she would mention it. In any case, there was no hurry. The marriage was purely a business matter between her and Hakesby, and there was no reason why the news should interest Marwood.

Besides, it was not something she cared to think about, let alone talk about, unless she had to.

Marwood, she murmured aloud. James Marwood.

THE END